God's Rough Drafts

Robert Scott

GW00691157

More Praise for *God's Rough Drafts:*

"Robert Scott's *God's Rough Drafts* takes the overworked Young Adult Dystopian Future Fantasy genre and gives it a good shake. Where today people might sell organs on the black market, in Scott's future world, it's a legitimate, and big, business. He's depicted a world where the gap between rich and poor has widened to such an extent that almost everything is marketable. The result is an amazing adventure featuring three compelling heroes, frightening villains and an eerily familiar society. You won't be able to put it down and will be left wanting more."

--Richard Marcus, *Seattle Post-Intelligencer* and

Blogcritics.com

"A thrilling chase, woven (with) threads of social commentary, friendship, self-discovery, and the dangers of treating people as commodities. These are characters you will care about as they struggle to overcome every obstacle and make some disturbing discoveries along the way...Dark, charming, foreboding, sharp, witty, and suspenseful in equal measure. A must read!"

-- Phil Leader, book reviewer for Goodreads.org and

Twitter, UK

Also Available
by Robert Scott

The Hickory Staff, Book 1 of the Eldarn Sequence
coauthored with Jay Gordon
Gollancz, London, 2005

Lessek's Key, Book 2 of the Eldarn Sequence
coauthored with Jay Gordon
Gollancz, London, 2006

The Larion Senators, Book 3 of the Eldarn Sequence
coauthored with Jay Gordon
Gollancz, London, 2007

15 Miles
Gollancz, London, 2010

Asbury Park
Gollancz, London, 2012

Emails from Jennifer Cooper
PJPF Press, Manassas, 2015/2017

Business Cards
PJPF Press, Manassas, 2017

Tom Parker's Confession
PJPF Press, Manassas, 2018

God's Rough Drafts

Robert Scott

God's Rough Drafts
© Robert Scott 2019

All rights reserved. Red Dashboard LLC Publishing
retains right to reprint. Permission to reprint stories or
poetry must be obtained from the author.

ISBN: 978-1-970003-45-1

Cover Artwork © Caleb Fletcher
Cover Design © Frankie Lopez, Jr.

Published by:
Red Dashboard LLC Publishing
Princeton NJ 08540
www.reddashboard.com

For Hadley Scott, my favorite adventure protagonist.

And special thanks to Allison Kieffer,
who told me this story years ago...
Nice work, Al.

Acknowledgements

I owe a debt of gratitude to many who helped me tell this story.
I hope you all know how much I appreciate your assistance.
This book came into focus over such a long stretch of time—
interrupted by other projects and responsibilities—it wasn't
until my students (and my son) demanded an ending that I
dragged Fallon, Emma, and Danny across the finish line.
Thanks to everyone who helped make this journey so enjoyable,
especially...

Gavin (Wake me when we're done.) Saul
Olivia (I stopped listening to you 5 minutes ago.) McCarthy
Sami (Are you going to eat that?) Gordon
Grace (Just take the damned derivative already.) Sheehy
Sam (It's 3:00 in the morning; let's watch *Moana*.) Scott
Neil (I have no idea what keeps me from firing you.) Beech
Christine (One more ellipsis and I'm kicking your ass.) Baker

and, as ever,
Karen (I'll raise the kids while you're typing.) Scott

See you all soon for Fallon's next adventure.

Robert (Someone bring me a double espresso.) Scott

Haymarket, VA
December, 2018

Epigraph . . . Epigram? Epidermal . . . EpiPen . . .

you know what, forget it.

This space is generally reserved for the writer to quote Cicero or some obscure, long-forgotten philosopher, scholar, or trapeze artist, words so esoteric they generally serve to make you (the important one in this relationship) feel stupid.

This isn't that kind of book.

So while I had a groovy quote selected from Abraham Lincoln's dry cleaner's hairdresser, we're going to leave it out and just get started.

(I'm in Alexandria, by the way, out back. Come find me. But be mindful of the dogs. They're here, too, waiting.)

Table of Contents

Fallon Westerly, the City Diner, and a Cinnamon Muffin

Claire Felver tried tiptoeing across the scuffed checkerboard tiles of the City Diner. Her sensible shoes made such a clacking, like a tap dancer in a twentieth-century film. Claire disliked disturbing anyone. Although, at 10:45 on a Tuesday night, there was only one other customer, an elderly man drinking coffee as he peered through reading glasses thick enough to moonlight as lenses for a deep-space telescope. At his age he must've been backwoods poor or he would've dealt with that vision problem years ago.

Claire couldn't see exactly what he was reading, but it looked to be one of those travel downloads with color photos of sandy beaches, tan families, and contented couples holding hands as adorable children goof around in the surf.

Do families like that exist? Maybe just on those lovely travel downloads and immersive sim journeys.

Claire's family had vacationed in Florida a few times back in the '80s. And what she remembered was sunburn, gritty energy paste sandwiches, and long hours listening to her brothers complain that there was nothing to do, or that the water was too chilly, or the air was too hot, or whine, whine, whine.

No one held hands.

No one looked tan, unless Claire counted splotchy, red burn marks as über tan. Nicely tanning skin was at a premium on beaches Claire's family could afford.

She'd been fourteen or fifteen back then, too thin, too pale, too shy, and too self-conscious to make any real friends. Sure, she'd chat with a couple of ugly ducklings on the beach, maybe go with them to get ice cream. But she never worked up the courage to talk with any of the boys. Even when one of them (*muscular, athletic, shirtless, gorgeous*) happened to connect with one of her beach friends – because that's what they were: beach friends; Claire Felver couldn't recall having any *regular* friends – she'd turn away, her mousy face reddening to a color even the Florida sun couldn't replicate.

That'd been a long time ago, over forty years, decades in which Claire had not done or owned or worked at anything of importance. Well, except for the referrals she'd sent to those nice people over at the Prevotel lab. But that'd been a while back.

Now she half tiptoed, half clickety-clacked to a booth against the diner wall. She stood beside the table for a breath or two, deciding whether to sit facing the street or facing the rear of the restaurant, where old movie posters of Gary Cooper and Rita Hayworth bookended a short hallway to dingy bathrooms. Gary, the City Diner's proprietor and late-night cook, host, waiter, and janitor, had decorated the walls with Hollywood film posters, some of them over a hundred and fifty years old. Claire didn't believe they were originals, just reprints. Gary wasn't broke, but he couldn't afford art from the 1900s. When asked about them he'd always answer the same: those movie stars had been among the most beautiful people when beauty was born, not bought or cobbled together like parts for a used electrobus.

Gary whispered that bit, even when he and Claire sat alone at the cracked Formica counter.

And only those old films ever played on the City Diner's projection screens. Gary paid for a run-of-the-mill Prevo account and all the downloads available on any interactive device. Yet he seemed content with nothing but old films.

Real beauty.

Claire considered both sides of the booth, matching red, vinyl benches held together here and there by patches of peeling duct tape. She didn't want to sit facing the rest rooms, because she liked to face the door in case anyone unseemly or dangerous-looking came inside. She rarely came down here with anyone, so the choice was hers to make. Claire usually sat facing out.

Tonight, she hesitated.

She hesitated to sit facing the street, because it had been pouring rain, awful sheets of Old Testament deluge, and she was certain she'd get one look at her grim reflection in Gary's polished front windows and begin to cry.

A drowned rat. That's what she looked like. No, worse. Worse than a drowned rat, a drowned rat that'd never been able to keep a boyfriend, or a drowned rat who had always been chosen last for soccer and who'd never had boys ask her to Rat Homecoming or Rat Prom.

If rats have a prom.

They probably don't.

Claire didn't want to stand too long, looking from the front bench to the rear bench in her regular booth beneath the dreamy poster of Harrison Ford playing Indiana Jones.

Talk about one of the beautiful ones!

She didn't want Gary, the only one on duty at 10:45 on a Tuesday night, to wonder if this time the old girl had truly blown a gasket. But she couldn't sit facing the rest rooms, because as soon as she sat facing the rest rooms, a hideous group of nasty teenage boys – chop-shop rejects and Stormcloud addicts – might arrive and start making fun of one another in noisy voices with noisy insults. And those noisy voices and noisy insults would invariably make their way across the checkerboard tiles and into Claire Felver's favorite booth beneath the dreamy poster of Harrison Ford, where she'd be sitting...

If you would just make up your mind!

But she couldn't sit facing the street, where she would see the ghastly teenage bullies coming down the sidewalk and could brace herself, or maybe even escape before they noticed her—because boys almost never noticed her.

Yet if she sat facing the street she'd have to make eye contact with herself in those wretched, lying, distrustful, polished-glass windows. And see herself, the drowned, dateless, lonely, blue-and-brown-eyed, too thin, too pale rat who'd never

3

had a boy rat ask her to dance at the prom or take her up on the boardwalk – those blisteringly-hot Florida boardwalks – for ice cream.

And too soon, Gary, the only one on duty tonight: Thursday, September 23, the eve of Claire's fifty-seventh birthday, would think that finally the old girl had finally cracked her shell.

"Gone down the road Bozo!" That's what he'd say as he flipped eggs and bacon and chatted with cute waitresses who hauled hash, paste cakes, and waffles through the morning rush. She supposed Gary was a chop-shopper himself, not a thunderhead, but a brokerage house barfly often enough. With one short leg, a deep-Africa-brown arm, and only one eye, greenish, Gary'd spent his share of nights in a chop shop. But that too had been long ago. She'd watched one morning as he bent to clean up shards from a broken mug. His T-shirt rode a few inches up the pale skin on his lower back, enough for Claire to catch sight of an erratic pink line, like a child's drawing of a scar for a Halloween costume: a kidney, probably how Gary had paid off the loan on the diner. Yet with a pink scar, a sloppy job, he couldn't have gotten full Prevotel credits for it, just storefront chits or E-credits. That was too bad. Gary'd always been kind to her, not like the people she'd seen stumbling in and out of those storefront shops.

Claire wanted to ask about it, how he'd made the decision, or if he'd just done it on the spur of the moment, simply walked in, rode the storm, and left with his mortgage paid off.

Claire couldn't do it; she'd try, after her Cleanse, maybe. But for now she knew it'd be too much to ask. She struggled to decide where to sit in the stupid booth. How could she possibly make the decision to ride the storm, to Harvest, to set up Bonnie and her kids...

Decide! She told herself. *Decide right now! Pick a seat. Just pick one, you ninny!*

4

She slid into the booth, her shabby, tweed skirt catching briefly on a sticky bit of duct tape. Avoiding her reflection in the front window was like trying not to look at a wreck on the Interstate. Staring back at her was the same bandy, sickly, tired-looking mouse of a woman, and tonight that reflection sported a tangled mass of matted hair, thanks to the storm soaking the downtown streets.

Her hands trembled. She clutched an empty coffee mug two-handed, like a third grader, in an effort to quiet them. Claire watched herself grasp the mug, her nine fingers holding it firmly before the paisley blouse she'd worn for her last seven birthdays.

It might be eight, actually.

In the diner's diabolical fluorescents, the old shirt looked more like a cutaway from some cheap curtains than the Labor Day special it had been back when she'd bought it at Prevo-Mart for sixty credits.

She tried focusing on Broad Street, staring through her depressing reflection. With rain falling in belligerent waves, the window seemed impenetrable, making her reflection all the more crisp, as if she sat before a spotless mirror in a beauty salon for hopeless causes.

Only brave light from one streetlamp brought any illumination to the street. So Claire concentrated on that hazy cone of dim yellow, watching as bits of trash and a few leaves ran through the gutter toward the inlet.

No one passed outside. Besides the rain, nothing moved.

Gary appeared at her booth, his white chef's uniform stained with grease and energy paste. "Hey, Miss Felver. Out late tonight. Aren'cha?" He poured coffee.

Normally, Claire drank it with one creamer and one sugar, but tonight that combination felt so lonely, she stirred two sugars and two creamers into the mug just for company. Upstairs in her apartment, she had a favorite mug, bright blue with cartoon red hearts printed all over it like a happy rash. She wished she'd brought it. Gary wouldn't have minded.

5

He watched her patiently. "Rough night out, huh?"

"Pretty dismal, yeah. The whole downtown's waterlogged."

"You okay, Miss Felver?"

Claire didn't tell him that she had to visit again this year, because she couldn't stomach the idea of another birthday without a card, a present, a phone call, a stranger bumping into her on the E-bus, anything. And Gary had no idea that Claire would turn fifty-seven the following day, or that she'd begin her Cleanse with a mug of green tea and a plate of egg whites with vegetable energy paste – Day 1, Meal 1, Screen 1 on the *Cleanse & Harvest* software download required of all fifty-seven-year-olds beginning the process. How could Gary know about such things? He'd turned fifty-seven years ago, had no reason to Cleanse, no grandchildren...neither did Claire. Bonnie's kids would have to do.

That's fine.

She said, "Yeah, Gary. I'm a bit hungry is all. I didn't have anything to eat in my apartment, and it's raining too hard to wait for the bus down to the Prevo-Mart."

"Well, what can I getcha?" Gary didn't offer a menu or encourage her to use the interactive tabletop to submit her order. He knew that she had the City Diner bill of fare by heart, like a pianist who never forgets a favorite piece of music, no matter how many others she might cram into her head. He also didn't mention the rain or the fact that Claire looked as though she had been dunked head first into the Ugly Pond. She appreciated it, didn't want him bringing her a towel or a hairbrush or a pair of industrial clippers. Rather, Gary just waited, a pen tucked in his shirt and a pack of illegal Bolivian cigarettes forming a near-perfect rectangle in his uniform pocket.

Contraband smokes. Gary had clearly decided against Cleanse & Harvest. Good for him.

Claire smiled, hiding her teeth. She hated her teeth, yellowing fangs. "I guess I'll have the number-three omelet,

6

with extra garlic, and maybe a cinnamon muffin, but Gary, if you can, please, cut it in half for me, and wrap up half, so I can have it tomorrow. You know?" She had no clue whether half a cinnamon muffin might be on the approved list for Day 1, alongside green tea and egg whites.

She doubted it.

Gary didn't write anything down. He'd dropped out of school in eighth grade, but could remember short-order requests for parties of twelve. Claire thought he might be the Autistic savant of lower downtown diners, but she'd never said as much. He wiped his hands on his apron. "Extra garlic? You celebrating something, Miss Felver?"

Claire sat up, struck by an idea. A bolt of undiluted determination rushed through her. "Yes. Yes, I am, Gary. And I'd like *triple* garlic!"

"Triple?" He looked as though she'd asked him to perform brain surgery. "You sure? That's a lotta garlic."

"I'm sure," Claire said. "It's a celebration after all."

"Well, what'rya celebratin', Miss Felver, if ya don't mind me askin'? It ain't the Cleanse, is it? You can't be that old."

"It's...the end of something." Claire checked her reflection in the diner windows. She stared the drowned, dateless rat down. "Yes, the *end* of something."

Again, Gary looked confused, then smirked. "A number three, triple garlic, God bless ya, with wheat toast, right?"

"Please."

"Any energy paste? I got seafood, grilled beef, and...um, I think Russian chicken."

"Not tonight."

"So, just a cinnamon muffin, cut in half, with half wrapped for tomorrow."

"Please."

"On its way," he hustled behind the counter. The old man reading the travel download had left. Claire hadn't seen him go.

She unwrapped smudged silverware from a forest green napkin and spread the cloth across her lap, careful to cover her tweed thighs. The booth smelled faintly of beef gravy and bleachy cleaning fluid. She held her mug close, happy to let Gary's coffee shove other aromas aside.

Claire checked her wrist: 10:53 p.m. Sixty-seven minutes to go. She could make it, even though the decision, this last first step, fought back. Garlic would help, particularly when—at Midnight—one corner of her bio-screen menu would begin blinking its countdown: 180:00:00:00.

179:23:59:59. And on and on until the end. Nothing could stop it.

From across the counter, she smelled sautéing garlic and mushrooms. *Garlic. God bless garlic. Green tea and egg whites it ain't!*

Watching rain fall through the cone of light spilling from the lamp across Broad Street, she whispered, "Yes. The end of something. I'll eat my omelet, eat my muffin, walk up the street, and at 12:01, one minute into my fifty-seventh year...yes, one minute into my fifty-seventh year, I'll...well, I'll just—"

She stopped, her decision draining unfinished into her coffee.

The man simply appeared. Claire'd been staring into the blurry light puddling on the sidewalk like colored rain. She'd not taken her eyes off that spot; there was no way her mind was playing tricks on her. She'd seen him, been watching that very place beneath the lonesome streetlamp.

Yet, he couldn't have just...taken shape? Fallen from the sky? Emerged from the darkness?

"How..." she started, then froze. The stranger stared at her through the diner windows. Claire couldn't make out the details of his face, but from here...

He's watching me.

Unconsciously, her hands went to her throat and the simple, wooden cross she'd worn every day since her first communion back in 2083. She'd had to replace the chain several times in the decades since, but the cross had held together. It used to mean more than it did now; somewhere along the line it'd just become an old wooden cross.

She thought there might be a hymn about that but couldn't think of it just now and didn't want to log in to Gary's tabletop just to look it up.

The man—

He can't have just materialized like that. Can he?

—approached the diner's front entrance.

"Oh, my," Claire gripped the cross tighter. "My, but...but he's handsome. So...handsome, more handsome even than Dr. Jones up there. And...and born from the looks of him, born beautiful. Gracious. Even his eyes match."

He shook water from his raincoat. Inky black, like a cape, it dripped on the diner's tattered WELCOME carpet, then seemed to dry out, as if impervious to the torrent. The man wore a black suit, an elegant cut, obviously tailored to fit his tall, lean figure. His dress shirt and tie matched, all black; even his cufflinks—they captured the diner's garish light, flickering onyx. He draped his coat over a stool at the counter, then ran his hands through his hair. The man had exquisite hair that rose and separated under his touch, then fell back into exactly the right place, as if it knew how to behave.

"Gracious," Claire whispered. Heat seeped through the porcelain mug to warm her fingers. She even felt it in the missing finger, the ring finger on her right hand. Missing these thirty-six years, Claire could still sense heat, cold, even pain in the place where that finger should have been.

Gary sidled from behind the counter. To the stranger, he called, "Hey, buddy. Have a seat anywhere. I'll be over in a second to get your order." He carried Claire's food on two platters, one for the eggs and toast, another for the two halves of muffin. One half had been wrapped neatly in white butcher paper, Claire's only birthday present.

He delivered the plates. "Here ya go...triple garlic."

9

Claire didn't look up. Instead, watching the newcomer as he fiddled with his shirt cuffs, she thought she might have seen a look of distaste pass over his face.

Maybe he doesn't like garlic. She cursed herself for ordering it.

"Look okay, Miss Felver?" Gary asked, waiting beside the booth. "Miss Felver?"

"Um," she stuttered. "Um...oh, sure, Gary. It looks great. Thanks." She wiped nervous fingers on her napkin, felt tweed through the cheap cloth.

The stranger brushed invisible lint from his suit lapel, looked Claire in the face, and then, just slightly, tilted his head toward the diner phone. An old-fashioned model Gary kept just for fun. It hung on the wall beside the cash register at the far end of the counter. (The register didn't work, but it quietly heralded a simpler time in a simpler America.)

On cue, the phone rang. Gary looked surprised. "Well, whaddya know? Who's callin' me at this hour? Probably Lizzy." He wiped his hands again then left Claire alone with a man, draped in immaculate black, an apparition who seemed to materialize out of nowhere, emerging as if from the storm.

Now that's silly. Claire sipped coffee. *Right? Just silly. He didn't appear; he just stepped into the light, either from the alley or from the sidewalk. That's all.*

He looked into her pinched, fifty-seven-year-old face. "Claire Felver, are you ready?"

"Am I...am I ready? For what?" Behind the counter, Gary answered the phone; she couldn't hear what he said.

The newcomer grinned, and Claire's stomach dropped like it had one summer when her father took her to ride the Lightning Bolt on the boardwalk at Seaside Heights. Or maybe it'd been Point Pleasant. Right now, it didn't matter.

"I don't...understand. For the Cleanse? I'm only just starting..."

His smile evaporated. "It's September 23. Are you ready? You look ready."

10

Claire peered into her mug: two sugars, two creamers, so they wouldn't be lonely. She sipped again: sweeter than normal. She let her eyes pass over her reflection, realizing with discomfort that the stranger, whoever he was, hadn't dripped or trailed water across the checkerboard tiles. For a moment, she thought her heart might seize right there in her chest as an icy sense of dread tightened around it. She felt herself overcome by the desire to flee, to run like she sometimes ran up the stairs after turning off the basement light. Fifty-seven years later, there was little that frightened her as much as the possibility that a drooling, axe-wielding madman might be lurking in her basement.

Until now.

Claire checked the street again, this time hoping that a pack of noisy, rowdy teenage boys might come in looking for trouble. She'd welcome them. Coffee warmed her nine fingers; she regretted she'd forgotten to bring her mug: happy blue with cartoon red hearts like a rash.

"Claire?" He asked, his hair already dry.

She didn't run, didn't flee from this…man, if he was a man. Instead, she raised her eyes to meet his. "Um…yeah… sure. Just gimme one second."

He didn't sit, didn't look away, but he didn't stare her down either. Instead, he simply stood, impervious to the goings-on of lower downtown, the inlet, the storm, the City Diner, and Gary.

Claire carefully swiped her napkin several times over the blotchy, water-stained knife. She repeated the gesture with her fork. For all his exquisite short-order creations, old Gary sometimes cut corners washing cutlery.

She sliced away a generous triangle of triple-garlic omelet, gently shoveled the portion inside her mouth, and savored the bitter, smoky flavor, chewing slowly until the smelly combination of eggs, vegetables, cheese, and glorious Italian herb nearly disintegrated. She swallowed, dabbed at the corners of her mouth with the napkin, took a final gulp of coffee, and said, "Okay, yeah. I'm ready."

Sixty-three minutes later, at 12:01 a.m. on September 24, Claire dove headlong through the west-facing window in her twelfth-floor apartment. That had been her favorite these past twenty-seven years, because from there she could see a narrow sliver of lake between two quayside restaurants. From time to time, when she was lucky, Claire caught sight of a family on a canoe trip or a colorful kayak, paddling somewhere she was never invited to go.

Tonight a storm worthy of a horror movie raged outside. No one in the apartment complex heard the glass shatter. No one saw her bandy, too pale, too thin form, still clad in her favorite tweed skirt and her paisley blouse—only sixty credits at Prevo-Mart eight birthdays ago—launch into the night above Broad Street. And no one saw or heard her strike the pavement with an unimpressive slap. She didn't bounce; she didn't groan, or roll over, or offer up a last confession or any long-held secrets. Even her blood, which flowed freely for a few seconds in an enthusiastic river, got itself organized and fled into the gutters, politely, as any retired librarian's blood might.

Claire Felver died simply in a twisted, tweed-and-paisley-covered heap.

Tom Whitehouse, part doorman, part security guard, part superintendent, and part dog walker, watched an old Richard Matheson download in his ground floor apartment, near the foyer. He sipped from a can of beer, nibbled cheese toast that had cooled into something he might have seen once in the 3-D wing of the art museum over on Union Avenue. He wondered if he ought to check the sump pumps.

Tom didn't watch the security screens, assembled in a tic-tac-toe pattern on his wall display.

Rather, tossed like a load of rumpled laundry into his favorite lounge chair, he watched as Will Smith and his dog harvested corn in New York's old Times Square – his projection screen wafted the smell of fertilizer and German Shepherd into

12

Tom's apartment. If he'd seen his security screens, he might have observed a handsome man in a dark raincoat leave old Miss Felver's apartment, 12-E, and walk unhurriedly toward the elevators at the end of the corridor. If the neatly-dressed fellow caught Tom's attention, he might have watched as the stranger disappeared from camera 12-2 and failed to reappear on camera 12-3, directly above the elevator.

Rather, had he not been watching Will Smith battle a city full of mutant vampires, Tom Whitehouse would have witnessed the inexplicable appearance of a teenager, a high school kid from the looks of him – or her – in tired blue jeans and a gray hooded sweatshirt. And while camera 12-3 didn't capture a perfect image of the hooded teen inexplicably waiting for the elevator outside Miss Felver's apartment, it did capture enough that Tom would have been able to make out the letters ORGE and OOL clearly.

No matter. The recording device on Tom's Prevo hard drive caught every stain and unsightly carpet runner along that corridor. The investigating officers would puzzle over it together the following day.

1.63

A Quick Interruption

Just a quick interruption...sorry.

That's how Fallon Westerly found herself in Warrenton, Virginia.

Who's Fallon Westerly? Don't worry; we'll get to that.

She'd simply gone to bed about 10:30, had awakened to rudely persistent thumping at the trailer door—the red-eyed clock beside her bed read 3:09—and been handcuffed to an aluminum table in the Old Forge Juvenile Detention Center by 5:30. The sun hadn't even risen, and she'd already been dressed neck-to-ankles in a baggy orange jumpsuit that smelled of sweat and industrial detergent.

Like most teens slated for dismemberment in Herkimer County, she'd spent ten confusing minutes with a frumpy clerk of the court and three incoherent minutes in front of a hungover judge who stank of blackberry brandy. She'd not been given an opportunity to speak, had not been appointed a lawyer – naturally, court records would note that she'd been represented by Kyle P. Shoemaker, an Old Forge public defender who'd been dead since 2098 – and been convicted of killing Claire Ellen Felver, fifty-seven-year-old librarian found dead (and later torn to pieces) in a flooded street, just a block off the inlet, near a diner famous for its cinnamon muffins.

How'd she get to Virginia? The bulls drove her, two of them, in a Lake Placid City Schools bus, one of the short ones, probably seventy-five years old, that had been converted for prisoner transport. A titanium grate separated Fallon from nearly twin Neanderthals who drove the 485 miles with her in the back. From her seat in what had been the last row, Fallon could just make out the red, POSITIVE pole of an oily car battery beneath the driver's seat. It was attached to a rusty set of jumper cables that ran the length of bus floor to welded points at the bottom edge of the prison grate.

Primitive, sure, but holy cats effective.

Granted, the shock probably wouldn't kill her. But it would sting something special.

Fallon sat still, didn't speak, didn't complain, cry for her mother, or even ask to pee until the bus reached the Warrenton School for Juvenile Student Management. It never did any good to upset bulls. For about an hour, somewhere in central Pennsylvania, she removed her handcuffs and her leg irons, just to stretch and keep her blood flowing. She put them back on when the bulls stopped for coffee and smelly seafood paste outside Harrisburg, then removed them again in Maryland, just for grins. She hadn't decided yet how she'd get back home. Stealing this bus was out of the question; it'd stand out like a Neon sign blinking: COME ARREST ME. Rather, Fallon thought she might try to find one of those new F-cycles. They looked like great fun and couldn't be too difficult to operate. The ride home might even be enjoyable. Although the odds that she could find a nuclear-powered cycle in the boondocks of western Maryland wore dangerously thin as the rust bucket bus groaned and farted up and down rural hills. She'd have a better chance of tracking down a hundred-year-old Schwinn Continental than a Prevosaki F-class fusion cycle.

But great gods what a ride she'd have...assuming the bulls didn't insert a blinker. Those were a damned nuisance, and Fallon Westerly could not afford another visit to a brokerage house even if it was only to pick up a blinker insert. *That* she had to avoid at any cost.

When their mini-bus finally reached Warrenton, Virginia, the bulls did not drive directly to the school for intake and registration. Having been on the road for the better part of twelve hours, they pulled up to Martin's Café & Sundries, a combination lunch counter and catch-all country store that looked to have been in business since the discovery of fire. And while another roadside pit stop doesn't merit mentioning in detail, I will list just a couple of things Fallon noticed while waiting for her escort to order and pay for dinner:

15

1. Old Ms. Martin, while easily pushing ninety, appeared to rule Martin's Café & Sundries with an iron, albeit liver-spotted fist.
2. One of her grandsons had recently purchased a brand new Antonelli Marauder.
3. Yes, that's a cool car. You can't afford one.
4. Martin's Café & Sundries made what smelled like the planet's most delicious brisket pastries with mushroom gravy (well, mushroom paste sauce, anyway).
5. The bulls ordered two each, nothing for her. Fallon would eat leftover grits and a cold pork chop after her intake meeting with Headmaster Connor Blair.
6. Yes, you'll meet him soon. Try not to get ahead of us.
7. Ms. Martin, while proud of her grandsons (several of them helped out behind the counter), seemed distrustful of any car that needed to go so fast that it required Hydrogen gas. "What's wrong with your grandfather's old Grey Panther? That car's been on the road since before your parents were born!"
8. And while distrustful of expensive new automobiles and Hydrogen engines, Ms. Martin appeared even less trustful of the Herkimer County Bulls delivering Fallon Westerly to Headmaster Blair.

As the old bus bumped up the dirt drive beneath the trestle arch and the rusty, wrought-iron letters – *WSJSM* – overhead, Fallon made certain her wrist and ankle cuffs were snugly in place.

A school. Sure.

But now I'm getting ahead of myself. We'll return to Fallon soon enough. Don't worry; she'll be fine without us for now.

Off to Jackson, Mississippi.

2

Danny Hackett, a Talking Squirrel, and a Brazilian Vacation

Arlen Howard had considered riding the storm when his wife, Shari, left him for a Hinds County sanitation worker in 2098. He figured with his connections at Prevotel, he could get top-of-the-line credits for a thirty-seven-year-old lung. Arlen was already short one kidney, or he'd have gone down that road first. But since he couldn't survive without a working pee filter, he decided to sacrifice a lung. Lungs weren't hearts or pancreases, but they often brought in as much as a kidney. Born with two, bright green eyes, he'd brokered those decades ago, had used the credits to take Shari on a whirlwind tour of Rio de Janeiro. They'd sipped tropical drinks on Copacabana Beach, hiked in what remained of the rain forest, and even took an E-copter ride up and around the broken shards of the old Corcovado. The pilot explained that it'd once been a 125-foot statue of Christianity's Messiah, Jesus Christ, but had been hit by a missile back in '38 when insurgents tried taking the city.

These days Arlen had two eyes, one brown and one watery gray. He picked them up cheap from a storefront over in Jackson. They weren't bad, weren't great, but weren't bad. He could drive. Arlen didn't do much more than drive these days anyway.

He'd calculated that with credits for a lung, Arlen could escape, flee from Shari, her garbage truck driver, Hinds County, and everything about the humid wilds of Nowhere, Mississippi. He spent evenings thumbing through brokerage house downloads and dreaming of a small, attached condo near Fort Lauderdale. Miami, Key Largo, Sanibel, those places were too expensive. But Fort Lauderdale…he might just score high enough to pull it off.

And he'd never look back.

At thirty-seven, Arlen's lungs had some mileage on them but not so much that he'd have to barter or worry that the brokers would chew him down. A healthy lung in 2098 ran upwards of 600,000 credits, Prevotel credits, not those phoney-baloney storefront chits that might be gold today and tin tomorrow.

But Arlen hadn't planned on failing the scan, and not just failing but tanking it like a blind gymnast dismounting a balance beam.

Arlen smoked. A lot.

He hadn't noted that bit of doggerel on his brokerage house application, so when he went across town to try his luck at a questionable storefront, even they kicked him out. Apparently, the broker had been irritated enough at Arlen's lies that she'd uploaded a nasty assessment to his wrist bio: Inserting one of Arlen's lungs into a paying customer would be akin to opening his chest and dumping in a shovelful of burned garbage.

Arlen couldn't sell those lungs to an illegal offshore dealer collecting organs for a sub-Saharan cancer clinic.

Fort Lauderdale would have to wait.

Angry, Arlen had ramped up his efforts referring healthy, high-demand bits and pieces to the Jackson Prevotel Brokerage House, mostly children from the elementary school on Cardiff Road, just outside the city. As the school's lunchtime custodian, he had a front row seat to a daily parade of robust pink or chocolate brown flesh in disease-free, poison-free, six- and seven-year-old packages.

Arlen Howard worked part time as a monster.

Before the Hinds County school board terminated his contract in 2107, Arlen had made dozens of referrals, most based on skin tone or eye color but a few for leg length or foot size. He'd been paid well, but not well enough for an escape to sunny Florida.

Instead, he took a job with the county road crew, driving up and down rural byways and country lanes with a shovel, a clutch of thirty-gallon cans, and a cardboard box filled with plastic trash bags. Arlen didn't collect garbage, not him. Trash collection, he believed, was a chore reserved for lesser men. Rather, Arlen's responsibilities included criss-crossing Hinds County and gathering up roadkill animals for disposal in a special pit adjacent to the landfill.

Deer, possums, snakes, raccoons, black bears, even a harmless Pteranodon from time to time, when one of God's woodland friends got waffled by a passing electrobus, Arlen arrived on clean-up duty. He'd pull to the side of the road, his hazard lights flashing as he selected an appropriate tool (shovel, spade, scraper, rake, whatever) and a bag or bags large enough to accommodate the corpse.

Although admittedly, Pteranodons, with their vast leathery wings, were an unexpected present. Somewhere, some billionaire had clearly left the gate open on the aviary.

With orange safety cones in place, Arlen would meticulously scrape, package, and secure each victim, placing the bags into sealed rubbish bins in his truck bed. This step was particularly important on summer days when temperatures in the Jackson area might top 105 with stifling, putty-thick humidity.

Roadkill animals tended to stink, especially those that had been out in disagreeable sun all weekend.

After a few months on the job, Arlen too began to stink. Redolent of rotting polecat, his welcome at local restaurants and bars wore thin, and only the chop-shop mongrel at the Prevo-Mart would serve him, bagging beer, whiskey, and under-the-counter cigarettes while breathing through his mouth.

After five years, Arlen stopped communicating with people entirely, even the Prevo-Mart mongrel. Rather he carried on his most animated conversations with a broken, partially dismembered squirrel he called Bullwinkle. He'd collected Bullwinkle out on Route 31 near a stand of pines that might have been squirrel heaven. Arlen often drove that way, imagining Bullwinkle trying to cross the street, his little squirrel imagination transfixed by the woodland contentment he'd find in those evergreen branches.

Bullwinkle proved to be excellent company. A brilliant conversationalist, the squirrel's personality and sense of humor made up for the unnerving way that most of his miniature skull had been crushed and one foreleg torn off, probably by a logging truck hauling clear-cut scraps to the river.

The squirrel materialized on the pickup's dashboard not long after Arlen began his daily rounds. The two friends would chat, laugh, share jokes, even sing along with the satellite signal, Bullwinkle offering up a chirrupy imitation of all the best country stars. Together, the two navigated the intestinal coils of rural Hinds County, ever vigilant for roadkill victims in need of a burial.

The roadkill cemetery had long ago been the final resting place of household appliances, dishwashers, clothes dryers, and refrigerators. Several of those relics still poked through the sandy bottom of the cemetery, looking like the cracked bones of a subterranean god. Arlen and Bullwinkle buried their day's victims in a pit two-hundred feet across and about forty feet deep. It lay a quarter mile off Route 529 near the base of Barton's Hill, a half-mile spill running steeply from the main entrance of the dump to the crossroads at Cardiff's Junction and the dirt road out to the picnic area beside Mountain Lake. Arlen and Shari had visited that very spot on their first date back in '81 or '82.

With a break in the chain link and a crushed gravel trail leading all the way round to Bullwinkle's graveyard, Arlen rarely used the landfill's main gate near the top of the ridge. Rather, he simply steered through the fence and drove beneath the oaks and elms—Bullwinkle preferred coming this way as well—to the roadkill cemetery. He and the squirrel would deposit whatever bags they'd collected during that shift, say a prayer, then toss a few shovelfuls of lime down, more as a makeshift burial ceremony than anything.

20

As long as they yielded to the juggernaut sanitation trucks, like runaway nightmares by the time they reached the base of Barton's Hill, Arlen and Bullwinkle enjoyed the solitary existence of men on a mission. Like knights questing through rural Mississippi, the duo spent their days ensuring that every one of Hinds County's roadkill animals enjoyed a respectful internment.

And so the months and years passed. Arlen forgot that he'd ever dreamed of a condo in Fort Lauderdale or that his lungs—thirty years ago—had been likened to a shovelful of incinerated trash. He and Bullwinkle became best friends. Often of one mind on an issue, they rarely disagreed and preferred one another's company to anyone else...or any *squirrel* else.

Near the end of a shift one August evening, Arlen pulled up beside the sandy pit and began preparations to bury the day's victims: a possum, two squirrels (Bullwinkle didn't recognize either), a cottonmouth moccasin with a flattened head, and a baby deer that so resembled one Arlen had seen in an animated movie sixty years earlier that he avoided looking at it until he'd double-knotted the trash bag. What had started as a warm, blustery day had settled into a muggy, still afternoon. It'd most likely rain later, buckets and buckets to scrub the humid skies.

The two friends didn't mind the rain. They'd be safely in Arlen's trailer by the time it started. Bullwinkle would watch old cartoons off the satellite feed, while Arlen tried swimming to the bottom of another whiskey bottle.

At sixty-seven, he used a step stool to climb into the pickup's bed. He'd just reached the first of the trash bins and unlatched the soiled bungee cord when he saw the dog, a putrefying German Shepherd he'd buried two months earlier. It stood on broken legs, hefted its head on a cracked neck, and stared at Arlen from the far side of the pit. Flanked by silent evergreens, the dog might have wandered in from the forest behind the landfill. This possibility made sense to Arlen until

21

he considered the dog's legs and neck and the fact that he remembered hauling the animal out of a drainage ditch beside Route 31.

Arlen recalled most of his customers.

"Hey, what? Hey..." he started, surprised at the raspy catch in his voice. "What're you...what?" He looked for Bullwinkle. "Bully? Bully! You seein' this?"

The squirrel didn't respond.

Arlen stood up straight, pressed a hand against his lower back. He screwed his face up into what he hoped was a look of genuine compassion and called to the dog. "Hey there, boy...hey...are you...all right? You okay?"

At first, the shepherd didn't answer, and Arlen blinked, hoping that perhaps the sunset was playing games with him or that he'd just had a momentary hallucination, what his grandmother had called a hibbity-bibble. It had been a scorcher of a day after all. Rains were coming.

When the dog tottered unsteadily to face him, Arlen nearly fainted. It glared across the pit, dared him to say anything.

Arlen kept his mouth shut, sort of shrugged dully. A half-dozen scavenger vultures took off from the pit, winging toward the river. The shepherd ignored them. "Join us," it called in a clear baritone that sent a dribble of warm pee down the inside of Arlen's threadbare Dickies, dampening the already stained fabric the color of mud.

"Wha...what?"

"Join us," the dog repeated, still staring with a doll's dead eyes.

"Go on now," Arlen mustered a thimbleful of courage. "You git! Git on!"

The shepherd cast him a withering look, then collapsed, its broken forelimbs failing, its neck flopping to an unnatural angle. The dog tumbled into a decomposing heap near the rusted husk of a dishwasher.

22

Arlen managed to light a cigarette with trembling fingers. "Bully! Where you at, Bully?"

The squirrel appeared atop one of the sealed bins. "What was that, Arlen?"

"Dunno," he said. "Dunno. C'mon, let's get this done and scram. I'ma...I'ma thinkin' maybe we'll...dunno...maybe we'll takea day off tomor'. Whadya say?"

Bullwinkle grinned, as broadly as he could with one side of his head caved in. "That sounds just great to me, buddy, just fine and super."

"Good then. C'mon, le's get this done."

That night, furious rains threatened to wash all of lower Mississippi into the Gulf of Florida. Bullwinkle drowsed contentedly on a carpet square Arlen had heisted from the elementary school. From the satellite, a baseball game filled the trailer with the sound of fans shouting, families enjoying a night out, players hitting the ball, running, jumping, catching.

But no aromas. Arlen couldn't afford one of those televisions, not yet. He'd seen one in a display over at the Prevo-Mart, had watched a commercial about a citrus farm in southern California and had smelled the oranges and grapefruits, the smoky flavor of the rich soil, even a bit of sea breeze, all while sitting five feet in front of the screen.

Arlen's television picked up the satellite feed, the three-dimensional images and the eight-layer sound, but that was all.

He thought one of those aroma screens might be nice, especially when watching some of the cooking downloads from New Orleans.

Tonight however, Arlen ignored the game. Instead, he sat without moving in his favorite lounge chair and stared at the rusty brown liquid in his whiskey glass.

Not much scared him. The dog had. He'd been scraping up roadkill animals for over eighteen years and never had one stand up and talk with him...well, except for Bully, but Bully was different. Bully was family.

23

The dog had spoken, had encouraged Arlen to join them. "Join who?" he whispered. "Join them critters? I don't...I don't understand." He shrugged again and gulped another swallow. "And you peed yo'self," he said, more embarrassed than angry. "Peed right in you' pants, you sissy." He poured two fingers of whiskey from the near-empty bottle. "You ain't never peed yo'self before...you aint never been so scairt—"

That was a lie. Arlen knew it and shut up. He had been frightened enough to wet his pants just once before.

He and Shari had stayed at a beachfront resort in Rio de Janeiro, a comfy hotel just off the sand, where they ate fresh fruit and seafood, drank rum punch and listened to local music, energetic stuff called samba. It'd been a dream vacation. They'd been in love. Shari, his wife, the woman he'd loved since fourth grade, had been in love with him...

She wasn't any more; she'd fallen for that truck driver. Arlen saw him now and again, careening down Barton's Hill near Cardiff Junction.

...but that'd been their time in the sun, their moment of deep-blue happiness—until one morning when Arlen went out early while Shari slept. He wandered deep into the city, a mile or two off the beach, where the State Department's online tutorials had warned them not to visit. On a hillside, behind a block of industrial-looking buildings, he found the *favela*, a rag-tag community of ramshackle huts, cardboard shacks, and shelters constructed piecemeal from whatever bits of rubbish could be found in the gutters.

There were people living here. Tens of thousands of Brazilian people, all of them existing in abject, crippling poverty. They climbed and crawled from hut to shack to wooden box, across the hillside like circus performers, some using bits of rope for support. Others balanced carefully on plank bridges connecting one side of their village with another. They were ghosts. There was no way that the Brazilian government could account for all of them. They might be born, grow old, and die right on this massive hillside, never knowing

24

that places like Jackson, Mississippi with its electrobuses and its eight-layer sound systems and retractable, 3-D aroma TVs even existed.

Arlen watched them for a long while, thousands of people moving like ants about a hill or bees in a hive. He'd never imagined anything like it, and struck dumb, he stared, unaware that a group of young men approached from behind an abandoned tractor trailer buried to the axles in soupy mud.

Too late to flee, the gang surrounded him. Two held machetes, rusty and chipped, but deadly-looking nevertheless. They spoke a mumbly Portuguese he couldn't decipher. Several had missing eyes; another hobbled on one foot and had fixed up a few handfuls of padding inside an old cigar box to get around. The stump of his ankle disappeared into the padding as if he had stepped into a box of dirty cotton balls. Two of his assailants were missing hands. These had been recent procedures, because both wore plastic grocery bags over scabby stumps, secured by duct tape around their forearms.

Arlen understood in a moment that they meant to disassemble him, brutally, with the machetes, but he couldn't run. Too many of them had managed to get behind him. He turned clumsily on his heel, nearly tripped, then turned back, wanting to keep the awful blades in view. Someone shouted, shoved him toward the larger of the machete wielders, and for the first time in his life, Arlen Howard wet his pants in fear.

Growing up in Mississippi, he had been raised a token Baptist, but his grandmother's deep-seated faith had never gained a foothold with Arlen's generation. That afternoon, he found a church near their hotel in the safe, sunlit streets beside the beach. It'd been a Catholic church, but Arlen figured any port in a storm and spent a good half hour praying. He thanked God again and again for getting him out of the *favela*. But before he was done, before he left the church for the nearest *carioca* bar, Arlen thanked Prevotel Industries.

Prevotel saved him.

With only seconds to spare before being chopped to pieces and disappearing into whatever broke-down shack doubled as this nightmare's storefront, Arlen heard the approaching roar of a truck engine, a big one.

The smaller of the machete wielders heard it too. He commented to the others, nothing that would have saved Arlen, but just enough to stay the grimy blades another ten seconds, three ragged breaths.

The truck rounded the corner, drew up in the muddy street beside the buried eighteen-wheeler, and stopped. Painted clean heaven-sent white with crimson letters, the PREVOTEL INDUSTRIES vehicle parked not fifteen feet away. Its driver set the air brakes with a noisy whoosh that squeezed another dribble of warm urine from Arlen's bladder.

What they were doing at the *favela*, he had no clue. But they saved him.

As quickly as they'd closed on him, the homicidal gang broke and hustled for the swinging, rear doors of the truck. They were joined by a wild, shouting mob from the hillside slum, hundreds of them, hands raised, entreating the Prevotel representatives (several of them quite well armed) for something: food, credits, clean procedures, eyes, lungs, kidneys. Arlen didn't know, didn't care.

Only Cigar Box stayed, standing a halfhearted guard, as if saving the American for later like a human dessert course.

Arlen lowered his shoulder and charged, knocked Cigar Box off his one good foot, albeit bare, filthy, and callused, and sent him and his box sprawling in the mud. The last thing Arlen noted as he sprinted away was the jagged, irregular pattern of scarred tissue where Cigar Box's foot had been.

Sloppy work.

Even the cheapest storefronts in Jackson did a cleaner job, left patients with smooth salvageable scars, places to attach another limb once they'd scrounged enough credits.

Not here. Nothing would attach to that ankle, ever. The kid couldn't have been fifteen, and he'd already given up walking on two feet for the rest of his life. All for a few credits. Most feet weren't worth one fifth of a green eye or one twentieth of a healthy kidney.

Now Arlen slugged the last of his whiskey and tried to blot the images from his memory. Bullwinkle slept soundly as rain battered their lonely trailer all night.

By morning, he felt better. He'd slept in the lounge chair and decided that the rain had done him wonders. If it could scrape the filth out of Jackson's skies, he and Bully could scrape the filth off Jackson's streets. By noon they'd gathered up two snakes and a skunk, and Arlen was feeling good. He hummed a few tunes, even sang along with Bullwinkle when one of the squirrel's favorite songs played on the radio.

As evening chased them down Route 31, however, Arlen's buoyant mood began to leak. The thought of visiting the roadkill graveyard crept into his imagination. He dreaded the day's internments. The German dog would be there again; Arlen knew it. Yet he couldn't come up with a plan of attack, no creative idea how to get this shift's victims buried without being confronted by the shepherd. He didn't realize how he'd underestimated his dilemma until he and Bullwinkle drew up beside the sand pit. The August sun fell slowly behind them, stretching the shadows and darkening the still places beneath the evergreens and the elms.

It was worse than he imagined.

Using his step stool, Arlen climbed into the truck's bed, unfastened the bungee cords, and dug in the first bin for the snakes and a blackbird that had been struck hard, probably by a logging truck.

"Join us, Arlen," someone...*thing*...whispered.

He nearly tumbled from the tailgate. "Who said that? Who's there?"

The sun slipped another hundredth of an inch, nudging the shadows farther across the graveyard of crushed and broken animals.

27

The shepherd stood in his same place, staring again. "Come along, Arlen," it said. "Come down here with us, into the pit."

"Come down." Other voices now, several of them hissed and croaked, rasped and begged, a chorus of rotting creatures speaking together. "Come on, Arlen. Join us."

He dared a glance over the sandy edge into the roadkill cemetery. A skunk, half crushed, a broken housecat, a bear cub, torn nearly in two, chipmunks, squirrels, a family of opossums, raccoons, even the baby deer that had looked so much like Bambi it'd broken Arlen's heart, all of them stood, hobbled and struggled up to stare at him. In unison, their corpses joined the old shepherd in hoarse whispers, "Down here with us. Come on."

Arlen ignored the warm stream of urine soaking his Dickies. He ignored Bullwinkle, who stood on the pit's upper edge, waving him in. Arlen ignored the lengthening shadows and the muggy breeze conspiring to frighten and confuse him. He missed the step stool and fell hard. Bright shards of pain spiked through his shoulder and lower back. Using his elbow and knees he crawled gamely to the truck's open door, hefted himself inside.

He jammed his foot on the accelerator, leaving the animals' graveyard with twin rooster tails of sand. Arlen drove one handed. His shoulder ached, so he left his right arm limp in his lap. It didn't matter. He'd driven the path beneath the trees so many times he could manage it blindfolded with no hands.

The rattly pickup reached fifty, then sixty miles per hour along the winding trail, and to Arlen's horror, he ran over an innocent red fox, the first animal he'd killed in nearly twenty years.

"Ah, God, no!" he cried. "No, not...no!" Tears flooded his eyes, blurring the forest. Barton's Hill, Cardiff Junction, Route 529, they were only seconds away, just two turns: one past the great hickory and one through the chain link fence. And he'd be free, safe from whatever ghosts haunted the cemetery. Those animals had been his friends, his responsibility. He'd buried them with dignity, even a prayer in a world that had forgotten how to pray. He never spoke an unkind word to them, about them, to Bullwinkle, to anyone. How could they? Why would this happen? What did they want from him? Arlen couldn't guess, but something deep in his mind, some primitive part of him understood that he could never climb down into that pit and return alive.

Bullwinkle appeared on his passenger seat. "It's okay, Arlen. Really, it is," he chirped. "They didn't mean to scare you, old buddy."

"Don't talk to me!" He roared, spinning the wheel to the right, then back, barely missing the hickory and the fence. "Leave me alone. You're not really...you're not..."

Bullwinkle smiled, again as much as he could smile with half his skull caved in, and waving once with his good forepaw, he squeaked. "Okay, buddy. See you around."

Bullwinkle went a bit fuzzy, then disappeared. "God!" Arlen shouted. "God! What have I—"

He had spent eighteen years watching for sanitation trucks as he made the left turn onto Route 529 at the bottom of Barton's Hill. Some of those trash trucks, especially when loaded full, came down the hill at wild, unchecked speeds, nearly out of control until they crossed Cardiff Junction near the dirt road to the picnic area where Arlen and Shari had gone on their first date.

He didn't check this time, didn't realize until it was too late. A Hinds County garbage truck, one of the big ones, bore down on him like a prehistoric hunter.

Too fast, too late, too heavy to stop or to change course, the sanitation truck slammed into Arlen's old pickup, shattering it to bent shards and torn bits of metal that splayed crazily across both lanes, into the same drainage ditches, and along the same soft shoulders that Arlen and Bullwinkle had so often checked for woodland friends who had passed away.

29

The last coherent thought to find a grip in Arlen Howard's addled mind was that the driver had an old cigar box filled with something, maybe even cigars, on the high dashboard. There was something about cigar boxes; it eluded Arlen for a heartbeat then came into focus a moment before he was slammed through the truck window and two hundred feet down Barton's Hill: the man who'd stolen his Shari away all those years ago, he smoked illegal cigars, even kept them in a box in his trash truck.

Later, surveying the damage with a pair of uninterested Hinds County Bulls, Carl Montrose, the cigar smoker who'd married Shari Howard after she ran out on Arlen back in 2098, noticed the kid in the torn jeans and the hooded sweatshirt sneaking over the fence down near the corner where one of the bulls had draped a tarp over most of Arlen's remains. The bulls hustled down there and collared him before he could disappear too far into the woods off Cardiff Junction.

2.26

Sorry! Just a Moment, Please

Sorry! Sorry, just another quick interruption. I promise not to do too much of this. However, *that* is how our friend Danny Hackett managed to get himself shipped off to the Warrenton School for Juvenile Student Management. And I'm sure you've guessed that once he arrived and got himself settled, he met Fallon Westerly.

Unlike Fallon, Danny wasn't convicted of murder. They could never pin crazy Arlen's death on him. The wreckage on Route 529 looked and smelled so much like a freak accident, the bulls didn't even wonder if Danny might have wanted Arlen dead. Rather, Danny got himself packed off to the WSJSM because he'd been trespassing on Hinds County property (the landfill) and because he allegedly resisted arrest in the woods near Mountain Lake. Apparently, one of those bulls came away with a bell-ringer of a concussion, while the other finished his shift with a broken wrist and a separated shoulder.

No one believed them at the kangaroo trial, but both testified that the forest itself rose against them. If one of the bulls hadn't managed a lucky blow to the base of Danny's skull, the kid might have escaped.

See? It's all coming together.

Oh, and whether or not Danny wanted Arlen Howard dead...yeah, we'll get back to that later.

While I have you distracted from the story, I suppose I ought to fill in a few of the details that're probably confusing you at this juncture. Much of the strife and turmoil we've covered has a common origin, albeit one over a hundred years old.

Both Claire Felver and Arlen Howard owe their untimely deaths to a controversial piece of legislation and litigation that took place way back in 2026. (That's a fancy

31

way of saying one group tried to pass a law and another group took them to court to make them stop.)

In 2026, the executive staff of the Kastner Group, a fat, American-based multinational corporation with hundreds of billions in investments around the world, decided to use the fledgling Internet to connect customers, investors, and suppliers interested in the formerly-overlooked market for buying and selling human body parts.

Yeah, body parts.

Think about it. Let's say you've got two good kidneys and your next-door neighbor needs one. In the past, charitable foundations worked hard to find donors who would—free of charge!—give up a kidney to a needy patient. Others were encouraged to donate their organs after they died, so patients with failing organs or organ systems could receive the 'gift of life' and have a second chance at survival in an otherwise nasty and inhospitable world.

What the Kastner Group proposed was quite simply the buying and selling of organs from willing donors...*suppliers*... and in turn selling them to interested patients...*customers*... often for lots and lots of money. Lungs, kidneys, hands, feet, even eyes would all be premium items, and the Internet would make marketing, connecting customers and sellers, and transportation of the organs simple for everyone involved.

The Kastner Group's executive staff anticipated resistance from lawmakers, religious leaders, and other corporations, especially those behind the times who would gripe that they'd missed out on such a lucrative market. To prepare, they hired enough lawyers to fill a football stadium, a regular battalion of legal resources led by one visionary genius, Amos J. Oakton, Esq.

Oakton organized doctors, chemists, surgeons, researchers, and more lawyers to plan Kastner's defense. His teams worked for months preparing statements, running public relations and information campaigns on television and across all the social media sites of the time. He used millions of dollars—Americans called money *dollars* back then, in the years before every nation on Earth transitioned to the Internet Credit Standard—to bribe federal judges, congressional leaders, even US senators. Oakton bought yachts, mansions, slick European race cars. He even paid for a few children and grandchildren to go to some of the finest colleges in the country...all of it to protect the Kastner Group's legal right to market, harvest, and sell human body parts.

And they won.

The legal battle emerged as one of the most divisive times in American history, by some accounts even worse than the Civil War back in the 1860s. Christian leaders condemned the Kastner program as an abomination before God. Liberals and university professors fought noisily in protests and with eloquent speeches against what they believed would be just another opportunity for rich Americans to exploit and take advantage of poor Americans. The nation's disadvantaged poor rose up in riots—as they always do in situations like these—but were beaten down by police and national guard soldiers under orders from wealthy government leaders who'd already been paid millions by Amos J. Oakton and who stood to make millions more protecting every American's legal right to have a body part removed, iced, transported, and attached or inserted into another willing American's body.

It's a free country after all, under God, pretty divisible and all that silliness.

Protestors started with rocks, burning cars, and a few Molotov cocktails. Later, they escalated their efforts, forcibly taking over government buildings, hospitals that performed transfer procedures, even sent a suicide bomber or two to disrupt press conferences the Kastner Group organized to share information—some called them *lies*—on the progress of their innovative research into the human organ trade.

But that bit's boring. We can get back to it later. For now, suffice to say a group of powerful, wealthy people decided that it should be legal to buy and sell body parts in the United

States. They convinced other wealthy people, the right wealthy people, to support them. Over time, the process became quick, relatively painless, and as widespread as the buying and selling of used cars.

Nope, not kidding. I'll tell you more after we've checked in with Fallon and Danny at the Warrenton School for Juvenile Student Management.

Oh, in case you're thinking ahead: yes, greedy people saw this undertaking as a chance to become ponderously rich, and poor people ended up providing most of the body parts traded and sold online. Not everyone lived, despite laws stating that no extraction could take place if it meant the donor would die. And it didn't take long for other nations, other corporations, other governments to understand the great potential for them and their citizens. Other protestors arose together; other civil wars broke out, and other wealthy officials abused their power to quiet those protests, often violently. The more things change, the more they stay the same, I guess.

And just one last bit before I let you get back to Virginia...once the legal battles quieted down—it was after the Corn War, about 2049—this colossal, yet newborn global industry needed a drug, something to make the extractions and insertions as pain free and speedy as possible.

(Wars always end with a new drug or two. Look it up. You'll see. The rich get richer selling weapons and then selling pharmaceuticals. The poor get shot before getting treated with the latest in pain medication. Lovely old cycle; isn't it?)

Anyway, in the wake of the Corn War, and with the advent of legal, transferable body parts for sale on a worldwide market, Diphenobenzadraconamine-72, Stormcloud for short, was born.

Oh yeah, who am I? Don't worry; we'll get to that, too.

3

Cast Iron, the Marrow Sucker, and Danny's Detention

Fallon covered her wrist screen with one of Monica's socks. While strictly forbidden for students at the Warrenton School for Juvenile Student Management, she couldn't afford to have the Headmaster's techie clown, Carter Somethingorother, decide to run a blind check, not just now anyway.

Here two weeks, Fallon had only spoken with Carter twice and didn't think the bio-wire jockey truly had the skills to pull off a blind check. If he did, he probably wouldn't be working here for 180 credits an hour. Regardless, she draped the bristly wool over her wrist, could always pretend it had been an accident, that she'd been reaching into a drawer to borrow a pair of socks.

Fallon leaned across Monica's cheap, pressboard dresser, gazed at herself in the small mirror Headmaster Blair had approved for the nine women in Lee Hall, Dorm C. With the cavernous chamber to herself this morning—unexpected October sunshine had lured her dorm mates outside before roll call—Fallon decided to give herself a haircut.

Not that she cared much about her appearance; these days vanity was reserved largely for the wealthy. Rather, Fallon wanted a haircut as an opportunity to exercise. On lockdown, she couldn't afford to get lazy, had to stay sharp, despite the tiresome predictability of her current, if temporary, schedule.

Hair grew at about one-half inch per month. She had no intention of remaining an inmate at the WSJSM another month, but what the hell. Chopping off her hair would provide a focal point, a target center on which to train her concentration for long hours each day, like a marathoner maintaining a steady pace per mile.

A half inch per month. Shouldn't be too difficult.

The trick for Fallon wasn't re-growing her hair. Instead, it was growing her hair in such a way as to convince everyone that she grew hair like a normal teenager.

Granted, she had people's everyday expectations in her corner: no one suspected that she could shave herself entirely bald and then regrow shoulder-length hair in seconds. So the illusion wasn't too difficult to pull off. Keep the growth slow and steady, like a man's beard or nubs of spring flowers. It could prove to be an excellent exercise in concentration.

Still with the wrist screen covered, Fallon ran her free hand up the bridge of her nose and across her head, erasing light brown tresses as if they'd been sketched in colored pencil.

Her hand lingered on the back of her neck.

She didn't turn around; there was no need to see it again. It had been there for nine years, long before she'd picked up the muddy-brown eye and discovered her gifts.

A miniature tattoo: **E2 13420 18**.

E2: her original left eye, a brilliant multi-colored gem, a living kaleidoscope, nothing at all like the dun-colored leftover she'd collected on her thirteenth birthday.

13420: the regional zip code for Old Forge, New York.

18: her next birthday.

E2 13420 18: Fallon's left eye would be removed at the Herkimer County Brokerage House on or about her eighteenth birthday. It had been purchased nine years earlier by a middle-class family who paid for it on time, the eye and any resale or distribution rights at a measly 800 credits per month. The tattoo on the back of her neck informed any Brokerage surgeons or storefront chop-shoppers that Fallon's eye was already under contract. Removing it for any reason was against federal statutes. The tattoo went on the back of her neck, out of sight beneath Fallon's hair. Most Draggers had tattoos: the inner thigh, inside a wrist, above the ankle, discreet places.

Fallon's eye would be exchanged for whatever the Herkimer County docs had in their bio-trays and soup bags out back, another muddy brown most likely. Brown eyes were fleas on a dog up there. Hazel, blue, and bright green were harder to come by, more expensive.

And that would be the end of it. Fallon knew. She could feel it in her bone marrow. When that eye was exchanged, her 'gift'—because that's what the poor, the disenfranchised, America's lost souls called it—would disappear forever.

No one knew, not even her mother.

Fallon stared into her last allocation, that muddy-water eye. It had been the one to change her. She'd felt that in her bone marrow, too, had been frightened of it for weeks before she learned to make friends with it and use it to her advantage.

She'd been to the Herkimer County Brokerage House twice and to a storefront once. A broken left foot—she'd always been clumsy!—had been exchanged for a Somali-brown, nearly black, African model that Fallon loved for its graceful, long toes. She'd had a kidney extracted at age six when she and her mother had been kicked off the Gerhard estate and needed credits to buy their trailer. And Fallon had made a quick trade, a day-patient swap of her right thumb—wildly fortunate, now that she thought on it—for a few credits she'd needed to buy clothes for school. When her thirteenth birthday arrived and her mother escorted her to the Brokerage House on Harvey Street, Fallon had wept. She'd kept matching eyes thirteen years, longer than most Draggers, and felt a sense of hollow loss when she woke to discover the turd-brown replacement her mother selected while Fallon had been high on Stormcloud.

It'd been the cheapest eye available for a teenager; she couldn't blame her mom. They'd had nothing, two or three red bars of credits blinking on her mother's wrist. The shit-colored eyeball would have to do. Fallon had sworn for days that she'd wear a patch, that she'd replace the ocular poop stain as soon as she'd saved up enough Prevotel credits, that she'd never look anyone in the face, never even open that eye again—

Until it happened.

Unexpectedly.

37

She had been in the trailer's tiny bathroom, brushing her teeth and wanting a swallow of water to rinse out her mouth. Nothing earthshattering, just a quick wish that her mother had left the plastic cup beside the sink.

Fallon had seen the cup in the kitchen nook, awaiting a wash with plates from dinner the night before. She finished brushing, spat foamy toothpaste into the sink, and then thought...no, *wished* she'd grabbed the cup on her way into the bathroom.

Just to rinse out my mouth.

When she lifted her hand to wipe her face, it was gone.

Not *gone* entirely; rather, Fallon's hand had transformed into a pink, plastic drinking cup with cheerful yellow daisies embossed around the upper lip. Without thinking, she took a swallow of cool water, gargled, and spat before realizing what had happened.

She screeched; the spell broke, and Fallon's hand morphed back to normal, all without her trying.

Her mother banged open the loose, fibro door, cried, "What? What is it, baby? You hurt? You cut yourself? Tell Mama!"

Fallon gulped a deep swallow of her mother's morning aroma—fried bacon and cheap shampoo—bought herself a few seconds.

"Fallon? What is it?"

She lied. Nearly five years later, she still didn't know why. "I'm fine, Mama, just a spider, a big one. He dropped down from the light and scurried through that crack there by the floor."

"A spider?" Her mother let go with a breathy sigh. "Sweetie, you're gonna have to toughen up some before you get to high school. Or those bigger kids are gonna eat you on a cracker." Fallon reddened with embarrassment. She didn't enjoy lying to her mother, but this...whatever this was...she'd have to think this through before telling anyone.

38

Her mother chided, "C'mon now, hurry up. Breakfast's almost ready."

Fallon looked into the trailer's bathroom mirror, into the brown eye she hated. "I'll be right out." She recalled a commercial jingle on the retractable screen they drew down each morning to watch cooking shows from France, *you're never in the weather when you're in weather guard!*

Now, peering into that same eye, Fallon hummed the silly tune. She understood that the combination of her missing kidney, her Somali foot, her spur-of-the-moment thumb, and that mud-colored eye...those together, along with all her original features, what her mother called, 'stock inventory,' somehow that recipe of procedures, replacements, and trades had worked together to provide her 'gifts,' making Fallon Westerly one-in-twelve-million. A *gifted* individual.

That's what Draggers called it anyway.

The Bloodsuckers called it a 'curse,' and dismembered any *gifted* Dragger they discovered.

They didn't always tear the gifted to pieces. Granted, that happened sometimes. Instead, they'd remove one part, a pinkie, an eye, a ring finger, something simple, and the powerful individual's talents would fade faster than morning fog.

That Fallon hoped to avoid.

She'd turn eighteen in three months. If she was still an inmate at the WSJSM, Headmaster Blair would hire a transport of bulls to take her home, forcibly if necessary, to the Herkimer County Brokerage House, where her left eye, that sunburst of rainbow color would be removed.

And everything would end.

"Not if I can help it," she promised her reflection. "No way."

Monica had uploaded the Lee Hall, Dorm C schedule into their mirror's interactive vid-screen as a reminder for the women who shared the sparsely decorated room. With a few area rugs to ward off the chill, the wide, low-ceilinged space had only a few sketches, a scattering of family photos, and a large map of the world, circa 2085, on the walls. More décor than that had to be approved by Headmaster Blair, and he rarely agreed to much in the way of homey additions to dormitory walls.

Fallon scrolled to Tuesday's schedule, and grimaced:

7:30 am: Roll call in the Quadrangle.

8:00 am: Breakfast

8:30 – 10:00 am: **Fundamentals of Service and Duty**. *Yawn!*

10:00 – 10:15 am: Break

10:15 – 11:45 am: **Cleanse & Harvest.**
Make your 57ᵗʰ birthday a gift that keeps on giving!

11:45 – 12:30 pm: Lunch

12:35 – 2:05 pm: **US History from 2026 to the Present.**
Lies, lies, and more lies!

2:15 – 3:00 pm: **Required Reflection and Daily Lessons.**
Get scared and stay scared!

3:00 – 4:00 pm: **Required Study Hall.**

4:00 – 5:30 pm: **Required Competitive Athletics.**
Bleed for your Dorm!

5:30 – 6:00 pm: Return to Residence Halls.

6:00 – 7:00 pm: Dinner in Linden Hall.

7:00 – 9:00 pm: Quiet Study and Tutoring.

9:00 – 10:00 pm: Personal Time in Residence Halls.
AKA: Lockdown!

10:00 pm: Lights out.

She wondered what Bloodsucker students studied at school: literature, mathematics, engineering, leadership, business, poetry, creative arts...so many possibilities Draggers would never know. Rather, Fallon and others like her, donors...*sorry, suppliers*...enrolled in the same sorry slop that their parents had studied, even some of their grandparents:

Fundamentals of Service and Duty.

Cleanse & Harvest.

Sure, sign me up for those.

Fallon drew her face close to the mirror. "Not ever. You understand? Not ever." She dragged a fingertip across the polished surface, smearing an X over her shit-colored eye.

With a thought, she grew a few dozen strands of wavy, brown hair. These she yanked from her bald scalp with a muffled cry, then scattered the loose strands in and around one of the shared sinks at the rear of the dorm room. On the sink's edge, she left a worn, disposable razor, and a few blots of shaving gel from Monica's bathroom supplies.

There. They'll think I was at it all morning.

She dressed in the required uniform of all Lee Hall women. Fresh from the sub-basement laundry, her dungarees felt as though they'd been spackled with starch, but she struggled into them regardless. Her corresponding, light denim shirt didn't seem to have been starched at all. Wrinkled here and there as if it'd been run down by an E-plow, Fallon regretted whiling away the morning. She should've been ironing. If Bastard Blair caught sight of her in this, she'd be marching off detention points from 7:00 – 10:00 as sure as the fake eggs in the breakfast line.

"Damn," she checked her wrist screen: 7:28 a.m., not enough time. She had to be in the quad for roll call in two minutes.

Fine. Whatever. I'll take my chances. Maybe Bastard Blair's busy today anyway.

But Headmaster Blair wasn't busy, and Fallon earned four detention points before 7:35.

41

An hour of marching, 7:00 – 8:00 p.m.

She bit back a curse when he called her number from the podium, didn't want another four, or more. While sunny and downright pleasant for 7:30 on an October morning, Warrenton had a tendency to sneak down into the lower forties, even periodically into the thirties after dark. Fallon didn't relish the notion of marching off detentions in forty-degree weather.

She vowed to keep her mouth shut and her head down all day.

It was her head, however, that drew Bastard Blair's attention—everyone's attention—that morning.

Should've come up with something else, she stared down at her uniform shoes, conservative, black leather with stodgy laces. *Could've gone with leg hair, armpit hair, any goddamned hair, but you had to grandstand, really challenge yourself. Well, get ready, sister, because this crew's going to be all over you today. This was a mistake!*

Anyone close might have seen Fallon's lips move as she mumbled curses and death threats to herself.

Danny Hackett wasn't close enough to read Fallon's lips; he'd lined up with Meade Hall, Dorm A, the young men's company, on the west side of the quad.

He did watch her, however, intrigued that the pretty girl he'd noticed several times had shaved her head.

He decided to ask her. Why not?

Near the end of second lunch, Meade Hall, Shift B, Danny requested permission from the grumpy cafeteria monitor to return his tray to the conveyer belt that carried it back to the scullery, where presumably, other students— *inmates*—would wash and stack them for dinner. With permission granted, he placed his water glass among others, upside down in a molded plastic tray that rolled directly into a washing machine. He dropped his fork into a cutlery bin, then placed his lunch tray on the main belt, his spoon still standing in an uneaten mound of mashed potato energy paste. Like a

42

miniature conqueror's flag, it stood, boldly catching light from the incandescent bulbs.

Danny started out, managed three steps before the monitor's whistle cut him off.

For a moment, all conversation ceased; nothing in the dining hall moved. Only the conveyer belt's lopsided squeal broke the silence. When the others realized it was just another Dragger pulling detention, they returned to their lunches, ignoring the new kid. He'd figure things out soon enough; they all did.

The monitor called, "Hackett, 137! Hackett."

Feigning surprise, Danny crossed to the podium. "Yes, ma'am?"

She nodded toward the disappearing tray, her hands already punching a code into the podium's interactive screen.

Danny's bio-wrist blinked on:

4 det. dem. TL137. 7:00 pm.

He asked, "Detention points, ma'am? Can I ask why?"

"Your spoon, Hackett," she answered, bored. "It goes in the cutlery bin with the forks."

"Oh, I'm sorry," he said, "I'll never do it again, ma'am, I swear. I'll keep that in—"

She cut him off. "I don't care, Hackett. You think about it tonight while you walk off your points."

"But ma'am, that's an hour of walking for one spoon—"

"Move along, Hackett," she frowned, one brown eye and one blue glaring over the titanium rims of her projection lenses.

"Yes, ma'am," Danny pretended to mope dejectedly toward the doors, ignoring the few jeers and whistles directed at him from the others. He ducked out of the cafeteria, beyond the watchful eye of the security cameras, and laughed.

Twenty minutes into second block, **Cleanse & Harvest**, Fallon noticed the empty bio-wire desk, three rows over and two rows back.

43

That kid, the little one...what's her name? Emma
Carlisle, with the silver pen around her neck all the time.

She'd been in their first block, **Fundamentals of
Service and Duty**, but hadn't contributed anything, hadn't
answered any questions or jumped into the discussion. Rather,
the petite redhead appeared visibly shaken, even frightened.
Not that this surprised Fallon. The WSJSM provided its
guests with a well-stocked salad bar of perfectly good reasons
to embrace fear.

But not many of them halfway through a knuckle-
scraping lecture on all Draggers' fundamental responsibility to
serve and meet the needs of the affluent, educated,
Bloodsuckers...blah, blah, blah.

Fallon glanced to her left, then tilted her head, just
slightly, to peer behind her: one row back, two desks over.

"Wha'chu lookin' at, Dragga?"

Bear. Of course. Only that half-human, half-woolly
manatee could terrify a fellow student during *one of Professor*
Clarke's lectures.

Bear. Rumor around campus contended that her real
name was Beatrice, but no one called her that. No one dared,
not even Beatrice's parents, if she had any. Fallon figured that
Bear might just have sprung, fully-formed, from some murky
bayou outside New Orleans. Nothing that large, that
disagreeable, and that downright violent could have had a
childhood with a mother, a favorite blanket, and a Barbie doll.
Not a chance.

"Huh, Dragga?" Down one eye, at least part of Bear's
homicidal countenance was hidden behind a WSJSM-issued
patch: Punishment for some prior offense.

Fallon shrugged. "Nothing."

"Well, you just keep on lookin' at nothin' bright eye, and
we won't have ourselves no problems." Bear didn't rise from her
chair, but she did lean her considerable bulk far enough
forward that Fallon detected her smell, the pungent aroma of

whatever roadkill Bear had scraped up for breakfast. "Ya hearin' me, bright eye?"

"Yup," Fallon didn't turn again.

A few minutes later, Headmaster Blair, Carter Whatshisname, the tech specialist, and little Emma Carlisle entered the classroom together, interrupting Professor Clarke's notes scrolling up the interactive wall and across the bio-wire desks.

"Excuse me, Mildred," Blair said while Carter escorted the shivering, quietly weeping Emma to her desk, then inserted the interactive wire into the tiny girl's wrist screen. On his own screen, Carter tapped a series of codes, then looked to Headmaster Blair, who simply nodded, all the while staring at Bear with scorn.

Two seconds later, Bear's own wrist buzzed faintly against the interactive plasma screen. Fallon sneaked a quick peek, just long enough to see it blink green twice, then flash a steady red.

Bear rose, angry enough to eat her own young. "Oh, no y'all didn't."

"I did," Blair retorted. While wiry and thin, handsome at forty something, the headmaster struck Fallon as much tougher and more resilient than his expensive suit suggested. He stared Bear down. "Care to go again?"

"How ya know it was me?"

No one spoke. None of the other young women in attendance dared to look up for fear that they'd find themselves near the top of Bear's menu. Sure, Old Blair had her by the short hairs for now, but it wouldn't be long before Bear was back on the prowl in the corridors, bathrooms, and recreational areas of the WSJSM. An errant comment or a whispered joke could mean serious injury, crippling humiliation, or worse the following weekend.

"If you truly want an answer to that question, Miss Guenard, we can discuss it in my office after class." Blair adjusted projection glasses up the bridge of his narrow nose.

45

"I'm not about to have that conversation here in the middle of Professor Clarke's lecture." The headmaster left without another word.

Bear called after him. "This is bullshit. Tha's what it is, bullshit! I aint done nothin' ta her, Blair, and y'all can't prove I did. Bastard Blair!" This last she shouted at the empty corridor outside the classroom. A moment later, Bear's wrist hummed again; Fallon heard it despite the fact that Bear was standing now, gesticulating angrily at the retreating headmaster.

She wheeled on Emma. "You! Y'all and me, Ginger. We got ourselves a problem."

Emma whimpered, her hands in her lap, her face turned down. The pen she wore around her neck dangled on its chain, swaying gently in time with the girl's sobs.

Bear shoved her desk to one side, started up the narrow aisle. "Oh yeah we do. Yeah, we got us a problem, Ginger."

Beside Emma's desk, Carter idly tapped another code into his wrist monitor. With his finger poised above the screen, he said calmly, "I suggest you have a seat and calm down, Miss Guenard. Right now."

"Y'all shut yourself up, skinny, or I'll take care of y'all's ass, too. Ya just clear outta my way, before I decide ta—"

Bear never made it past Professor Clarke's desk. Shrugging, Carter pressed what Fallon guessed was a green ENTER command on his wrist screen.

Instantly, Bear froze; a loose runner of spittle dangled limply from her chin. Catatonic, her one eye bulged so wide that Fallon half expected it to pop free and roll into the corridor. Bear's muscles locked as 2.5 milliamps of direct current lanced through her body. When Carter finally released her, Bear offered her wrist a confused look, then crashed over two front row desks, to land in a heap at Professor Clarke's feet. Her flaccid bulk twitched unnervingly a few times before she finally lay still.

At her desk, Emma continued to weep. She knew she'd climbed to the very top of Bear's hit list. She'd never sleep

46

soundly again, never be able to go anywhere, the showers, the toilet, *anywhere*, alone. Bear would find her. The one-time Emma wandered into some corner where the security cameras didn't reach, that's where it would happen. And Bear would make it last through the afternoon.

Unfazed, Carter adjusted his necktie, rolled down his shirtsleeve, and spoke calmly to Professor Clarke. "Sorry Mildred. I'll have someone up to take care of this mess in just a few minutes."

"Take your time, Mr. Hodges." The professor hadn't moved from behind the podium. "We'll carry on."

"Very good." Before turning to leave, Carter shot Fallon's bald scalp a quick glance. He cocked an eyebrow, then followed Headmaster Blair toward the main office. He did not offer any consolation to Emma.

Fallon slowly rotated her own wrist, examined the bio-engineered flesh holding her flexible, information and communication screen in place. She scraped a fingernail over the juncture between the light brown skin of her forearm and the soft, polymer housing of the device. *Huh, didn't know they could make it do that.*

Up front, Bear hadn't moved.

Fallon tapped the screen twice. It woke with a faint buzz that vibrated along the nerves and muscles of her wrist. From the miniature menu, she pressed HOME; the screen morphed quickly to display:

TUESDAY   October 12   10:41 A.M.

Cleanse & Harvest – Clarke.
Room 2039

YOU HAVE 14 NEW MESSAGES.

CALENDAR   P-CREDITS
DEMERIT/DETENTION

MAIN MENU

She scrolled through a few of her messages, mostly reminders from teachers to complete homework assignments or to submit essays and assessments on time.

I wonder where it says, Electrocute My Ass to a Burning Cinder.

She clicked the screen OFF, then peeked over at Emma. The petite redhead still hadn't looked up. Fallon guessed that Bear had forcibly transferred P-credits from Emma's wrist to her own. Some of the students had figured out ways to share documents, songs, photos, or other information simply by bringing their bio-wrist monitors into contact with one another. A convenient means of cheating on tests, the students most likely got away with these minor transgressions, because the faculty and administration of the WSJSM understood that none of their current enrollees were in any danger of attending tier I colleges. A few shared paragraphs or a Geometry quiz didn't represent any real threat to the integrity of the American collegiate admissions process. WSJSM students didn't graduate and attend college, not often anyway.

Fallon wondered how Bear had managed it.

Emma probably came from one of the nicer, middle class neighborhoods, had most likely got herself into trouble with a Brokerage House. Many first-time misdemeanors went up the river after offering to trade or broker a body part that they couldn't deliver. It happened all the time. Emma would do six-to-twelve months on expulsion from her home school. What parents didn't realize was that they should just keep kids like Emma home for that year. Sending her to a place like the WSJSM—despite the colorful brochures and promises of a thorough, comprehensive education—did little more than put innocent waifs like Emma on the menu for marrow suckers like Bear.

Mommy and Daddy had no idea that when they transferred P-credits to Emma's wrist account, they were actually funneling credits directly to Beatice *Bear* Guenard.

Would Emma tell? Would she complain to Headmaster Blair?

No way. Not if she valued walking around on an intact skeleton, she wouldn't.

Fallon guessed that Bear had threatened or extorted the process from another of the middle-class kids slumming for six-to-twelve. Bear didn't look like the type to get too involved with the intricacies of complex software programming, but she clearly knew how to beat information out of weaker, smarter inmates. She wondered how long it had been going on and why Emma had chosen today to finally spill her guts to the administration.

Unless she hadn't.

That was probably the case: Headmaster Blair or Carter Whatshisname had encountered the frightened redhead sneaking into Professor Clarke's class without authorization and had rubber-hosed the truth out of her.

Fallon ignored the professor's notes, didn't bother plugging her wrist into the bio-connector on the plasma screen desk. Instead, she clicked back to her monitor, selected MAIN MENU, and then scrolled down to find the link for the WSJSM CODE OF CONDUCT. The file opened, and Fallon read leisurely, wondering just what Blair might decide to do with Bear once the Neanderthal regained consciousness.

Infractions and punishments appeared on Fallon's wrist:

Infraction	Punishment
--Excessive Tardies	Hobbled, 1 Week
--Disruptive, Disrespectful, Defiant	Hobbled, 2 Weeks
--Excessive Absences	Non-Dom Hand, 2 Weeks
--Smoking	Dominant Hand, 1 Week
--Unauthorized Use of Technology	Dominant Eye, 2 Weeks
--Fighting (Mutual)	Blind, 2 Weeks
--Assault	Blind, 4 Weeks
--Drug Use	Dom. Hand & Foot, 4 Weeks
--Drug Distribution	Dominant Arm, 6 Months

Damn, Fallon thought. *That's a nasty list; I might have to bug outta here earlier than I'd planned.* She clicked back to the Main Menu, found Professor Clarke's page, and uploaded the notes through her bio-wire. *Read 'em later, while you're walking off your points.*

Bear groaned dumbly and rolled into a puddle of her own drool. As if waking from hibernation, she mumbled a few incoherent phrases, then slipped onto her back, one arm cast awkwardly above her head. Her ill-fitting blouse rode up a few inches, loosing an unendearing roll of ugly flab held captive by the snug waistband of her jeans.

Fallon watched until Bear regained enough composure to cover her bulging midsection. *Heh, look at that...old Sasquatch has a soft spot after all.*

At her desk, Emma removed the pen from its delicate chain and scribbled notes in a miniature pad she had stashed in her pocket. Fallon wondered why the odd little girl didn't just write on her wrist like everyone else.

Inmates of the Warrenton School for Juvenile Student Management guilty of minor infractions—an un-ironed blouse, for example—were afforded the opportunity to attend Evening March and walk off their detention, rather than have their demerits accumulate to the point where they'd have to sacrifice a foot, a hand, even an eye for a week or two. Thanks to the proliferation of Stormcloud throughout every culture on Earth, alterations and physical adjustments had become relatively easy. However, some degree of risk remained every time a Brokerage House technician removed or traded a body part, especially an organ or an eye. So school administrators often employed other options as discipline, particularly for lower class students, affectionately: the Draggers.

Evening March began with the on-duty staff member's whistle at 7:00 p.m. and ended spot on at 9:55 p.m., five minutes before lights out. For every detention assigned or every demerit point earned, students could walk for fifteen minutes. Eventually, even the simplest infractions, Danny's overlooked spoon, for instance, resulted in the assignment of four demerits, an hour of marching. The administration, faculty and staff of the WSJSM appreciated nice, round numbers like that; it made the math easier for less-talented inmates.

Women marchers assembled on the west end of the quadrangle; while male students gathered in the east. Women marched in a truncated square, counterclockwise, to the quad's crushed gravel midline; while the men marched clockwise, passing the women – without speaking to them – when chance, pace, or just blind luck brought them to the midline together. From the dorm rooms surrounding the quad like an arroyo, male and female marchers formed an amoebic pair of crooked parallelograms, each rotating sullenly as the faculty monitor tallied students, numbers, and fifteen-minute increments in an online database.

The DETENTION/DEMERIT link on marchers' wrists flashed green, three times, after each fifteen-minute block: *Another point down. Keep walking!*

Apart from the narrow midline path and the chance to walk a few paces beside a member of the opposite sex, Evening March tended to spiral rapidly into tedious boredom, particularly for inmates who owed eight or twelve demerit points.

Get caught chatting with another marcher? Add two points.

Get caught holding hands or reaching for another marcher along the midline? Add four points.

Get caught talking with a member of the opposite sex, particularly while pacing the midline? Add four points.

The midline was a famous stretch of crushed stone, only twenty-seven paces long. It was this narrow pathway that Danny looked forward to, especially tonight. Professor Bins had pulled Evening March duty. Bins had gained acclaim among inmates because she often needed at least one, sometimes two-

51

bathroom breaks in a seventy-five-minute lecture class. Bins regularly shouted across the quad during Evening March, "Keep at it, children. I'll be just a minute!" before disappearing for up to ten minutes of quality, *alone time* with her aging bladder and sagging colon.

Molly Bins, forty-three years in the classroom, sixteen of which had been devoted to teaching **US History from 2026 – Present** right here at the WSJSM. Tonight, Professor Bins ranked as Danny's favorite teacher. He silently hoped that the old cow helped herself to three extra cups of tea after dinner and filled that droopy bladder to bursting.

That'd do it.

Danny watched Fallon for the first few laps of the quad, speeding up or slowing his pace based on his best guess as to how to create an opportunity to pass her on the Evening March's only co-ed path. If he could get in sync with her stride, it would be easy to check at each of the outer corners and ensure he'd have another chance to march beside her for the twenty-seven paces along the midline. As long as he turned the outer corners when she did, he'd be on track to meet her at the midline turn.

And eureka!

Tonight, Bear marched as well. Danny couldn't imagine how many demerit points she'd racked up; it had to be in the tens of millions. Why the staff at the WSJSM didn't just take both of her legs for six months and be done with it, he couldn't understand. Most nights Bear marched. Rain, sleet, snow, air-to-ground lightning, great white sharks, not much in the way of natural disasters frightened her. Bear walked miles each week, slogging a trench in the western quad; it was a wonder to Danny that the bayou monster didn't lose more weight.

By lap two, Danny saw that Fallon continually adjusted her pace to avoid walking near the beefy criminal. That made sense; he wouldn't want to march near Bear either. The smell alone would have incapacitated him.

By lap four, he'd figured out Fallon's strategy, and matched his stride to hers.

Only two corners to go before the midline.

Danny wished he'd fixed his hair, then laughed. *Sure, to impress a girl who shaved her head this morning!* He rounded turn three, the southeast corner of the quad and leaned far enough to see Fallon's naked scalp turning left in the southwest corner.

Perfect.

At the midline, Danny had to stutter step twice to keep from turning too quickly and starting down the shared path five or six feet in front of the intriguing girl from Lee Hall. Dragging his right foot an interminable second, he glanced up at Professor Bins, standing her post on the first-floor balcony outside the double doors of the Women's Dining Hall. Almost directly beneath her, Danny had been able to drag three precious seconds while waiting for Fallon to catch up.

When she turned left, avoiding eye contact with him, Danny almost lost her and had to half jog three steps to catch up. He rarely felt thankful for his limp, particularly when trying to outrun a van load of heavily armored bulls. But tonight, his weak ankle made stutter stepping, limping, and toe dragging appear natural, and he soon came into pace beside the tall, pretty—albeit bald—girl from Lee Hall.

Shoulder to shoulder, Danny kept his gaze straight ahead, whispered, "Hey, Cue Ball, why'd you do it?"

Fallon ignored him. Twenty-six paces later, she turned left without so much as a "Go to hell" for Danny Hackett.

Damn! Heh. She's a tough one. Danny passed through a cone of sodium arc illumination. With a light bounce in his step, he might have been dancing off his mashed-potato demerits. *No worries, though. We've got another chance coming around in about ninety seconds, Cue Ball. See you soon!*

Side by side with Fallon again, Danny whispered, "So...you have any plans Friday?"

Again, the imperturbable young woman ignored him.

53

"C'mon, huh?" he pressed. "We've got fifty-four more minutes of this. Are you really going to make me shovel that many pick-up lines?"

Fallon turned without a glance and disappeared into the gloom of the western quad.

Rats! C'mon Hackett...think of something.

Two minutes later: "You ever been to Jackson, Mississippi?"

Nothing.

Two minutes after that: "What's a nice Italian girl like you doing in a dump like this?"

No response.

Another two minutes, another lap later: "Who do you like in the upcoming election?"

Not a wrinkle.

And two minutes later: "I'm sorry, but I seem to have forgotten the quadratic formula. Do you know it?"

Again, nothing, not a smirk.

Finally, Danny decided on honesty. "I don't have any friends in here. Whaddya say?"

And Fallon Westerly peeked over at him, just for a second. It was a gesture that on ten million other occasions would have meant nothing, but to Danny on that evening, in that quad, marching off demerit points he'd collected stabbing a spoon into a handful of dry potato paste, that solitary glance meant hope. He could have hope.

For another two minutes, anyway.

But on their next lap, Danny noticed that Bear had come up behind Fallon. Less-than ten feet behind the curiously-attractive bald girl from Rural Ass, New York, Bear moved in close enough to whisper.

When they turned the midline corner this time, Danny checked over his shoulder, Bear had narrowed the gap between her and Fallon to less-than six feet.

Why's she staying on this pace? She's gotta know that Bear's coming up...gotta know that—Danny's thoughts locked up in his head, like gears in an old clock. *Oh, no. No...she didn't hurry; she didn't speed up; she's waiting—*

They reached the northern intersection of the midline path; Fallon peeked over at him again, just for a second before turning left.

"See you," Danny whispered, too loudly. "Be careful."

And in that moment, Fallon Westerly grinned at him, a devilish, just-you-wait-and-see grin that made Danny's stomach clench up with an uninvited case of nervous butterflies.

He almost stopped, then thought better of it. "Be careful," he whispered again, risking another four demerits from Bins.

The north side of the WSJSM quadrangle ran parallel to the men's dormitories: Meade, Grant, and Jackson Halls. Outside the first-floor rooms, a wrought iron gate kept intrepid young men from sneaking out during the night. As she turned into the murky shadows, Fallon checked to be sure that Professor Bins's attention was focused elsewhere: one of the Meade Hall boys was complaining of a blister. Unobtrusively, she ran a fingertip along the iron gate, just long enough to get the feel for the metal, the heart of the forged iron, the waterproof, plastic layer that kept it from rusting in Northern Virginia's swampy weather.

Just a fingertip over a few inches of wrought iron.

Having turned east into the men's quad, Danny didn't see Fallon reach over and touch the iron gate. He didn't see her slow and then stop in the darkness near the quad's northwest corner, and didn't see as she turned to face Bear—who happily confronted the bald, bright-eyed girl who'd dared to look at her with disdain in Professor Clarke's class.

Danny didn't see any of that.

What Danny noticed when he turned corner three, in the southeast end of the quad, was that Fallon no longer kept pace with him. Something had happened.

Panic seeped into his bloodstream, poisoning the hope he'd harbored for an enjoyable—and maybe romantic—connection with the odd girl from New York.

Bear's got her. Damn! I never should've—

Professor Bins's whistle echoed from the quad walls like a gunshot. "Freeze!" she cried, "All of you freeze! On the ground. Get down on the ground! Now!"

Around him, inmates dropped, face-first to the dirt.

Danny did not. Instead, he squinted into the darkness. "Fallon!" he shouted, then regretted it when Bins wheeled on him.

"Hackett! 137! Get down, now!"

Danny moved as if to prostrate himself on the crushed gravel walkway; Professor Bins punched codes into her network tablet. From above, ancient air-powered claxons began squawking their decades-old yowl. Lights flicked on in dorm rooms about the quadrangle, lighting the WSJSM with the alacrity of a prairie fire. Searchlights, sun-bright beams mounted atop the dormitory roof brought noonday brilliance to the northwest corner, where Fallon stood defiantly, with fists clenched, over the immobile form of Beatrice *Bear* Guenard.

Danny blinked against the unexpected glare. Still halfway between standing and lying face down, he fought the urge to shout for Fallon.

Then, strangely, he realized that he didn't need to. With disagreeable light glaring from her smoothly-shaved head, Fallon ignored Bear's inert body and instead stared across the quad, directly at him. Before lying down beside Bear, Fallon, still looking over at Danny, tilted her head to one side. Gesturing toward the unconscious bully, she smiled, clearly showing off.

Having witnessed the fight—however one sided—Professor Bins frantically pressed codes, buttons, alarms, and pointless links on her interactive network tablet. Too old for all of this technological communication and security, she

56

missed the days when one simply opened the door and shouted, "I need some help down here, thank you very much."

Finally something worked, and the overhead lights, the claxons, the entire security apparatus of the WSJSM roared to life.

"Oh, dear. Dear, I didn't need quite that...quite that much. No, now...no—" Frantic, she pressed links and entered her best guess at half-forgotten codes in an effort to shut down the alarms if nothing else.

It didn't work, and Molly Bins only grew more confused, more frustrated with every throaty scream from the security claxons, old Corn War missile-strike sirens if her memory served.

Her wrist screen buzzed, then Headmaster Blair's voice called through the miniature speaker. "Molly, what the devil's going on out there? Has someone escaped?"

She understood her bio-screen well enough to respond and pressed the com-link icon. "No, sir. A fight, a bad one. I think that new girl, Westerly...oh, I can't remember her code, sir...I think she's seriously injured Bear...sorry! Beatrice, sir. Beatrice Guenard."

Blair understood; his voice dropped to a pleasant, even soothing tone that put Molly Bins's heart at rest. "Well, Professor Bins, that's fine. That's perfectly okay. Please just stand your post. I'll have security there to take care of things in less-than thirty seconds. Okay?"

"Yes, sir. Yes, I...well, don't you think that I should—"

Blair cut her off. "No, no. Now, there's no need for you to do anything, Molly. Don't worry. We don't go through these things alone. Help is on the way."

"Yes, sir, but Beatrice, sir, she's not moving...at all."

Again, Blair's voice smoothed the wrinkles in Professor Bins's fear. "That's fine, Molly. We'll take care of everything."

"Yes, sir," she took a long stabilizing breath, and looked across the quad where dozens of student inmates lay, face down, praying that no one from the WSJSM's security detail would decide that they had anything at all to do with whatever had happened in the darkness near turn two of the women's Evening March.

Molly remembered her place, her role as the teacher and authority figure, and stood a bit straighter, even approached the balcony railing. After another deep breath, she called above the noise of the claxons, "Just stay where you are, all of you! Assistance is on the way! Just stay where you are! Keep calm!"

She searched the quad again, and felt strangely as if she had missed something, as if the light had shifted slightly, casting part of her recent memory into shadow. Something wasn't right. Something had changed. She calmed herself further, leaned heavily on the balcony railing. It matched the wrought iron design of the first-floor gate on the north side of the quad.

What's different? She wondered, then decided it was nothing. She'd just been a little agitated; that's all. *It's nothing to get aflutter about, after all…just a fight, albeit a nasty one from the looks of Bear down there.*

From her position on the balcony, Molly Bins could see that Fallon Westerly had lowered herself to the ground and lay, spread-eagled beside Bear Guenard, who lay in a shapeless heap near the lower dormitory rooms.

Good God, she must have hit her hard…must have used a weapon, an iron bar or something. Bins shook her head, enjoyed another deep gulp of cool October evening, then worked to put the whole disquieting incident, her overreaction and embarrassment, out of her mind.

She felt a sudden, powerful need to pee. *Too much gosh-darned tea after dinner again, Miss Molly. Too much tea!*

At that, she even managed to chuckle, standing there with her legs clenched together. Below, a team of security staff flooded the quad like an invasion of neatly-dressed conquerors from a khaki and denim kingdom. Molly chuckled again. That was funny. It was funny to watch security assistants herd students back to their dorms, to watch as one coded Fallon

58

Westerly into his wrist screen and electrocuted the bald girl into dumb, frozen submission, funny to watch as three of them struggled to get Bear's dopey mass onto a stretcher. Molly giggled at all of it.

She never realized what had seemed out of place, however, never recalled shouting at that new fellow from Mississippi, Danny Hackett, 137. She'd even remembered his code. That'd been a feat, given how upset she'd been.

Professor Bins hadn't realized as she looked across the quad, watched the security detail restore order to the Evening March: Danny Hackett had disappeared.

3.19

Yeah, Okay. But Just For a Second

I can read your mind. So I thought I'd drop in for a second and clarify.

Clarify what?

The problem with hard-wired versus wireless wrist screens. It's what you're thinking. Isn't it?

Of course you are.

It's pretty simple. There are wireless signals for wrist vid-screens almost everywhere, all over the country. Granted, a few native American reservations don't have the full wireless option quite yet, but we've been pretty thoroughly screwing the Native Americans since the Federal Communications Act was ratified in 1934. I mean, if we can't get them frigging cable TV, how on Earth are we supposed to ensure that they have access to their vid-screens?

Whatever. That's a rant for another day.

For now, you're wondering why students at the WSJSM have to hard wire their wrists in order to access the daily curricula, their online accounts, library and news downloads, social media, taco recipes, South American dictator speeches, lewd videos, takeout pizza menus, bank accounts, you know what I mean. Yes, the rest of us can do all of that wirelessly. Instant access comes with the monthly subscription, available for 250 E-credits from most Prevotel Internet hosts.

Easy peasy.

However, students at the WSJSM aren't really 'students' per se.

Notice the quotation marks around 'students' in that previous sentence.

Because they're not students.

They're prisoners...no quotation marks necessary.

And prisoners don't get wireless access or voice-activated software, or decent pizza, nice soap, voting rights, or all-water routes to the West Indies...whatever those are. No way. Carter Hodges, the tech specialist at the WSJSM, uploads a wireless 'governor,' basically a software bug that shuts down the Wi-Fi option for all student vid-screens at the WSJSM. And it's good software. No, Carter didn't design it; some geeky, loser programmer at the University of Arizona created it.

I know: Arizona! Heh.

But anyway, none of the students, going on three generations with some form of bio-wireless hookup, have been able to beat the U-Arizona software. It's an airtight, no bullshit, shut-me-down-and-shut-me-up download that Carter inserts into all wrist screens when criminals join the student body at the WSJSM.

Yeah, I know that doesn't sound like much now. But later, when our friends might benefit from wireless access, they're not going to have it.

That's all for now, kiddos. Peace.

4

A Breakout, an Exploding Dog, and a Rusty Water Pump

Fallon grabbed her own lapels, dragged herself bodily up through sticky paste, the grim sludge restricted her breath, gripped her ankles and wrists. She had to wake, needed to for unsettling reasons she didn't care to recall.

But this...this was relaxing, restful, such a placid and quiet place just to drift without a care. Peace. A peace like she hadn't known, not since her thirteenth birthday, her thumb, that turd-brown eye. Just peace.

She pulled again, harder this time, struggling upward, then heard him, his voice encouraging.

"C'mon...that's it...you can do it."

Blair. Sonofabitch.

Suffused through with adrenaline, a burst of mad determination carried her in a yelping rush upward through the last of the pasty muck.

Back to consciousness, and the WSJSM, and Bear Guenard, and Headmaster Blair.

"What?" she tried, then decided on, "Where?"

The headmaster understood, "Shh, shh, shh. Easy now. Easy. Just rest, Miss Westerly. Rest." Fallon felt his hand, the gentle palm flat against her breastbone, then sliding down, over.

"No." Her eyes blinked open to cold, brash light, examination lights, a chop-shop. "No, not—"

Blair released her breast, pressed again, harder this time, against her shoulder. She'd noticed previously how handsome he was in his suit, tall and athletic. But now the headmaster's good looks modulated from sexy to threatening, as if he might smile casually and then run off with the contents of her life's savings. Blair was clearly used to getting his way.

Skin on skin. Shit, I'm naked. What's happening? What's...

"Please, Miss Westerly, please relax. Nothing bad's going to happen to you. No one's going to hurt you."

She tried moving, her arms, legs. Nothing. *Strapped down? Why am I*—She couldn't see him, had to squint to keep the deafening light from cracking her skull and spilling her brains. "Lemme up."

"No," Blair's silhouette momentarily blocked half of one bank of lights. He'd leaned over her.

Bite him. Bite his nose off.

He didn't come close enough, didn't descend to kiss her or to lick her face or whatever he had in mind. "Lemme up," Fallon said.

"Not yet," Blair soothed. "You're much too weak. You should try to sleep, my dear. We're going to have a brief chat, and then you can rest. Okay?"

"No," Fallon closed her eyes, found it easier to get her thoughts together without obnoxious light in her face. "Cover me up."

"Soon, soon," Blair said, his hand at her breast again, not squeezing or twisting, just cupping it gently. "I must say, Miss Westerly, I adore that foot. Where'd you get it? Old Forge? The Herkimer County Brokerage House? It's Maasai; isn't it? You know they produced some of the world's greatest runners once, long, long ago. What color, like rich chocolate. Are you a runner?"

"Stop," she fought the restraints. "Let me up."

Change. Just change. You can do it. Relax and shift. You can be out of here in two minutes.

Fallon concentrated, then failed. She'd let herself panic and couldn't get centered. Her shift would have to wait. Just two minutes. That's all she'd need. If Blair left for two minutes, she'd manage it, and be free. She moved her head, needed to know if her hair had grown back. That'd mean Blair knew.

He can't know. She moved again, felt imitation leather rub softly against her scalp. *Still bald. That's good.*

Blair coaxed again. "Miss Westerly, please, just listen for a moment." His voice oozed faux silk. Fallon wondered if women actually fell for it. She guessed they must, or he wouldn't be relying so heavily on it, like a lecher in a cloud bar. Students, too, she assumed; he must have used that voice on students, young girls all undone by his trim body and salt-and-pepper hair.

Blair continued, "You needn't worry. I'm not going to hurt you. I'm actually quite pleased that you took care of Beatrice." He snorted a derisive laugh. "Truth be told, I've often wished that someone would shove her in front of an E-bus. It'd have to be a big bus, one of the cross-country models, and moving fast, too, if it was going to do any damage to her. Good lord, but she's built like a football stadium. We could drop her out of a plane at 900 miles an hour, and only the sidewalk would get bruised."

Blair chuckled at that, amused himself. His laughter reminded her of an adolescent boy about to rip the wings off a butterfly.

Fallon felt one of his hands, still gentle, lift from her shoulder and press warmly against the taut flesh of her upper thigh. It rested there a moment, then began an infinitesimal stroking, as soft as gossamer thread, but insistent.

And at that moment, Fallon knew what he'd done. She wasn't sober enough yet to truly feel it. Rather the dull throbbing resonated deep between her thighs, distant, like a summer squall still miles off. The moment would arrive, however, when she'd feel and know and regret, and that moment would be awful; she'd brace for it. Then, without question, Fallon understood that she was going to kill this man.

Headmaster Blair had no idea that he had signed his own death sentence. "What I can't understand, Miss Westerly...Fallon...can I call you Fallon?"

Stroking, stroking, falling inside, down, closer, still stroking.

"What I can't understand is how you managed, in two quick strikes, to break three of Bear's ribs—I'm convinced they're made of kiln dried two-by-four—and her jaw. It's shattered, you know. We're going to have to install a new one. It's not worth wiring for ten weeks; although, how I would love to shut her up, and that'd do it. No, the doctors—"

Blair used that term with a ready ease that made Fallon want to vomit. They both knew the WSJSM didn't employ any genuine doctors.

"—assure me that her jaw needs replacing."

Stroking, still stroking, insistent stroking…Fallon tried ignoring Blair's gentle touch, focused instead on his silky voice.

"Two punches. That's all you needed to clean her clock. Wham! Bam! I tell you, Fallon, you should hear Professor Bins go on about you." Blair's hand lifted from her thigh; he needed it to gesture in the air above her chop shop gurney. Fallon saw it flitter in the examination lights like a drunk sparrow.

Blair mimicked the elderly History professor, cackling like a crone. "I've never seen anything like it, Charles. She just spun on her toes, then one-two! And *whump*—she actually said that, just like that: *whump*—Bear fell like a bag of wet cement!"

Fallon swallowed dry sandpaper. "Let me up."

"How'd you do it?" Blair's voice dropped an octave, threatening now. "How'd you cripple a girl nearly a hundred pounds heavier than you in two seconds, without a weapon? Yes, I checked, had the security team search every student on tonight's Evening March. And you know what they found? What some of them claim they saw?"

"Let me up." Fallon tugged against the restraints.

Shift. Do it now. Beat him to death. Show him. He wants to know.

It didn't work.

Drugs. Shit. This bastard's given me something.

"You know what they found, *Miss Westerly*? Nothing. Not a loose brick, a garden stone, an iron rod, or a hand grenade. Nothing. And what's worse is that the two students closest to you and Bear, interviewed separately, both claimed to have heard and seen the same things: Bear came up on you, called you 'Bright Eye,'—which I can understand; that is a wonderful eye you have—and you simply turned, punched her once in the ribs and once on the jaw, and Bear collapsed, unconscious for seventeen minutes." He paused, turned this number over in his mind. "Seventeen minutes! Do you have any idea how difficult it is to hit someone hard enough to knock them out for seventeen minutes? Do you know how close that is to death, Fallon? Do you know what I *should* do to you for nearly killing another student?"

Blair waited, then shouted, "Huh?"

Fallon swallowed as much spit as she could manage, coated her throat to speak louder, "Let me go!"

"Heh. No, my dear, not a chance." He began pacing.

Fallon counted his steps in an effort to determine where she was, how far this room stretched.

The headmaster walked at least five steps behind her, then ten steps back, out beyond her bare feet. *It's big, could be an empty dorm. Those sleep up to twelve on cots.* Even squinting through the glare, she couldn't see far enough to determine if anything hung from the walls, no art, schedules, mirrors, or shelves of chop equipment. *Shit.*

Blair mused aloud as he paced. "I suppose I should dismember you entirely, take that lovely, chocolate foot and that gorgeous, rainbow-colored eye you've got. And this leg—"

He paused long enough to fondle her thigh with both hands, teasing her.

"—this one, this supple length of tasty flesh. Yes, Miss Westerly, I ought to take you apart like an Electro-car engine and sell you to Brokerage Houses from here to Kentucky." Blair sat beside her again, traced a fingertip up and down her bare stomach, between her breasts and along the thin line of her neck. "But I won't. Will I?

"Let me—"

66

"Shut!" he roared. "Shut up! Can't you say anything else? Here I'm trying to have a pleasant conversation with you, trying to reassure you that I'm not going to hurt you, that I'm not going to punish you for attempted murder, not going to hobble you or sell your liver to a Chinese dealer, an offshore friend of mine who just happens to be in the market for fresh, pink livers. At 700,000 credits a piece I'm crazy to miss out on such an opportunity, but I won't. I won't, Fallon, because I like you. I do. I like you, and we're going to be close. Close friends. We are."

His hand again, inside her thigh. "Close friends."
Stroking, stroking, stroking.
"But…as my bad luck would have it…I can't just let you return to your classes without some punishment. Oh, it's not because I worry that you're going to start beating all our students into comas. Nonsense. No, it's the faculty and staff. If I let you, an adorable, misunderstood, lonely teenager, return to classes with no punishment at all, they'll think I've gone soft, or that you promised me inappropriate favors for my leniency, or that I requested inappropriate favors for my leniency—which I entirely plan to do, mind you, so brace yourself—and I'll lose their respect and their fear, and I just can't have that. Can I?"

Fallon didn't respond. Instead, she tried calling up the memory of a tempered steel kitchen knife, a top seller with sociopaths. Her mother had used it to chop onions in their trailer. Fallon shut her eyes tight against the glare, remembered her mother beside the kitchen counter, chopping, that steel blade rising and falling, a steady metronome against the cutting board.

Damn. Damn it. I can't…can't get it.
Blair leaned over again. "Fallon? Are you listening?"
"Going to kill you," she growled.
The headmaster laughed. "Ha! No. No, you're not. And do you know how I know you're not going to kill me?"
Again, Fallon refused to answer.

"Because, my dear, I am going to blind you. As soon as Dr. Greeves arrives tomorrow—"

He checked the clock on his wrist screen.

"—*today*, later today, this morning, I am going to have him remove both of your eyes. That lovely color burst...I plan to sell that for enough credits to buy myself two weeks in Buenos Aires next winter. It's summer down there when it's winter here. Did you know that? And the brown eye, well, that one we can leave in the soup for you. Let's say...six months? How's six months of blindness suit you Fallon? That should be enough time, plenty of time—"

"For what?" she asked, not wanting to have a conversation with him, but needing time to get focused, to clear the medicinal cobwebs and zero in on that kitchen knife, and her mother's chopping.

"For what?" Again, Blair chuckled. "For you and me to enjoy our close, meaningful friendship, and for Bear to...well, I guess for Bear to do...whatever it is that Bear does. But I wouldn't know anything about that."

You can't have my eye. Sharp, exquisite panic caught up with Fallon again, and she knew she'd lost. If Dr. Greeves arrived in the next few hours, it might not be enough time. She might not be able to blow out the fog, to find that knife, and to gut this pig from balls to brains. *Shit, shit, shit, shit! You gotta calm down. Stop listening to him. Calm. Breathe. Just breathe, and let it come to you.* Fallon inhaled deeply through her nose and exhaled slowly out her mouth. Again. Again. She did it slowly, tried to hide it.

Then he was gone.

She heard him moving about, opening and closing metal drawers, like stainless steel, something she'd expect in a Brokerage House or a chop shop. The WSJSM had a chop shop; it wasn't any secret. For the number of inmates walking around with a body part missing, two weeks, four, whatever, they had to do the removals themselves. No dumpy reform school could afford to send criminal kids to an actual procedure center in an actual Brokerage House, no way.

She tried a different tack, removed any threat from her voice and went for innocent, frightened. "What are you...what are you doing?"

Blair took the bait. "Nothing much, my dear, just getting something to help you sleep until Dr. Greeves arrives. It's nothing scary, just a quick sting and you'll sleep soundly until it's time to administer the Stormcloud. And after that...well, you know...it's all wonderful after that."

"No!" Fallon screamed; her throat ached. "No! No, you can't have my eye! You can't...I'll kill you, Blair, you motherless prick! I'll gut you and I'll eat your heart. I swear to God, I'll—"

The headmaster reappeared by her side. Even in silhouette, his shadow seemed to enjoy watching as Fallon, naked, fought the straps snaring her to the gurney. "Shut up!" he finally shouted. "This is boring. Go to sleep." And he gripped her thigh again, not gentle this time, but firm, squeezing the flesh steady with one hand while jabbing a hypodermic needle into it with the other. "There. Now shut up, and go to sleep. I'll see you later, Fallon Westerly," he said, and she swore she'd cut his heart out and hang it from his wife's Christmas tree. "Sadly, though, you won't see me, not for six months." Amused by this, Blair bent over her, took her lower lip into his mouth, sucked on it briefly, then added, "But you'll feel me. Don't worry, my dear, you'll *feel* me."

Fallon felt the sting where Blair had injected her, felt the cold infusion of whatever poison he'd administered to knock her out, and felt the gentle, moist tug at her lip. She wondered what it might have been, then drifted off, plans for murder forgotten.

The world smeared into a runny amalgam of soft colors. Fallon enjoyed drifting again, would have been content to drift forever.

No stress no questions no anxiety no mother no school no stealing money no foraging no breaking into Prevo-Mart no secreting a cache of food money food clothes food supplies or food no hiding by the lake no sneaking in and out of their trailer no shifting no shifting no…just drift. The WSJSM ceased to exist. It fell away from her, here above the world at night, here in the darkness, the WSJSM, a school, a prison, it rose suddenly—a block and mortar monument—then crumbled to dust, just collapsed. And Fallon rode the drift.

Content.

Until…

Voices. That nice voice. The boy, the one who'd tried to make her laugh. The boy, his voice. His touch. Not so gentle as Blair. Rough, firm, jostling, rolling, lifting, then shuffling her. His touch. The boy, the one who made her laugh.

He didn't know that.

She hadn't let him see.

That boy, the nice boy. Pretty boy. With the funny walk.

He didn't touch her gently, not like Blair. Blair had been gentle. Not this boy. He rushed. Hurried. Pushed pulled shoved carried stumbled—he had a funny walk—carried stumbled.

Fell.

She fell far. Landed hard. Didn't care.

More voices, shouting. The boy's voice, what a nice voice.

Saying her name.

"Help me out here, huh?"

"Huh?"

"Help a little? Maybe? Get your feet under you, for shit's sake. Huh?"

Shit's sake. That's funny. He's funny. The pretty boy with the nice voice.

Then sunlight. Noisy, screaming, shouting sunlight, blinding her. Again. Can't see again. The wall. It's electric. Can't touch it.

A buzz in her wrist. The girl holds her hand. All better.

70

She has red hair. I want red hair, maybe next time I can have red hair.

No hair now.

Those dogs are coming. Blair's dogs, coming fast.

The girl's there. She knows the dogs. One bursts, the mean one from Germany.

Dog burst. Dog's burst. I burst; you burst; he she it bursts. Dog bursts, just pops.

How does that happen? The boy didn't see.

And voices. The boy and that girl.

Others too.

Angry, and dogs barking, except for that one. He popped. Pop! Pop goes the German dog! No more biting, Karlheinz.

It's all right. Just drift. Just...

His touch is nice, not gentle, but nice.

The girl. I know her.

The wall and that tree, the big one.

Shouting shouting. Who's shouting.

Running stumbling carrying.

"Help me out, huh? For shit's sake."

Shit's sake. Let's go again, huh? For shit's sake.

Does shit have a sake? It should. That tree, the big one. That tree scared them.

Shouting.

He has a funny walk.

The boy, that pretty boy, the one who tried to make her laugh.

What's a nice Italian girl like you doing in a dump like this?

I'm sorry, but I seem to have forgotten the quadratic formula.

That tree. I love that tree, the big one.

Carrying.

"Help me out, for shit's sake."

The sun's nice on my face. Warm.

Don't touch the electric wall.

"Under it! Go!"

Don't hurt any more dogs. Don't pop them.

Dogs pop. Burst.

Hmmmmmmmmmmm. Like a train.
Hmmmmmmmmmmm.

Sleep. Sleep on the train. That's nice. What a nice boy.

Funny.

What's a nice Italian girl like you doing in a dump like this?

Fallon rolled over, blinked her eyes clear, waited, listened. Somewhere, not close by, an engine coughed and sputtered, noisily finding a rhythm.

She didn't recognize the room, the tattered carpet, peeling wallpaper, cheap patio furniture, a screen door with a gaping tear. Puddles of spring sunlight spilled through a broken window, half happy yellow, half stained the color of piss by a grimy stretch of plastic, duct taped over missing panes.

She swallowed more sand paper, couldn't remember her last glass of water. Turning onto her stomach, she let the headache come, knew it would. Like distant thunder, it was just a matter of time before it rolled across her bald dome, crippling her.

Someone had draped a blanket over her; it smelled of grandmothers and mildew. But her arms and legs were free. She moved each in turn, waited for the sharp pain of a muscle tear or the dull throb of a broken bone.

Nothing. Just exhaustion and the hazy uncertainty that follows in the wake of uncompromising sedatives.

I'm all right.

She swallowed again, tried to remember what had happened, then croaked weakly, "Anyone? Did someone...did anyone blow up a German Shepherd? Because I..." She didn't know how to explain it. "...because I think I saw a German Shepherd explode. Did that happen? Anyone?"

72

Behind her, the screen door squeaked open then slapped shut, a noisy punctuation mark. A voice she remembered: "Well, hey! Look who's finally awake!"

The girl, that little redhead.

"Emma, right?" Fallon lifted her head, waited for it to crack open, maybe make someone a nice omelet. "Emma…"

"Carlisle. Yeah, that's me." She pulled up a folding patio chair with torn, nylon straps. It squealed across the untreated hardwoods.

"From…"

"Professor Clarke's class," Emma rubbed a hand over Fallon's bald head. "I love your haircut. Why'd you do it?"

Fallon buried her face in the cushions, got another whiff of grandmothers and housecats. "I dunno. Just wanted a change, I guess. Where are we?"

The younger girl glanced toward the screen door. Fallon blinked her vision clear. A connect-the-dots map of endearing freckles came into focus across Emma's cheeks and nose. Her eyes matched; that was rare.

Her family's gotta have money.

"Emma?"

"Um…I'm not entirely sure," she started. "I think maybe…"

Fallon remembered, sat up suddenly. Her vision tunneled and she worried she might faint, so she let her head loll back, her mouth open. "Where is he?"

"Outside," Emma said. "He's looking around, trying to see if maybe one of the old trucks might start, something to get us out of here. There's a barn out back. I didn't want to go in. It looks like it could collapse in a light breeze. You want some water?"

"Yeah, please," Fallon listened as Emma hurried into an adjoining room. Water splashed amicably from a pitcher or a basin. Whatever this place was, it no longer had working faucets—maybe a pump somewhere. She took stock again. Her arms and legs ached, but they'd follow orders if necessary. Her

73

eyesight seemed determined to disobey for the time being, but the listless, dilapidated room continued pulling itself together. She figured her vision would return, given time.

Only Fallon's head felt as though it had been dropped off a building.

Maybe the water will help.

Emma returned with a large tumbler filled with suspicious-looking fluid. Fallon cringed, "It's yellow."

"Yeah, um...sorry about that. It's all we have for now."

"No thanks."

"No, no, it's okay. Um...well, I'm pretty sure it's okay. I had a bunch of it yesterday, and I feel fine. So, I think it might just be a bit...I dunno."

"Stained?"

"Yeah, stained. Sure. That'll work."

Fallon drank. It tasted coppery, like a life-threatening tumor waiting to take root in her liver. "Thanks," she said. "It's good."

Emma seemed pleased. "Good! I'm glad you like it. We were worried about you for a while there. I don't know what old Mr. Blair gave you, but you were out of it for a while, really gone."

"How long?"

"Almost two days."

"Shit."

"Oh, no," Emma held up both hands to alleviate Fallon's anxiety. "This place seems pretty remote, really off the grid, to hear Danny describe it. I guess he saw it on his way in, you know, from Mississippi, when the bulls brought him two weeks ago. They made a wrong turn and ended up out here." She gestured toward the broken window. Fallon couldn't see outside, just the muddy dooryard through the torn screen. "Anyway, he kept track of the roads, and when we broke you out, he'd already figured that we just needed a bus to a little town across a couple of fields." Again, she pointed uncertainly.

"Then we half walked and half carried you out here. It wasn't too much trouble. And now you're safe...we're safe."

Fallon nodded toward twin network ports mounted on the wall, near the window. "Those work?"

Emma shook her head. "We don't really know, and we can't find out."

"How come?"

She tried for a workable explanation. "You see, I'm not entirely sure what Mr. Hodges loaded on our screens—"

Fallon understood. "Damn. You're right. We can't plug in."

"Not until I figure out how to disable the school's software."

"Wait," Fallon said. "Wait a second. How'd you get us out of there in the first place? Why didn't Carter or Bins or Blair or any of them just fry all of us to burnt bacon? Why aren't they doing it now? Does the network have a range? I've never heard of a range before."

Emma gestured nervously. "It's okay. Lemme explain."

Fallon let her head fall back again, closed her eyes. "Sorry. Go ahead."

"You remember the other day when Blair and Carter hauled me in after first period?"

"Fundamentals of Service and Duty. Yeah. You looked pretty upset."

"I was. I mean, anyone would be. Bear was going to break my legs, because she thought I'd told on her for stealing my P-credits."

"I figured as much. How'd she do it?"

"Oh, that's easy," Emma started. "Basically, she beat up a kid, a fourth year from Pennsylvania, David Bryce. Do you know him? Anyway—"

"Wait," Fallon groped blindly for her, missed. "I don't care."

"Oh...um...well, okay."

"Blair and Carter brought you into the office..." Fallon twirled two fingers. "Start there."

"They made me tell about Bear," Emma picked up the narrative. "The Headmaster was pretty angry about the whole thing; I guess he gets messages from parents who are upset about credit transfers and then having some Neanderthal half-wit steal them."

"So Blair knew."

"Suspected anyway," Emma went on. "But when he and Carter went into the other office to whisper about what to do to Bear—shoot her, drop her from a skyscraper, force her into hibernation, who cares, right?—I was able to sneak a quick look onto Mr. Carter's interactive vid-screen, and I—"

"You found his network password?"

"Yeah, I wish," Emma snorted.

"So how'd you turn off the tracking or the electricity or the death ray or the tractor beam or whatever the hell else they've got on these things?" Fallon felt for the power switch on her wrist screen, then thought better about it.

"I un-enrolled us."

"What? You what to us?"

"Un-enrolled us," Emma said. "I saw the screen in Carter's office. When Danny decided to break you out, I offered to help. I sneaked back in, and—"

"Wait. He told you he was gonna come after me?"

"No," Emma waved her off. "But I could tell. He was all sorts of agitated that morning. He telegraphs his punches, that boy. I'm surprised Headmaster Blair and the teachers didn't notice. We were all at Blair's morning muster. Danny could barely stand still."

"So you..."

"I asked him," she said. "Before breakfast. Well, not so much *asked* as offered to help."

Fallon blinked the adorable redhead into focus. "How'd you get into Carter's office? Onto his terminal?"

76

Emma shrugged. "Walked in. Easiest thing ever. I guess they don't figure anyone will be bold or stupid enough to try something that outrageous.

"So you...un-enrolled us?"

"Deleted us," Emma said. "Truth be told. I had just a few seconds. It's all I could think to do at the time."

"So...what if Carter decides just to reactivate us?"

"That'll be difficult to do." She drew her sleeve back, exposed her wrist screen. "I attached a virus to the files, had it saved in a folder called *Jane Eyre*. Basically, it's software that tells our files to delete themselves if anyone tries to retrieve them from any network or storage cloud. They call it a *Zombie Cannibal*. I love that nickname. Can you believe it? Carter and Blair never bothered to check. Boneheads."

"So. Carter probably deals with those all the time."

"Not like this," Emma explained. "It's wicked sneaky; I got it from a programmer at the University of Zurich."

"Oh, of course," Fallon rolled her eyes. "Why didn't I think of that?"

"Hey, don't make fun."

"What's a zombie cannibal?"

"An unpleasant little virus that makes it virtually impossible to upload a file—"

"Because it eats..."

"Itself. Yes, basically."

Impressed, Fallon said. "When Carter tries to reactivate us, he..."

"Won't find us," Emma nodded. "Anywhere."

"Because the folders eat themselves."

"Yup."

"Suppose Carter is familiar with your Swiss criminal—"

"Programmer."

"Whatever."

"We're not thinking about that just yet," Emma admitted. "The consequences could be bad...and surprisingly unexpected."

"Shit," Fallon lifted herself from the couch, collected the water glass, and hobbled for the next room. "I need another drink."

"It's just in there, on the counter by the big sink, the blue jug."

Fallon found the decanter, tilted it, and poured another glass of amber-colored liquid. "We gotta find clean water. We can't keep drinking this."

Emma waited in the front room. "I know what you're thinking, and I don't blame you for being upset, but the way those files appear on Mr. Carter's rolls, I don't know that he'll catch it...right away."

"Right away," Fallon drank. "So what you're saying is that if we try to access our accounts, to contact anyone, to plug in anywhere, and maybe, on the off chance that Mr. Carter or that sonofabitch Blair has checked our enrollment, seen that we're no longer students at the Warrenton School for Juvenile whateveritis...and decides to download an anti-zombie-cannibal-whateveritis program, we might just click on our screens and..."

Emma frowned. "Yeah, get fried. Sorry."

"Sorry."

"It's all I could think of at the time."

Fallon slid a hand over her scalp. "It's all right. You did fine. It got us out of there, and, as luck would have it, I don't think we need much time off the network anyway."

"Why's that?"

She changed the subject. "Hey, Em...Um, I was naked in Blair's chop shop. At least I think I was. Do you...did he?"

Emma winced. "Danny?"

"Yeah."

"Yeah. Sorry."

Fallon sighed again.

Emma continued in a rush. "But not for long, and there was a blanket, so he got you wrapped up, and really...come to think about it...when we were running, there wasn't anything, you know, sexual about it at all. I mean, he was carrying you more like a sack of potatoes than a…well, a naked girl. And he's got that limp, you know, so I think he was more worried about his ankle holding up than whether or not you were dressed." Reading the sour look on the older girl's face, Emma thought about continuing, then gave up. "Sorry."

"Who dressed me?" Fallon considered her clothing: denim jeans, a WSJSM work shirt, wool socks, utilitarian stuff, about as attractive as burlap on a swimsuit model.

"I did," Emma said. "Once we got you clear of the fence, Danny found a place for us to hide, just some bushes near the highway. I dressed you there."

"In what?"

"Oh, he thought of everything."

Fallon waited.

"Before Danny broke in to rescue you, he put on multiple changes of clothes."

"Wait," she dropped the glass to the table. "How'd he know I'd lost my clothes?"

"He didn't," Emma explained. Outside the light had shifted. Late day sun burrowed through her Irish curls. "I think he was just stealing as many pairs of pants and shirts as possible. If it hadn't slowed us down when those dogs arrived it would've been pretty funny, him trundling along like a chubby marshmallow man." She laughed at the memory.

Fallon pressed her eyes tightly shut, tried to recall their escape. "The dogs. I remember the dogs, but—and this is going to sound crazy—I could've sworn I saw one of them…"

"What?" Now Emma waited.

"You know what, never mind."

"Okay. Hey, look at the bright side; at least we're out of there, and we got you away from Mr. Blair."

"That's true," Fallon said. "But I'm going back."

Danny appeared, framed in the screen door. "No you're not. Sorry."

From her place on the couch and with the fog of Headmaster Blair's pharmaceutical clubbing still billowing behind her eyes, Fallon had to work to see him clearly. After a few seconds, she decided she must look feeble-minded and gave up, deciding to get a good look later.

At a loss for something to do, Emma stood, then sat down again. "Hi Danny. You find a car or something?"

"Hi Em," he joined them in the farmhouse. "Or something."

"A truck?"

"A peach grader."

"A what?" Fallon asked.

"A peach grader, well, apple grader, fruit grader. Whatever." Danny reached out his hand. "Hi, I'm Danny Hackett."

Fallon watched him with suspicion. His hands were greasy with some kind of dirty mechanical oil. He'd carelessly slopped some of it onto his cheeks, chin, and forehead, decorating his face in grease monkey war paint. With his unwashed hair tugged into a miniature pony tail, Danny looked like the promise of a season in Hell. Yet, when he smiled, his eyes, matching blue, another rarity, lit up his face with boyish enthusiasm.

He noticed his hands, wiped them nervously on his T-shirt, also diabolical. "Sorry."

"It's okay," Fallon shook his hand. "I'm Fallon Westerly."

"I know," he sat heavily in a worn lounge chair. Its exposed springs groaned as it coughed up a cloud of dust.

Emma covered her face.

Danny brushed the turbid billow away. "Sorry."

"You do a lot of that," Fallon said.

"What?"

"Apologizing."

"Whaddya mean?"

"Well, you've been in the room for less than thirty seconds, and you've apologized three times."

"Sorry."

"Four." Now she did smile, just a quick one. "But I suppose I should be the one apologizing to you, thanking you too."

"Nah," Danny said. "Don't worry about it. I'm sure you'd have done the same for me."

"Broke into Blair's private, illegal chop shop, found you insensible, wrapped you in a blanket, carried you—while running from the possibility of electrocution, truly irritated watch dogs, and almost certain dismemberment—broke through the wall, hid your unconscious body in the brush, dressed you in clothes I'd stolen for myself, transported you by bus to a place I remembered from a wrong turn the bulls took two weeks ago, and then protected you while you slept for nearly two days?"

"Yeah," he said, "That's about right, except that I didn't dress you. I'm sure you'd have done the same for me if I'd been the one trapped in Blair's happy house of horrors."

Emma giggled. "It sounds a lot worse when you string it all together like that."

"Um..." Fallon finished her water, shook her head. "Let's hope we never have to find out."

"Deal," Danny slapped both palms down on the chair's armrests, loosing another noxious cloud of old farts and stale cat hair. "Sorry," he coughed.

"Five," Fallon tallied on her fingers.

"Anyway, since I agree with you—that testing the limits of your affection for me would be a mistake this early in our relationship—"

Emma groaned, "Oh, please."

"—we are not going anywhere near the Warrenton School for Juvenile Dismemberment and Dissection again." He stole her water glass, tried to get a last drop or two into his mouth. "I can't imagine why you'd wanna go back there. I'm

81

thinking that if we can get a car or a truck or something running, we can make for Richmond, and maybe steal a better car or enough credits for bus fare to Mississippi or even a software package we can download that will ensure these wrist screens won't—"

"No," Fallon shook her head. She didn't look up at him, didn't want to disagree with him. He had saved her life—*and your gifts, dummy. Don't forget that!*

Danny stood, threw greasy hands into the air. "Why? What on Earth could possibly motivate you to go back in there? The whole county will be crawling with bulls just waiting for us to access even one frigging P-credit for a cup of coffee, and blam! We'll be in leg irons again. I say we get lost in a hurry. C'mon, Fallon, you're gonna like Mississippi. It's warm year-round. There's lots of great open country, plenty of abandoned houses out in the hills, no one to pester you all day, and...hell, we could take some time, get settled, and then decide what to do, maybe make some credits, get an E-van or a houseboat. I always wanted a houseboat." When she didn't respond right away, he asked, "Or do you have family somewhere? Emma does. We gotta get her home, but I didn't know if you...I mean, I don't, and so I sometimes just figure—"

"I can't go with you, Danny. I'm sorry, but not yet."

"Why? Did you leave something in there? Something you sneaked past the bulls? Past Blair and Carter?"

"Nothing like that," she tried to explain. "You saw that place, his chop shop. It's gotta be—"

"What?" He interrupted. "Destroyed? Burned down? He'll build another one. He's a sociopath, a full-on, falling-down-the-stairs-loop-de-loop maniac. You wanna go head to head with him over a chop shop he'll have up and running two weeks after he sees your arms and legs and kidneys and...that one heartbreaking eye...sold to drunk Panamanian dealers?"

"I'm going to kill him," her voice cracked. Fallon cursed herself for sounding weak and uncertain.

Danny sighed through his nose. Tossing his hands again, he spun on his toes, spoke through the rusty screen to the yard outside. "Of course you are. Of course, Fallon Westerly, you're going to kill Headmaster Blair...after sneaking back into the detention center, into the residence, past the guards, the security monitors, the on-duty staff, the hundreds of teenage felons who might just say, 'Hey, look! It's Fallon! I wonder what she's doing here!' and somehow find your way into Blair's apartments, murder him without raising the alarm, then sneak to the chop shop and...what...blow it up? Set it on fire?"

"Do you always do that?" Fallon asked.

"Apologize? No." Irritated, Danny still spoke to the dooryard.

"No," Fallon said. "Do you always speak in long exaggerated lists like that?"

Leaning against the screen, he fussed with the stained T-shirt he'd ruined working on the peach grader, whatever that was.

"Huh?" Fallon asked.

"Yeah, actually," Danny said, "come to think on it, I do."

"Well, knock it off. That's gonna get boring."

"Hey, you started it."

"I did not." She felt ridiculous, engaging in such an infantile pissing contest.

"Sure you did." He turned to face her, any hint of boyish enthusiasm evaporating from his face. Fallon missed it already. "You and all your *found you insensible, wrapped you in a blanket, carried you—while running from the possibility of electrocution, truly irritated watch dogs, and almost certain dismemberment—broke through the wall, hid your unconscious body in the brush*...and whatever else you said just then. Yes, you started it."

Fallon gave up. "You're right. I did. But that changes nothing. I'm going back to the school. I'll go on my own; I don't care."

He looked to Emma, willing her to side with him, but the younger girl just shook her head, unwilling to take sides this early in their misadventures. Danny pressed the fleshy ball of his palm hard against his eye, then sighed, turned and kicked open the door. He left without saying anything.

"But thank you," Fallon called, hoping he heard her. She stripped all the animosity out of her voice. "I mean it, Danny. You really...saved me."

Emma fidgeted with the pen around her neck. "He did, you know."

Fallon watched out the torn screen. A cloud passed overhead, throttling back sunlight across the dooryard. Danny didn't reappear. "I know."

From the barn, the barking wheeze of the gas-powered engine started up again. "That's gotta be the peach grader," Emma said. "C'mon, let's go see."

"All right."

"And maybe play nice this time."

"Yeah." Fallon followed her into the yard. "Where's the water pump?"

"Around the side. I'll show you."

"No, it's all right. I can find it," Fallon followed a weedy flowerbed toward the corner of the house. "I just wanna...clean up a little."

"Whatever you need. We'll be in the barn."

Fallon guessed the antique pump had been fashioned from cast iron at least two-hundred years earlier. Rusting in Virginia humidity, it was a wonder the thing still worked. She understood why the water was such an unappetizing yellowish brown. Given time, the three teens wouldn't have to worry about Fauquier County Bulls hauling them into custody. Rather, they'd all die from heavy metal accumulation in their organs. The pump stood crookedly in a concrete slab beside a bowl-shaped spillway adorned with an anachronistic, pitcher-toting cherub who'd been decapitated in a grim accident some decades earlier. "Just as well," Fallon glanced back the way she'd come, listened a moment. "You don't wanna see this anyway."

Priming the old cistern with a half-dozen pumps of the creaky handle, she waited for the first trickle to spill into the concrete bowl before she kicked off a boot and unfastened her jeans. Pressing them down just far enough to step free from one leg, Fallon let the other hang in limp folds around her ankle.

The first sobs overtook her when she realized that she wasn't wearing underwear.

"Of course you're not, dumbass." She pumped again, loosing a steady flood into the spillway. "You really think Danny was gonna steal you a fresh pair of panties?" She let water splash over her hands, reveled in the fierce cold as she scrubbed herself clean.

She cried, aching for her mother and her mother's silly warnings. So many nights when Fallon had left their trailer with a boy, just for dinner or a sim movie in Old Forge, Helen Westerly had warned her. It'd been fun, an amusing game. What would Mama offer as sage advice tonight? Something awkward but underpinned with just enough seriousness to stick with Fallon through the evening.

You know how long it takes to make a baby? About 15 seconds. And that's what he'll give you, honey...15 seconds of pleasure in exchange for 25 years of responsibility and grief.

She'd never had sex with them, never found the right boy.

Right man.

Fallon pumped again, aggressively yanking the iron handle until a stream of unsanitary-looking water filled the concrete bowl and spilled into the uncut grass.

She wept in sloppy crying jags that shook her whole body. Scrubbing her hands and face, Fallon splashed water between her thighs, rubbing her skin raw and crying for her mother. Still scrubbing, still splashing and pumping, she collapsed to her knees and wrapped an arm loosely about the old pump.

"Why?" She rinsed the last of Headmaster Blair's insidious touch from her thighs, her abdomen, her arms, face, and neck. Then Fallon rested her cheek against the rusty pump, closed her eyes, and let grief have her. Naked and kneeling in eight inches of stale smelling water, she leaned over the grass and vomited. She spat, coughed up stomach acid, then scooped a handful of water into her mouth. Washing the very taste of the WSJSM from her throat, she spat again, then promised, "That's it, Blair. This is the last time you break me, you sonofabitch."

Pulling herself upright, Fallon struggled into her wet jeans, wiped her face clean and spoke to the empty dooryard. "I'm gonna kill you."

Only the headless cherub heard her.

5

Bulls, Peaches, and a Nest of Irritated Insects

The abandoned farm's ancient fruit grader could have doubled as the fossilized skeleton of a prehistoric creature— something hungry and generally pissed off. It stood center stage of the barn's rotting plank floor. A row of empty stables, walls filled with hanging harnesses and cracked leather saddlery, and a nearly unidentifiable stack of disintegrating hay bales rounded out the tableau, seemingly undisturbed for decades. Redolent of mown grass and a hundred years of accumulated dust, the barn's musty aroma didn't improve as Danny's roiling clouds of oily exhaust choked the place to its rafters.

"Christ, what's he doing?" Fallon shouted to be heard above the yelping bark in the confined space. "Do we need to sort fruit this morning? Why don't we just invite a van load of bulls out here to gas us?"

Ignoring Fallon's wet clothes, Emma paced slowly from the feeder end of the grader to the slowly turning, lazy Susan outwash at the far end, twenty feet away. To Danny, she called, "How's it work?"

He didn't hear. Rather, the already filthy teen contented himself by tinkering with one of the grader's engines, this one particularly boisterous and smoking.

"Danny!" Emma cupped her hands and shouted.

Seeing them, he hustled to the feeder chute and slapped a once red KILL switch. The grader chugged to a stop with a backfire that sounded like a gunshot in the enclosed barn.

"Huh?" Danny said, too loudly. "Sorry."

"That's six," Fallon commented, hoping to hide the redness in her eyes.

"How does it work?" Emma asked.

"And why did you need to turn it on?" Fallon added. "Why not plug into the wall network and invite Blair and Carter over for lunch?"

He noticed her wet jeans and dripping shirt, shook his head. "See, Emma, if you were a peach farmer—"

"Or apples."

"Apples...sure," he slid a hand down the grader's load chute. "You'd dump bags of apples in here and the machine would do the rest." Walking the length of the antique monstrosity, Danny paused at each grate and dump chute. "Here, it'd drop out the three-inch apples, the biguns. Down here, the two-and-a-half inchers. From here, you'd collect the twos, and on down the line."

Emma tried spinning the final chute, the broad circular tabletop, like a music record she'd seen in an old 2-D movie. It didn't budge. "So what's this for? Just the babies? The throw-aways?"

"Not throw-aways," he explained, "just the smallest of the apples, less than two inches."

"Wouldn't it fill up and overflow?"

"Nope," again, Danny shifted from chute to chute. "Some farm worker or kid would stand at each of these stations and fill boxes."

"Wait. I get it," Emma said. "It's how they'd know what sizes to sell and how to price them for the stores or the markets. Right?"

"Yup," he said, "but farmers don't use these any more. They just deliver the whole harvest to some Prevo-Mart Co-Op factory somewhere, and it's ground up and processed into paste or juice or whatever stores need for staples that week. Think about it; when's the last time you ate an actual piece of fruit with a stem?"

Emma stuck a hand down through the now silent, two-inch grate to the chute below. "You wouldn't have much time...or space...if you had to clear a clog."

"No kidding. Although after a while, I'd bet most workers got pretty good at it, pretty fast."

"You'd have to," Emma inserted and removed her tiny hand through the grate sorter as quickly as she could, seeing how fast she could reach the chute and still clear her wrist. "Maybe two seconds is all."

Danny did the same through the three-inch grates. "Yeah, huh...and then it'd be bye-bye hand."

"At the wrist."

He stepped back, looked over the grader, taking it all in. "Yeah, at the wrist, if no one got to the KILL switch in time, it might even carry you all the way to that turn table chute there at the end...tear you apart slowly."

"Yikes."

"No kidding."

"So why are we fussing with the thing?" Fallon asked. She'd found a wooden ladder against the back wall of the barn and stepped tentatively around the dusty, uncertain loft.

"Fallon!" Danny called. "You gotta get down. That won't hold you. Jesus, you'll crash right through."

She tiptoed along a splintered, two-hundred-year-old beam, her arms extended like a trapeze artist. "I can't be up here, but you can jolly around with a noisy, smelly, pointless old machine that can only...literally only...offer us the opportunity to be torn apart? I gotta admit: I don't understand you."

Emma caught Fallon's eye, mouthed the words, *Play nice!*

"I think better when I'm working on something is all." He didn't rise to the bait. "Fixing things calms me down, helps me get focused."

Fallon sat gingerly on the beam, her legs dangling from the hayloft. "So, whaddya think?"

"About what?"

"You're thinking," she said. "What about?"

89

"Well…" Danny rooted around for a good place to start. "Well, I guess I'm sorry I said that about Mississippi. I've been on my own for so long I don't always remember that other people have ties…you know, family and stuff."

When Fallon merely scissored her legs below the beam, he pressed on. "And as much as I'd like to go back to Mississippi, we can go anywhere. I don't mind, but I do think we oughta stick together. It's gotta be safer, at least until we get Emma to Baltimore and you back to…"

Fallon hesitated, saw disappointment in Danny's eyes, then said, "Old Forge, New York. Herkimer County. You'll like it, Danny. Lots of lakes, pine forests, rivers, a lot like rural Mississippi, I suppose, except without all the heat."

He looked up at her. "Downright cold from time to time, I'd bet."

"And snowy."

"Snowy? I haven't seen snow in a while, years I guess."

"We get plenty," Fallon went on, "feet of the stuff. You can bury yourself in it from about November to March."

"But first…" he prompted.

"But first, I'm going back for Blair."

"Don't suppose I can talk you out of it?" He wiped his face on his shirt sleeve, smearing more grease across his cheeks. "Can't convince you just to pack up and motivate outta here for New York or London or the Mars Colonies…I don't care."

"Nope."

"Even if I'm charming?"

"You've got a five-inch splash of motor oil on your face. There isn't any amount of charming that can outdistance a five-inch splash of motor oil."

Danny sighed. "All right, but Emma stays here."

"Done," Fallon said.

"Hey!" Emma protested. "How about if we don't discuss me as if I'm not here."

"He's right, Em," Fallon said. "It's safer for you here. I only need one person to watch my back. Danny and I'll get in and out of there in no time. You'll not even know we've been gone."

"No," the younger girl folded thin arms across her chest. "I'm not a child to be bossed around by seventeen-year olds. I'm only a year younger than you two."

"A year?" Danny prompted.

"Okay, two, but still…"

"Tell you what," Fallon said. "We'll need to get outta there in a goddamned hurry. How about if you wait for us outside the wall on some street nearby, and drive us away?"

Emma's eyes widened to Irish green saucers. "Drive?"

"Drive," Danny shot Fallon an appreciative glance. *Nice work!*

"Done!" Emma said.

"Done," Fallon pushed off the beam, dropped gracefully to the barn floor, falling twelve feet as if stepping off her back porch. "Now we just gotta steal a car."

"Steal a car?" Danny unleashed his bright, albeit greasy smile. It grew on Fallon with each appearance. "That part's easy."

"Then what're we waiting for?" She started for the dooryard. "C'mon Emma. Let's see what else we can borrow from this place."

"Good idea," Danny turned toward the rear storage closets. "I'll look for gas cans. Maybe we can siphon some useable fuel out of this thing."

"Okay. We'll be back in ten minutes."

The second floor of the ramshackle farmhouse looked to have been decorated in Post Bombing Rubble. Fallon truly hoped that whoever owned the place had abandoned it years ago, because if they still lived here, they existed in abject squalor. Fallon and her mother had never been wealthy and had shared a trailer with their on-again-off-again cat, Banjo, ever since they'd been evicted from the Gerhard estate for a

91

rich, snot-nosed, whining brat of a silver spoon Bloodsucker boy's lies.

But she didn't let that bother her.

Her mother was all right, with enough credits coming in from Herkimer County to afford the monthly fees on the trailer and the Prevo accounts.

Fallon would get back there soon enough. Besides, with Claire Felver's murder still in the Old Forge news and Herkimer County Bulls still patrolling the lakefront trailer park from time to time, it made sense to stay away.

Although she did feel sharp pangs of guilt that she couldn't send a message home or call briefly to let her mother know that everything was all right…if everything was all right. But plugging in to any network, even the broke-down, rusty-ass boxes providing signals to the Fauquier County farm community off whatever dirt path Danny'd taken to get them here would be a mistake.

She was being unfair.

He'd saved her.

He had.

If Blair had forced her to ride the storm, had removed even a pinkie toe…Fallon didn't like thinking about it.

And he was cute.

I don't have time for cute, not now.

Heh. Nonsense. Make time, dummy.

The upstairs bedrooms had been stripped of just about everything except for a toss of stained mattresses and a chest of drawers that yielded little of use to the three fugitives: several pairs of decent socks, a wool sweater, two pairs of denim pants that could possibly fit Danny or Fallon, an E-battery that might retain some charge, and a map of New Hampshire, circa 2086.

In the kitchen, Emma and Fallon discovered a collection of plastic plates decorated with sunny, happy tulips—Fallon decided immediately to leave them behind—and a few pieces of useless silverware.

Emma insisted on stealing three forks, said it made sense to be prepared to eat if they happened to scrape up any food in the foreseeable future.

Fallon tossed the forks into Danny's backpack. Although she remained a bit squeamish on the subject of food and would need a few more hours to recover from Headmaster Blair's sedatives.

"You know," Emma began. "You might think about giving him a bit of slack. Without him, I'm not sure we'd—"

"Down!" Fallon whispered. "Get down!" Dropping the bag, she cursed when the forks and the stolen battery clattered lightly on the peeling linoleum.

"What?" Emma crawled to her. "What happened?"

"Bulls," Fallon tilted her head toward the kitchen window, then pressed a finger to her lips.

Emma's hands shook. Fallon whispered. "In the pantry. Go. Quiet. Close the door."

Emma slithered across the dingy floor and into the closet-sized pantry. Curled up, she just fit beneath the bottom shelf with the scattered mouse turds and dry husks of dead cockroaches.

Close the door, Fallon mouthed silently, then winced when the screen door slapped open.

She crawled behind the long dead refrigerator, unplugged and quiet, but large enough to shield her from view if the bulls only peeked into the kitchen. She nearly yelped when a spider, a homely brown sucker large enough to eat Miami, skittered over her shoe and brushed up against the bare skin of her ankle. Flicking it away, she pulled her knees in, rested her chin on them, and tried to relax. She remembered the carving knife she'd failed to envision while insensible on Blair's chop shop table. It came to her readily now, easily taking shape in her imagination, her mother chopping onions.

Yes, it would be easy; she'd have two deadly knives at her disposal, just had to strike beneath or around the bulls' armor.

Where's that?

The belly. The armpits. The neck.

That'll do.

But where was Danny?

Get him out of your head, dummy. You're no good to anyone if you're all worked up about some boy.

But where is he? What if they take him? I can't have that...can't, not sure what we'll—

Voices reached her from the adjoining room:

"This place is deserted, a dead end. C'mon, let's check the barn then get outta here. I'm hungry."

"Hold on...hold on."

"What?"

"How long you figure this place is empty? How long since anyone lived here?"

"Dunno...years anyway."

"This water glass," Fallon heard the bull drop it back on the coffee table beside the sofa. "There's still water in it."

"And?"

"*And?* Dumbass. How long you expect water stays in a glass? Years?"

"Oh...um, no. Sorry."

"It's all right. They're here, or they been here."

"Whadda we do?"

"You check upstairs. I'll go through this floor. Then we gotta check the basement and the barn, the fields, anyplace they mighta been."

"Gotcha."

"They put blinkers in these kids?"

"Obviously not."

"Whaddya mean?"

"We're here...searching, bonehead."

"Yeah, right."

94

"Probably too expensive anyway. How many kids make a run for it? A couple, maybe five in a year? Not worth the cost of blinking all of them."

"All right. I'm goin' up."

Fallon felt heavy boot steps as one of the armor-plated half-humans trundled up the wooden stairs. She held her breath when the other clumped into the kitchen.

Carving knife, carving knife, carving knife, carving knife.

Shaking, she breathed through her mouth, figured they heard it in Saskatchewan.

The bull, armored, robotic, part human, shuffled into the kitchen, his boot steps resonating through the linoleum to tickle Fallon's quickly numbing ass. His uniform, part cloth and part bio-engineered protective gear, smelled of summer roadkill. She only caught a glimpse of his pants, gathering in wrinkles above his boots, but they seemed to be rotting away. This was no ordinary bull, not a government-standard, taxpayer-funded law officer anyway.

You can kill him. You can.

He opened the refrigerator. "Anything to eat in here?" And liberated such a dense, crippling stench of long dead, long rotten, long putrefied food that Fallon bit down on her wrist to keep from dry heaving. The cruel smell wafted about like the ghost of Christmas in Hell.

"Great mother of Christ," the bull shouted. "What are these Draggers eating?"

Leave! Leave already. Why won't you leave? Jesus, it smells like a frigging autopsy. Just go!

The bull stayed, left the refrigerator door open, ironically loosing more of the foul stink, while conveniently shielding Fallon from view. If she lived another hundred years she would never know why he'd not closed the door, shut off the stink.

"Try the pantry, eh? Maybe some canned bits anyway."

Fallon silently drew her feet beneath her, prepared to spring, to strike swiftly and repeatedly until the bull either lay dead or until he electrocuted her, gassed her, or just crushed her skull between his meaty paws.

She erased the salad of gruesome images from her imagination. She couldn't let them have Emma, couldn't stomach the idea of the little redhead in custody. She'd talk; they'd torture her and she'd talk – not that it mattered – because Fallon would come for her. She'd kill any of them, this stinking motherscratcher for starters. She had no recollection of Headmaster Blair between her legs; she'd been unconscious, riding the storm most likely. Yet, strangely, she wanted to know, wanted badly to remember.

Perhaps killing a few bulls would help to jog her memory.

With the pantry door standing open, the soldier growled, "Meh, nothing. Figures." Turning, he slapped it closed, slammed the refrigerator, and called, "Bentley! Let's go! There's no one here anyway! Let's check the basement, then hit the barn."

Still cowering, but shivering with adrenaline and fear, Fallon waited until she heard the heavy duo tromp downstairs before whispering, "Emma...are you in there?"

The pantry door slid quietly open. Emma crouched where she'd been hiding. She snapped her ever-present pen into its cap and shoved the card-sized notebook into her back pocket. Fallon couldn't imagine how the bull had missed her. But for now, it didn't matter. They'd dodged the bullet. Next, they had to warn Danny. And although every cell in her body wanted to stay put until the deadly bloodhounds drove away, she crouched and motioned for Emma to follow. Sweat beaded on her forehead and ran in salty trickles down the side of her nose. But she didn't hurry, couldn't risk a creaky floorboard.

Fallon nearly pissed her borrowed jeans when the godfusticating screen door squealed faintly. "C'mon," she whispered. "We gotta run!"

96

Not two steps inside the barn, Fallon understood that they were cooked, and all her efforts to hide had been a pointless waste of time. The unmistakable aroma of burning oil and gas exhaust filled the space with clear evidence that someone had been here in the last hour.

She figured they had about two minutes to get clear of the farm. "Danny!"

Nothing.

Emma ran to the storage closet in the rear wall, peeked into the darkness. "Nope, not in there."

"Good," Fallon said. "He took off."

The younger girl looked as though her mother had just confessed to delivering Christmas presents and Easter eggs. Everything about Emma Carlisle slumped dejectedly. "And left us? He left us?"

"I dunno, but we gotta hustle. Let's go. Now. Out the back."

Fallon had to shove Emma to get her going; the smaller girl might have stood dumbstruck in the barn all afternoon. They hurried into the anonymity of tangled brush in the adjacent field. The barn quickly disappeared behind them.

They pressed through stinging nettles and barbed thistles, and while Fallon had no idea where Danny had hidden, she dared not cry out for him again. She decided to hide until the bulls left, wait to see how many more arrived and then, perhaps, return to look for the infuriating boy.

The good news, if it could be called such, was that they hadn't been tagged with blinkers. The bulls had confirmed at least that much.

The officers didn't summon backup. They didn't call in a grizzled old timer with a team of woofing hounds to search the fields, stone rows, and creek beds south and west of the farmhouse. Rather, the two officers simply searched the house, searched the barn and realized that someone had started the peach grader that morning. They stood in the muddy dooryard and sent messages via their wrist screens.

97

"What're they doing?" Emma brushed a fly from her face.

Fallon pressed a prickly raspberry bush aside, then sat where she could make out the dooryard, the back porch, and the rear of the barn. "I think they're calling in the fact that they've found something, but they don't know if it's us, some kids from town goofing off, or the actual owners of this place, whoever they are."

"They searched the barn." It wasn't a question.

"Yeah," Fallon said, "didn't find him. That's good."

"You think he's out here somewhere?"

"I hope so."

Emma squirmed uncomfortably, "I wish we could hear what they're saying."

"Sit still," Fallon said, then regretted it. "Sorry, Emma, just try to…"

"These pricker bushes are all stabbing me. How much longer do you think?"

"We'll see soon enough."

The larger of the officers moved to the front porch, stood half inside the screen door, and withdrew a nearly invisible retractable bio-wire from his wrist screen.

"Look!" Emma pointed. "He's plugging in; the Wi-Fi must be dead. Not surprising."

"Downloading something," Fallon grabbed Emma's wrist, lowered it gently. "Please try to stop fussing around. Okay? I'm not thrilled with the idea of getting chained in the back of their van."

"At least we know the network's still on."

"Lotta good that does us," Fallon rotated her own wrist, considered her vid-screen. Either Emma or Danny had powered it down when they carried her out of Blair's chop shop. She wondered if Carter Whatshisname could activate them remotely, especially after he found out that the three runaways had been deleted from the rolls at the WSJSM. She asked, "So what'd you do?"

98

"To get shipped off to Warrenton?"

"Yup."

Emma paused a beat, just long enough for Fallon to wonder whether she was about to get fed some well-rehearsed lie. Eventually, she said, "nothing much. I made some promises about merchandise I couldn't deliver."

"Or decided against delivering?" Fallon asked. "I noticed your eyes match, figured it meant your parents had plenty of credits in the bank. What'd you need money for?"

"To run away."

Fallon nodded. "That bad?"

"Yes and no," she said. "My mother's remarried, and Edward's a bit of a...handful, I guess."

"I get it."

"Hey, look!" Happy to change the subject, Emma pointed again toward the dooryard. "They're coming this way."

"Nah, they're turning."

The bulls, their eyes hidden behind dark interactive E-visors, reached the edge of the overgrown field and turned left, skirting the brush. Fallon could only imagine what sorts of orders flashed inside those helmet screens, nothing useful. While they searched the mass of chaotic bushes, neither of them ventured into the field to look for the escaped inmates.

Emma whispered. "They don't wanna come out here either."

"You're right," Fallon said. "This is good; this is all good."

The younger girl frowned. "I'm not sure I share your enthusiasm, buddy. Especially if they have infrared detection software on those lenses. Some jurisdictions do."

"Think about it," Fallon explained. "They know we're gone, and they're looking for us. But they don't believe we're anywhere near this farm. If they thought we were hiding out here, they'd get dogs and E-copters and a whole battalion of bulls out here tramping the bushes flat. That's good."

"Um...how?"

"We've got the upper hand, Em. We know they're after us, and they've sent bulls, not your everyday bulls either. That smelly sonofanightmare who came into the kitchen, he's not normal."

"He did look and smell like he had a bit of a glandular problem," Emma agreed.

"Anyway, if they leave, this farm is now the safest place in the Universe for us. They've given it a look over, haven't found us...yet...and moved on."

"Well—"

"Right, not yet," Fallon whispered. "Just stay down, and we're home free."

"Um..."

"Okay, that's overstated. Fine."

Twenty minutes later, Fallon realized that she'd been right: the bulls walked the length of the field, turned down the eastern stone row, checked the small creek bed between the brush meadow and a fallow stretch of dirt behind them, and then wandered back to the dooryard where they started toward the barn again, apparently for a last look.

Near the door, they were set upon by an unexpected colony of hornets. Fallon watched, amused as the beefy officials in tactical helmets and body armor flailed at a cloud of pissed off insects.

"Damnit! Where in all Hell did these bastards come from?" One yelled, still swatting like a man having a full-on seizure.

"Must've stepped on a nest." His partner shouted, shoving the other toward their van. "C'mon!"

With the hornet cloud in angry pursuit, the bulls sped out the dirt driveway, leaving an impressive cloud of dust over the dooryard.

"Holy shit!" Fallon said. "That was lucky."

"Yeah," Emma stood upright, still three feet shorter than the half green, half brown-husky corn stalks. "I hope those wasps hit them hard. But just to be sure, let's not go back yet. Okay? Just stay here a little longer?"

"Yeah," Fallon pressed stalks aside, hoping to find Danny. "Sure, kiddo. We'll wait."

Emma insisted that they remain hidden for another fifteen minutes. In that time, they neither heard nor saw any sign of the bulls.

Emma pointed to the back of her own neck. "I noticed your…"

Fallon tugged an ear of corn free, began shucking. "Oh, that. Yeah. It hurt; I remember the day they did it."

"It's for your eye?"

"Yeah. My eighteenth birthday present."

"It's gorgeous."

"It's a pain in my ass." She sniffed the corn, nibbled, then spat into the dirt. "Been nothing but trouble for Mom and me since I was a kid."

"You wish you'd been born with just two brown ones?"

"Green, I guess."

"Green. Yeah, they'd be pretty with your hair."

Impatient to look for Danny, Fallon focused on the lengthening shadows along the grimy whitewashed wall of the farm house. She realized that for every few minutes they waited, the barn's shadowy outline swallowed a few more inches of abandoned homestead. When the screen door disappeared entirely, its last corner sliding silently inside late afternoon shade, she stood with a curse, brushed prickles from her clothes and hair, "I think we're about good, Em. Let's go."

Not three steps across the trampled lawn, Fallon heard the barn door creak open. She shoved Emma toward the driveway and the dirt road beyond. "Run!"

She'd no idea how one of the bulls had managed to remain behind, didn't care. Unless he succeeded in sneaking past her, somehow sprinting to the road, Fallon would get in front of him, cut him off.

Then deal with him.

101

Emma didn't wait to be told twice and tore up the driveway at a hysterical sprint.

Fallon spun on her heel, her mother's carving knife and the wrought iron gate in the WSJSM courtyard clear in her mind's eye. Squinting into the afternoon sun, she growled, "Okay, you smelly mother—"

Danny stepped into the dooryard, his hands extended. "Whoa, whoa, hold on a second. It's just me."

Anger and relief warred for possession of Fallon's heart—a sensation she didn't relish. She clenched her teeth, banished the vivid images of knives and rib-cracking iron fists. "Where the hell were you?"

"Whaddya mean?" His hands still out, palms up in apology, "I was in the barn the whole time. Didn't you see the bulls? I mean, sure, you had to see them. Right? Did you hide? Where'd you go? Are you okay?"

"Danny," Fallon's tone threatened his very life.

"Fallon," he hurried to her, considered hugging her, then just pressed his hands down on her shoulders. Leaning close, he looked earnestly into her eyes. "Are you okay? Did they hurt you? Did they hurt Emma?"

"Em!" Fallon shouted without turning around. "C'mon back. It's just Jackass."

The redhead actually hadn't run all the way to the county road. Rather, Emma huddled behind an evergreen shrub alongside the farm's rutted driveway. Fallon could have sworn she saw Emma note something in her pad.

Danny asked, "What's the matter?"

"Where were you?" Fallon glared. "Where'd you go?"

"I was in the barn."

"Don't lie to me, Danny." She heard the pleading overtones in her voice and just about broke down. "Please. I can't do this if you're lying to me."

He squeezed her shoulders tighter, clearly wishing he could summon the courage to hold her close. "Look at me." He gave her a gentle shake. "Look, I...I was in the barn. I hid in

102

the loft. The bigger of those bulls, that godfrigging giant, he sniffed, actually smelled the air, like he could sniff out my fear or something. Then he tried coming up the same ladder you used. He got about three rungs up, and it splintered under him. He didn't fall, but he gave up, figured either of them would come crashing down if they managed to get up there. So they left. That's it. I waited, listened for you the whole time." He considered her carefully. "Why? What happened?"

Tears slipped from Fallon's eyes, cleaned twin paths through the sweaty grime on her cheeks. "Please, Danny, don't lie to me."

"I'm not lying," he insisted. "I can show you right where I hid...in the hayloft...behind that pile of rotting bales."

"We called for you," she shook loose from his grip. "We were in the barn. Why didn't you answer? What's going on? You're hiding something, and it's making me nervous. Can't you see that?"

"I dunno what to say. You must not have called very loud, because I was there."

She saw it: the faint, almost indecipherable shift in his gaze. Danny Hackett was lying to her. Fallon's heart broke, but she decided in a moment not to let him know it. Instead, she wiped her eyes on her sleeve. "We hid in the brush. The bulls gave a half-assed look for us, then left. They know we're gone, but they don't believe we're anywhere near this farm. It's the best place for us. We can set up here, use this as a base, you know, as we get ready."

Danny's shoulders slumped. "What's the matter?"

Again, Fallon dragged a sleeve across her face. "Nothing. I'm fine, just worked up a bit. That's all. We thought you were gone. Emma, especially, was scared you'd left."

At that, Emma dove into Danny's arms. "You're here!" she hugged him close. "I thought you'd left us. I was so scared. Where'd you go? Were you in the field?"

Still looking at Fallon, he said, "I was in the barn, just in the hayloft. I dunno what happened. I guess I didn't hear when you came through. I was pretty scared, too."

Emma forgave him immediately. "It's okay. We were sort of whispering anyway."

Fallon pressed her lips together in a grim smile. "So what's next?" She felt brief pride that she'd kept the wrinkles out of her voice this time.

"Next," Danny looked about the dooryard, as if the answer might be scribbled some place they'd overlooked. Sunlight lit his hair making Fallon want to lace her fingers into it, then maybe rip some of it out. "Next...I guess we make our way into town, try to catch the local news, and..."

"Steal a car?" Emma finished for him, all at once ready to drive them both to safety.

"Yeah," Fallon said. "We steal a car."

5.07

You've Never Met a Bull? Be Glad

Psst. Hey, sorry. I'm back. But this time, I promise I'll be quick. We've got all kinds of things going on with the story, so I don't want to keep you on this siding too long.

However, if you haven't met a bull, particularly one of the big, ugly, garbage-truck models they have in cities like Baltimore, Washington, or Philadelphia (hot beds of pretty acrimonious discontent during the Cloud Wars), you ought to have a thumbnail lesson.

Oh, and 'acrimonious'? Cool vocab word. Look it up. You'll be glad you did.

Anyway, bulls.

About two generations ago, the United States of America was involved in what essentially amounted to World War III. We generally refer to the conflict as the Cloud Wars, waged entirely because of the global proliferation of Stormcloud and its bedfellows: the Internet credit, the offshore body parts dealer, the soup bag—nasty bit of genetic engineering technology—and the international organ and beauty features trader, essentially heartless, soulless smugglers.

But we're not here to discuss the Cloud Wars just yet. We need more time and space for those. For now, let's just focus on bulls.

Biomechatronic Urban Law Enforcement Sentry or 'Bulls' for short. Yeah, I know: It really ought to be 'Bules,' but one shouldn't underestimate the sometimes-paralyzing stupidity of Congress in session.

What are they?

That's challenging to answer.

Bulls are domestic federal agents, mostly human, part robotic armored device. They have been bred (and injected with such an array of growth hormones and steroids) to be massive, almost always in excess of three-hundred pounds. Although, I

105

have acquaintances who claim to have seen bulls who stand over seven feet tall and weigh in at over four hundred pounds when wearing their tactical gear.

They have the authority to suspend your Constitutional rights (all of them) if they have reasonable suspicion that you've been up to no good. Granted, most federal agents can't intervene unless there is evidence that crime has taken place across interstate lines or that criminals involved have violated others' Constitutionally protected rights. Bulls, however, weren't in attendance the day they taught federal law in the Sisters of No Frigging Mercy Grammar School third grade.

No chance.

And given that most 'interstate' lines were essentially erased during the Corn War (yeah, another nickname. We'll get to that.), bulls have staggering power almost everywhere they go. Federal officials send in squadrons of bulls when America's disenfranchised or downtrodden masses rise up, demanding equity of access to resources, better food, hospitals, schools, roads, salaries, you get the idea...the same list the disenfranchised and downtrodden have been bitching about for two-thousand years.

Bulls have an array of AI, thought-controlled weapons affixed to their tactical vests and can quiet a street riot in a matter of minutes. No one messes with them. They travel in old vans, school buses, and gas-powered delivery trucks, because they want to maintain a low profile in some of the worst neighborhoods in the nation. They fear (almost) nothing, are difficult to wound, and nearly impossible to kill without a flame thrower or a tactical nuclear device.

I can hear you already: C'mon...you're telling me that the federal government breeds three-hundred-pound, part human, street soldiers to control domestic disturbances and investigate federal crimes. They're armed with guns, tasers, and noxious gasses. They wear projection screen visors that carry comprehensive state and federal crime data, and they're scared off by a few angry hornets?

106

Yes, that's exactly what I'm saying. Everyone's afraid of angry hornets, even bulls.

6

Mr. & Mrs. American Perfect, a News Broadcast, and Another Exploding Dog

The towns of Warrenton and Culpeper, Virginia existed as anomalies among residential areas within fifty miles of Washington, DC. Most towns, villages, and cities within commuter distance to the nation's capital had been overrun by cookie-cutter, suburban sprawl homes over the past three generations. Trees, which had grown in abundance when Robert E. Lee and George Meade led armies about the region, were now such a rarity that counties near the old DC Beltway passed contentious laws punishing anyone who even considered permitting their domesticated animals to urinate on a naturally-growing tree.

But domesticated animals had become pretty rare, except for the über rich or the über rural.

Fake trees, porcelain, ceramic, even plaster—the cheapest versions—dotted gated community lawns and greenways. But real trees, roots-in-the-ground, leaf-changing creations of nature, those were a rare sight within fifty miles of the White House.

Farther west, beyond Warrenton, zoning laws established in the 1700s still held on with a gnarled, weakening talon. Farms that had been operating for over four-hundred years were protected by a Constitutional amendment and could not be developed, even if they were sold. Because families couldn't subdivide land for suburban developers, they lost out on the opportunity to make a massive return on their great, great, great, great, great grandparents' investment. In turn few farms sold. Why would they? By 2050, the Commonwealth government realized that if they didn't provide some financial subsidy to farmers, nothing but tobacco and twelfth generation corn-not-corn would ever be planted in Virginia soil.

Some farmers did relatively well, took the state kickback, and grew corn-not-corn or soybeans. Others gave up, let the ground go fallow, and took punch-in, punch-out jobs in the nearest town. Rich farmers grew tobacco for export. Rich farmers had always grown tobacco. Cigarettes had been illegal for thirty years, not that these statutes kept people from smoking.

Walking in single file toward the closest of Fauquier's gated sprawl neighborhoods, the three teens avoided unnecessary chatter. Fallon wanted them listening for approaching vehicles in case they needed to dive into the brush. Two miles later, they'd not seen even a tractor along the nearly deserted roadway. Across fields and between creek draws, they noticed lights coming on in kitchen windows and above porch doors. The October sun hesitantly gave up its hold on the day and sank in a majestic orange and purple display behind the rank of uniform Shenandoahs in the west.

Fading into the gloom, Danny finally said, "So whaddya think? Should we try to get into the town center and hit a café or a bar for some news? Or should we try one of these Bloodsucker neighborhoods, maybe get lucky and find a car?"

"Won't it be harder to steal a car in town?" Emma asked, "with people around?"

"Nah," Danny said. "There's gotta be plenty of dark parking lots or side streets where we can find something."

"I'd rather hit one of the snooty neighborhoods, if we can get inside the wall," Fallon said. "I'm not sure how we talk our way in, especially if the guard's been watching the local news and recognizes us."

"That'd be bad," Emma said, "to hide from bulls trained to rip our spleens out and then get collared by a rent-a-cop watching baseball highlights in a community guard house."

"That's true, Em, but I can get us in."

"And in the dark, maybe we can find someone with the news on their retractable. Right?"

"Sure," Danny said. "It's a nice night. If we're really lucky they might even have a window open, so we can hear the broadcast."

"But first we have to get in," Emma reminded.

"I'll worry about that," he said.

"How?" Fallon challenged. Walking in silence had given her time to think over why she'd been so upset when Danny suddenly appeared in the dooryard. Why hadn't she believed his story? And if he'd not really been in the barn, why had he lied about it? Danny certainly wasn't working with the Fauquier County Bulls. She'd overreacted, just stress or nerves or heebie-jeebies, and figured she should apologize once they were alone. Yet simultaneously, some rarely-tapped instinct continued to suggest that he'd lied, for whatever reason. So Fallon wasn't about to follow him over an electrified fence just to land in leg irons and a ten-by-six solitary confinement chamber at the WSJSM. She asked again, "How can you get us in?"

"I've lived on my own for a few years now," he said. "I've learned some things about fences and cars."

Emma didn't detect the tension between them. "Even the F-models?"

"No, sorry," he replied. "You're not going to get to drive an F-car."

"Damn. I was hoping."

"Probably just an E model, or if we're really lucky, one of those Prevo junkers. Those are easy to hot wire."

"Like the Texarcana Siesta?" Emma asked. "My mother had one when I was little, vomit beige. It had just about enough power to get us across town to Aunt Madeline's. But you could hear it working extra hard when we went up the hill at Belvedere Avenue, by Sally Cassidy's house."

Fallon allowed herself a chuckle. "You had a problem with Sally Cassidy?"

"The bitch," Emma said. "I hated her and hated that she saw us driving in that old thing. I swear my father's lawn mower had a bigger engine."

Danny slowed to walk beside her. "Well then I promise we will not steal a Texarcana Siesta."

"Deal," Emma wrapped her arm around the tall boy's waist but didn't hold on to him long. Danny's curious limp made walking that close difficult; his hip sidled a few inches to the right with each step, knocking Emma off her stride.

Watching the two of them in the twilight, Fallon noted that Danny hadn't answered her question about breaking into a guarded neighborhood, over an electric perimeter fence, to watch television and steal a car.

The fence, weathered colonial brick, stood at least twelve feet high.

Emma whistled through her teeth. "Damn, that's up there."

"No kidding," Fallon agreed.

"And it's electric on top?" Emma asked.

"Yeah," Danny said. "Get this: they implant the electric bands into that decorative concrete cap running the whole length of the wall. But they don't do it because they give a shit about anyone who tries to climb over. The minute you put a hand on that smooth peak, you're dead...or at least shocked into next Thursday." He slapped a hand flat against the bricks. "And that's not to mention the damage you do falling twelve feet as a catatonic rag doll. Not good, puppies, not at all!"

"Good Lord," Emma whispered.

"And you know what's funny?" Danny went on. "These rich Bloodsucker slobs don't give a pinch of giraffe poop that I get fried when I get up there. Nope, not for one second. The reason they embed the electric bands in the upper edge of the concrete is because they don't want their neighborhood looking like a maximum-security prison."

"Doesn't it kill squirrels and birds and stuff?" Fallon asked.

111

"All the time," he replied. "There's not a squirrel within a mile of here that hasn't had a foot fried off."

Emma folded her arms. "I don't like this place."

"Well my dear, these people don't like you, either." He ruffled her unruly curls with one hand, then repeated the gesture with both, just for amusement. "So it's mutual."

"How're you getting in Evel Knievel?" Fallon asked with unmistakable skepticism.

"Who?" Emma looked confused. "What's an Evel...whatever you said?"

"Never mind. How about it, Knievel?"

"Sounds like an ice cream flavor."

Danny zipped his jacket, his now clean face enthusiastic in the moonlight. "Not for you to worry about, my alarmingly bald friend. You and Emma just make your way around that corner. Head for the main gate. There should be a doorway, just a regular, wrought-iron door somewhere near the guard house, where cars pass in and out." He walked them to the corner, peeked around to check for patrolmen. "I'll meet you there in five minutes."

"What about dogs?" Emma asked. "I heard that some of these places have dogs trained to bite anyone whose wrist screens aren't giving off some kind of special pulse. Is that true? I mean, what would these people do if their power went down for a few days? If there was a blizzard or something and their batteries died? They'd be trapped in their homes with a pack of man-eaters roaming the streets like great white sharks?"

"Sharks are in the ocean, sweetie," Fallon took her hand. "C'mon, let's go."

"But what about the dogs?" Emma resisted. "I don't like mean dogs, even worse than those XX-Reptiles. Have you seen those things? What the hell are we thinking, breeding those things like Labradoodles?"

Fallon flashed to her hazy impression that a German Shepherd exploded while bearing down on them. She shook her

112

head, dismissed the memory. "It's all right. Danny will protect us. Won't you, Danny?"

"From trained killer dogs?" His voice cracked.

"Um…sure. Yeah, sure. I'm not…you know, afraid of dogs."

"And the XX-dinos," Emma added.

"They're harmless," he said. "I knew a guy who worked on some billionaire's estate where they had a whole bunch of them, Triceratops, Pteranodons, even an Allosaurus, big as a frigging garbage truck, and, get this, the neighbors' cats used to scare the snot out of them."

"Of the Allosaurus?"

"Yup. They've been in-bred so many times, they're like massive, overweight frogs, just stupid and hungry."

"All right." That seemed to placate Emma. "But either way, watch for dogs."

"Right," he said. "You don't like mean dogs."

Fallon smiled in the darkness, hoped Danny noticed. "Five minutes. Meet you there."

"Wait," Emma pulled up short again. "What do we do if you're not there?"

"I'll be there."

"Wanna bet?" Fallon teased.

"Name your terms, Baldie," he warned, "but you better be ready to pay up. I am, in fact, dazzling at breaking and entering."

"Five minutes?"

"Five."

"And if you're not there, you will buy me breakfast tomorrow. My choice." Fallon said, entirely uncertain how any of them would access credits for food, shelter, electricity for their stolen car, weapons, timeshare condos, investment management opportunities, new summer fashions, anything.

"Done," Danny clapped his hands. "And if you lose, Fallon, you will spend forty-eight hours responding with 'Yes, dear' every time I refer to you as 'Baldie.' How's that?"

"Done," Fallon pretended to check her still-dead vid-screen. "You'd better hustle; time's flying." She and Emma turned the corner, started for the distant lights of the community guard house a hundred yards away. When they'd moved about fifteen paces along the wall, she turned and hurried back to the corner, needing to know. "Danny, where are you?" But the charming boy had already disappeared. "Damnit."

Less than four minutes later, Danny appeared at the wrought-iron doorway reserved for pedestrian traffic into or out of whatever community this was. From inside, he was able to open the door without a key card, a code, or a bio-wire plug.

It opened with a metal squeal. Fallon felt a quick pang of tension, then realized that the guards wouldn't give the pedestrian gate a second glance. People came and went through here all the time. They might not even hear the hinges any longer.

Danny bowed low. "Table for two on the veranda?"

Emma took his hand. "Yes, please, and I'd like a shrimp cocktail when you have a moment, good sir."

"Coming right up." He reached for Fallon's hand. When she stuffed them both into her pockets, he said, "Ah, c'mon, Fallon—excuse me...Baldie—but you gotta admit: that was pretty good what I just pulled off there. Doncha think?"

Fallon frowned. "You're a criminal."

Danny feigned offense. "How dare you make such an implication?"

"It's not an implication, jackass, if I say it outright."

"Well," a little uncertain at this, Danny said, "okay, fair enough, but so are you, Baldie. I'm sure you didn't come all the way down to the Warrenton School for Juvenile Truckstop Bathroom Maintenance for fun. Didja...Baldie?"

"No, Danny, I—"

"Nope," he wagged a finger, cutting her off.

"Oh, come on, already. We've got work to do." She tried pushing past him.

114

"Nope," Danny stood frozen, only his finger wagging. "It'll have to wait...Baldie."

Fallon sighed through her nose, shook her head, then said, "Yes, dear."

Danny raised his hands in triumph, shouted, "Yes! Yes, I do believe she called me *dear*. You heard her, Emma Carlisle. Didn't you?" He tumbled backward into the neatly trimmed grass, his fists still raised to Heaven.

Emma couldn't help but laugh. "I did. She called you *dear*."

Fallon ignored them, started up the sidewalk. "You're a criminal...gonna get yourself killed. And you're too damned loud. Put a lid on it, dumbass."

Emma waited beside the still open passageway through the bricks. "Did you...did you see any dogs? I really don't like mean dogs. I mean...I get—"

"Nope," Danny lowered his voice, "not one."

"But there might be patrols," Fallon said. "So we find a car, find someplace where they're watching the news, and then get the hell out of here. And if we can't find someplace with the broadcasts downloaded, we'll drive into town, and one of us can go into a café or a bar to see what kinds of coverage we're getting."

"Good idea. And you're right: there's probably patrols. This place is pretty nice. They've got credits here for a whole army of rent-a-killers."

"Lovely," Fallon said, "because I haven't been naked and strapped down for almost three days."

"What time's the news on?" Emma asked. "Must be about six, right?"

"Yeah. Unless they're just running downloads." Danny started after Fallon. "But I don't have any idea what time it is, haven't had my wrist live since we broke out."

"Rats," Fallon stopped, turned. "Okay, let's find some places with interactive screens visible through the windows. It's gotta be close to six by now."

115

"Or later," Danny started.

"Don't," Fallon interrupted. "Let's just go."

They snaked stealthily between and around the big-boned, but closely-constructed homes in the wealthy community. With full darkness shrouding them now, the fugitives found it relatively easy to move without being seen. What worried Fallon was that after four blocks of creeping and backtracking in search of an interactive wall unit with the sound turned up and a window cracked slightly, they'd not encountered one family dog, no cats, not even one of Danny's dismembered squirrels.

"There's gotta be dogs," she whispered after another two homes and no news projections.

Emma pulled up short. "Why? Why do you say that? Did you hear something?" Nervously, she clutched her pen. "Fallon?"

"No, Emma, it's nothing like that," she said. "I just haven't seen any other animals, no dogs on porches, no cats sneaking around. Why is that?"

"Because they're on the menu," Danny said. "Good catch. We gotta be extra careful."

Fallon let him take her hand, even reveled in the non-romantic, rough grasp of his fingers across her palm.

"C'mon," he said. "There's light in that window, over there, just beyond that little pond. Let's check it out."

They ducked behind a hedgerow, skirted the edge of a large, in-ground pool, dimly illuminated for after-dark swimming, and circled around a small pond offset from the neighborhood by a circle of massive hardwood trees, like supplicants gathered round sacred waters.

"Wow," Emma paused to run her hands over an immense elm, its branches an impenetrable canopy above. "We don't have these where I live. This thing's gotta be three-hundred years old."

"It's a tree," Fallon said. "There's forty million of them out behind my mother's trailer. You can come over and build an apartment in one if you like. Let's keep moving."

Danny agreed. "Trust me, Em: there are places with plenty of forest left."

"Sure," she whispered, "in rural Mississippi. Who wants to live there?"

He motioned for her to follow through a flower bed. "I do."

Fallon sneaked ahead, ducked low beneath a row of dark windows, and crept on her hands and knees, carefully avoiding the splash of light from the large windows of the mansion's main sitting room. She reached back with one hand, gave a thumbs up, then turned and sat with her back pressed against the siding. "The news is on," she whispered. "There's two people in there, plus the reporter's projection, but I can't hear what she's saying."

Danny leaned close, spoke directly into Fallon's ear. "We need them to open the window, just a crack."

Fallon said, "They're moving like they're bringing dinner plates or trays in from another room. Maybe they're cooking...I mean, if we time it just right, maybe we can reach up, push the glass open when they're out of the room."

"Unless it's locked," Emma said.

"It's worth a try," Danny slid past Fallon; he didn't risk a glimpse into the room, not from directly beneath the glass. "Can you see them?"

Fallon held up one finger, "Wait...wait...one second...okay now!"

Danny pressed upwards against the window frame. Nothing. He adjusted his hands, tried for a better grip along the synthetic trim but still couldn't get it to budge. Risking a quick peek into the room, he saw a massive, interactive video screen, nearly the size of an entire wall, and easily ten feet across by eight feet high. From a row of small apertures in the screen's lower corner, a series of beams projected the three-dimensional image of a local news reporter, an attractive brunette woman in a tasteful suit, into the family's sitting room. She sat at her desk, shuffled papers, even took periodic sips from a mug of tea or water. When the family entered the room, the reporter continued her broadcast, noting various points in the news as graphics, statistics, or images scrolled or flashed on the wall screen. When family members left the room, the reporter fell silent again, seemingly contenting herself with notes or pages until the viewers returned.

"Whoah," Danny whistled softly. "Now that's a television. Look at the clarity of that avatar. I can see individual gem stones in her broach. Ah, I want one."

"Sure," Fallon said. "I'll get you one. You can hang it in your...oh, wait...you're homeless."

"No one likes you," he said.

Emma giggled.

"Can we focus?" Fallon asked. "What're we gonna do?"

In the wash of multi-colored light from the video screen," Danny's expression shifted from uncertainty to reckless, daredevil stupidity.

Fallon didn't like it. "No."

"No, what?"

"No, whatever you're thinking you're about to do."

"Don't," Emma said. "Let's just try another house."

"It's okay," he said. "Just wait here, two minutes."

"Wanna bet?" Fallon forced sarcasm into a whisper.

"I'm a criminal." Projection screen color flashed across his teeth. "You said so yourself, Baldie."

"Don't—"

"I'll be right back." He crawled toward the front of the house, keeping low and quickly disappearing into the shadows.

"Well," Emma said, "I guess it's good that I kind-of always liked Professor Clarke."

"Why's that?"

"Because we'll probably have her for second period tomorrow."

Now Fallon laughed, tried to hide it, then let herself go. "Em, you made a joke."

Emma looked ready to vomit into the tulips. "Heh, sure, I made a joke."

From images and graphs on the wall screen, Fallon figured the reporter avatar was passing along information about a pirate attack on a cruise ship somewhere off the coast of Mexico. United Nations military personnel had apparently intervened, sank the pirate vessel, and incapacitated all of the would-be hijackers with a sonic missile. She wasn't able to determine whether anyone on the ship had been injured in the botched attack.

"What can you see?" Emma asked.

"It's world news. We might be too late."

"Nah, it's probably headlines. Right?" Emma said. "They do those first. But it's awfully dark, might be the later news, like eight o'clock."

"Does that matter?"

"Dunno. I only normally watch the news at six. It's often just lies and propaganda crap anyway."

"Bugger," Fallon whispered. "We need these two to go back into the kitchen for a refill or something." The couple, young professionals from the looks of them, ate from fancy dinner plates as they lounged in their living room, drinking wine and chatting. To Fallon, they looked as happy, healthy, and prosperous as members of the Bloodsucker class should be allowed to get. The husband wore an eye patch—*probably waiting on something pale or aquamarine to arrive in a soup bag from Helsinki.* The wife, a white woman, thin with a shapely neck, had replaced her Northern European legs, both of them, with lean, athletic African legs, chocolate brown and muscular. *A matching set. Those must have been expensive. And somewhere in Africa, there's a former runway model now dragging herself around on a frigging skateboard.*

Emma broke her spell. "Can you see him?"

"Where?"

119

"I have no idea. Is he in there somewhere?"

"No, he's gotta be out front, completely undone by the lock on their—" She stopped. In a darkened corridor off the family sitting room, Danny crouched, just out of sight of Mr. & Mrs. American Perfect. "Holy shit!"

"What?"

"Shhh."

"Sorry."

"He's there," Fallon couldn't fathom it. "Great humping dogs, that crazy sonofabitch made it in there. I can't frigging believe that boy. I can't believe him."

"What's he doing?"

"Hiding, sweating, peeing his pants. I don't have any idea."

"No," Emma pointed over Fallon's shoulder. "Look, he's...oh, wait...I get it."

"What?"

"Don't worry," she said. "I'll be right back." And Emma disappeared behind the house.

"What the hell?" Fallon rubbed her temples. "This is not good, not good, sister. You're in deep tonight. Let's see what's gonna happen next. Huh?"

On cue, Mr. & Mrs. American Perfect stopped eating, looked questioningly at one another, and then placed the dinner plates on their ornate granite coffee table. Mr. American Perfect motioned for Mrs. American Perfect to stay put as he rose from the sofa and headed into an adjacent room, presumably their kitchen where Emma was banging on a side door or window. "Oh, shit," Fallon said. "Get up, stupid. Get up! Go on; use those expensive African legs, you dopey, suburban slob. You gonna make your husband do all the heavy lifting? C'mon, clear outta there...just for a second..."

Mr. American Perfect peeked back into the room and said something to Mrs. American Perfect that prompted her to follow him out. As soon as she disappeared, the three-dimensional news avatar entered vamp-and-wait mode and began fussocking with her notes and coffee mug. Fallon stood, waved frantically for Danny. "C'mon, now. Now, stupid. You got about ten seconds."

Danny ran for the window, unlatched it, and in two breaths had it open a half inch, enough for them to hear the broadcast, but not so much that Mr. & Mrs. American Perfect would notice when they returned to their dinner plates. Through the glass, Danny offered up such a confidently smug grin that Fallon seriously considered murdering him in his sleep. Bending close, he whispered, "Not bad, huh? Jesus, but a guy's gotta work to impress you, Fallon Westerly."

She didn't answer. Behind him, in Mr. & Mrs. Perfect's sitting room, the brunette news avatar had detected the presence of another person and begun her broadcast once again.

"Shit!" Fallon said.

"What?" Panic rose in Danny's face.

"The reporter! Get the hell out of there!"

He dove for the hallway. The moment his feet disappeared into the shadows, Mr. & Mrs. Perfect's news avatar quieted again. But not before Mrs. Perfect frowned into the room. With the window open, Fallon heard her clearly. "Winston, the news started up again. I hate it when it does that. We have to fix this thing."

From the kitchen, Mr. Perfect's response came back muffled. "Yeah, okay honey. I'll look at it tomorrow."

"Thank Christ," Fallon sank back into the shadows. "One down. Now, where's—"

Reading her mind, Emma appeared, traipsing through the tulip beds. "Hey," she said as if ordering takeout from a sushi counter. "Is Danny okay?"

Fallon bit back a reprimand. It wouldn't do anyone any good. "Get down!"

"Okay," Emma kneeled.

"You bang on the door?"

"No. Gimme some credit. Will you?"

121

Fallon's shoulders rose. "Then how did you get both of them out of the room?"

"That big oak tree on the other side of the house," she explained. "I just made it seem like this breeze had broken one of the branches, and it was banging against the window."

"Not bad, but what do we do if Mr. American Perfect decides to wander out and check the tree?"

"Dunno," Emma said. "It is on the other side of the house, and the branch is broken…I hated doing that…so hopefully if he goes outside, he'll just cut off the branch and then hurry back in to keep eating whatever it is that beautiful billionaires eat when they're watching the news on the couch."

Fallon gave up. "Yeah, I'm hungry, too. Whaddya think they've got?"

"Probably something wonderful and exotic."

"Dinosaur steak."

"Giraffe testicle."

"Yeah, I hear that's pretty good grilled."

Danny appeared, as much phantom as teenager. "Not bad, huh?" He sat beside Fallon, ostensibly to hear through the window, but close enough for their shoulders to rub whenever either of them moved. He carried on in exaggerated whispers. "I'm betting you're thanking your lucky stars that I came along and hauled your pasty, naked, insensible self off of that operating table."

Without looking, Fallon said, "Danny?"

"Um…yeah?"

"Don't make me kill you."

Abashed, he frowned. "Yeah, okay."

"Listen," Emma interrupted. "It's on."

Through the cracked window frame, they heard the avatar projection report in an engaging, conversational tone:

In local news, Fauquier County authorities remain on the lookout for three fugitives from the Warrenton School for Juvenile Student Management they believe to be in the area. Among them are Daniel Hackett of Jackson, Mississippi who is wanted for resisting arrest and assaulting two members of the Hinds County Law Enforcement Division...

"Bulls," Fallon muttered. "He assaulted bulls, the dumbass."

A three-dimensional image of two rural, redneck officers, both of them visibly injured, floated out from the wall screen and hovered over the Perfects' coffee table until the news avatar said:

Also at large tonight is seventeen-year-old Fallon Westerly of Herkimer County, New York, wanted for the murder of Claire Felver, a librarian and cleanse candidate on her fifty-seventh birthday. Given the brutal nature of her crime, on the advent of Felver's cleanse, Westerly is considered a political extremist and extremely dangerous by local officials. Citizens are encouraged not to approach her, but to contact the crime hotline via the **FCPD code available on any bio-wrist screen.

Hovering over the coffee table now was a 3-D representation of Fallon with shoulder length hair and wearing an OLD FORGE HIGH SCHOOL sweatshirt beside a disquieting image of an older woman in a conservative tweed skirt and cheap Prevo-Mart blouse. Thick glasses and an all-business hair bun gave Claire the sympathetic look of a woman who had been victimized her entire life. There wasn't a circumstance, a class, a job, a boyfriend, a restaurant waiter, or an auto mechanic who hadn't taken advantage of poor, dead Miss Felver at some juncture during the past fifty years.

Fallon cringed when she saw her own face, her former face, with attractive hair, floating guiltily beside the murdered librarian.

Emma inhaled sharply. "No, please, tell me—"

"No," Fallon said. "No."

Danny took her hand. He squeezed tighter than she'd ever imagined a handsome boy might hold her, and said, "You know...I don't—"

"I didn't," she said.

He nodded.

123

Don't let go. Don't let go. C'mon, Danny, you've come this far. Just hold on. Just...

He dropped her hand. "Good. I believe you."

Emma said, "Okay, guys, let's get out of here. Huh? Don't you think we've been here too long anyway? I mean, we heard the news. Right?"

Through the window, Mr. & Mrs. Perfect's 3-D avatar, still seated at her laser-generated mahogany desk, smiled to the Perfects as they ate their Perfect triceratops t-bone steaks and giraffe testicles, grilled to exquisite deliciousness, and said:

Also assumed at large in Fauquier County this evening is fifteen-year-old Emma Carlisle of Baltimore.

"Guys," Emma tried again. "C'mon, we should go. How about it? Huh?"

"What's the matter, Em?" Danny asked. "You in a hurry?"

"Whatever," she feigned boredom. "So they're looking for us, and we gotta hide. Right? So...you know...let's get a car and get outta here."

She'd spoken too late. Whether she hadn't truly anticipated what she'd do if they succeeded in hearing a broadcast, if she'd just come along for the adventure, or if she hadn't wanted to abandon her new friends, Emma gnawed on her bottom lip, disconcerted, as Mr. & Mrs. Perfect's avatar reported:

Carlisle is wanted in connection with multiple acts of domestic terrorism, including the firebombing of Baltimore's Penn Station, the 2127 assault on the Baltimore County Brokerage House, and the sinking of the German cargo ship Himmelstoss *in Delaware Bay. Captain Dietrich Hess of the German import-export company* TransAtlantisch *had been suspected of carrying illegal body parts to offshore South American and African dealers with satellite distributors in Reykjavik, Iceland. Carlisle, while only fifteen, is considered extremely dangerous. Fauquier County citizens are encouraged* *to use caution if they should encounter these individuals and code **FCPD on any bio-wrist screen for assistance.*

"Em," Danny's eyes widened. "Holy shit."

"It's not like that." She defended herself. "It's not true."

"Three counts of terrorism?" Fallon asked. "What'd they get wrong? Not because I care so much, but...you know...Danny and I have been treating you like a...like a porcelain victim, and maybe we ought to be letting you take the lead, maybe staying out of your way."

Emma's lip began to quiver. "No, guys, c'mon now, I'm serious. It's not like they're saying. It's why I didn't want you to hear. I haven't done...well...too much of that, anyway."

Through the window, the news avatar detailed a terrorist attempt on an unknown number of body part recipients:...*Alfred James McMurphy, Cleanse & Harvest patient from Anacostia, Maryland, had been working with accomplices who gained entry to the facility on M Street mere hours before McMurphy's harvest, and injected the fifty-seven-year-old with plague bacteria...*

"You're a terrorist?" Danny asked.

Fallon elbowed him in the ribs.

...in hopes that McMurphy would develop septicemic plague unbeknownst to the medical personnel conducting the harvest and thereby ensuring the onset of—at least—local plague infections in a variety of Brokerage Houses that had purchased McMurphy's organs for distribution...

"What?" Danny wheezed.

"No," Emma said.

"But you told me you'd been picked up for—"

She cut Fallon off. "I told you I'd made a deal for merchandise I couldn't deliver. And that's exactly the 100% truth, Fallon. I promise."

...growing problem among Cleanse & Harvest patients, prompting even more security measures at medical facilities and hospitals in the region...

"So what's with the German cargo ships and Iceland and all that?" Danny asked.

The growl, low and guttural, cut their conversation short.

Emma shrieked and bolted past the others, her cry alerting both Mr. & Mrs. American Perfect that someone had been huddled just off their flower beds. Mr. Perfect dropped his fancy dinner plate; it shattered on the obnoxious coffee table. When Fallon saw him again, he was hurrying down the same hallway Danny had used to escape.

Out front! Fallon raced after Emma.

Danny hurried along behind, the frothing dog on his heels. "Run!" he shouted, not wanting to pass Fallon and leave her as dog food but panicking nevertheless. He shoved her hard into the evergreen bushes beside the street-side stoop. Not expecting to get pushed, Fallon tumbled into the shrubbery as Mr. Perfect burst through the front door, his one eye assessing the threat. "What the hell's going on out here? Who are you?" He shouted as Danny tripped, sprawled in the grass, and Emma disappeared between two cookie-cutter mansions on the opposite side of the street.

The dog, a famished-looking Rottweiler, bounded after her, rapidly making up ground.

Fallon rose in a rage, seeing *wrought iron fence* as clearly as any vivid nightmare. Mr. American Perfect took her by both shoulders, realized that she was a young girl, and sought to hold her tightly, not hurt her, just detain her for the police.

That was his mistake.

With both fists transformed, Fallon punched him twice in the ribs, felt them crack, heard him bark wet cries of breathless pain before doubling over, his arms tight at his sides.

Change back, she thought, and her hands shook loose with the familiar pins-and-needles sensation she'd grown accustomed to in the past few years.

"Danny," she hefted him up. "Let's go. C'mon, that dog's after Emma." And ensuring the daredevil boy had regained his feet, she dashed across the street where she assumed Emma had led the heavy-bodied watchdog. "C'mon! She's in trouble."

But Emma wasn't.

Fallon no sooner entered the dark, grass-lined stretch of no-man's land between the two mansions that she slid in something viscous and slippery. "What the hell?" She nearly fell, then caught herself against the siding. "What's this?" She ran a finger across her ankle; it came away warm and wet. She listened, didn't hear anything. "Em? You okay, sweetie?"

From the grassy yard behind the homes, Emma replied faintly. "I'm back here. I'm okay."

Still in hurry and acutely aware that she'd seriously injured Mr. American Perfect, Fallon jogged the few yards to the open stretch of lawn. Emma sat there, huddled and shivering. Light from a nearby porch illuminated her enough that Fallon could see the younger girl with her pen gripped in one hand like a recovered artifact. When light fell across Fallon's shoes, she realized that they were splattered with a generous helping of blood, gore, and dog hair.

"Emma?" she spoke as gently as she could, given their immediate need to get the hell out of that neighborhood and her unnerving fear that she might burst at any moment.

"Yeah?"

"Can you tell me what happened to the dog?" *But you don't need to; do you? Because I know what happened to him. He came after you, and you detonated a tactical incendiary device in his ass. Didn't you?*

"Em?"

Danny pulled up beside her, panting. "We gotta go guys. Mrs. Sexy Legs is already out front, and she doesn't look happy."

Fallon ignored him. "Em?"

"Can I explain later?"

127

"Sure," Fallon said. "That'll be fine. Let's go." She reached down warily, genuinely frightened of the smaller girl.

Smiling against her tears, Emma took Fallon's hand. "Okay, let's go."

6.47

I Can Read Your Mind

Nope, I'm not magic. Not too magic, anyway.

But I can read your mind.

You're wondering about all of this technology. Right? If we have 3-D projection screen TVs with an aroma setting, bio-embedded interactive video screens and network access in our wrists, self-driving cars, satellite-guided autonomous drones, recycled automobile tire highway lanes, fusion-powered motorcycles, and full-immersion movie theaters, why don't we have all of it, everything tech engineers imagined back in 2025 or 2030? Why don't we have dream readers? Artificial intelligence kitchens that cook whatever we're imagining? Fully robotic surgical procedures? Self-bagging dog poop?

Heh.

You wanna know why?

Sure, technology and innovation were on a meteoric trajectory in the early twenty-first century. We were headed at light speed toward every wildly innovative gadget that Captain Kirk ever drew from his utility belt.

But it didn't happen, not all of it, anyway.

Again, I bet you wanna know why. Right?

War.

War leaves an indelible poop stain on lots of our best laid plans. Back in the mid-1800s, the American Civil War resulted in about six-hundred-thousand dead. It changed everything. Art, music, literature, cultural innovations, industry, essentially every fundamental pillar in American society at the time had to shift. And that was with only six-hundred-thousand dead. Forgive me for using 'only' in that sentence. The American Agricultural Conflict (that Corn War you've been reading about) left nearly forty-million Americans dead and disrupted the evolution and revolution of just about every cultural value, tradition, myth, expectation, and dream in our nation at the time.

Yeah, things changed. For some, it was tragic. For others, it was a chance to sweep up great garbage bags full of money.

Was there any good news? Sure. Sort of.

For generations American culture divided too often along racist lines based on skin color or ethnicity. That doesn't happen anymore—well, not nearly like it did. These days, culture divides along the lines of the information rich and the information poor. It's that simple. A wealthy suburbanite might showcase a half dozen ethnicities in the body parts she chooses to buy, rent, or have replaced. It's pretty difficult to be racist when you're a walking salad bar of multi-cultural editions. But stand that same individual up beside a poverty-stricken kid with no wrist screen, no network access, no credits...and boom, you've got Bloodsuckers and Draggers, as culturally inappropriate and insensitive as an old game of cowboy and Indian, cowboy and African, or cowboy and Muslim.

(I'm thinking those cowboys have some anger management problems.)

Disappointing. Aren't we?

Yeah, it's a disappointing world. Get a helmet.

7

A Stolen Clunker, an Honest Chat, Some Staggering Odds, and an Unexpected Visitor

Back at the farm, the two women searched the house for candles—Emma had used the last nub watching over Fallon the previous night—while Danny set about tinkering with the car they'd stolen, a 2108 Canadian Chevron. At twenty years old, the Chevron was ideal, and Danny nearly peed his trousers when they stumbled upon it after fleeing from Mrs. American Perfect. On their way back to the countryside, he explained that cars over fifteen years old no longer had use of factory-standard, anti-theft devices, such as: automatic shut-offs, home GPS codes, silent police alerts in the event that the vehicle is hotwired, or monthly point-to-point tracking subscriptions popular among newer models, especially F-cars.

"I can't believe this old clunker was even in that neighborhood," Danny explained. "It's like finding a cracked plastic fork in a China shop."

"Must be some kid's first car," Fallon guessed.

"Either way, it's easy to steal—especially when some dumbass leaves the starter codes beneath the floor mat. It's easy to drive, and, if we want, we can turn on the autopilot when we're riding on the main roads, and they still won't be able to find us, because the home codes shut down after twelve years. I suppose it's the auto companies' way of getting people to upgrade."

Emma spoke up from the back. "Lemme remind both of you that this is my car, for me to drive after you two commit murder and arson or whatever you're planning, and we will not be turning on any autopilot. I don't need any stupid satellite driving for me while I nap or watch cooking downloads on my wrist."

"Gotcha," Danny checked the rear-view mirror. While still haggard, the younger girl's spirits seemed to be rebounding.

"I'm driving," she said.

"You're driving," Fallon agreed, "just not tonight."

Danny figured that after a bit of work, he could teach Emma the fundamentals of driving one of the older models. He'd owned...stolen...a '06 Chevron outside Biloxi two years earlier and had learned a metric ton about keeping rust buckets road worthy. Despite her unexplained encounter with the neighborhood watch dog, Emma maintained that she was excited about learning to drive. She wanted to stick with the older runaways as long as possible. Helping them escape after their assault on the WSJSM would be her final contribution to Danny and Fallon's frantic life on the run.

Later, while Danny worked on the Chevron, Fallon gave a half-hearted attempt to search through drawers in the farmhouse kitchen. She didn't hold out much hope that they'd find candles, just orphan spoons, a pencil stub, and a clutch of unused paper clips.

Emma rifled through cabinets, giving a more concerted effort, while avoiding conversation, even eye contact with Fallon.

Eventually, the older girl gave up. "I can...do things, too."

Emma paused, then resumed her search, as if she hadn't heard. Kneeling, she mined in a cardboard box stuffed beside the stove.

"Em," Fallon crouched. "I want you to know. It's okay. We've all heard about people, read about people...you know; it's just the right mix of—"

"It was my kidney," she said. "It's the only work I've ever had done."

"Why?"

"My parents got into credit trouble, nothing too serious. Mom still had two kidneys, but the Baltimore Brokerage House offered them nearly five times as much for one of mine."

Fallon understood. "Sure. Sometimes wealthy parents will pay anything for a kidney. It saves their child. Why wouldn't they?"

"Anyway, my mom and dad thought it over...for an hour at least...and decided to give up one of mine," Emma sat on the linoleum, peeled at a loose corner. The room still smelled of whatever had rotted inside the refrigerator. "I think it's why I've never had anything else done. Mom and Dad were so torn up by it, selling off their four-year-old daughter's kidney just to get their business back afloat, that they never even considered making any adjustments with me again." In the near darkness, she motioned to her face. "It's why my eyes still match. That's a rarity these days."

"And afterward..."

"It took a while," she said, "but eventually I learned to control it, sort of."

"Your pen?"

"How'd you know?"

"How many fifteen-year olds have a fancy, expensive pen permanently dangling around their neck? It's the obvious first place to look."

Emma held it aloft, the chain fixed to a makeshift metal loop in the cap. "My poems sometimes come to life."

"Poems?"

"Not really poems, I guess, more like my writing, phrases, a few lines I'll jot on a piece of paper. I don't know if I can do it without writing them down; somehow the writing focuses my thoughts and then things just happen the way I want them to. I call them poems, because it's how I remembered the important phrases when I was small."

"Poetry," Fallon said, "you'd memorize it?"

"Yup."

"Like how to deal with mean dogs."

133

"Yup."

"Whatshername…Sally Castillo?"

"Cassidy."

"She had a dog." Another tumbler clicked in Fallon's mind.

"Rufus, a mean sucker. That's when things started to change for my parents and me." Emma's voice rose slightly, as if she meant to say more.

Again, Fallon understood. "I get it. Trust me."

"How about you?" she asked. "Is it how you beat up Bear so easily?"

"And how I shaved my head." With a thought, Fallon let shoulder-length hair sprout from her scalp.

"Whoah!" Emma ran both hands through it. "You know; you're gorgeous. You should leave it."

Fallon tossed her head toward the window and Danny outside. "He'd have a heart attack." She wiped her head bald again, leaving only a few days' stubble.

"Wow," Emma's mood improved. "I'm not that good, and when you think about it, this is great. What are the odds that we'd ever find one another? They've gotta be amazing. Right?"

Fallon said, "One in twelve million."

"Holy crap."

"And those are just the odds that we exist," Fallon explained. "I'm not much for math, but I think the odds that we find one another are pretty remarkable."

"Should we tell Danny?"

"Why would we?"

"To explain how I killed that dog." Emma found another stash of paperclips and was straightening them one at a time.

"Nah," Fallon tried to look nonchalant. "Just stick with your story that you ran and hid, and something else managed to get to the dog first. Granted, it's not the best lie, but it's what's out there now, so we have to stick with it."

"What could have done that to a dog?"

Fallon shook her head. "Dunno. A grizzly bear? Do they still have grizzly bears?"

"Just in pictures."

"Well we shouldn't go with that. Should we?"

Emma laughed, clearly feeling better. "No. I suppose not. Maybe those homes had one of those taser fence things. You know? The bad ones that fire off a blast of whatever it is...to stop people from breaking in."

"So how'd *you* get past it?"

"I saw the beam, the electric eye, and jumped."

"Then how'd I get by?"

"It takes a minute to reset."

"Does it?" Fallon asked, genuinely interested.

"How the hell do I know?" Emma dropped another straightened clip into the growing collection.

Fallon slid an empty drawer closed. "What happened to the Baltimore County Brokerage House?"

Emma peeked into the sitting room, just to be certain Danny hadn't come inside. "It blew up."

"That's where you..."

"Lost my kidney. Yeah." She toyed with the last clip.

"And that German cargo ship?"

"It sank," she said.

"Why?"

"The captain, that German guy they mentioned on the news –"

"Dietrich Hess."

"He's a bad man," Emma said. "He's been funneling tons and tons of illegally farmed, harvested, and stolen body parts and organs through an Icelandic middle man for decades. There are poor children all over South America, Mexico, hell, even poverty-stricken cities and towns right here in the United States of Deception who'll never walk right, never breathe right, never see or stand or catch or throw or run right. They make these kids ride the storm, get them all hopped up on

135

meds that make them feel better than they've ever felt in their lives, literally ever, and some of them are..."

"Four years old," Fallon finished for her. "And losing kidneys."

Emma didn't cry, just set her jaw. "That's right."

"And you decided to stop him?" Fallon stifled a chuckle at the improbability of a hundred-pound, cute-as-a-button, teenage redhead declaring war against an illegal organ dealer.

"Yup," Emma said. "I figured if not me, then who?"

"How'd you do it? Do you just sit somewhere and write a poem and a ship sinks off the coast of Maryland?"

Emma snorted through her nose. "I wish. I'd be like a god, just lounging in front of a cup of coffee and writing my judgments on all the guilty, the cruel, and the dishonest."

"So...no?"

"I have to be there, to feel the place, the walls and floors of the place. Or the person, if it's...more serious. After that, it's easy."

"And the dogs?"

"Like I said, some verses have been working for me for a long time. They're like reflexes."

Fallon made a mental note never to be downwind from one of Emma's reflexes.

"I snuck onto the boat. A dockside security camera caught images of me afterward. At first, no one thought anything of it. I was fourteen, just a kid, maybe some officer's daughter saying good-bye. But..."

"What?"

"There was a man on the dock when I left. I was sure no one had seen me. I damned near crawled the length of the deck to stay under cover. It was dark, rainy, windy; no one was out, and then all of a sudden *Blam!* there he was, asking me questions and moving me sideways into the light from a streetlamp, just far enough for the cameras to get a good look at me."

Fallon took Emma's wrist, squeezed. "The man, was he tall? Dressed all in black? Good looking, I mean like really, drop-your-panties good looking?"

"That's him!" Emma cried. "But...how'd you know?"

"The security video." She remembered a brief surveillance film the Herkimer County prosecutor had displayed at her bullshit trial. There'd been a man outside Claire Felver's apartment. He disappeared from view only seconds before Fallon stepped into the image, her high school sweatshirt giving her away.

"What video?"

"God damn."

"Fallon? What's the matter?"

She let go the younger girl's wrist. "What do you think the odds are that we find one another, especially if the odds are one in twelve million that we even exist?"

Emma said, "I have no idea. One in a gazillion or something."

"That's too much. Right?"

"Oh, shit. I get it."

"We gotta go." She helped Emma to her feet just in time to be tackled to the kitchen floor. The weight of Danny's body, the impact, and Emma's bony elbow all conspired to knock the wind out of her. She rolled to her side, sucked in an agonized breath, wheezed, "Why?"

Emma shouted, "damn it, Danny! What the hell are you—"

He clamped a trembling hand over her mouth. "Shut up! Stay down!"

"What is it?"

"Shhhh," he hissed, then shifted Fallon to her back, pressed her legs flat across the linoleum, and gripped the button clasp of her pants in his fist. "Try and breathe normally," he ordered, and lifted her hips and midsection about eight inches off the floor.

Still sucking wind, Fallon tried to push his hand away, particularly the ends of his fingers, now curled precariously close to her bare stomach.

Danny whispered, "Just breathe." He lowered her hips and ass to the floor, then lifted again, slowly.

It was the most sensual thing anyone had ever done to her, but she erased the delightfully inappropriate thoughts. Danny was in mortal terror; Emma visibly shook, and Fallon couldn't get a full breath. Whatever waited for them outside had frightened Danny Hackett, crazy-as-hell daredevil and breaking-and-entering specialist more than the electric fence, the American Perfects' mansion, the bloodthirsty watchdog, or the locks on that old Chevron. Not much frightened him; whatever had driven him inside had to be abominable. *So breathe stupid. Just breathe, and don't think about the fact that he's got his hand in your pants. Just breathe.*

And breathing got easier.

Danny lowered her hips. "You okay? Sorry."

"Yeah," she managed. "But...what is it? Who's out there?"

"Not who," he pressed them both into the shadows beside the refrigerator. "What."

"Oh, my God," Emma whimpered.

This from a kid with a notebook full of poems that sink cargo ships. Fallon thought, then gripped her elbow. "Write something."

As if slapped, Emma broke free from her panic. "Yeah, okay, but what? I dunno what's there."

"Do you have, like, a general one? Something for just garden variety devastation?"

"Why are we talking?" Danny asked. "What the hell are we talking about? Keep your voices down."

Fallon squeezed tighter.

Emma understood, drew her pen, and dug in her pockets for the notepad.

Probably won't be worth a damn, but it'll shut her up.

138

Danny looked ready to pass out. "What're we doing? Practicing our letters? Writing to Congress?"

Fallon took his face in her hands, brought it close, then whispered. "Just trust me. It'll keep her busy. Now...what's outside?"

He shifted his weight, allowed his cheek to rest gently on Fallon's. "I don't know. I...felt it...come up the road. Something heavy, cold, shrouded...yeah, *shrouded*, I guess...in all black and fear. It's big, powerful, and—I think—dragging part of itself in the dirt."

Content to stay here on the floor, with the memory of his warm knuckles against her stomach, Fallon ignored the first tendrils of sublime fear uncoiling in her heart. Instead she let her cheek brush against his, whispered again, "What *was* it, Danny?"

He's going to kiss me. Jesus, of all the times in my life to have a cute boy decide to kiss me. This is about the worst.

But he didn't. Instead, he exhaled slowly, a languid, warm caress against her ear, trying to calm down, to remember what he'd seen and felt outside. "Fallon, I don't know. It just—"

The wall in the living room, perhaps the entire side of the house, collapsed inward with a rending, shuddering crash, as if the farmhouse had been torn open by a guided missile.

In a moment, Danny was on his feet, pulling them both up, shoving them toward the screen door. "Run! To the car, now!"

Fallon led them through the kitchen's side door as the thing, whatever it was, lumbered into the farmhouse. She smelled it before actually seeing it, a ponderous hulking mass of animated shadow, easily twelve feet tall and darker than the surrounding night. It smelled powerfully of summer roadkill, dead animals left to rot in a ditch beside a highway.

It swung for them with a hand as broad as a frying pan; Fallon ducked, dragging Emma with her. She was faintly aware of Danny diving to his left, drawing its attention and throwing an old lamp at it.

139

Emma shouted; Fallon couldn't make out what she said, but in the moment before bursting through the old screen door, she heard the faint whistling sound of tiny arrows knifing through the darkness to strike the creature somewhere near its head – if it had a head.

It's those paper clips! She fired those clips like miniature spears. Pushing Emma outside, Fallon cried, "Nice work! I think you hit –"

The thing bellowed in anger or pain; it was impossible to know which.

Fallon yelped when she heard it shout at them in incoherent, runny sounds like a condemned soul tumbling backwards into Hell. Blind now with fear, she staggered across the dooryard to the Chevron. Emma yanked open the door and crawled into the back seat.

"Where is he?" Fallon called, too frightened to turn around. Inside, the dark colossus shattered and crashed through the lower floors, pursuing Danny or simply pulling the house down upon itself. "Danny!" Fallon screamed, wanted to go back for him but couldn't make her muscles follow directions.

Think! Think of something! Get something clear…a spear, a rock, a flame, a heavy wind, something…hurry!

Danny saved her the trouble. In a headfirst dive and with a madman's banshee wail, he crashed through the front hall window, rolled clumsily into the driveway, and stumbled to his feet, his face, hands, and forearms already sloppy with blood. "Holy shit!" He ran for the car. "What the hell is that thing?"

Fallon sobbed with relief. "I dunno! I dunno! Quick, get in. Are you okay? Did it get to you?"

He climbed in beside her, started the engine. "What is it?" Sounds of rage and devastation roared out through the broken windows and collapsed wall.

"I have no idea," Emma said, "but let's go. Go now!"

140

Danny stomped on the accelerator; the old Canadian sedan responded with a groan, but then leapt to the task. Its rear wheels churning up mud, the Chevron fishtailed, gripped, and started up the driveway.

The creature broke through the side wall of the farmhouse, and in two tottering steps, stopped in front of the fleeing teenagers.

"Hit it!" Emma cried.

Danny stood on the brakes.

"Just hit it!" the younger girl yelled again.

"It'll wreck us," Danny said. "We can't." Yanking the car into reverse, he backed toward the barn. The thing followed, stomping after them with eight-foot strides.

"Danny, turn the lights on," Fallon said.

"What? Why?"

"I wanna see it," she said. "C'mon, just do it."

He found the switch, and the thing that had crashed headlong through the farmhouse was cast all at once into brash white light.

It yowled, and Fallon thought her head might cave in. "High beams!" she shouted, covering her ears.

"Got it," Danny flipped the toggle to HIGH.

The monster turned away, bent low at its oak-thick waist, then wheeled on them, low to the ground, reaching forward, its neck stretched long as if to gnaw the offending headlights into darkness.

"Holy mother of Christ," Fallon whispered. "It's human." The creature's head looked to have been pulled awkwardly into place from a block of pasty wax. Its...*his*...facial features only approximated a man's countenance. Smeary and wrinkled, his cheeks, chin, jawline, and forehead looked to have been melted together over a campfire. Only his eyes, insane and bloodshot, and his mouth, large enough to devour a watermelon, opened wide and snapped shut with all the alacrity of a fast-moving case of holy, frigging dead. The few wisps of hair sprouting from his head grew in here-and-there patches of tangled, three-foot, greasy strands. Several fell across his face, even into his open maw, as he barked his senseless cry at the fleeing teenagers. When he groped for them, stretched his neck and arms, erratic pink scar tissue around his wrists and just beneath his chin roadmapped a history of grim storefront procedures. Somewhere, someone worked on this thing like an old peach grader.

But his eyes matched.

Danny revved the car backwards almost all the way to the barn. He killed the headlights, and the dooryard, driveway, and ruined farmhouse fell once again into darkness.

"What're you doing?" Emma cried. "Are you crazy?"

"Might be," he pulled the Chevron into neutral, pressed down on the accelerator, and waited. Outside, the man...thing...had nearly reached them. Still staggering drunkenly, he roared and shrieked, flailed his tree-trunk arms, and stomped the dooryard mud into stupid submission.

"Danny?" Fallon said. "Are you gonna fill us in here?"

Ignoring her, he spoke instead to himself. "Just...about...NOW!" In a fluid motion, Danny jerked the Chevron into drive, prayed audibly that the transmission wouldn't decide to drop, smoking and dead, into the mud, and flipped the high beams on.

The colossus, nearly on top of the car, took the full force of the headlights directly into its eyes. Blind, it bellowed outrage, stumbled a drunken foxtrot toward the dooryard, and Danny was able to maneuver the erratic fishtailing car around its thick legs, up the driveway, and away from the farm.

On the county road, Danny killed the lights and pulled to the shoulder. Opening the window, he, Fallon, and Emma listened as the monster laid waste to the farmhouse and the barn, rending them to splinters.

Flipping the lights back on, Danny wiped blood from his forehead. With his vision clear, he used the car's interior lamp to remove two shards of glass from his forearm, wincing as he pried them loose.

142

In the back seat, Emma groaned. "My God, that's awful."

Danny tossed the glass bits out the window and drove slowly away. With the devastation still audible in the distance, he said, "We need to talk."

7.92

Yeah, I'm Back…Like a Bad Penny

Pennies. Do we still have pennies? I don't know why. It takes a hundred of the worthless things to make a dollar. And we don't have dollars anymore!

Anyway, I've chosen just about the worst possible time to interrupt. I mean, good grief, can you believe the sloppy rotten luck these three have?

The monster? That colossus? You're wondering about him; aren't you?

Colossus. Another great word.

Anyway, sorry. The colossus. I can't tell you too much about him right now, except that it's pretty clear someone, somewhere has a keen interest in Fallon or perhaps Emma.

Or it might be both of them, now that I give it some thought.

You heard Fallon's rhetorical question: What are the odds that two gifted individuals would find one another in middle-of-nowhere Warrenton, Virginia, particularly when the odds of gifted individuals existing are already one in twelve million?

I don't have any idea. I was always more of a Humanities student than a math whiz. But from where I'm sitting, those are some steep, steep odds. And when we couple those absurd figures with the fact that both Fallon and Emma were taken into custody shortly after the appearance of a staggeringly good-looking fellow, dressed all in black, with perfect hair and a nice suit…well, you get the idea. This is feeling less and less like a coincidence. It's as I said: someone, somewhere wants these two together.

That's my guess anyway.

All right; all right. I'm not guessing. I know.

But you probably had that figured out; didn't you?

The *someone, somewhere*, that's Susan Wentworth-White. Suffice to say, she's not a nice person, but we'll get to her shortly.

I'm uncertain how familiar you are with the geography of the nation's capital, so I'll fill in a couple of important bits for you here:

As the Potomac River flows south from Washington, DC, it passes the ruins of the Alexandria waterfront, which, if you believe the news broadcasts for the past seventeen years – you shouldn't – is just a few signatures away from a complete remodel and rebuild. I'm not buying it for a second. What had been an upscale, millionaires' neighborhood a hundred years ago has gathered dust as an abandoned pile of unwanted rubble ever since the war. I'd love to see it returned to its former American Colonial glory, but I'm not holding my breath.

Although there were some top-shelf pastry and coffee shops down that way when I was young. Ahhh, memories.

Anyway, below Alexandria, the river wanders beside the old George Washington Parkway until it passes Mount Vernon, Mason Neck, and Occoquan Bay before turning nearly all the way back round, just about changing its mind but then giving up and spilling into the polluted waters of the Chesapeake Bay. While the Alexandria waterfront was almost entirely reduced to splinters and pebbles by the British navy during the Cloud Wars, the estates between the ruins and Mount Vernon—about ten miles of riverfront—remained undamaged. Through the past generation, estate owners, some of them powerful political figures in the Alexandria reconstruction disagreement, have allowed the waterfront ruins to act as a convenient barricade between their billionaires' playground and the DC suburbs, a disagreeable place for anyone. Just trust me on that.

Having a mile of war demolition cutting off the great unwashed supplicants looking to Congress for a better life, the riverfront billionaires expanded, rebuilt, doubled, even tripled—

Trebled? I don't know.

145

—the size of their mansions, constructing a row of massive, über-modern castles overlooking the aromatic waters of the Potomac. Anyone boating down river from DC to Occoquan Bay would see them, seventeen egregiously ostentatious palaces, each sporting its own boat house with underground tunnel access, speed boats, sail boats, and unwieldy yachts of various sizes, shapes, and price tags.

While devastating to many, the war was downright profitable to a select few. An even *selecter* few—if that's not a word, it should be—chose to showcase their wealth, their family's wealth, their pets' wealth, in an appalling display of medieval architecture, modernized with every imaginable gadget and technological advance, including those tunnels, a convenient way to get from the palace to the yacht without having to step outside.

Susan Wentworth-White, however, had not been treated especially well by the war, not that her mansion was any smaller than the other sixteen along billionaires' row. On the contrary, Ms. Wentworth-White owned one of the largest private homes in the world. With a quarter-mile façade, the Wentworth-White estate could have housed thousands of people in relative comfort.

It housed exactly two.

You guessed it: Susan Wentworth-White and her…companion…Edward Wilson. You've already met him: the colossus.

(Alright, if I'm being entirely honest, a third lived out back in a guest cottage with the dogs. But we'll get to him later.)

Anyway, I can't tell you much more about Ms. Wentworth-White, except that her family did not get rich from the war. Oh, I'm sure they picked up a few credits. Absurdly rich individuals are always finding ways to get more absurdly rich on the misfortunes of others, poor others especially. Rather, Susan Wentworth-White made her first real money marketing, souping, packing, and shipping body parts all over

146

the world. It's a lucrative business, and Ms. Wentworth-White oversaw her empire with an acumen that bordered on pure, unbridled genius. Legend has it that she rarely slept, rarely ate, rarely left her palatial apartments, but knew the inner workings of every nook and wrinkle in her corporate holdings down to the employee, the daily production, the shipping manifests, even the custodians.

(I don't know if I believe that, though.)

Over time, Ms. Wentworth-White did not content herself with simply marketing and shipping body parts. Nope. She set her sights high, and eventually purchased the majority share of Prevotel Industries. (This is not surprising, actually. All seventeen of the mansion owners along that elite stretch of riverfront own some percentage of Prevotel.) However, Ms. Wentworth-White controlled Prevotel, the company that designed, manufactured, and mass produced essentially all of the household products sold in the United States, including Prevo-cars, Prevo-buses, Prevo-washing machines, Prevo-bicycles, and Prevo-toilet brushes.

But those products, the cars included, amounted to comparatively little of the empire's annual profits. The majority of the Prevotel stock holders' wealth came from the production and distribution of one product.

But I bet you'd figured that bit out as well. You strike me as a pretty sharp individual.

Prevotel Industries produced Diphenobenzadraconamine-72. Stormcloud. This made the corporation as powerful—or perhaps more powerful—than any nation, any government on Earth.

Yet that's enough out of me for now. Let's get back to Fallon, Danny, and Emma. Shall we? In the time that I've been chatting at you, they've been driving that rickety Chevron toward Baltimore. Oh, and while it might sound lovely to you to have heisted a self-driving car, Fallon decided against using the auto-sat option, fearing that their route would be catalogued on a navigational server or satellite somewhere

147

after someone reported it as stolen. So instead of navigating to Baltimore in the self-driving, recycled-rubber lanes at over 120 miles per hour, our fugitive friends were forced to remain in the traditional lanes, which in 2128 meant significantly slower travel.

Ah, well...they say crime doesn't pay (which is utter nonsense, by the way; crime often pays quite well.)

Oh, and the dogs out by the carriage house...yeah, they were unpleasant. Don't forget about them; they might be important later.

8

Penn Station, Cold Italian Food, and an Ill-Tempered Intruder

Even in the slowly gathering dawn, with the building blanketed in shadow, Baltimore's Penn Station looked like a timeless testament to tasteless architecture. Everything about the building yawned. Fallon figured it might be because she was so tired; she and Danny had been up nearly all night. Emma slept in the back seat, having overcome the adrenaline rush of being pursued from the farmhouse by…whatever that had been. Regardless, Penn Station was about the most featureless, flavorless structure either of them had ever seen. Even the retro-fit expansion wings—designed to accommodate P-drones and E-copters—appeared to have been constructed to match the apathetic look of the original, twentieth-century building.

"Damn, look at this place. Will you?" she said, just to keep Danny awake.

"What about it? The drone towers? Those are pretty awesome. You ever see one up close?"

"That's not what I meant."

"Yeah, okay, but you ever seen one up close?"

"No."

"Me neither."

"It's just a boring building," she said. "Doncha think?"

"It's a mass transit station in a major American city." Danny turned onto a side street, hoping for a place to park. "Who cares?"

Fallon adjusted the uncomfortable shoulder belt. It had been pressing into the side of her neck for the past three hours. Of all the Chevron's features that had either broken, been discontinued, or run beyond their factory-required activity dates, mandatory seatbelt ignition remained active in the old rattler, and because the 2108 model still used x-cross belts,

149

Fallon wasn't able to duck beneath the buckle without the car automatically shutting down in the middle of Interstate 95. Instead, she contented herself with yanking the belts side to side every fifteen minutes of the three-hour journey from Warrenton through the DC suburbs and into the nearly incessant traffic—even at 3:00 a.m.—north and south along the cracked and broken macadam lanes of the interstate highway.

Throughout the night, E-trains and E-buses sped north on their closed tracks of forbidden, trowel-smooth highway. Virginia, Maryland, and DC leaders often failed to agree on governance questions, but highway traffic remained an issue on which every elected or appointed official had an accord: Make Them Ride Mass Transportation. Even families with auto-sat installed in their cars could ride in those lanes, just program in their destination, convert the bucket seats into fold-down beds (not the most comfortable, but better than driving all night), and sleep, play cards, watch films, or video downloads on the rear vid-screens...all the way to grandma's house. Easy peasy.

Not for Fallon, Danny, and Emma.

A Baltimore city bus, an express from the suburbs, roared north at nearly 150 miles per hour. Yet it still lost ground rapidly to an F-cycle, its fusion powerplant pushing the bike close to 200 mph, barely a blur. "Sheesh, those things go fast."

"I know," Danny craned his neck to check another questionable side street. "You see any spaces down there? I don't wanna turn that way, get stuck and not be able to get back."

"Why don't we park in the station lot?"

"No credits," Danny said. "Can't get the car out later without money."

"Damn. Well, I guess we could always steal another one." She tried to sound hopeful.

"This car is perfect," he explained. "With anything newer, we'd have to spend an entire day finding all the computer chips to turn off the safety features."

"And with anything older…" she started.

"We'd have to push the damned thing."

"Yeah, okay," she said. "So we gotta find a space."

"A legal, free space," he said. "There are probably about eight of them left in the city."

Emma stirred in the back, yawned noisy assonance. "Hey."

"Good morning," Fallon said.

Sunlight sneaked down an east-west alleyway to illuminate Danny's face with the color of dawn. "Oh, ouch," Emma reached over to touch the lacerations above his eye. "Are you all right?"

He winced away. "Fine. I'm fine, but no touching. Okay?"

"What's with him?" Emma asked Fallon.

"Him," Danny interrupted, "is wondering why that… thing…came looking for us. Him is tired and starving and needs a bath and a long nap." He turned along another street, behind the station, and had to double back when the roadway ended abruptly beside a wide swath of E-train tracks and wires. "Damn," he said, cranking the wheel over and pulling the car into reverse.

"Where are we going?" Emma asked.

"We have to find a place to leave the car," Danny explained, frustrated. "We have to be able to get—"

"Just park on the side of the building," she said, still rubbing sleep from her eyes. "There are three spaces reserved for Luigi's Continental Express. You can take any one of them and leave the car there as long as you like."

"What about the workers? The staff? Don't they park there?"

"Not today."

"And how do you know?"

151

"Because most of the dining area was destroyed in an explosion."

Exhausted, stressed nearly to the breaking point, and frightened for all of them, Fallon couldn't help but laugh. "Em, remind me not to cook for you."

Danny turned down the side street. "Yeah, heh. What'd they do? Burn the chicken?"

"Something like that."

Emma was right: there were three spaces marked with fading signs reading RESERVED FOR *LUIGI'S CONTINENTAL EXPRESS*.

She led them up a flight of metal stairs along the outside wall of the original building to a fire door nearly forty feet above the staff parking area. Fallon held her breath at each creaking, whining step, hoping that she hadn't fled Warrenton just to break both of her legs on a ramshackle Baltimore fire escape.

On the miniature landing, Emma tried the door, cursed when she found it locked.

"You got a key?" Danny asked.

"No," she seemed upset. "It must be that this wing is shut down until they finish rebuilding the damaged stores and restaurants."

"So what's the problem?" Fallon asked. "Can't we just go in the front?"

"I don't have a commuter card," she said. "None of us do."

Fallon shrugged. "So?"

"So...that means we can't access the foyer elevators." She gripped the door handle, gave it another yank. "We have to cross the main hall and go up the service steps to the second floor. I know where they are and how to get in, but we'll have to get there first." She cast an uncertain glance toward the sunrise, still waking slowly over the harbor. "At least it's early. That's good."

Fallon elbowed Danny.

152

He asked, "What's inside, Em?"

"Oh, you'll see." She started down the stairs, hurrying now. "Just stay close to me. Don't drag your feet."

Fallon followed in silence. Near the station's once-grand entryway, she used Emma's comment as an opportunity. "Danny?"

"Huh?"

"Why don't you have someone fix that limp? It wouldn't cost much."

Realizing that she'd been watching him walk, he made an almost imperceptible adjustment to his gait, minimizing his limp. Fallon regretted bringing it up. Embarrassed, she asked, "How'd you get it, anyway? I mean...was it an accident?"

Without looking back, Danny echoed Emma. "Something like that."

"Oh, sorry."

"Nah, it's all right. I just never thought it was worth the credits to get it done in a Brokerage House, and I didn't want to risk it in a storefront, particularly with some of the hacksaw sociopaths we have in downtown Jackson."

"Guys?" Emma heaved open one of the heavy double doors.

Fallon let her interrupt, was glad for it and avoided looking at Danny. "Yeah, we're ready."

"Stay close." She disappeared into the dim gloom of the station's surface level house of horrors.

Not fifteen feet across the yawning entryway, Fallon pulled up short. "What's wrong with them? What is this?"

"They're cloud addicts, thunderheads." Danny took her hand. "C'mon, keep moving. Don't make eye contact, but don't run. Just follow Emma; keep steady."

Their passage through the bowels of the Baltimore train station might as well have been a descent into a senseless lunatic's hell. Lit only by intermittent bulbs in once-decorative wall sconces and the morning sun, still inching above the Atlantic horizon, the cave-like depot echoed with the grunts,

farts, babbles, yelps and unsettling murmurs of nearly a
hundred lost souls. Stormcloud junkies lined every wall,
crowded every smooth wooden bench. Some lay about the chilly
concrete floor like life-sized dolls, first disfigured, then tossed
aside by a disinterested toddler. Behind a plexi-glass fortified
ticket booth, now empty, a handful of more lucid addicts had
dragged a crooked stack of stained, threadbare mattresses.
Some sat up, watching the three strangers like pack hunters
waiting for an exposed ankle. Filthy, broken, some of them
literally in discomforting stages of dismemberment, the cloud
victims had clearly taken possession of this infrequently used
level of the station and would not hesitate to attack unwanted
visitors.

Forty feet overhead, multicolored lights flashed in
geometric patterns off the venerable blown glass and lead
frame of the station's massive atrium windows, beside which
twin, twenty-foot waterfalls fell into faux lagoons featuring
authentic imitation tropical plants, even a few seashells and a
carpet of picturesque white sand. Digital melodies, commercial
advertisements and perky jingles overlapped, conspiring with
the waterfalls to drown out the intermittent sound of
Baltimore's earliest commuters clickety clacking in hard-soled
shoes across the vast concourse. Without a commuter card, the
clean, well-lit second level might as well have existed on
another planet. Security guards standing sentry behind
retractable grates only permitted commuters or paying
travelers access to second floor elevators. Without a confirmed
ticket or an active Baltimore County E-Commuter subscription,
no one could talk, beg, or shoot their way in. Protecting the
anonymous integrity of the elevator foyer, implacable security
staff had the option of electrocution, gas, sonic cannons, even
acid spray to deter unwanted incursions from the long-
abandoned bowels of Penn Station.

Fallon glanced at the lights overhead, caught a few
notes of a commercial tune she'd heard back home, something
about grab-and-go sandwiches, and worried that it was as close

as she'd get to a real Heaven, even one without pretend waterfalls and fake beaches.

Farther on, she and Danny discovered that most of the addicts didn't see them, didn't see anything. Some danced about, sang, mumbled and giggled to themselves, as if replaying all of their fondest recollections over and over as their bodies were disassembled in secret, like old Chevrons, for spare parts. One grotesque woman, bandy thin in a torn dress the color of fresh mud, danced in awkward pirouettes, her one foot doing the brunt of the work while her ragged, scarred ankle stump provided a makeshift pivot each time she twirled.

On a colorless tear of old carpet, a young boy, no older than Fallon or Danny, wept in all-over crying jags, howling up at the inaccessible light from the second floor as if it truly was the impossibly close entryway to paradise.

"God, make him stop that," Fallon said. "What's he –"

"He crashed." Danny slid between her and the wailing teen. "He's probably been riding the storm for weeks. Look at how he keeps reaching for his left hand. That poor sonofabitch doesn't have any idea what happened to it. Holy Christ, that's a lousy thing to learn when you sober up, probably has no idea he traded it."

Fallon stopped. "I'm gonna throw up."

He pressed her forward. "Not here you're not."

"Look at them. How did they get like this?"

"Government and industry, your vote and your tax dollars at work." He pulled her a stutter step to the left, narrowly avoiding another ballet dancer in a threadbare Penn State sweatshirt and nothing else. Her outstretched arm, while oddly graceful, was a poorly sawn stump of filthy pink tissue – her wrist screen amputated as well. The woman hummed a piece of orchestral music Fallon recognized, something from a ballet she'd seen on a 3-D projection screen down at the Prevo-Mart in Old Forge one winter, *The Nutcracker*, a story about a young girl's Christmas dream.

155

*Goddamned ugly irony if that...*thing...*is dreaming of sugarplums.* She thought as Danny led her deeper into the darkness. Ahead Emma faded to an indistinct blur. Fallon pointed just to keep from losing sight of her.

Danny whispered, "You never been in a big city before?"

She reached an arm around his shoulders, not really needing his help but relishing the comforting warmth of his presence beside her, even with his awkward gait. "Not that I can remember, and certainly never any place like this. I can't believe this. I've seen cloud addicts. We all have. Old Mr. Cranford—he lives down by the lake—he's a thunderhead, but he's nothing like these people. Most of them don't even realize we're here."

"I know," he checked over his shoulder. "That's good."

"Why?" Fallon squinted to keep track of Emma. The smaller girl hurried toward a set of code-protected doors leading to the train platforms.

"Because the ones who don't realize we're here won't bother coming after us."

"Whaddya mean?" Fighting panic, she turned as well, saw them. A loose clutch of about fifteen, ragamuffin cloud addicts had formed up, blocking the exit. There'd be no escaping to the street; they were either going to reach the second floor by whatever stairway Emma claimed to know, or they were going to be mauled and most likely dismembered by the wild-eyed pack.

"Oh, shit," she said. "C'mon, we gotta hurry."

"Yeah, I saw." He picked up his pace. "Stay with me."

I'm not going anywhere. Fallon thought, then called, "Emma! What the hell are you doing? We got a big frigging problem back here."

The younger girl saw the hungry group closing in. "C'mon!" she shouted, ignoring her own order to keep quiet. "Hurry!"

Fallon and Danny broke into a run. Behind them, thunderheads began hooting, shouting and snarling, waking others to their insidious pursuit. Breakfast was served! For every eye, foot, arm, or liver they managed to harvest, the feral group would be able to ride the storm for a week. The consequences for the three fugitives came suddenly into sharp relief: if they were caught, there'd be almost nothing left for Baltimore officials to mop up.

Danny sprinted ahead, cut off an elderly woman in a knit apron who'd shambled from the shadows in an effort to slow them down. Without stopping, he punched her hard across the jaw, shattering it audibly and leaving her sprawled over an old bench. "This way!" he shouted, cutting to his right, toward the near wall and the abandoned wreckage of rolling coffee-and-donut cart.

Behind him, Fallon swallowed the terror rising from her chest. Focusing her imagination, she considered *butcher knife*, but then let it pass. These people didn't need more of themselves sliced away. Instead, she remembered her mother's fire pit. Just a truncated 55-gallon drum out behind their trailer, the pit had provided the Westerly women many autumn nights' pleasure as they sat talking, singing, telling jokes, or just enjoying the flames. She often wandered into the woods adjacent to the trailer park, hunting for deadfalls and firewood. Her mother had made the same offer each chilly evening: *We'll keep the fire burning as long as you gather the wood.*

It was an armful of logs she recalled now and soon had one, an extension of her right arm, a built-in maple club, perfect for crowd control. What Fallon hadn't expected was what she discovered in her left hand: a fireball, compact, brilliant, blisteringly hot. Yet it didn't burn. Like the maple branch, the fire in her palm had become part of her. And for a paralyzing moment, the fear threatening to cripple her was supplanted by stark, unabridged wonder: With a thought, she could bring down the entire building, leave the city a smoldering pile of ash.

"Holy shit!" She thought to shake the flames off, but then decided to keep them at least until the others were safe.

157

All right you bastards, she exhaled slowly, allowed burgeoning anger to elbow her fears aside, *come and get me.*

Through the gauzy, dizzying sheen of her newfound talent, Fallon became vaguely aware of Danny, still running, still shouting, and still swinging left and right as thunderheads charged him. One, a middle-aged man dragging a useless leg, noticed her coming up fast and turned from Danny to cut her off.

It was a mistake.

Swinging her arm first forward then back, she struck him violently across both cheeks then rammed the wooden club into his soft midsection. The man crumpled, spitting bloodstained yellow teeth and coughing up frothy grunts.

Wheeling back, Fallon looked for another victim, another cloud junkie dumb enough or stoned enough to attack her or threaten her friends.

That ballet, The Nutcracker, *it was beautiful. Graceful. Like a three-hour break from the ten-thousand hours of stress, uncertainty and anxiety she and her mother shouldered together every year.*

A teenage girl took advantage of the break in Fallon's stride. She attacked from behind. Fallon ducked, shoved the wiry assailant away, then brought the wooden club down on the girl's knee.

Better not be a ballet dancer. Better not have any Christmas dreams, bitch, because you're done dancing.

She'd never imagined doing anything this brutal—*except for killing Blair; I can't forget him*—and felt mildly sick with each swing of the club. *Worry about it later, dumbass. For now, fight.*

Then Danny fell, his bad leg buckling beneath the weight of two muscular men in denim pants, denim shirts, matching belts, boots, and haircuts. One grabbed the teen's wrists, held them in a frantic dance, as the other managed to get behind the boy and snake a hand around Danny's throat. Smirking, he squeezed.

158

Escaped inmates, Fallon thought, then let go the tenuous hold she'd kept on her anger, let go the strangely pleasant memories of the Christmas ballet. Bright, delicious rage scrubbed away any regrets she might have had after breaking the teenager's knee. "You better get off him," she said calmly. When they ignored her, Fallon shouted, "Get off him! You'd better get off him right now, assholes!"

They didn't. So Fallon set them both on fire.

Their screams filled the old station with enough unnatural terror and agony that upstairs a few of the city's morning commuters, middle-class business travelers in conservative suits, took a moment to peer over the second-floor railing. Fallon only glanced their way for a moment, but several of them clearly enjoyed the unexpected entertainment this morning.

You motherscratchers can be next for all I care; just gimme a reason.

Whatever discomfort she'd felt at clubbing the girl and the crippled man had washed out with the tide. Fallon extinguished the flame and dropped the firewood before Danny noticed. She took him beneath one arm. "C'mon, that'll slow them, but we gotta get out of here. This is nuts."

He rubbed feeling into his neck, sucked a hoarse breath. "Thanks. Where's Emma?"

Fallon pointed. "There, just by those doors."

The writhing, screaming convicts didn't die, but they both had difficulty rolling around enough to smother the flames and smelled powerfully of charred flesh. Eventually, the pack of feral cloud addicts, distracted by their burning conspirators, returned to the pursuit.

But by then, the three teenagers had disappeared out to the platforms and through a key code security door to a stairway leading up to the second floor, the middle-class floor, the commuter floor, every thunderhead's fantasy Heaven and safety. As the door slammed closed behind them, Fallon heard the burning convicts scream again. The mob's bloodthirst had found another target.

The friends crashed through the upper fire door and into another country. Level II of Baltimore's Penn Station smelled of freshly baked pastries, morning coffee, frying bacon, and clean-filtered HVAC air—no smog, no pollution, no human perspiration, agony, despair, or regret to offend anyone at this early hour.

The flickering colors they'd seen from the Level I dungeon were cast about from wall-sized advertisements, interactive billboards that spoke to commuters, tempting them with actual scents, sounds, or three-dimensional images of products hawked by mostly-naked models, computer-generated based on statistical assumptions of what represented physical perfection in the minds of Baltimore, Maryland's Bloodsucker class. Still early for a Friday, only a few dozen commuters crossed the marble canyon, most of them ignoring the come-hither stares of larger-than-life models pitching clothing, local restaurants, virtual reality, cheap flights to Africa, and spare parts: legs, arms, eyes, smooth brown hands, delicate fingers, taut breasts, even feet—all of which could be grown to fit, pre-ordered, bought on credit, or transferred in easy, day-patient procedures at the Howard County Brokerage House.

There were no advertisements for Baltimore County's own Brokerage House. Emma Carlisle had seen to that.

His hands shaking, Danny staggered, then slumped to the wall. Taking in what he could of the colorful, clean, absurdly safe second floor, he opened his mouth to say something, but only an odd smear of yelpy vowel sounds spilled out.

Fallon leaned beside him, then slid, panting, to the floor.

Two well-dressed commuters hurried by. Both distracted themselves with some film or download on a monocular projection lens. Neither gave the teens a second glance.

160

Emma warned, "We shouldn't just sit here. Eventually someone will notice. We gotta keep moving." She reached for Fallon. "C'mon, it's just down that hall, beneath Drone Tower III."

Danny didn't hear her. "I hit an old lady. Jesus Christ, I just punched an elderly woman in the face."

"Guys!" Emma repeated. "We can't stay out here."

"Okay, okay," Fallon sighed. "Just lemme—Christ, I'm out of shape. I gotta start running or something."

"Wait," Danny grabbed her wrist. "How'd you do that? How'd you light those two up? It was so fast. I couldn't—"

Fallon's eyes widened. "I...uh, I had some matches. I found matches back at the farmhouse, old ones in a box. I stuck them in my pocket, had no idea even if they'd work." She looked to Emma for help. "When those guys jumped on you, I didn't know what to do. I grabbed some scraps of cloth, something one of them must've dropped, just a grimy bit of T-shirt. It lit right up, must've been pretty old, dried out. You know?"

Danny's eyes locked onto hers. Fallon couldn't have pulled her gaze away with a commuter train. Finally, he said. "Well, thanks. Thanks, I owe you."

Across the concourse, on a digital, interactive screen twenty feet high and forty feet long, enormous images of the three runaways flashed brilliantly in a massive all-points bulletin. Letters three feet high warned Baltimore's Friday-morning commuters that Danny, Fallon, and Emma were wanted for terrorism, mayhem, and murder.

Stumble-stepping to the nearest trash can, Fallon threw up. She'd have been content to remain there, inhaling whatever ropy strands had been left in her stomach after three days without eating. But Emma quickly pressed her back against the wall, took her roughly by the elbow and guided her to the far corner of the concourse, and then along the streetside windows to the gaping corridor and the tracks and bus platforms beneath Drone Tower III.

161

"Where're we going?" Fallon managed between dry heaves.

"We're staying out of camera view," Emma said. "Just keep your head down and hurry."

Behind them, Fallon heard Danny shuffling along with his crooked limp.

Emma said, "We need to feed her."

He answered, "We need to feed me."

Halfway through the corridor, with tunnels, tracks, and E-buses lined up on either side of the elevated access ramps, Fallon allowed herself to be shoved roughly beneath a bright orange line of Baltimore County Police tape and into a section of Level II that had been closed off to the public.

Again, from behind her, Danny whispered, "What's this?"

"Bomb damage," Emma said. "There'll be workers later, construction guys and bulls mostly, but for now we can get inside without anyone knowing."

"We'll have to hunker down all day," Danny said. "We need food."

"There's food."

While the front sitting room, plate glass windows, and security gate at Luigi's Continental Express looked to have been involved in an air raid, the kitchen and storage areas behind the walk-up, interactive countertop remained in passable working order. Scorched and dusted with a generous helping of rubble, Luigi's kitchen needed little more than a cleaning crew to be operational again. Fallon couldn't decide if the bomb had been detonated to assassinate guests in the dining room or to jeopardize key supports in the drone tower overhead. Killing fat commuters noshing on cannoli was reprehensible enough; bringing down a two-hundred-foot drone tower would have been an Old Testament catastrophe.

Luigi's kitchen was small enough to fit in most suburban homes. With every available inch of space dedicated to the rapid mass production of inexpensive, takeout Italian food, sous chefs, chefs, and wait staff would have been elbow to elbow, hip to hip all day. From twin refrigerators at the rear of the kitchen area, three-foot prep stations, four-foot grills, and four-foot stove tops – mirror images on either side of a five-foot aisle, led to stainless steel warming hoods where plastic containers of eggplant parmesan, chicken cacciatore, or pasta bolognese waited all of ten seconds before being distributed to some middle class commuter looking forward to a hot meal on a 260-mph E-train out of the city. With gaping steel hoods hovering over each stovetop and grill, the kitchen might have fallen out of the pages of an old Dr. Seuss poem.

"Damn," Danny followed Emma up the narrow aisle. "This is tight. Claustrophobics wouldn't have lasted twenty minutes." With his arm around Fallon's waist, he had to shuffle step just to pass through without banging his hip against the stoves.

"You have no idea," Emma said. "When things got busy, there'd be four people on each line, with two others working the scanners out front. Granted the place only accommodated about twenty customers at the tables, but it wasn't really a sit-down restaurant. This place lived or died by its takeout. For 150 credits, a commuter going home could get dinner for her entire family."

"Not bad," Danny said. "But did it taste any good? Some of these grab-and-go places all taste like salt, sugar, or dog food."

Emma led them between the refrigerators, past a freezer large enough to keep a basketball team on ice, and into a storage room, lined from floor to ceiling with all the accoutrements and non-perishable canned foods, pastas, tins of flour, bags of sugar, and five-gallon containers of *Luigi's Special Marinara Sauce* that one mass transit station could hope for.

"Eureka," Danny helped Fallon to a seat on a plastic tub of tomato paste, "The motherlode! Let's fire up the grill. I'm starving."

163

"We can't," Emma said. "After the attack, station managers re-routed the battery feeds to the stoves. There's no juice."

"Bugger," Fallon said, coming around at the mention of hot food. "I'm pretty hungry."

"Let's cook over a fire," Danny suggested.

"Um...yeah. Why don't you call me from prison and let me know how that worked out," Emma teased. "We'll have to make do with food we can eat without cooking. There's plenty here."

Danny looked crestfallen. "There's gotta be a way, Em. I'm starving. What about those flame hoods out there? Can't we work up some way to build a fire under those?"

"Sorry. But they vent out back, between this level and the drone tower upstairs. Someone would see the smoke, smell it, something, and we'd be cooked . . . literally."

"You're right," Fallon agreed. "But this is good. There's plenty here. We can make do just fine, eat, and maybe figure out how to get some credits, so we're not breaking into bombed out restaurants every afternoon for lunch."

"Good point," Danny said. "Accessing our accounts. That's gotta be our top priority."

"If there's anything left," Emma said. "I'm sure that with half the authorities in the mid-Atlantic states trying to find us, they're gonna know as soon as we plug in anywhere."

"True," Fallon said. "We're beyond just worrying about whether or not Carter Whatshisname can fry us from Warrenton."

"I've been thinking about that," Emma said.

"Me too," Danny added. "I don't think he can."

"Right."

"How do you know?" Fallon asked. "If we don't plug in, how can we know?"

"Because if he could fry us remotely," Emma explained, "he probably could turn on our bio-screens remotely, track us, do whatever he wanted from his office tablet."

164

"I think you're right," Danny said. "It's like stealing a new car. It's about the dumbest thing you can do, because the tracking company can give the VIN number to the bulls, and they can shut it down, lock you in, even electrocute you in some of the newer models, right there in the seat."

Fallon tapped absently at her wrist screen with a fingernail. "So before we leave here…whenever we leave here…we've gotta plug in. Someone's gotta try it before we walk out."

"Sprint out is probably closer to what you mean, but yes," Danny said. "Because we can't know what we have unless we try—"

"But we'd better try right before we exit the premises, because about five minutes after we press the ON button, the drones will be overhead and the bulls will be on the street."

"Then why would we even try it?" Fallon asked.

"We have to," Danny said. "We can't go on like this. We've gotta have access to credits. My accounts are in Jackson, Mississippi. If I can hit them from here or DC or somewhere out in Virginia, and we can beat feet out of there before the bulls arrive, we can make purchases, locally of course, for food, clothes, a battery charge for that car."

"We've gotta be quick every time, though," Emma raised a finger. "Less than five minutes in and out."

"Less than two, if we can," Danny added. "And we'll buy food and battery charges in rural places, off the beaten path, places with crap network access, dog slow stuff, so they take longer to lock onto us, maybe not lock onto us at all, if we're lucky."

Fallon said, "It could work. My mother and I used to go to a restaurant on the lake where their access was so bad that you'd not see your account debits until the next day. They ran them overnight."

"Exactly," Emma agreed. "If we can find places like that, we should be able to get in, get what we need, and get out before the bulls have us in chains."

165

"I hate that," Danny said, "the chains bit, I really hate that."

"Fine," Fallon slapped both hands on her knees, tried to appear peppy despite that fact that she felt like curling into a ball and crying for her mother, who was probably worrying over the news feeds right now. "But let's eat first."

"That's gonna be tough," Danny reminded, "with no juice to the stoves."

"Actually," Emma disappeared into a walk-in pantry lined floor-to-ceiling with well stocked shelves. "I might have an idea to heat a few things up."

"We gonna rub two sticks together?"

The red-haired criminal emerged holding what looked like a miniature bottle of compressed air affixed to a well-worn, blackened metal nozzle. "Crème Brûlèe!" She beamed. "One of our specialties. We use these to caramelize the—"

"Wait," Danny interrupted. "Whaddya mean, *our* specialties? I thought you...well, I dunno what I thought." He tugged at the crew neck of his sweatshirt, considering. "Is this your family's place? But I thought you were the one who...well, who..."

"Blew it up, Em," Fallon interrupted. "Why?"

Fussing with the silver nozzle, she said. "It is, and I did, and I guess it's complicated." Cranking a small lever a half turn, she held a sparking device to the nozzle tip, and several inches of searing blue flame appeared with a sibilant cough. "Yeah, I suppose it's complicated. I'll explain after we eat."

Thirty minutes—and several awkward starts and stops—later, the fugitives basked in the afterglow of the first, mostly-hot meal they'd enjoyed in days. Italian bread (still sort of frozen on the inside), spicy chicken sausages stuffed with gruyere cheese (burned on the outside, mostly frozen on the inside), room temperature canned pears with heavenly syrup Fallon drank directly from the canister, and room temperature tomato sauce (seasoned liberally with garlic powder, the best they could do) served in a bowl into which they dipped

166

sausages and hunks of cold bread. Emma hunted in the pantry until she found a tin of mostly-stale Italian deli cookies, which Danny ate as if they'd been invented the previous afternoon, and an old box of individually-wrapped dark chocolates which tasted, to Fallon, like a momentary break from every stressor she'd ever known.

Danny burped and patted his stomach. "I feel like my drunk Uncle Dave."

Fallon tossed a crumpled napkin at him. "You don't have a drunk Uncle Dave."

"I know," he admitted. "But if I did, I'd want him to feel like this."

Emma dipped the last of the bread into their waning puddle of tomato sauce. "Fat and happy?"

"Exactly," Danny flashed matching blue eyes. "Let's agree that we make it a short-term goal: to live until we're fat and happy."

"Done," Fallon elbowed him softly. *Why? What are you doing, Baldie? Huh? Flirting? With half...no, three-quarters of the bulls in the mid-Atlantic region hunting for you, you're flirting?*

Danny sat leaning against a pastry oven. "What time is it? I don't imagine we can stick around here this morning and nap. Right?"

Emma craned her neck to peer inside the closet-sized office between the kitchen and the fire exit out back, presumably to the corridor above the parking area where they'd left the Chevron. "Um...it's 7:12. We've got about fifteen minutes to clear out of here without being seen."

Fallon crossed her legs on the cramped floor. "What if we stayed here? I mean, there's plenty of food. Granted, we'll get tired of pears and sausages after a while, but with another couple canisters of natural gas, we could regroup, spend our days in the city, anonymous and maybe picking up a few things—"

167

"You mean steal," Emma said. "We can't plug in, not in the city. The connections are too fast. Drones'll be on us in seconds."

Fallon tilted her head left to right. "Yeah, well...you know—"

"Absolutely," Danny rescued her. "We'd steal. No sense trying to access credits until we have to, no sense giving Blair and Carter any idea where we are. We risk that every time we plug in."

"Exactly," Fallon added. "I like your idea: we only plug in out in the sticks, rural places. We have a car. Why not? We can test our wrist screens way out in western Maryland somewhere, not here."

"So we steal," Emma confirmed. "That's fine. I mean...I'll get used to the idea."

Danny's brow furrowed. "Em, you're a...well, kid, you're actually a terrorist, like a legitimate, domestic enemy of the state. You sank a cargo ship, blew up a brokerage house, and firebombed your own parents' better-than-average Italian restaurant." He raised his hands in uncertainty. "And you're concerned that we might steal a couple of natural gas canisters and a new battery for that old clunker."

Emma smirked. "Hey, that's my car your bad-mouthing, mister. Knock it off."

"Yes, Emma," Fallon added. "We're going to steal what we need in the city."

"Leave that to me," Danny said.

Fallon said, "Then we'll come back here at night, maybe...after 6 or 6:30, when we're sure the work crews are gone." She gestured toward the small dining room. "That walk-up counter is cover. As long as we don't get too brash, we can stay hunkered down, eat all we need, get our strength back, take turns sleeping, and—"

"And plan our escape?" Emma interjected.

"And plan our assault on the Warrenton School of Juvenile Student Management."

Danny's smile fell. "C'mon, Fallon. You can't possibly want to go back there. Carter and Blair...our bio-wires? We might already be living on stolen time. When they figure out how Emma deleted us from the roster, they might fry us from 150 miles away."

"It's a mistake," Emma agreed.

"I'm going," Fallon didn't budge. "You saw that room. You know what he was about to do to me, what he's been doing to kids for who knows how long." She ran a hand over her bald scalp. "I'm going to bring the place down, going to free everyone. Sure, they'll probably get rounded up and sent off to the next place, but that place, the WSJSM...that's closing down forever."

"How?" Danny began collecting up crockery and utensils, stuffing it all into a plastic container he found in the pantry. "You're going to get yourself dismembered or killed. Us too."

"You don't have to come."

Emma squeezed Fallon's forearm. "Yes, we do."

Danny ducked into the pantry, then emerged holding what appeared to be key cards on nylon lanyards. "What're these, Em?"

"Oh, yes, right, brilliant!" She distributed one to each of them. "These will get us into the door out back—"

"The one above the parking area?" Glad for the distraction, Fallon asked, "So we don't have to navigate through that godforsaken lower level again?"

"Exactly. We can come and go as we like through the door at the top of the fire escape. It opens to a service hallway."

"That's good news," Danny draped the lanyard over his neck. "Now, what about credits? Who's got some?"

"I've got plenty," Emma tossed her ginger mop. "I've got them stashed in an account my father set up for me. It's in my uncle's name, so my mother's new husband would never know about it."

"Edward?" Fallon asked.

169

"He's the one," Emma said.

"Hidden credits," Danny said. "That's the best news we've had all year. I've got a dummy account, too. A friend and I set them up a couple of years ago, just to have a place to dump the odd credit here and there, like a savings account...you know...in case our main ID logins got pulled, emptied by the Hinds County attorney's office."

"Maybe we can move some credits from your uncle's account into Danny's hidden trove."

Abashed, he blushed. "I wouldn't call it a trove, precisely."

Fallon sighed. "I was being sarcastic, genius. While I love the idea that you both have accounts you think we can access, I worry that Blair or Carter or the Whateveritis County Bulls have already located all of those account codes and are just waiting for us to plug in."

"That's why we do it out in the boondocks, maybe get wildly lucky with an overnight update," Danny said. "And...I'll have you know...yes, there are a few surprises in that account."

"Dirty socks?" Emma teased.

"A couple, yeah. Multiple colors. You never know what you might need, especially for evening wear."

"My dad gave me all the numbers for my account," Emma explained. "They're not programmed into my notes. I've memorized them, so no one could hack in and transfer any credits."

"Ah," Danny cocked an eyebrow at her. "So that's why old Beatrice Bear wanted to eat your liver."

"Exactly."

"Poetic," Fallon said. "Even in prison Bloodsuckers can hide their credits from us Draggers."

Emma flushed. "I'm not rich."

Fallon held up the gas powered caramelizer. "Crème Brûlèe? You sure aren't from Herkimer County, New York."

"Or Jackson, Mississippi," Danny said. "Sorry, I hate to take old Baldie's side on anything, but Bear must have choked on her own drool when you walked in."

Fallon laughed. "Yeah, little did she know that you'd just as soon launch her Neanderthal ass into space with one of your bombs as make a cup of tea for her."

Emma smiled. "Yeah, well, that's true, but I'm not rich."

"Where d'you go to school?" Danny asked.

"Ugh, you'd hate it." She toyed with the remote gas igniter, flicked it on and off. "Grayson Academy, out in Towson. Ghastly place."

"Academy?" Fallon pursed her lips. "Sounds poor to me."

Emma blushed. "Yeah, well...okay. But I was doing lousy in math, and I'm absolutely awful in science, Chemistry especially."

Danny looked to Fallon. "You ever take a science class? Chemistry?"

She pursed her lips comically. "Not a one. I took Principles of Servitude or some such baloney on rye."

Danny nodded. "Me too. A whole class load last year, basically: how to be of use to wealthy shitheads."

"Where's your dad now?" Fallon hung the keycard around her neck like Danny. "Your mother?"

"Baltimore County lockup," she lit the igniter, watched the flame dance. "They're being held until I turn over the people who helped me, you know, detonate those bombs."

"Wait," Danny tugged his lanyard like a pendulum. "Your parents are split, but they're both in prison? Did they work this place together?"

Emma hesitated. "Yeah...this was a good business, um, for both of them...like I said, it's complicated."

"Why don't you give the evidence they're asking for?" Fallon asked. "Do you think they'll just arrest everyone and keep your parents in lockup?"

"Well, that," Emma started. "And...well, you see, there weren't really—"

171

"Hey," Danny cut her off. "What's that smell?"

Instinctively, Fallon ducked beneath the counter. Pulling Emma down, she said, "Whaddya mean? I don't smell any–" She inhaled, deeply. "Hey, yeah. What is that?"

"Cucumbers?" Emma offered, uncertain. "Yeah, I think that's it. Cucumbers."

Hunkered down as well, Danny whispered, "Down south, when you smell cucumbers, you know there's gotta be—"

"Snake!" Emma screamed and leaped clear of the counter. She landed in a heap, rolled, and reached frantically for the notepad in her sweater.

Not having seen it, Fallon fell to one hip, landed on her elbow, then turned to see the creature coming fast over the counter. Big bodied, heavy, and fast, the snake – she had no idea what kind it was: speckled brown, with a sinister, triangle-shaped head and insidious eyes – could have bitten her multiple times where she lay on the tiles. But instead, it made directly for Danny.

Seeing it come, he simply reacted, and like Emma, dove into the pantry.

"No!" Fallon cried. "Not in there! Danny, there's no way out."

Carrying its head two feet above the floor, the snake slithered rapidly into the narrow storage chamber after the fleeing boy. Fallon heard him banging and clattering and assumed he was dumping or tossing cookware and heavy tins of marinara sauce down at the monster. Fallon watched as the snake's head disappeared into the pantry, watched its powerful body, as big around as one of her thighs, continue to spill over the counter, across the floor and into the panty. "Good god, it's gotta be twenty feet long...twenty-five!" Her mind pinged from useless idea to useless idea. Somewhere far away, she heard Danny shout, then scream, but before she could settle on a decision, Emma simply attacked the snake, wrapped her seemingly useless child's arms about its body, and began yanking.

172

Fallon rolled to her feet. "Emma! No, honey, don't grab it. Don't!"

The snake was faster. Coiling back, it struck with mind-numbing speed, a nearly invisible blur of prehistoric death. It bit the girl deep in the side of her neck, injecting God only knew how much venom.

"No!" On her feet now, Fallon closed on the creature. She didn't need to look down to know that both of her hands, her wrists, and nearly half of her forearms were engulfed in molten-hot flame. "No you don't, you motherless—"

The snake rose several feet above Emma's inert body, glanced once at Fallon, seemed to grin at her, flashed sinister eyes as if inviting the older girl to watch as it killed her friend. Then it struck, slamming downward to sink its fangs into Emma's cheek.

Fallon heard her voice, as if from across a street. "Not today, you homely prick. Come get me."

Sensing an approaching threat, the great serpent, coiled protectively between the walk-up counter and the pantry door. With half its bulk slithering beneath the ovens, Fallon worried for a moment that they'd never get it out of there, and they'd be forced to flee, two of them badly injured, poisoned or worse, as the snake struck and retreated to the relative protection of the stoves.

But it didn't hide.

Instead, it made one error in judgement.

And Fallon Westerly ensured that it regretted that error for what remained of its exceedingly short life.

Too confident, too angry, too bloodthirsty, the snake— now coiled like a 700-pound clock spring—released the full strength of its considerable sinews and the full toxicity of its needle-sharp fangs at the approaching woman.

"Fine," Fallon growled. "Eat this." And she caught the snake's striking head with incalculable speed. As large across as the serving bowl they'd used to dip Italian bread into room temperature marinara sauce, the beast's fangs never reached

173

her, never punctured Fallon's outstretched hand. Rather, the snake's head simply melted, dripping into a foul-smelling puddle of ichor, burning blood, and teeth as large and blackened as the nozzle Emma had used to caramelize Crème Brûlèe, a French dessert in an Italian restaurant.

The snake's body writhed and tumbled violently, shattering plates and cracking the sturdy glass in one of the restaurant's oven doors. Still Fallon advanced, grabbing at it with both hands, burning through its now clumsy body with unaccountably hot flame that severed the snake into writhing sizzling pieces that lay scattered about Luigi's kitchen floor like so much spilled meat.

Remembering her friends, she reached into the very center of her consciousness and convinced herself to calm down, to extinguish the flames and to help the others. It took a few moments, time she used to survey her surroundings, ensuring no one, nothing, no other snakes, no massive, sewn-together colossal men had followed the serpent into their hiding place. *Their* hiding place. That miserable swamp dweller had invaded their only shelter, the only place the three fugitives had to hide. It had forced her to employ powers she'd never imagined, but in doing so, she'd raised such an unholy stench, the first construction foreman to show up this morning was going to have Baltimore County authorities here in two minutes.

"Shit." The fire in her breast quieted and the flames on her hands flickered out. "We gotta get out of here."

On the floor, Emma didn't move, even when a largish chunk of seizing snake carcass flopped onto her stomach, leaving a reddish-black stain of burned blood and organs on the girl's sweatshirt. "Get off her," Fallon kicked it away, then kneeled, cradling Emma's head in her lap. She dropped her face down to within inches of the smaller girl's, hoping to feel even the slightest breath on her cheek. "C'mon, sweetie. C'mon, gimme a breath, just one good one. Show me you're still on this side of the fence."

There it was; a gentle puff tickled her nose. *Thank God.* Trying not to look at the cruel punctures in Emma's neck and cheek, Fallon peeked into the pantry, ground her teeth together as she fought off a wet sob, then choked, "Danny? Are you in there? Can you help me? I need help, please."

"I'm here." His voice came from behind her. Fallon shrieked, jumping so violently that Emma's head all but bounced on the tiles.

"Jesus and dogshit, Danny!" She wheeled on him. "How did you get out here? How'd you..." Fallon gestured into the pantry, across the unholy snake carnage, to the small space beside the restaurant's office. "I didn't see you. How's that—"

"Did it bite you?" He asked without moving.

"No," she shook her head. "You? Are you okay?"

"I'm..." He started.

Squeezing blood and clear, runny fluid from the bite marks in Emma's cheek, Fallon wiped it up with a sleeve. "How'd you get past me? I thought you were bitten, trapped in there."

"You were...gone. You were..." As badly as Danny wanted to help, he remained pressed against the wall, uncertain whether to approach the dangerous girl. "I don't know what..."

"I'm fine," she lied. "I had a hold of that caramelizer. I just...you know...cranked up the gas. It made a great blow torch." She didn't want to lie directly to his face. 'C'mon, please. Help me. I don't know what to do. I think she might—"

"Tell me the truth."

"I told you the truth. I had that torch. I just turned up the gas as high as it would go, and it—"

"Fallon," Danny's voice sounded oddly disconnected, calm given their circumstances.

She turned slowly to face him.

"You have hair. Your hair grew almost two feet in fifteen seconds."

175

Oh shit, oh shit, oh shit, oh shit. She let her mind race about a moment or two, hoping perhaps to find a viable lie in the soupy quagmire of her imagination. But coming up empty, she said simply, "I promise, I'll explain. Just help me."

Breathing in ragged gasps, he whispered. "You have hair. You have gorgeous, brilliant, sexy brown hair, and you grew it in fifteen seconds."

"Danny?"

"Yeah, right. Right." He fell to helping with Emma.

"What're we gonna do?" Fallon asked. She cradled Emma's head, was all she could think to ease the girl's suffering.

Danny pressed fingers to Emma's carotid artery. "Her heart's beating fine. I don't like the look of her neck or her cheek. That's the start of necrosis. If we don't get her some antivenin that'll get a lot worse. It could paralyze her nervous system, cause her heart to shut down, her lungs, diaphragm, I dunno."

"You're scaring me." Fallon fought tears again.

"I'm sorry, but it's true." He had little comfort to offer. "What's worse is the first work crew that shows up…any second now…is gonna smell your little snake barbecue and be down here with torches and pitchforks."

"I know," she said, "I couldn't help it, couldn't…"

"Don't worry about it. I'm glad you killed it. It might've left all of us paralyzed and taking turns having nasty seizures all day if you hadn't."

Now tears did come, just a few as hopelessness threatened to leave Fallon curled up beside Emma on the bloody tiles. "Is she gonna…"

"Nope," Danny worked to sound confident, needed it to be contagious. "Nope, she's gonna be all right."

"How do you—"

"You remember what I said right before that big bastard came after us?"

"About the cucumbers?"

176

"Exactly," he reached across Emma's body to roll the hunk of charred snake flesh onto what had been its stomach. "See that?"

"What?"

"That's a copperhead. We've got them all over Mississippi." He turned the speckled, chocolate-colored chunk and winced. "Granted, ours are all about two, maybe three feet long at the longest, and timid, almost never aggressive …certainly never thirty-odd feet long, 700 pounds and homicidal. But it's a copperhead, nevertheless."

"And?"

"And there's antivenin for copperhead bites. Almost nobody dies from them." Again, he considered the inconceivably massive creature laying in charred pieces about the kitchen. "Of course, I've never seen one this…this goddamned huge. Jesus, look at the size of him."

"There's antivenin?"

"Yeah, it's called CroFab…we've been using it for decades. It's good. But you've gotta use a lot of it over a period of about twelve hours."

"Who are you? Who knows this sort of thing in passing?"

Danny smiled. "About eight-million Mississippians. It isn't laser surgery."

"How quickly does she need it?"

"As soon as possible after the bite," he wiped a napkin over the punctures in Emma's neck. "We should be quick. I have no idea how much that thing pumped into her."

"And you're gonna pick this stuff up in a train station in Baltimore? We can't just go to a med-dispenser and insert a prescription. I can't imagine any of the auto-dispensers could even cook up this CroFab whateveritis, anyway. Are we gonna find this here?"

He shook his head ruefully. "Well, no. We're gonna have to get her to a hospital or…I dunno, maybe break in. I can do it, but it's gonna take some time. I think I saw a county clinic,

177

one of those state-sponsored places down the street just a couple blocks."

"Really, Danny, how much time do we have?"

"With that much venom in her? I promise you I don't know." He examined her wounds again. "Damn, it bit her hard. This is an unbridled frigging tragedy. We should hustle."

Fallon grabbed his wrist, forced him to face her. "We don't have any credits; we don't have any identification. We can't just drop her off on the clinic's doorstep and hope they get the diagnosis right. There're no copperheads in Baltimore. They'll think she was stabbed, bitten by a raccoon or a werewolf or some goddamned thing, but not, never, not ever an impossible, frigging-goddamned-impossible, gargantuan copperhead out of a horror story nightmare." Her voice rose, trembled. Fallon pressed her temples to keep from passing out.

"I know," Danny had sweat through his clothes, looked like a sprinter after a hard race. "Okay, here's what we do." He took in the abominable mess Fallon made when she unleashed the fires of Hell on their slithery attacker. "You get as many of the pieces as you can into the ovens, just stuff them in there tight, and close the doors. That'll keep the stink down, at least for today."

"What're you gonna do?"

"I'm gonna get her a few hits of Stormcloud. Emma can ride the storm for a few hours. She won't feel a thing, won't die, and won't know that she's slowly succumbing to snake venom."

"And then what?"

"Then I'm gonna break into the pharmacy at the clinic."

"What if it's automated? One of those robo-pharm places? You'll get gassed, electrocuted; you're gonna end up back in lockup before lunch."

"Nah," he assured. "I had some friends back home who managed it, or at least claimed they did. I dunno. Their story sounded pretty plausible. I'll have a go at it."

"Oh, Jesus Christ, this isn't good." For all her abilities, Fallon couldn't think of a way to help. She knew the odds of success would improve significantly were she to go along for the break-in but couldn't bring herself to leave Emma.

Danny read her mind. "No."

"No, what?"

"You stay with her; we can't leave her alone. Hide in the pantry. Just close the door tight and stay in there." He sucked his lower lip, certain a rogue mountain gorilla or a legion of poisonous tarantulas might charge over the interactive counter screen any second now. "It's dangerous. Right? I know. Someone knows we're here. That big bastard in the farm yard. This snake..."

"Yeah," Fallon agreed. "Someone's tracking us... somehow. And someone is sending these...nightmares...rather than just sending in the bulls or drones. Why is that?"

"I have no idea." Now Danny's voice trembled. Tears spilled over his cheeks. "Listen, we can't help it. We gotta risk it. I hate leaving you here, maybe even to watch...you know."

"No."

"Right. Sorry. No. No way." He backtracked, "I hate leaving you. I do. But I can get into that hospital. I know I can. I know what I need to find, and I know how and where to find needles and first aid supplies to have her up and on her feet in just a few hours. But I've gotta go by myself, Fallon. I'm a lot faster, a lot...by myself."

Recalling the alacrity with which the limping, exhausted boy had managed to disappear over a twelve-foot brick wall with electrified wire and shards of glass, she didn't doubt him. "Okay, where you gonna find Stormcloud?"

"At the SPD, out there in the main concourse. I saw it when we came up earlier."

"An SPD? They sell band-aids and chocolate. She doesn't need a Prevotel calling card or a fashion magazine download. She needs Stormcloud."

"I know, love." He peeled off his bloody sweatshirt, and started for the main corridor. "I'm not going there to buy Stormcloud. I'm going there to steal it."

179

She folded the sweatshirt into a makeshift pillow, tucked it beneath Emma's mop of brash Irish hair. "They have it? How do you know?"

He grinned at her, and all at once Fallon wanted to kiss him, to hold and protect him, and to hide away with Danny, even if it meant huddling in the tiny pantry for the next six months. She rested a hand on Emma's damp forehead, hoped it brought the semi-conscious girl comfort. "How do you know they have Stormcloud?"

"Everyone has Stormcloud." He flashed the plastic key card. "Let's hope this works on all the outer access doors. And try not to worry. I promise you that most people don't die from copperhead bites."

She didn't seem convinced. "Okay, good luck. Don't get electrocuted, Daniel Hackett. We need you back here."

"Clean up the snake. Hurry, please. We don't have much time."

"Got it, and hey!" She called as he hustled out.

He pulled up quickly. "What?"

"I won't leave here. I don't care what happens, what shows up, or who comes for us. I swear I'll be here."

He grinned again. Two of the glass cuts in his forehead had opened. Blood seeped from both. Fallon didn't care and knew she could get quite addicted to seeing that grin every day. Danny said, "I know." He turned to go, then stopped again. "Oh, and..."

"What?"

"I love your hair." He shrugged. "Sorry. I confess. I could've gotten used to you bald, but this is better. Much."

From this far away, he couldn't see her blush. Fallon counted that among the very few good things happening right now. "Go. Be careful."

"Then we're gonna talk...for real this time."

"For real. I promise."

He started for the fire exit, then returned abruptly. "What were you in for?"

"What you heard in the broadcast...murder. An old school librarian, out her apartment window into the street, face first. Rumor is she spent years referring kids to Prevotel scavengers for spare parts."

"Did you do it?"

"No." She shook her head. "You?"

"I...resisted arrest near the site of an accident. It was an old school janitor utterly crushed by a garbage truck out in nowhere Mississippi. Rumor is that he also spent years referring kids to Prevotel."

"Did you do it?"

"Resist arrest? Yes."

Fallon pressed. "Why were you out there?"

"Because I was trying to kill him."

"Maybe tell me why some day?"

"Absolutely," He kneeled beside her. "I like it when we're honest."

"Yeah, me too." She smiled, wanting him to understand that they were all right. She dabbed blood from his face with her sleeve. "Now, go."

8.17

No, I Can't Help You

Hi all. I'm just checking in. I don't have much for you, except to note that I'm deathly afraid of snakes. I was raking leaves in my yard once about thirty years ago. (Yes, I still have natural trees in my yard; I'm fortunate.) I raked for a few minutes before realizing that I had raked up a snake, a deadly, man-eating, prehistoric monster. Truth be told, it was about a fifteen-inch garter snake, entirely harmless and terrified at the prospect of being raked around for the rest of his life.

Anyway, that was thirty years ago, and my rake is still out there, where I dropped it when I ran, screaming like a frightened third grader.

I think I'm going to take a break for a while, maybe breathe into a paper bag, you know, just until my head stops spinning.

See you in a few weeks.

Good luck!

9

A Robot Pharmacist, Punching Old Ladies, and a Whole Bunch of Arrows

Less than an hour later, Danny moved south along St. Paul Street toward the ruins of the city's old Inner Harbor. He crossed beneath a two-level trestle bridge. Multiple lines of traditional railroad and high-speed E-track crossed overhead, momentarily eclipsing the morning sun. A handful of thunderheads called the underpass home. None of them saw the teen as he hurried toward the state clinic at the corner of St. Paul and Biddle, an ugly part of the city that seemed to have irretrievably lost whatever charm it might have possessed generations earlier.

Danny passed within a few feet of two cloud junkies wrestling over what he guessed was a wine bottle and another who'd just awakened to discover that her right foot was missing, most likely traded for a few hits of Stormcloud at a local chop shop. All while the emaciated, hollow-cheeked girl—*woman?* It was impossible to know—howled in abject despair. She was in miserable shape: filthy, bandy-thin, with errant clumps of dirt-clotted hair, and leathery skin pocked with festering sores. Danny wondered how long she could live. Clearly, she'd recently crashed from whatever high she managed to secure in exchange for a foot—a ghastly foot no one could possibly purchase on purpose—and thought she couldn't have much time left among the living. Not long. How could she? How could any of them?

He didn't ponder the dilemma, however. Emma needed CroFab, and Danny had a hospital to rob. Lying to Fallon had been growing more and more difficult. He disliked having to convince her that he knew what he was doing. Sure, some friends back in Hinds County had dreamed of robbing a Robo-Pharm facility, but their security measures were nearly impossible to crack: automatic time-sensitive bolts on the doors and windows, individual medical drawer keys or combination locks, armed robo-pharmacists with gas jets, tasers, even built-in firearms in some of the big city hospitals. *What a mess.* Danny crossed St. Paul. *Just gotta hope it's an old lock-and-key place with a regular, flesh-and-bone pharmacist.* He hurried to avoid an electro-cab speeding north. *Baltimore County hospitals have the robots. Right? This old clinic can't afford anything that sophisticated. No way.*

By comparison, finding Stormcloud in the train station had been a snack. Danny left Fallon to clean up the gory bits of snake carcass and was thrilled to find Luigi's Continental nearly scrubbed clean of burned reptile remains when he returned with Emma's injection. He'd guessed right: The manager's desk at the SPD contained a motherlode of cloud tablets and a half-dozen ampules with built-in needles for easy administration. Danny pocketed a handful of about thirty tabs and all of the ampules. Not that he thought they'd need the drugs, but a few dozen hits might mean a lucrative trade were the fugitive trio to find themselves truly at the end of their collective rope.

He and Fallon injected Emma twice, plenty to keep the teen high as a crepe-paper blimp for the rest of the day. He didn't worry that it would hurt her; Emma had shown no signs of ever having been a cloud addict. So two injections weren't dangerous...well, not too dangerous.

She had awakened with the first needle prick, the cloud giving her a momentary burst of clarity. "Guys! Guys! The snake! There's a really big snake."

Weeping in relief, Fallon held Emma close, shushed her quietly. "It's okay, sweetie. It's gone. It's gone. Rest now. You just rest."

On cue, Emma tumbled back into unconsciousness, resting peacefully in the narrow quarters of Luigi's pantry. "Where'd you find this?' Fallon indicated the drawstring bag Danny left in case Emma needed another injection or in case he was unable to return.

"At the SPD," he said. "The manager's desk is a frigging pharmacy."

"The key get you in?"

"Yeah," he lied. "Nothing to it."

"We're lucky."

"We are," he agreed, looking away.

Danny moved carboard boxes, and folded tablecloths in hopes of providing Fallon as much comfort as possible before sneaking out the back exit and into a crowd of early-shift construction workers, drinking coffee and preparing for the day's schedule of projects.

None of the crews saw him, however.

He made certain of that.

Now, standing at the vast, ostentatiously arched doors of what had once been St. Sebastian Memorial Hospital (before the mid-Atlantic states joined liberal partisans in the Cloud Wars and much of Baltimore was shelled), Danny paused long enough to ensure that none of the morning commuters making their way up St. Paul to Penn Station noticed him. They didn't; they couldn't, not when he was this dialed in. Even the security guards astride the clinic's entryway only gave him a passing glance, as if some part of their minds could see him, but another part, a more determined lobe or bit of coil, convinced them that there was nothing of consequence to notice. Granted, traveling this way was significantly easier in Mississippi, where the weather was almost always warm, and he could wear less clothing. Layers of fabric made traveling as mist more challenging and required so much energy and focus as not to be worth the effort. His wrist screen and accompanying wires had never been a problem; they somehow shifted when he shifted, but heavy clothing, especially leather shoes, were a challenge.

With a moment's renewed focus, he drifted effortlessly toward the doors...and through.

The familiar, oddly comforting feeling of nausea rushed through Danny as he passed, like smoke, between, beneath, and above the oak door frame and into the dismal, anachronistic lobby.

A marble statue, clearly centuries old, stood in one corner of the foyer, St. Sebastian, Danny guessed. Why anyone would build a hospital in memory of a Christian saint who clearly had been martyred in a grim encounter with dozens of homicidal bowmen escaped him. Regardless, Danny wafted behind Sebastian's tormented, pin-cushion torso to retake his corporeal form. Seconds later, he, the teenage boy with the limp, that oh, so important limp, hurried up cracked and broken marble stairs in search of the clinic's pharmacy.

No one questioned him; he'd passed through security. Obviously he belonged here. And that limp...perhaps he was just a kid coming in for a new foot, a string of new ankle tendons, a nip, a tuck, an adjustment, and home in time for dinner, limp free.

He smiled at the overworked, exhausted clinic staff, talking with patients, comforting those in pain, those in the throes of cloud withdrawal, and those just too poor to afford one of Baltimore County's private hospitals. A doctor carrying an electronic chart passed; she'd drawn a monocular projection lens over one eye and spoke into a wireless microphone draped around her neck. From what Danny heard, she was directing a surgical procedure, albeit remotely. He wondered where her patient might be, perhaps Africa or a South American jungle. He wanted to ask if there was another surgeon on the line, or just a technician positioning a robot maybe in the back of a truck or in an airplane high above a rainforest.

The Baltimore County Brokerage House had been shut down for nearly two months. Cloud addicts and surgical patients had to come somewhere. Anyone low on credits for the high-priced hospitals—there were four in the city—would be here, in line with the desperate and destitute from the city's poverty-stricken lower classes. He grimaced at the sheer number of patients lining the halls with plastic grocery bags taped over wrist or ankle stumps, or the eye patches hiding the ragged, empty sockets of the sorry sods who'd given up half their sight to cover a few months' rent.

Danny was no revolutionary. He'd been in survival mode too long to give a damn about other people's politics. Yet he did feel a momentary pang of compassion and allegiance for Fallon's developing plan to kill Headmaster Blair and burn the WSJSM to ash. Having witnessed her killing that snake in less time than it takes to spell *copperhead*, he thought that the young woman, clearly special, powerfully so, might just be on to something.

Perhaps it was time to fight back rather than just duck and run. Seeing so many of Baltimore's downtrodden gathered here, each awaiting a measure of kindness or hope, an angry side of his personality tried surfacing. If only they could fight back, if only someone led them, if only they had a unifying cause around which to rally...

"Nah." Moving down the crowded corridor, he banished the irresponsible revolutionary ideas. He wasn't interested in getting killed helping some girl seek vengeance on a sociopathic headmaster. The world was full of sociopathic headmasters. Killing one wouldn't make any difference to anyone. Danny had been on his own too long to fall for pointless causes.

Even when those pointless causes were championed by women with heart-stoppingly gorgeous hair.

He dodged a group of young doctors, clearly high on speed supplements—what Monique LeFevbre at the Mississippi Mud Café called 'double-shifters' as she poured coffee and slung waffles eighteen hours a day. A passing gurney caused Danny to pull up for a moment. He ducked into the hollow beside a wall-mounted wellness scanner and watched as the patient, a strikingly healthy-looking woman, obviously fifty-seven, rolled past, clear-eyed and smiling dumbly on whatever mind erasers they injected into cleanse patients wheeling into their harvest procedure. Her reed thin wrist lay naked on the starched blanket; a technician or nurse had removed her interactive screen in a hasty, sloppy procedure. Danny absent-mindedly rubbed the numb skin around his own vid-screen, swallowing dryly at the older woman's raw, open flesh.

"Long life to your family." He whispered the traditional greeting.

"Thank you, young man." The woman stared half at him and half through him, awash in sedatives. "I won't be coming back this way."

"Be brave, mother." Danny gave her blanketed foot a pat as she passed. "You're doing a good thing, better than most of us ever will."

"Thank you," her voice tried to break. She fought it. "Thank you, young man." This time with no quiver. "I know."

Better you than me, sister. Jesus, how some people eat, drink, and believe the hype. He wanted to call after her, "Hey, lady...you're rolling to your death!" But it wouldn't do either of them any good. Cleanse & Harvest patients were zealots. Six decades of struggling through a crappy-ass life, an hour as stoned as St. Sebastian's statue, and twenty minutes of no-nonsense dismemberment.

Done. Game over. Family set for life.

Well, for a few years anyway.

Actually, the lady rolling down the second-floor corridor of the Baltimore County Bullshit Grimy-Ass Public Clinic looked pretty good. Her spare parts might bring a nice nest egg to her children and grandchildren. Healthy, obviously fit, a non-drinker, non-smoker, swimmer, maybe a bicyclist...she'd bring maybe two-million credits, if this clinic had connections with the right brokerage houses.

Danny hesitated a moment longer, wished he'd asked her name.

Then, remembering Emma, he hurried toward the pharmacy.

"Bugger," Danny spat. "Nothing's ever goddamned easy."

He couldn't check his bio-screen. The clinic didn't have any traditional clocks on the walls, and he wasn't about to ask any of the lonely losers lined up for meds, drugs, or doctor-prescribed happiness come 9:00 a.m.

He grabbed a passing nurse. "Hey, sis, sorry. But my vid's uploading software."

"Whaddya need, kid?'

"Just the time."

She tugged her sleeve up a few inches. "Um...8:53. Still coffee hour."

"Thanks, sister." He turned back to the locked, plexi-glass doors of the clinic's fully automated, robo-pharmacy.

Over her shoulder, the nurse, a young woman in a stained, threadbare uniform called back. "They don't open until 9:00. Sorry."

"Seven minutes," Danny feigned amused frustration. "I'll just wait, thanks." When she was out of earshot, he muttered. "Shit. Gotta hurry." He wandered farther down the corridor, ducked into an open doorway, faded to the nearly invisible smoke he'd perfected years ago when he received a faulty ligament in his ankle, a cheap, thirty-minute procedure at a Cincinnati storefront—all his mother could afford at the time—and drifted back to the robo-pharm gate.

And inside.

The automated pharmacist, a boxy, multi-armed robotic device that looked nothing at all like the robots Danny had seen in downloads of old science fiction comics, sat quietly behind the pharmacy counter. Affixed to a single rail that ran like E-trolley track through the medicine and drug shelves and cabinets, the pharmacist, in overnight shut down mode, didn't stir when Danny passed through the narrow slit between the plexi-glass entry panels. Armed with what appeared to be multiple tasers, gas nozzles, and even a short-barreled, semi-automatic firearm, the robot would 'awaken' should any intruder pass behind the electric eye beam separating the

189

stores of valuable medicines and painkillers from the throngs of delirious addicts and patients seeking solace in the clinic.

And that won't be good, Danny thought, eyeing again the laser-guided tasers and gas jets. He'd been gassed once in a food line outside a shelter in Titusville, Florida. It had taken days for his vision to return and even longer to get the acrid flavor of chemical poison from the back of his throat.

He hoped he could float past or over the security beam, find the CroFab—if there was any—and hide nearby until 9:00 when the robo-pharmacist would hopefully be busy negotiating with and filling prescriptions for the clutch of customers already lined up.

Danny also knew that most of the scripts could be filled from the auto dispensers beside the counter. Patients would either slide their prescription chips into the wall unit and await their meds, or they'd plug in to the robot's terminal, and the pharmacist would dial up the ingredients without ever moving from its perch.

Five minutes. Gotta hurry.

He moved like fog through the shelves until he located a few items he, Fallon, and Emma might need in the coming weeks: More Stormcloud ampules, Prevocodone for pain, gauze bandages, first-aid tape, Travoxycillin, which he abandoned when he found the good stuff, Prevoxycillin, and then finally, on a corner shelf, tucked nearly out of site and dusty, Crotalidae Polyvalent Immune Fab, CroFab antivenin, distilled from the venom of the country's deadliest pit vipers, twelve miniature ampules in a handy, plastic carry case.

Perfect. Now, I just gotta get it all out of here.

There was no way he could carry the meds in his insubstantial, smoky form, couldn't even get the good stuff— the cloud ampules and the Prevocodone—out of their drawers.

But if he got wildly lucky, and all the drawers unlocked automatically at 9:00, when coincidentally, the robot of frigging death parked out front would also fire up, he might be able to retake his corporeal form, steal the meds he needed without

190

the pharmacist (or anyone else) noticing, stash them together somewhere, and...*then what?*

Then, dummy, you've got to create such a holy ruckus, that everyone gets plenty distracted, even old Metal Head out there.

Danny had no idea how he might manage it. *Just have to cross that death-defying chasm when you come to it. Gotta remember Emma. She needs this.*

He positioned himself in front of the CroFab shelf.

And hope that robot doesn't have an auto lockup program default in the event of a 'Ruckus.' I need it to keep these doors open or I'll be stuck in here like Pooh's little black rain cloud all morning.

With that last swallow of irritating uncertainty, Danny allowed his teenage self to re-establish, taking form quickly in a low crouch behind a tidy row of medicine bottles and pill boxes. Near the entrance, he heard the robot's gears, turbines, battery packs, whatever they were, begin firing up. As they did, several hundred prescription medicine drawers clicked to the UNLOCKED position at once.

Perfect. Danny stayed low, moving silently between the racks.

"GOOD MORNING BALTIMORE. I AM YOUR BCS CLINIC 17 ROBO-PHARMACIST, MODEL 98-665. BUT YOU CAN CALL ME *NINER*." Danny couldn't tell where the polite, curiously-human voice came from. Niner didn't have anything that even remotely approximated a human head, human face, even a mouth, and figured there must be a hidden speaker in the thing's chest...if it had a chest...beside the camera lenses that passed for its eyes.

For a paralyzing second, Danny froze, then peeked warily out from behind a stack of Travoxycillin boxes to confirm for himself that old Niner didn't have a camera in the back of its...body, whatever.

It didn't, not one he could see from here. And if he couldn't see a camera, he assumed that Niner couldn't see him.

191

But you have no idea how many security beams, floor sensors, overhead cameras, or touch-sensitive devices it might have wired to fry your ass back here.

Niner kept speaking, so Danny continued sidling through the cabinets and storage containers, taking what he needed and stacking it all in a corner, just out of sight of the front counter.

"I AM HAPPY TO HELP YOU WITH YOUR PHARMACOLOGICAL NEEDS THIS LOVELY MORNING. PLEASE FORM AN ORDERLY LINE HERE AT THE COUNTER OR AT THE SELF-SERVICE DISPENSERS TO MY RIGHT." Niner gestured dramatically with one, jointed arm. "I AM SURE THAT TOGETHER WE CAN HAVE YOU ON YOUR WAY IN JUST A FEW MINUTES. THANK YOU FOR YOUR COOPERATION AND PATIENCE."

Polite fellow, isn't he? Danny slid the stolen supplies into a cardboard box, slid it even closer to Niner's electric eye beam, then concentrated his attention inward, breathed easily through his nose, and disappeared.

Drifting back to the recessed doorway he'd used earlier, Danny re-formed, pulling himself back from what he always thought of as the edge of the solar system, a depressing sensation, but a necessary one. Traveling as nearly-invisible smoke made a life of crime easier, but not altogether easy. He rested against the doorjamb a moment, made up his mind, then turned and half jogged back to the pharmacy.

Have to do this before I lose my nerve. He thought. *Emma. Keep thinking: Emma.*

A tall, muscular man in a hard hat, coveralls, boots, and a flannel jacket waited patiently in the queue to pick up medications. An elderly woman, maybe 65, too old for Cleanse & Harvest, waited in front of him, just one place back from the counter and the über-polite robot drug peddler.

He'll do. Danny hurried, picking up the pace so as not to chicken out. *Shit, friends, this is gonna hurt. Fallon, I hope you're good with broken bones!*

192

And jogging up beside the large man, even larger now that he'd gotten in close, Danny shouted, "I told you before, Buford, stay away from my mother!"

The big man held up his hands, one clutching a yellow prescription chip. "Hey, kid...wait!"

Danny reared back and slugged him. He had no idea if the punch actually hurt the burly construction worker. But it surprised him enough that the bigger man staggered backward into a wiry, teenager, a thunderhead, sweaty and jonesing, but probably in line to fill a doctor-prescribed battery of step-down pills. Whoever he was, Danny figured his family had mega credits, enough for cloud detox. Otherwise, this loser would be under the E-train tracks or wandering around the basement of Penn Station with the rest of the lost generation.

"Hey, man," the cloud junkie pushed Gigantor with grimy paws that seemed to offend him as much as Danny's punch. "Git off me, butchy bitch!"

Gigantor took a swipe at the cloud loser, knocking him halfway across the corridor. He then pivoted smoothly for a man his size—*this guy's a fighter*—and came for Danny, a delicious love for brawling clear in his eyes.

Shit. I'm too far over.

From behind the counter, Niner cranked up the speaker volume and cranked down the polite attitude. "WARNING ALL. WARNING BALTIMORE. IF YOU DO NOT DESIST, I WILL BE FORCED TO EMPLOY CORRECTIVE MEASURES! I REPEAT: DESIST AT THIS MOMENT, OR I WILL BE FORCED..."

Out of position, Danny tried moving to his right, Niner's left, near the electric eye and the box of stolen supplies, but the old woman, *Grandma Pain In My Ass*, had moved to intercept him, as if she was going to hold him until the bulls arrived.

She started, "Now, young man, that's no way to—"

Danny punched her hard across the face, laid her out like a prize fighter with a glass jaw.

Jesus, Jesus, I've gotta stop punching old ladies!

193

When he turned back far enough to see Gigantor coming for him, Danny Hackett offered up a wily grin and dropped his hands to his sides. His last hope, before tumbling backward through the pharmacy electric eye security beam was *I hope he doesn't break my jaw...or kill me.*

He took the punch, saw a brilliant constellation of fiery supernovas, then tumbled backwards, focusing every cell in his body on changing over to smoke before striking the scuffed tile floor.

It almost worked.

Landing in a heap, he needed a faction of a second to focus his attention—Gigantor had really tagged him and for a moment all he could think was *Mary had a little lamb, and we ate it.* He found excellent motivation when he turned his head and, through blurry eyes, caught sight of Niner turning on him, gas nozzles focused, tasers blinking blue to red.

And he was gone.

Niner was still warning the entire city of Baltimore away from its pharmacy. "I WILL BE FORCED TO EMPLOY CORRECTIVE MEASURES..."

When Gigantor broke the pharmacy's electric eye beam (hoping to beat Danny to greasy soup), Niner needed only a hundredth of a second to adjust his tasers away from the bloody boy who had just disappeared – which did not calculate in the robot's security programming – and train his weapons on the large man who had intruded behind the counter.

Niner fired.

Gigantor's body froze for an instant, twitched violently in a mad shiver, and then launched itself catapult-like into a corner, where it continued to spasm as the robo-pharmacist rolled smoothly over.

"REMAIN WHERE YOU ARE, OR I WILL BE FORCED TO ENGAGE ONCE AGAIN. THE BALTIMORE COUNTY AUTHORITIES ARE EN ROUTE TO THIS POSITION. REMAIN WHERE YOU ARE..."

Gigantor couldn't have moved from where he lay, arms and legs awkwardly jutting like so much useless tidal flotsam. Rather he slumped loosely as the last of Niner's electric charge left his body. Drool spilled over his lips while contrails of bloody snot seeped from his nostrils. Niner seemed to consider these, weighing them as evidence that the large man was still alive. Behind them, Danny reformed, grabbed the box of stolen goods, and forced himself to walk calmly away.

It didn't work. Apparently, Niner did have some sort of sensory device in the back of his torso box. Or perhaps Danny breaking the security beam a second time warned the robot again. Whirling on its rail-gyro fitting, it shouted this time. "STOP WHERE YOU ARE. STOP WHERE YOU ARE, OR I WILL FIRE. STOP IMMEDIATELY."

Danny considered running, just pelting Hell-for-abandon down the corridor, hoping not to get shot, but some ancient survival gene woke up at that moment and warned him. *Don't try it, dummy. That thing's got laser guided tasers and probably a dead-eye for center mass at 100 yards with that gun. Just drop the box and disappear. Get out of here. We'll figure it out later. Just disappear.*

He was about to, had convinced himself it was the right decision…when the strung-out cloud junkie saved him. Diving over the counter, the desperate teen rolled, crashed shoulder first into a twelve-foot rack of medicine bottles and ampules, and had no idea when it began swaying precariously. Crawling, scrabbling away from the robot guard, the junkie clawed his way between the racks, fingers and toes dragging him to freedom, when the metal shelf toppled with a gorgeous din that collapsed two additional racks and drove Niner into robot apoplexy.

Seeming to forget Danny entirely, Niner rolled smoothly back to the cross rail, selected a clutter-free approach that would take it close to the would-be thief, now buried beneath five-hundred pounds of medical detritus, and fired twin nozzles of acrid-smelling gas down at the teen's already unconscious

195

body. The plexi-glass doors of the pharmacy crashed closed with a slam that echoed to both ends of the clinic's main hallway. Hundreds of people, many of the them badly injured or suffering, turned to watch.

Danny didn't stay long enough to learn if Niner killed anyone. Rather, he fled at a gentle, non-hurried walk, despite his heart yelping 175 beats a minute, down the cracked and smudged marble stairs, past St. Sebastian (who hadn't recovered from his encounter with the Bowmen of Agincourt) and out the front entrance.

Passing through the arched double doors onto St. Paul, he waved to the security guards. "Hey, you guys might wanna know that there's some trouble up at—"

The taller of the two interrupted. Glancing at his wrist, he said, "Yeah, we just got it, kid. Up at the pharmacy. Huh?"

"Yeah," Danny forced a smile. "Looks like some thunderhead tried to get past that robo-guy."

The shorter guard, beefy and tough, laughed at this. "Past Niner? Heh. Well, I tell you what, kid, whoever that guy is...he's cooked."

"Yeah, right," Tallish added. "I wouldn't wanna try to sneak a stick of gum past that thing."

"Okay," Danny started down the stairs. "Just thought you guys should know."

"We're good. Thanks, kid," Shortish ushered him toward the street. "Have a good day."

"Yeah, bye." He didn't make it five steps up St. Paul before Tallish called, "Hey, kid...what happened to your face? You all right?"

Danny turned on his heel, held up the cardboard box of meds. "I'm good. Thanks. Had a bit of a scuffle is all...over a girl."

"Ha!" Shortish laughed again. "Aint it always the truth? Whaddya say; maybe duck next time, huh?"

"I will." Danny jogged up St. Paul feeling like a hero in an adventure story.

Two blocks north, he nearly slammed into a Maryland State Bull rounding a corner outside a run-down convenience store near the tracks. The bull, a massive specimen, over seven feet tall, took him firmly in one half-human, half-goddamned-whateveritis hand. It closed like a vise over Danny's shoulder.

"Hold on, kid." The generous stink of burned plastic and rotting meat wafted from his clothing and tactical gear.

Danny gagged. "Sorry."

"Where you going in such a hurry?" The officer might have weighed three-hundred-fifty pounds but in this close looked like a sanitation truck in jackboots.

"Just headed home," he lied. "I was running some errands for my dad and crashed my bike. So I'm hoofing it. Hurrying. You know."

"That how you banged up your face?" In his opposite hand, the bull held a large takeout coffee cup that looked like a thimble. Without spilling a drop, he extended a finger and pressed two buttons in his armored com-vest. LED lights that had been red now flashed green, and a single projection lens lowered from his helmet to cover the bull's left eye. Sipping noisily, he considered Danny through the eyepiece. "Just headed home?"

"Yes, sir." *Shit, oh shit, oh shit, oh shit.*

"Where'd you crash your bike?"

Danny's mind raced, decided that a little trouble was better than a lot of trouble. "Um..."

The bull's grip tightened. "C'mon."

"Down on Atlantic Avenue, by that old warehouse, just off the river."

"You know you're not supposed to—"

"I know," he interrupted, a calculated risk that, on the wrong day, might see him back at the county clinic, this time as a patient. "I figured if I told you the truth maybe you'd let me go this time. The old loading dock makes a great ramp. I lost it, rammed some pallets, bent my front rim and bashed my

197

face in those old barrels stacked out there." *You are piling it on, dumbass. You better hope this works.*

The bull pressed another button in his vest. Another LED blinked green, then flashed red. The bull gave him a healthy shake; Danny feared his teeth might come loose. "Well, my boy, you caught me on my coffee break. So I'm gonna let you go home to..."

Danny read his mind. "Lafayette, just on the other side of the station." He pointed north, grateful he'd paid attention to at least one street sign on their drive in.

"What's in the box?" The bull's projection lens folded back inside his tactical helmet.

"Some stuff I had to pick up for Dad. Parts. He's fixing a robo-host for one of the hotels out by the airport. I forget which one."

"Which class?"

"Um..." Again, his mind ran ten miles a minute. "R, I think. It's one of the friendly ones, polite all the time, with the creepy human face."

The bull let him go, drank more coffee. "I hate those things."

Danny had no idea what to say. "Thanks. Sorry. And...thanks." He hustled off, glad to be jogging as a means to hide the jelly-wobble in his legs.

"I punched another old lady." Danny tiptoed into the pantry to find Emma still sleeping on Fallon's chest. The smaller girl moaned restlessly. Sweating, she breathed in shallow, raspy swallows, but at least she was still drawing breath. Fallon had found candles which cast eerie light and made Emma's bite marks appear even more sinister.

"Did you get the meds?" Fallon shifted, uncomfortable on the cold tiles.

"Did you not hear me?" Still in a good mood following his harrowing escape from the robo-pharm facility, he said, "I punched another old lady. That makes two today, over 700 in a

198

year, if I stay on this pace, and it's only 9:30 in the morning. Who knows how many I might clobber before dinnertime?"

She noticed the bruises on his face. "Looks like she might've gotten the better of you, though. Huh, big guy? You get your ass kicked by someone's grandmother?"

He fingered the swelling above his cheek. "What? This? No...I got this on purpose."

"You got punched on purpose? Oh, this oughta be good."

"No, really," he began rooting in the box of stolen goods. "I had to let this monster of a guy beat the crap out of me to lure him past a security beam and distract the robo—" Fallon watched him hunt for the CroFab ampules. "You know what? Never mind."

"No, no," she wiped Emma's face, then shifted the girl's head to a cardboard box cushioned with Danny's folded sweatshirt. "I can't wait to hear."

"Hey," he pleaded his case. "It wasn't easy, getting this loot out of that place. Those robo-pharmacists are goddamned deadly."

"I know," Fallon admitted. "I'm impressed. I don't know how you do it. Who punched you?"

He passed her the ampules. "It doesn't matter. It was a harebrained idea that barely worked, and I almost got gassed, electrocuted, and shot...frigging shot...that thing had guns. And then I got stopped by a bull."

"Wait. What? Where?"

"Just down by the street level tracks, on the other side of the bridge. He was giant, even bigger than the ones that came to the farm."

She grabbed his shirt collar. "He let you go? Did he not recognize you? How could he not recognize you?"

"I dunno. I think the swelling in my face didn't match whatever software he was using. Or maybe the image they have of me is old. I've heard that works sometimes. You grow; you know? And the photo specs don't match the lens scans they do in the street."

199

"What did you say?"

"I lied like an Olympic gold medal winner, made up bullshit as fast as I could shovel it."

At that, Fallon acquiesced. "Okay. Let's hope. But Jesus, next time make sure you're not being followed"

"Hey," his temper flared. "It wasn't easy. You sneak past the armed robo-pharmacist next time, see if you can sweet talk your way in without getting tazed, fogged, and shocked. I'll take a turn watching from the cheap seats."

"You're right," she said. "I'm sorry. It's just that we're sort of sitting ducks here."

"Or maybe Emma was right. Maybe that zombie cannibal thing is working and the City of Baltimore can't pull up anything recent on us."

Fallon frowned. "Sure, or perhaps the City of Baltimore hired itself a lazy-ass bull who didn't wanna be bothered cross referencing the file during his morning donut run."

"Yeah, I hate this city." He passed her the box. "But on the bright side, there's a lot of stuff in here. I managed a pretty good haul."

Opening the cache, Fallon's mood shifted. "I'm impressed! Prevoxycillin? Prevocodone? This is outstanding. Truly."

Danny blushed. "Thanks."

She looked closer at his face. "Sorry you got punched."

"Meh," he shrugged. "It wasn't that bad. The guy was big as a mountain gorilla but he punched like my sister. And if I'm right, the swelling helped me get past that bull."

"How'd you get out of the pharmacy?"

"A thunderhead helped me."

"Really?" She withdrew the first CroFab ampule, broke the plastic seal, and held it up to their meagre candlelight. "So you're making friends and influencing people left and right."

"I think he's dead."

"Oh, shit."

"Yeah, he was in deep when I got out of there."

"Sorry."

"Whatever," Danny removed a second ampule, turned it carefully in his fingers, reading the tiny printed directions along the glass container. "It's not like we were exchanging holiday cards or anything. He was a junkie loser, desperate."

"Still..."

"Yeah, still."

Two hours and four ampules later, the swelling and discoloration around Emma's bites had gone down noticeably. Construction crews worked steadily in the halls, shops, and restaurants around Luigi's Continental. But after their noon break, there'd been nothing to suggest that anyone had started renovations or repairs on their hiding place.

"We can stay here tonight," Fallon said. "If they don't flush us out this afternoon, we can whip up another meal and give her as much time to recover as possible. Right?"

Danny sat with his back in a corner and Fallon's feet draped over his thighs. About thirty minutes earlier, he'd finally drummed up enough courage to rest his hand, without moving, on her crossed ankles. Fallon didn't complain, so he left them there, giving them both time to get used to the very real suggestion that friends in close company sometimes have to touch one another. Sliding one hand slowly just a few inches up her shin, he said, "I'm worried about staying. I think we gotta get out of here as soon as she's ready."

"The snake?"

"Yeah, jumping Jesus, and that frigging thing... whatever he was...that man-giant who came after us at the farm." He held his breath a moment, didn't want her to see him that frightened. Exhaling slowly, he confessed anyway. "I was scared. I don't know...what those things...what they are."

Fallon uncrossed her ankles, dragged one foot affectionately over his thigh. "Hey." He didn't respond right away, so she did it again, just a quick gesture that spoke volumes. "Hey. Listen..."

"Yeah?"

201

"I was scared, too. I've never been so scared."

"Yeah, I—"

"No, wait," she cut him off, "listen." The pantry, lit only by candlelight, boosted Fallon's courage. "I couldn't have managed today without you, Danny. And I agree: I think we get out of here as soon as she's up."

He didn't know what to say. He'd never been romantic, and thinking on their situation: trapped in an abandoned restaurant pantry for at least another six hours, with little hope, few prospects for success, a badly poisoned and heavily medicated friend riding the storm on the floor, no access to credits, and an antique car that might not start without some serious prayer, he realized that this might not be the most appropriate time for romance. Perhaps honesty would serve him better just now. He decided to go with it. "I'm scared, Fallon. That snake scared me. That man...thing, whatever it was...scared me. I don't wanna do this. I don't wanna go back, but...Jesus...I will. But only because that's where you're going, and you're the only thing that makes any sense today."

"Even though you..." She ran a hand through her hair, luxuriant tresses that hadn't been there six hours earlier, "...know more about me?"

"Yeah," he pulled her wandering ankle close, crossed it over the other, and draped both hands over her bare feet. "Yeah, that doesn't scare me."

"Good. I'm glad," she confessed. "It terrifies most people."

I'm not most people. Danny tried to say. Then didn't. Perhaps another time.

"I wish we knew about our accounts."

"Me, too," he agreed. "Even my phony one. Who knows what the bulls can do from a central terminal?"

"I hate the idea of stealing everything we need," she started, "hate thinking of you...you know."

"I'm fine," he said.

"You look like you got hit by a train," Fallon said. "We can't have you beaten every time we need a loaf of bread."

"Yeah," he said, then replayed their previous plan, just because it made him feel better. "If we can get someplace rural, like wicked, frigging rural, we can move Emma's credits to my account..."

"We should be okay."

"I think so."

"Then we just have to make purchases from rural places, country stores and backwater Prevo-Marts." She passed a finger through the candleflame.

"Exactly."

"You think it'll work?"

"For a while," he confessed. "But then, no. Carter seems pretty sharp. He's gonna figure it out."

Fallon ignored this, withdrew another ampule of CroFab. "She's due for her next dose."

"I'll do it." Regretfully, Danny shifted, moving her legs from his lap.

"Should we give her more Stormcloud? Keep her knocked out?"

He shook his head, crawled to Emma, peeled the plastic seal from the CroFab ampule. "Nah. She looks a lot better. Maybe we let her wake up, see how she's feeling."

"Yeah," Fallon agreed. "Then she can tell us why we drove all the way to Baltimore just to eat lukewarm Italian food."

Eventually, Emma woke. But it wasn't until late that night.

10

Robbery, an Unanswered Question, an Explosion, and Turning Eighteen

They took turns napping, took turns listening for construction workers and machinery. On a few frightening occasions, either Fallon or Danny woke the other, worried that an engineer or a foreman might be outside their door, assessing damage to Luigi's. Twice, Danny hurried to the pantry door, and for better or worse, held tight to the latch, figuring their last resort would be to pretend that the door was stuck. It wasn't the most inspired idea either of them had come up with in a tight spot, but with the sounds of construction staff clumping about outside, hanging on for dear life emerged as the only—hopefully temporary—option.

By 6:30, they relaxed. Fallon insisted that they remain in the cramped storage facility for another thirty minutes, without moving, only listening, as they ensured that neither of them heard anything from the rear corridor or the drone tower concourse beyond the restaurant's bombed out seating area.

At 6:34, Danny suggested, "They've gotta be gone."

"Two more minutes," Fallon replied. "Then we'll make dinner."

Emma had finished her battery of CroFab at around 4:00. Having been stabbed six times each, her thin thighs looked like pin cushions. Danny considered referencing St. Sebastian, then let it go. Dead Catholics filled to bursting with pagan arrows didn't strike him as the most productive topic for chit chat while cowering among tins of tomato puree.

"You wanna try to wake her?" Danny asked. "She oughta eat."

"Not yet," Fallon said. "Two hits of Stormcloud and who knows how much CroFab. That box said to administer all of it, but there's nothing on there to suggest that the dose might be smaller if the victim is only ninety pounds."

Danny stretched with a groan. "Yeah, or if the snake is twenty-five feet long and over 700 pounds."

"Let's make dinner," she joined him. "Maybe us moving around will wake her up."

He cracked the door an inch, peeked out.

Fallon pressed close. "We good?"

"Yeah," he whispered. "Let's go. But you know...that fire thing. That works."

She smiled. "I'm ready."

"Okay," he crossed into the kitchen. "Then, Madame, would you prefer the lukewarm sausage with cold bread and sauce or the cold bread and sauce with lukewarm sausage?"

"Hmmm...decisions, decisions." Fallon took two steps into the kitchen and the aroma of stale, dead serpent enveloped her. "Oh, crap."

"Yeah, you smell it? I was hoping it might just be me."

"They're gonna know."

Danny tugged one oven open. Wet, rotting slabs of snake meat waited inside like uncooked roasts for an annual zombie conference. "Shit. We should've loaded all of this into the freezer. What were we thinking?"

"We weren't." Fallon forgave them. "We were desperate and terrified."

"You wanna move it now?"

"I'll give you fifteen-hundred credits if you do it."

He laughed. "You don't have fifteen-hundred credits."

"I'll sell my body. I swear to God."

"Well, damn." He reached into the oven, withdrew a forty-pound cross section of charred, dripping copperhead. "Open the freezer, will you?"

She did. "Damn, what?"

"Damn," he tossed the snake meat inside. It landed with a disquieting splat. "I don't have fifteen-hundred credits"

"Do the math, genius." She grimaced as she hefted a slab from the oven. "I'm selling my body to get fifteen-hundred credits to pay you to carry this...thing."

"Yeah," he propped the freezer door open. "But you've gotta convince a customer first, love. I might require less convincing."

"Hey!" She tossed the snake at him. It left a gory stain on his t-shirt. "I'll have you know…I'm sure there are men lining up to buy a piece of this." Fallon struck a pose so absurdly un-sexy that Danny spluttered laughter, despite the fact that he had about thirty pounds of decomposing snake meat on his shoes.

"You realize that I'm gonna have to steal another shirt?"

"You're good at that." She drew another hunk from the oven.

He scooped up the piece she'd thrown. "You think we can eat this?"

"Clearly rotting, possibly supernatural, full-of-poison snake that tried to kill us?"

"Well…yeah."

"No." She tossed the grim armload into the freezer. It splashed down beside the others. "I'm having the lukewarm sausage. Thank you very much."

"Okay, well…you better enjoy it, because you're sleeping in the pantry tonight, dear. Cramped quarters. Sorry. All that sausage…things could get aromatic."

"Nasty. I'm sleeping right out here."

Night crept up on Penn Station. Fallon and Danny made sure that Emma rested comfortably on the tiles, then sneaked out the fire exit to watch city lights in their nightly tug of war with the encroaching darkness. Beyond the trestle bridges and layered, criss-crossing railroad and E-train tracks to the south, they could see the broad swatch of darkness that had once been the Inner Harbor, Baltimore's hub for tourism, good food, and family entertainment. Now the city's historic waterfront lay in ashy ruins, a gaping maw of nothingness flooded with three feet of pollution-choked, oily water from the Patapsco River.

Overhead, delivery and surveillance drones arrived and departed from Tower III with the predictable regularity of a military operation. Like bloated, buzzing mosquitos, they landed, charged, and took off again, forever in search of something or monitoring the city as it drifted off to sleep. The heavier drones, a neat row of KFG-49 models, sat mostly quiet on the uppermost departure deck. Only a few still operated, carrying the last of Baltimore's commuters home late to dinner. After about thirty minutes, a storm front rolled over the harbor, blowing a towering squall off the Atlantic in an inevitable cleansing wall determined to scrub Baltimore's sins out to sea.

"We're about to get clobbered," Fallon said, the first droplets splattering up St. Paul Street on a compass heading directly toward them.

"Yeah," Danny used his keycard, pulled open the fire door. "Let's go."

As Fallon crossed the threshold, a roiling orange glow lit the darkness a mile or so to the west. The muffled explosion reached them a second or two later. She felt the warm blast of air following in the wake of the noisy detonation.

"What the hell was that?" Danny pointed to where the upper floors of a high-rise housing complex had been seconds earlier.

Fallon watched, waiting for another explosion. "Damn, I don't know."

"Terrorists? Gas line? That high up, it's gotta be something nasty. All the main lines are beneath the street, in the basements, you know?" The building burned like a towering matchstick; flames danced in winds from the encroaching storm.

"This can't be good."

They lingered for a few minutes, watching and listening as sirens and PA announcements boomed throughout the city. Officials squawked incoherent orders and pedestrians hustled about like mice in a maze, scurrying desultorily in an effort to avoid the rain and the terrorists. When the flames weakened, the ruined high rise smoked like a blast furnace chimney. Danny followed Fallon inside as the downpour eventually engulfed Penn Station. Residual flames soon flickered out.

Inside the drone tower, Fallon located the back-corridor entrance of the sporting goods store adjacent to Luigi's Continental. She withdrew her plastic key card from the flannel shirt she'd stolen at the farmhouse. "C'mon, stinky. She's sleeping, and I owe you a t-shirt."

He followed without thinking. "Okay. But don't you think we should…"

"What can we do?"

He pressed two fingers to the cuts on his forehead, checked them for blood. "I dunno, I guess. But…I mean, that was probably a terror attack."

"And?"

"Yeah, all right."

She tried the key card in the store's fire door. It didn't work. "Hmmm…this one's a dud. Lemme try that one." The lock's red light flashed twice, then blinked out. "Crap." She turned the card over in her hands. "I thought you said this worked on the security access doors."

"I did," he swallowed. "It did."

She handed the key back. "Well, it's dead now, at least on this door."

Sweat broke out on Danny's face. "Um…sorry. I dunno. But listen, if you wanna steal me a new t-shirt—"

"I do," she said. "You smell like the reptile house at the zoo."

"You're no bouquet of flowers."

"We'll break in the front?"

"Yeah, he looped the lanyard back over his head. "We've got all night."

She looked askance at him. "You sure that card worked at the SPD today?"

"How else would I have gotten in?"

208

"All right, but I want you to steal me something nice."

"Heh. I will."

"C'mon," Fallon took his hand. "Let's go now. I've never had anyone teach me breaking and entering before."

He squeezed her fingers. "It should be simple getting in. There was some ugly bomb damage out front. The plexi-glass security doors are hanging by a few runners and only held in place by police and construction tape."

"Great," she tugged. "Let's go. I need new shoes, too. Boots maybe. Who knows where we're gonna end up?"

"And we'll get some Kleen straws. They're amazing. Not kidding, you can drink from a public toilet with one of those."

Fallon frowned. "There's no way you have a girlfriend. Just no way. Not one who isn't under some court order or who maybe lost a wager with the Devil."

"Kleen straws, dopey," he said again. "Your bowels will thank me when we're living in a drainage ditch in New Jersey somewhere."

"Heh, oh, yeah...women lining up." She shoved him; he didn't mind at all. "C'mon, Mama needs some new clothes! Oh, and maybe a couple of those inflatable mattresses they have. You know? Just in case we really do end up living in a ditch."

"Good idea."

"C'mon," she tugged again.

"Wait," he held back. "We have no idea if the security cameras are still on in the tower corridor or in the store itself."

"They're off in Luigi's."

"True, but Luigi's was also ground zero for the blast."

"Shit," Fallon dropped his hand. "So we can't go? Can't risk it?"

"We can," Danny reached for her, thought better, then started toward the tower's main fairway. "We just need to be aware of the cameras and maybe keep our heads down. There's been construction crews around all day, so no one is monitoring this end of the tower that closely—we hope."

"I get it," Fallon's enthusiasm returned. "We can go shopping, but we've gotta be all sneaky."

"All sneaky," Danny echoed. "Yeah, that about captures it. Follow my lead."

"Heh, doofus."

"What?"

"You just said *Follow my lead* like we're in a spy movie or something."

"You know what, Fallon? No one likes you. *And* you're wanted for murder...actual murder."

"I know," she tossed her hair over one shoulder. Danny thought his heart might seize in his chest. "But it cuts way, way down on the holiday cards I have to send out."

From a vantage point beneath a pyramid display of amino acid supplement canisters—the city's poorest inhabitants often stole these. Water soluble, they doubled as a healthy source of dietary protein. – Danny pointed out three cameras that appeared to be functional. Fallon nodded toward the east wall, *Women's Clothing and Exercise Wear.*

"We can talk," he said. "Those are just video. No audio. These," he gestured to two cameras above the Customer Service counter and the Prevo-Credit archway, "have audio. But they look dead."

"Okay," she said. "But that's boring. As spies and fugitive, international jewelry and underwear thieves, we should have to communicate with just sign language, mind-melding, and hand gestures." Keeping low, she started off between the clothing racks.

"I'll give you a hand gesture," he whispered and followed after.

Neither of them gave the amino acid canisters a second glance. But both remembered the fifteen-foot pyramid later, when it crashed down shortly after Midnight.

Emma woke when the first echoes of trouble rumbled from the commuter floor, the dank street-level basement clotted with thunderheads and the vampires who fed on them. Vibrating through the kitchen tiles as if a mild earthquake had occurred fifty miles offshore, those distant stirrings were enough to rouse her. For someone who'd been poisoned, passed out, or high on Stormcloud for fifteen hours, Emma woke in a panic, her face sickly pale in the candlelight. "What's that?"

Fallon sat up. Danny, who'd been maintaining a drowsy watch, propped against one of the ovens, blinked several times, then shook his head. "Em? You okay?"

"What's that?" She glanced about, her eyes wide. She seemed unaware that she'd been wrapped in stolen camping blankets and laid out on the floor of her parents' restaurant. "Did you feel that?"

"Feel what?" Fallon rubbed her eyes. "It was just a dream. Try and sleep."

Danny asked again, "you okay, kiddo? Feel all right?"

"I'm fine," she pressed both palms flat against the cold tiles. "Thanks. I mean, thank you, but yes, I'm fine." Closing her eyes, she slid her hands several inches out from her body, waited. "You didn't feel that?"

Fallon rested her own hand on the floor beside Emma's. "I don't...Em, I think it might just be—"

"Hey, you have hair again." She toyed with the ends, playing them through her fingers. "Don't you love her hair, Danny?"

An audible boom, a hollow thudding crash, echoed from the street level. Waves of disconcerting sound reached them through the HVAC vents. Danny froze. "Holy shit, I felt that one. What is that? Maybe the same people who blew up that place earlier?"

"Could be," Fallon offered. "But if they're terrorists or political insurgents, we ought to be okay here. No one's in this section of the tower. Right? No one to kill."

Shouts, screams, cloud addicts hollering in despair followed moments later, all of them underpinned with what was now steady, rhythmic thuds, booming crashes three

211

octaves lower, that shook all of Tower III as if a subterranean god had awakened in an ancient tomb.

Emma panicked. "It's him. He's back. Isn't he? He knows where we are."

"Him, who?" Danny knelt, took her hand.

"Damn," Fallon said. "From the farm. And yes, Em, I think he knows where we are." To Danny she added, "It was stupid to stay here."

"The car's outside," he pointed toward the fire door. "Quick, down the stairs. We can sneak away."

Fallon hesitated, not wanting to make a hasty decision that would see all of them pummeled to jelly.

Danny grabbed a nylon backpack they'd stolen along with blankets, clothes, and durable shoes. "Grab everything. Whatever we can pitchfork in here, and maybe some food. C'mon, we gotta go."

Emma moved as if through pasty mud. "We can't leave without my box."

Fallon stuffed clothing and supplies into a second backpack, too anxious to notice Emma crawling, staggering up, then stumbling into the pantry.

"Need my box."

A weighty crash, thick with the unmistakable sounds of spilling concrete rubble, exploded nearby.

"He's here," Danny tossed his backpack into the pantry, grabbed Fallon, shoved her in behind.

"Not in there. No!" Finding Emma on the floor, Fallon turned a full circle, struck dumb by a combination of fear and disbelief. "Are we kidding? We can't hide in here. He'll tear the door off the hinges, break through the wall, bring the whole goddamned restaurant down."

"He's out back," Danny whispered. "Just get down. Stay quiet."

Another roll of devastating thunder echoed along the corridor. Fallon clutched her backpack close, sat shivering on the floor, helpless and gambling on a miracle. "He's next door; he went through the wall."

The fugitives spent the next five minutes paralyzed with numb, prickly terror. Each remembered the colossus who'd attacked them at the farm. Twelve feet tall, rippling with preternatural muscle, utterly overcome with inhuman rage, the man...thing...from the previous evening wouldn't allow anything as paltry as a concrete drone tower to keep him from finding his quarry. He would bring the entire building down if he needed to.

The cataclysm quieted briefly; only the creature's heavy footsteps boomed along the main thoroughfare, in and out of stores, beyond the edge of the market to the drone lifts, back to the main concourse, where advertisements and interactive marketing billboards still hawked goods with cheery celebrity spokespeople—all in 3-D projections—and happy, upbeat, memorable, hummable melodies.

Danny strained to hear through the pantry door. *You're never in the weather when you're in your weather guard.* A once-famous rock and roll singer crooned the weather guard jingle from the station lobby. Danny said, "I think he's gone. I can't hear footsteps. Can't feel anything." He pressed his palms flat, as he'd seen Emma do. "You?"

Fallon tried. "No. Maybe we're okay."

Emma sat in the candlelight, clutching a small, wooden box she'd dug from behind a rack of gallon tomato sauce cans stacked three deep. She didn't say anything.

"Em," Danny asked, "what's that?"

The red-haired girl shook her head despondently. "It's why I wanted to come here. I need this, but I don't think...I don't need it so bad that we get killed for it."

Fallon nudged her gently. "Don't worry about it. The food here was delightful. I'm telling all my friends."

Danny played along. "We are all your friends, Fallon."

213

Through the wall, two-hundred aluminum canisters of amino acid supplement clattered to the floor. Fallon met Danny's gaze.

"He's near the front of that place," she whispered.

"Probably hiding right where we ducked down." Danny assumed that the hulking man-monster could smell them, had smelled where he and Fallon surveilled the security cameras next door. If he could smell them there, he wouldn't need long to home in on the aroma of lukewarm sausage and pasta sauce. For the first time all day, he was glad that Luigi's Continental reeked with the tragic smell of burned copperhead.

No footsteps. Fallon mimed.

He's waiting there. Danny tilted his head. "Watching the corridor out front."

"Can we make it?"

"Let me go first. I can hide." He didn't wait for her to argue. Rather, he sneaked soundlessly through the pantry door and out the rear exit to the service corridor. A clear path to the fire exit lay open, but rather than hurry back for his friends, Danny exhaled slowly, focused his concentration, dissipated to nearly-invisible smoke, and wafted next door to investigate.

The colossus was easy to locate. Hunkered behind the Customer Service counter, the creature's head, as large as an automobile tire, peeked clumsily up, the pale, stupid eyes roving left to right along the travelers' main thoroughfare outside. He waited, a hunter in a blind. The fugitives might have spotted him from a hundred feet away, but, Danny calculated, that would already be too close. About the floor, canisters of protein powder lay, evidence of the monster's collateral damage when it failed to make the leap behind the counter and kicked the entire display over.

Floating closer, he watched as the man-thing used a cigar-sized index finger to corkscrew two knuckles deep into his cavernous nose, withdrawing a toad-green booger the size of a hood ornament. Considering it as he might consider a piece of three-dimensional art, the colossus smeared the snot sculpture

214

on the Customer Service counter and resumed his vigil. Reaching up to deposit his treasure—the morning construction crew would marvel at it over coffee—the colossus exposed heavy, clumsy stitching where his muscular arm had been attached to his torso.

Like the Frankenstein monster, Danny thought, buoyed above the scattered amino acid canisters. *He's been assembled from parts, frigging, goddamned gigantic parts.*

Deciding not to press his luck, Danny drifted back to Luigi's, re-took his seventeen-year-old form, and quietly motioned for Fallon to help him support Emma out the fire exit. In the staff lot, the smaller girl barfed twice into the shrubbery.

"Too much medication?" Fallon asked.

"Yeah, probably. It's hitting her system hard. She needs to rest." He found a strip of old cloth in the Chevron and handed it over. "Here, wipe your chin."

She dragged it over her mouth, spat toward the bushes. "Where'd you go?"

"Whaddya mean?"

"When the snake chased you into the pantry, and I grabbed it, you weren't in there." A barrage of dry heaves shook her. Emma coughed up strings of slimy, yellow Italian food. Spitting again, she added, "That's three times, Danny. How'd you do it?"

"Three times what?" Fallon asked. But Emma was overcome by more shuddering spasms. Fallon searched in her pack for a bottle of water. "Here you go, sweetie."

Emma drank. The others helped her into the back seat, made sure she was comfortable, then hurried into the front. Fallon strapped herself in. She remembered Danny somehow appearing behind her after she'd killed the snake. She thought about asking how he'd managed it, figured that's what Emma had been after, then decided to let it go for now.

Danny backed the Chevron out and turned south on St. Paul toward the Inner Harbor ruins and the inevitable traffic

215

on Interstate 95. Neither he nor Fallon minded much tonight. Being lost in the anonymity of interstate traffic was fine with both of them.

In the back, Emma clutched the polished wooden box to her breast; her ubiquitous pen draped over it like a shiny pendulum.

Fifteen miles south of the city and slogging along at just under thirty miles per hour, Emma fell asleep, leaving the older teens alone in the Chevron's front seat. The steady flow of northbound traffic lit their faces with essentially uninterrupted headlights. Every quarter mile, state-sponsored trestle arches spanning the Interstate projected colorful information, news, and advertisements. While most commuters ignored the overhead ads, traveling so slowly made the periodic projections strangely compelling – nothing else to watch. Traffic alerts, weather information, missing persons bulletins, even ads for sim vacations one could download anywhere, even in the car, splashed across the darkness above the highway. For travelers as weary as Danny and Fallon, the laser-generated pop-ups just meant sledge-hammering sinus pain.

Danny rubbed his eyes with the back of his wrist. Fallon asked, "You want me to drive?"

"Nah, I'm okay. So wired."

"You wanna risk the auto-sat, just program in some random street in Manassas or somewhere close?"

"Yeah, but no," he said. "It's too risky. I mean, whoever's after us can't possibly know we've left yet."

"Unless they do."

"Trying not to think about that possibility." He tossed her a tired smile in the steady waves of northbound light. "We can't know how they've found us so far, but if we connect to a satellite and someone's reported this clunker as stolen, we're screwing ourselves."

"All right." She stretched as far as she could in the old car's criss-crossed safety belts. "I've never been this tired."

"Yeah," he agreed, happy to be discussing anything other than how he'd managed to escape the snake. "I feel like five miles of rutted dirt road."

"Got a lot of those down in Hounds County?"

"Hinds," he corrected. "And yes, almost as many as copperheads."

"That snake...I've never seen anything like it."

"Oh, yeah, I've stutter-stepped over a hundred snakes out in the nethers, you know, but nothing like that. My imagination doesn't even stretch that far."

"But you've seen XX-Reptiles? Those soup bag monstrosities they sell these days? Those Prevo engineers could easily make a snake that large if they wanted to."

"I've seen couple, even a Tyrannosaur," Danny said, "outside New Orleans. A bunch of gazillionaires down there have frigging herds of them, just wandering around the Garden District. But those things are harmless, Fallon, like great, stupid hamsters. The T-Rex I saw would chase a beach ball, popped the damned thing every time. That snake was smart, vicious, and...I dunno..."

"Following orders?"

"Yes!" he sat up, gripped the wheel two handed. "Exactly. Like it understood its mission."

"And then this guy, Bulldozer Man. What the hell is that?"

"I dunno," he said. "But I've gotta confess: I didn't want...you know..."

"Didn't want what?"

"You know, I didn't want this...all of this to end, not yet." He glanced over in hopes of catching some tell in her face, would've given up all his E-credits for any hint of agreement. Instead, he forced the point. "I don't want this to end, this...whatever this is...which might kill all three of us. I don't want it to end."

Fallon stared out the side window. Travelers, overnight commuters, and vacationing families—rich bastards—careened

217

past in the auto-sat, recycled rubber lanes. She wondered what it might be like to sleep all the way to a destination, any destination, just wake with the sun and be there, the beach, the mountains, anywhere. "I don't want it to end either."

"But..."

"But..." She turned; fatigue had left her drawn and pale. "I'm going back to Warrenton, Danny. I'm sorry. But I'm going."

"I wish you wouldn't."

"I know," she said. "And I love that about you; I do. But I can't stand knowing that self-indulgent, self-centered prick—"

"Blair?"

"Of course, Blair," she said, "is smugly running a chop shop in the back of that place, serving up Draggers, for what? He's probably making payments on a frigging boat. I just can't...I can't let it go."

"Well," Danny started, uncertain where he'd end up. "Well...I can't speak for Emma, but I've gotta tell you—"

"I know," she interrupted. "You're not a revolutionary. That's good. It's a great survival skill. I admire it in you. And once you drop me off in Warrenton, we might not ever see one another again, but I don't think you need me to confirm for you...that I've got some...resources at my disposal that might make this little adventure more feasible." She tugged the chest belt away from her neck, hated this goddamned car. "I might make it possible for us to get this done. You know?"

"That isn't what I was gonna say." He changed lanes, moving past a grimy sanitation truck slowing for an exit. "You have this irritating tendency to finish other people's thoughts. Has no one ever pointed that out to you?"

"Heh. No."

"Well, you do," he said. "And I'm not leaving you in Warrenton."

"Then let me out now, because I'm going back to—"

"I'm going to stay, to help you."

"You don't have to," Fallon said. In the headlights, tears rose in her eyes. "You don't..."

218

"I know," he said. "But I'll never talk Emma into leaving you, and maybe together we can get you out of there in one piece, without any missing parts." He let go with a long, slow breath, waited. "What he did to you. You know. I find that, well, it disgusts me that he thinks he ought to be able to prey on young girls like that."

Now Fallon did cry, almost silently. Her face ran wet in the wash of headlights and the overhead advertisements for SCUBA vacations in Bonaire, wherever that was. "How did you know?"

"When I got there, you were out of it, but almost reflexively protective of..." He gestured absently, unsure how to communicate it. "Of yourself."

"Yeah."

"And you're pretty well bruised up. Sorry. I couldn't help but notice."

Fallon dragged her palms along the length of her thighs, imagined Blair taking hold of her too tightly, with no regard for her pain. "I understand."

"Sorry."

"It's okay." She ran a sleeve across her face. "I'll feel better when I stand over his corpse."

"Yeah," Danny changed lanes again, sped up slightly. "I will, too."

"But you're right," she added, happy to be talking in the pretend protection of Interstate anonymity. "I can't lose any parts, not even a fingertip. Right?" A moment's silence between them ensured they both understood the implications for Fallon were she to lose even one toe to Blair's chop shop.

Interstate 95 wound lazily south toward the old Capital Beltway, the traffic unrelenting, even as 1:00 a.m. gave way to the middle watch. Eventually, Fallon said, "We'll go in across the lake, steal a boat or a raft or something. The defenses back there are a joke compared with the east and west perimeters—electrified barbed wire; that's a joke."

Danny shook his head. "You are something. You know that?"

"What?"

"Nothing. It's just that you must've had guys lining up to take you out for pizza." He mimicked her. "*Electrified barbed wire; that's a joke.*"

Fallon snorted through her nose, tried to hide it, then gave up and laughed out loud. "Boys like me, Mr. Lonesome. Not everyone wants to hide in the swamps of muggy Hounds County by themselves."

"It's Hinds, love. *Hinds* County," Danny said. "And you'd love it, the swamps especially. They're gorgeous...well, maybe not so much in the summertime."

"I'm just saying, the easiest way back into that *school* is across the lake out back. It's wide but short enough that we can cross in one night, attack before dawn."

"And then?"

"And then we walk out the front gate...whatever's left of it."

He turned from the slow traffic of the interstate to merge with the almost equally slow traffic of the Beltway. "I'm gonna need you to sketch this out for me, Fallon. Maybe even a couple of times."

"What's your line?" She stared into the darkness of the exit ramp. "*Leave that to me.*"

"You wanna go to the farm?"

"No," she said, "I think it's suicide."

"I disagree."

"I can tell."

"We were just there. They know we were; they found water in your glass," Danny explained.

"That wasn't water," she corrected. "But for argument's sake, let's say you're right. Why would we go back?"

"Because it doesn't make sense," he said. "They know we were in Baltimore. They sent two hunters to kill us. They probably know we're injured or worse because they got wind of my break in at the county clinic and the stolen meds."

"Okay? And?" She raised her hands as if to say, *you're not answering my question.*

"Of all the places in the world, why would we go to a place where they know they can find us?"

"That's the hundred-credit question of the very, very, very late show. Why would we ever make that decision?"

"Because it's lunacy," he said. "It's madness to go back there. However—"

"Madness?"

"Madness. Yes. But stop interrupting."

"Sorry," she rested her head on his shoulder. "Sorry. It's my nature to be a bitch."

Danny lay his head over, resting it on hers. "You're not sorry for a second, bitch. So don't pull my chain."

She sat up, smiling. "Good. See? I knew I liked you."

"If they send bulls...or worse...to the farm, we've gotta try and hide. We'll hide the supplies, hide the car, hide...everything...in the corn. We'll sleep in the barn, in the loft. We can rig a few ropes, so we can drop down if anyone comes into the dooryard. But my money, not kidding, I'm betting no one shows up."

"So..." Fallon sang the long vowel, leading Danny toward inevitable compromise. "Maybe we agree that if I risk death on the farm with you and Emma, you risk death bringing down Blair and Carter with me. Whaddya say? Deal?"

"Nope," Danny frowned. "Sorry."

"Jesus Christ, what now?"

"Professor Bins, the old lady, the one from detention supervision. Remember her?"

"Yeah," Fallon seemed amused. "What about her? She's about eight-hundred years old. Harmless."

"I'm taking her out," he said. "I hate that woman."

"You've got a thing for old ladies, Hackett. You ought to get that looked at."

"Oh, shit."

"What now? You know I was kidding about the old ladies thing."

"The farmhouse, the barn...they might be gone."

Fallon remembered. "You're right. Bulldozer Man...he was pretty well tearing the place apart when we left."

"Shit."

"Shit is right. We're returning to matchstick heaven. Great choice, genius. You're driving us back to a place that's currently in ruins. Why not take us to Pompeii?"

He turned to her. At twenty-six miles an hour, he figured they'd survive, even if he rammed the back of a logging truck. "Hey, do you...you know, back home? Do you have..."

Fallon brandished a disarming smile.

"Yeah," Danny turned back to the traffic. "Probably a moot issue about now. Isn't it?"

Still grinning, she said, "I think so."

"You look tired," he said. "Like you've just done about two weeks in a lifeboat off shore."

"I've never even seen the ocean. Never walked on a beach. I've never felt sand between my toes. None of it."

"Really? We need to fix that soon."

Fallon adjusted her seat back. "I'd like that, Danny Hackett, very much."

"Hey, when's your—"

"I'm sleeping."

"You closed your eyes eight seconds ago; you're not sleeping."

Again the embarrassing snort, this time from the shadows of the reclined bucket seat. "What?"

"You scheduled for your eighteenth birthday?" He glanced over, couldn't really see her.

She sighed. "Yeah."

"That eye?"

"Yeah."

222

"Figured," he said. "It's a good one. How long ago'd someone pick it up?"

"Nine years."

"Sorry." She didn't respond, so he asked, "When's your birthday?"

"Early January. About two months from now."

"Okay, so, well...that gives us two months."

Fallon sat up, interested in what tricks the young felon might have up his sleeve, but mostly irritated that he wouldn't let her nap. "You know a way around an Eighteen Subpoena?"

"No."

"Ever been around one?"

"Yeah, a friend back home," Danny checked the mirror, slid into the left lane and accelerated past rows of family cars, delivery trucks, construction vehicles, even a few military transports.

"Was it bad?"

"You haven't seen one?"

She shook her head.

"It starts with flashing, red. You can't shut it off, can't dim it, can't do anything. It just flashes, twenty-four hours a day." He slowed as traffic thickened to vehicular paste. "Next comes the frigging sirens. God awful. Two in the morning. Three in the morning, the things just starts wailing like an old air raid speaker. You can't shut it off. There's no sleep. And...I think that's what gets most people."

"Lack of sleep?" Fallon adjusted her seat up and down in a display of irony lost on Danny.

"Yup. People get crazy. They just give up, get the silence code to reboot their screen, and ride the storm. Gotta do it."

"I don't want to...for obvious reasons."

"That fire thing was pretty impressive."

"I don't want to go back."

"We'll figure something out," he said.

"You think so? Honestly?"

Danny set his jaw, gripped the steering wheel tightly, and felt as useless as he'd ever managed in seventeen years. "Yeah. There's gotta be a way. Someone has to know."

Fallon dropped the seat back into the shadows, rested. "You okay on your own for a few minutes?"

Determined now, invigorating adrenaline warmed his blood. "I'm fine. Sleep as long as you like."

An hour later, the fugitives were nearly across what had once been Lord Fairfax County, but which had since found itself ingested by the redistricted government of the federal capital in Washington. Most of the old signs and markers noting that this had long been an independent county of the Virginia Commonwealth were gone. Only a handful of battlefield markers and grave sites maintained traditions in the name of Lord Fairfax.

Needing a charge, Danny pulled the Chevron off the highway and drove aimlessly into rolling hills of clone, suburban townhomes.

Fallon woke from her power nap. "Where are we?"

"The Divided States of Let's All Be Exactly the Same," Danny said.

"Where you going? We can't plug in here. We'll be wearing local cops as a hat in about ninety seconds."

"We need a charge," he explained. "It was dumb to leave that parking space without one, was probably a charger cable right there, for Luigi's owners and staff."

"Yeah, well..." Fallon yawned. "We do make a habit of running for the exit."

"Not tonight," he said. "Actually, you know what time it is?"

"No idea. My vid screen hasn't been on in three days."

"I'm hoping it's still a good hour before dawn," he said. "You ever stolen a charge before?"

Watching rows upon rows of bedroom community housing scroll by out both sides of the Chevron, Fallon said, "No. Never had to. How can we?"

224

Danny turned down an empty street. "Here we go."

"Where?"

"The last house on either side," he explained. "Assuming it's dark, we pull up on the grass or into the greenway beside it, and..."

"And drag the charger cable over," she finished. "Danny Hackett, you might just be a genius, unappreciated in your time."

"I like to think so."

"But what if they have a lock on the charger? Even my mother has one of those."

"Here?" He shot her an incredulous look. "With fifty chargers along each block? Nah. These fat suburbanites are too goddamned lazy to hook it up with the locking device. Actually, I bet you credits to chocolates the cable is coiled neatly on the side of the house."

Fallon asked, "Why? Because they all take the E-bus? The train?"

"Yup. It'll take about twenty minutes to get us half a charge. That should be plenty."

"Let's do the whole thing," she said.

"Because you like tempting the fates? Risking death?"

"Because I like the idea of a fully charged car."

"Okay," Danny tilted his head, calculated. "Yeah, maybe forty minutes. Gonna be light in forty minutes?"

She yawned. "No way. We'll just have to hope that they're not early risers on the weekend."

He drew near the end of the road, killed the Chevron's lights, and drove onto the lawn beside a neat, three-level townhome that might have been a Xerox copy of two-thousand others within a mile in any direction. A hundred feet of neatly trimmed, common greenway, complete with a paved path, polite hedges, and a babbling, manmade stream ran between this row of homes and a mirror image across the street. Danny whispered. "Now, duck down." He shoved the car into PARK, set the engine on CHARGE, and sneaked out behind a runty evergreen bush probably bio-engineered never to need trimming.

Fallon watched until he vanished in the shadows. "You are a resourceful sucker. Aren't you?"

Thirty-eight minutes later, with the Chevron fully charged, the runaways drove back toward the highway, passing two dog walkers and one intrepid jogger in a glow-in-the-dark exercise vest.

Behind them, sun rose over the nation's capital. Neither Danny nor Fallon had slept in two nights. Regardless of how they felt about hiding out at the farm, both agreed that being within a half hour of the place moved it near the top of the list of possible hideouts in which to regroup.

And to sleep.

11

Kleen Straws, Too Much Corn, and One First Kiss

Fallon woke to congenial autumn breeze through the torn screen door and one nearly demolished retaining wall. She had no sense of how long she'd slept, but sunlight through the house's gaping wounds suggested the day had moved on without her. Danny had teased the previous night that she looked to have spent a few weeks in a lifeboat. Rolling over to test herself with the simultaneous challenge of breathing in and out while examining the cobwebbed ceiling, Fallon disagreed: This wasn't lifeboat exhaustion. Nope. This was dropped from an airplane, airlifted, packaged, flown over some barren desert and dropped like a crate of UN famine relief.

Through the shattered wall, she heard the others working in the barn, that silly peach grader again.

"…hijacked a super tanker. This was back in 2037 or maybe 38. Their plan was to ram it as far up onto the wharf in Baltimore as they could, by the refinery tanks, and set the whole thing on fire…"

"How is that eco-terrorism? Sounds positively awful for the environment."

"They were striking back against government, industry, factory farming, and approved preservatives, additives…all the shit people used to eat."

"But especially the corn?"

"Corn. Can you believe it? All of Baltimore's Inner Harbor burned for corn."

"So it worked?"

"Sort of…the supertanker ran aground…" The breeze picked up, drowning out Danny's story. Fallon wondered how a wayward orphan from Nowhere, Mississippi knew so much history. She craned her neck, listened. "…too shallow in there for a ship that size."

"They set it on fire anyway?"

"Yup. Burned for weeks."

"How'd that destroy the city?"

"One of those refinery tanks—they hadn't used them in years, decades maybe—had sprung a minor leak, just a trickle, but gasoline is gasoline."

"Whoah."

"Whoah is right...my dad said his grandfather told him the explosion broke windows five miles away, even brought down a plane!"

"Everyday people did this?"

"Everyone called them 'terrorists'...I think they called themselves 'everyday people.'"

"Why'd they never rebuild the place?"

"War, money, corporate greed, the death of tourism in Maryland, who knows? But I think it might be because of the rise in seawater."

"Really?"

"Sure. Most of the Inner Harbor was only a couple of feet above high tide. When the oceans rose—"

"Wait. I had a class. They said that the water level didn't rise as much as...I dunno...everyone feared."

"Not at all, but two feet...maybe thirty inches...that was enough to leave much of the old Inner Harbor under some pretty smelly, polluted, disease-carrying water."

"Nasty. But didn't some of the polar ice freeze again with some of that whateveritis up there...permafrost?"

"Yup, after the war, when the oil and gas reserves had been wiped out, most of them, anyway."

"When all those people died."

"Yeah, the planet tried...is trying, I guess...to fix itself. Pretty slowly, but it's working. Well, assuming all those environmental downloads are accurate."

"A plane," Fallon said to no one. "I fell out of a plane last night. It's all right, though. It's just the first day of the rest of my life...after having been dropped out of a plane." She groaned. "Okay, a really high-altitude airplane, one of those F-planes that gets from Philadelphia to Istanbul in four hours."

She sat up, her narrow ass nearly lost in the catacombs of the ancient sofa. Why Danny hadn't inflated their stolen camp mattresses, she also didn't know and promised to ask him, just as soon as he'd tugged her through a regimen of back and shoulder stretches, hot yoga, and perhaps a massage.

Danny. He'd saved her, twice. *Three times?* Who knew? She couldn't be irritated with him for forgetting the mattresses. He'd only broken her out of the WSJM, saved Emma from Beatrice Grizzly Bear McJackass, carried a half-conscious, half-naked Fallon to an E-bus station, clothed her in stolen duds, transported her here, helped her escape bulls and a homicidal mountain of a man bent on tearing her to pieces, broken into a gated community, a nearly-impenetrable house, stolen a car, driven them to Baltimore, heisted an array of medications and first aid supplies from an essentially impregnable robo-pharm facility in a county clinic, medicated Emma, perhaps saving her life (again), sneaked up on the Human Bulldozer after stealing clothes, supplies, blankets, shoes, knives, and weapons from a sporting goods store, then driven them back to the farm, and even ensured their crappy-ass car had a charge, so they would be able to make it even farther into the boondocks that evening to plug in their bio wires and transfer Emma's hidden credits to Danny's dummy account.

"Jesus, what hasn't he done?" Fallon rested her head in her hands, concentrated on breathing as pain and fatigue drained from her muscles. Sitting up, she said, "Fight the snake. He didn't fight the snake. I fought the goddamned snake!"

She stood, stretched, then sat back down. "Killed its ass. Deep fat fried that sumbitch."

Someone—*Danny, goddamnit*—had left her a large tumbler of questionable looking water with one of the Kleen straws they'd stolen. Fallon recalled the advertisements in her Herkimer County Schools feed. *Absolutely, positively kills*

99.9% of bacteria while filtering 96.9% of pollutants from any water, any time. She'd never tried one, never had to living in her mother's trailer. Water from the county facility had always been pretty reliable.

She withdrew the straw, considered the miniature digital display running up the cylinder's side: *100%* accompanied by a green light that blinked every few seconds.

"I don't believe you," she said but drank anyway. Why not? She'd drunk from the farm's old pump before, two days ago, if her ass-dragging mental calculator still worked. It felt more like two weeks. Stirring the Kleen straw around a few times—she didn't know if it came with directions—she sipped a few swallows. "Hmmm, not too bad."

Fallon gulped the rest of the tumbler.

Beside the water glass, someone—*Danny, goddamnit*—had arranged a clutch of wildflowers, just a splash of natural color in a world that grew more and more gray every day.

"Yeah, okay." She refilled her glass from the kitchen basin—whatever rotted in the farm's long-dead refrigerator was still in there (she was thinking: *entire buffalo*)—and went outside to join her friends.

The screen door slapped shut. From the dooryard, she could see that one side of the farmhouse lay in splintered ruins, clearly the work of Mr. Colossus after their escape.

"Hey!" Emma appeared through the ramshackle double doors. "Yeah, it's her." She jogged the length of the yard, hugged Fallon hard. "Good morning!"

"Afternoon, I think," Fallon hugged her back, then held her at arm's length. "Lemme see your face, your neck. You okay?"

Emma blushed. "I'm sorry. I don't know what I was thinking, you know, when I jumped on the snake. I just didn't want it to get to Danny...or you."

Scabbed now, the punctures looked healthier than the previous morning but were still turning immutably to necrotic scars. "You feel all right?"

230

"Just tired," Emma said. "And sick, but not like last night. I think I just had so much of that goop in my system, I wasn't ready to be up and running for my life quite yet."

"You and me both, sister." Fallon allowed herself to be led into the barn, or what was left of it. Bulldozer Bob had crashed bodily through three walls, tearing ragged holes in the plank siding and leaving the old structure on the brink of imminent collapse. "You two sure you're okay out here? This place looks like an unexpected gust of wind will bring it down in a heap."

"That beam," Danny pointed to an overworked, four-by-four holding up the barn's southwest corner. "If that one comes down, the whole house of cards is gonna collapse." He winked. "Be somewhere else when that happens."

Danny looked to have been dipped in grease from fingertips to elbows.

"What are you doing? Why do you need a fully-operational peach grader? You gonna stay here and go into farming?"

He clapped filthy hands together, clearly happy to see her. "I just might. And I'll tell you what, it'd be a helluva lot safer than traipsing around the country on your adventures. No giant snakes. No hormonal Neanderthal wanting to rip my arms off and make a charm bracelet. No German Shepherds chasing me through electric fences, no Rottweiler guard dogs hoping to eat my ass on a hoagie roll."

She waved him off. "You're having fun."

"Not dying? Yeah, not dying is always on the top of my list of fun shit to do with the afternoon!"

"Thanks for the water," she sipped from the Kleen straw. "And the flowers." To Emma she said, "I have you to thank for that; I presume."

"Nope," Emma started toward the farmhouse. "Danny. He walked the whole perimeter of the farm this morning, picked one of every flower that grows on the edges of the cornfields."

Fallon made eye contact with him over the greasy contraption. "Oh, he did? Well, I wonder why he didn't just pick some corn. Something we can eat."

"No corn!" Emma called from the wooden steps. "Tell her, Danny. I'm gonna get some water."

"Yeah, tell me." Having made up her mind, Fallon moved quickly. Leaving the water tumbler and flowers on the grader's rotating lazy Susan, she closed quickly on Danny, pulled him in by the tail of his t-shirt, and kissed him quickly on the mouth. Clumsy at first, the teens settled into one another. Danny's lips tasted of sweat and durable reliability. Fallon felt such an unexpected rush of sheer happiness, she pressed a hand on the back of his neck, held him close.

Surprised, he slipped away, looking equal parts stunned and stupid. "Wait. What're you...why?"

"Let's do that better." She pulled on his shirt again. This time, he helped. It was better, a soft, affectionate break, just a few seconds, from what had been a harried, terrifying time together. Sucking his lower lip gently into her mouth, Fallon held him captive another few seconds, then let him go.

Staggered, he breathed through his mouth, waiting for permission to move. "Um...so, yeah, there's nothing wrong with this corn. It's fine."

"I don't give a shit about corn, bonehead."

Danny reached for her; she shoved his hands away. "Not with those grimy mitts. I don't want Emma to see me covered in filth thirty seconds after coming out here."

"Yeah, um...yeah, okay." He backed away a few steps, found a rag, wiped his hands. "But why? What's that for?"

"Thank you." She looked into his face with as much genuine honesty as she could muster. "You saved me...I dunno...half a dozen times. I'd be dead—*we'd* be dead, or dismembered, or who knows what without you."

Danny surprised her. "I have something to tell you."

Emma hopscotched back into the barn, slopping water from two tumblers that matched Fallon's. "Tell her what? Did you tell her about the corn? The Corn War? Before Stormcloud." She handed a glass to Danny. "I never knew this guy knew so much about history."

Fallon played along, content to recapture their moment later. It would be nice anticipating something pleasant for once. "Yeah, how do you know so much about history? I didn't think they taught history in *Hounds* County."

He frowned, but didn't take the bait. "My parents were history teachers a long time ago, before they got rid of all that curricula, before the change over to the useless shit they teach the Dragger class nowadays: Fundamentals of Service and Duty or, my favorite, Cleanse & Harvest. Jesus Jumping Christ."

Emma asked, "Do they still teach?"

"Dad does." He grabbed a wrench, went back to tinkering with the grader. "At least he was teaching when I left two years ago. He didn't like the classes but felt he had to keep at it, was getting paid, keeping the family afloat teaching poor kids that it's their job to be dismembered at the whim of anyone with money, anywhere—"

"And often as a birthday present," Fallon said. "Adds that special warm feeling to the whole interchange: Turn twelve, and guess what! You get to trade in a kidney! Congratulations and happy birthday! Now, roll up your sleeve, kiddo. This won't hurt a bit."

"You sound like my mother," Danny said. "She quit, just packed up one afternoon and left her access codes, her key card, and about 50 terabytes of downloads with the office secretary, one of the robo models, R-class, I think. Damned thing just responded as if it was just another afternoon: *Good night, Ms. Hackett. Enjoy your evening.*"

"R-class. Those are the nice ones," Emma said. "We had one in the bakery by my house. They remember everything, ask nice questions, even make book and film recommendations or give restaurant reviews...you know, as if they eat food or watch movies."

"Yeah," Danny went on. "Mom couldn't do it, train kids that it's okay to give up a foot or a hand to some corporate sleezebag's daughter or worse, girlfriend, boyfriend…you know what I mean."

Fallon saw where this was headed, decided to give Danny a chance to change gears. "You think you can get this thing running, Farmer John?"

He sidestepped the topic change, finished his thoughts about his mother. "They took her. That's why I left when I did." He wrenched a bolt free, tugged a flywheel loose and examined the cracked and dried belt around it. "This thing's never gonna run."

"Where's your dad?" Emma sat on a hay bale left to rot, crossed her legs and propped her chin on her hands. Her pen dangled loosely between her knees. "Do you talk to him?"

"Not for about a year now. I'm guessing he's in Ohio, still teaching, keeping his head down, working diligently, steadily, reliably, whatever the hell might get my mom freed."

"That explains why you don't have an accent," Fallon said. "You're not really from Mississippi."

"No," Danny wiped grease from the flywheel, replaced it. "Ohio."

"So, why—"

"I kicked around for a while, just doing whatever damage I could, frustrated and trying to lash out at anything I felt was…I dunno…injustice."

Emma laughed. "That'll keep you busy."

"Yeah, no kidding," Danny smiled for the first time since Fallon kissed him. "Do you have any idea how much injustice you can find when you honestly go hunting around for it? It's everywhere. And I mean, here, there, and *everywhere…* everywhere."

"So Mississippi was just a stop over?" Fallon asked.

"Yes and no. I love it there, I suppose, if I love it anywhere. Nice people. Beautiful places to visit, some—a little—clean water and undisturbed natural resources—"

"Those swamps?"

"Exactly. I mean, I know I'll eventually get back home, but with my mother gone and my father…well, with him having let her go, just let her go, I dunno when I'll get back. I guess I'm not really in a hurry to go home for Christmas or anything."

Fallon understood. Danny wasn't ready to forgive his father for continuing to teach the very classes that got his mother hauled off to the local lockup, perhaps worse. She imagined him taking risks, tackling stupid challenges, and all the while working to reconcile his love for his steady, reliable, predictable, hard-working father with the anger he felt at his mother's arrest. Yeah, the whole thing, Danny Hackett, all of a sudden made a great deal more sense. Watching him replace the old peach grader's flywheel, fixing something broken, Fallon silently promised that she'd use whatever powers the universe had granted her to protect this delightful, complicated boy.

Emma broke the spell. "You guys wanna head west, out past Culpeper, and maybe find someplace to plug in? We can move some credits to Danny's account while the world is quiet and no giant snakes are trying to eat my face."

Fallon finished her water. "That sounds lovely. Yeah, I think we ought to try. The fact that we've been here almost twelve hours and nothing has tried to eat your face is a genuinely good sign."

"I agree." Danny pocketed the Kleen straw from his water glass, then dumped the contents down his greasy forearms. It didn't help.

"You two eat yet?" Fallon asked.

"After essentially no food for days?" Emma teased. "No. We were waiting for you."

"Hey, no one likes a smartass."

"Yes, we ate. We cooked some of the sausages over the firepit by the side of the house, and Danny had some of that green stuff you two stole from the sporting goods store."

235

"Energy paste," he said.

"Looked borderline to me," Emma added. "I passed."

Fallon raised her hands in surrender. "Fine, fine. Okay. I promise I won't sleep in again. But before we go, I need to eat something."

"I'll get cleaned up," Danny followed her toward the house.

As hungry as she was, it would be hours before Fallon ate again.

11.43

I Hate History. Don't You?

How's everyone? No snakes?

I'm sorry to keep interrupting with these distracting bits. But, alas, they're important. I'll try to keep this brief.

However, before I begin, don't you always wish you were the kind of person who could use the word 'alas' in passing conversation and not have anyone point or laugh?

You know what...try it. Later, when your mother, sister, brother, teacher, whomever comes to you with a question, see if you can answer with 'alas' and not have anyone spray milk as they collapse in laughter. Perhaps something like this:

"Tell me, (Insert Your Name Here), do you ever plan to pick up your disgusting laundry from the floor of your bedroom?"

"Alas, mother, not today. You see, I'm busy...splitting these atoms."

Or curing degenerative diseases, or fighting crime, or parallel parking a whaling vessel. Who cares? Whatever excuse you insert into that space will work because you effectively used the word 'alas.'

Heh. Isn't this fun?

I'm having a lovely time.

Anyway, history. I know you hate history. Everyone hates history. Well, okay, not everyone hates history, but statistically, the sample size is so large probability suggests that within a fairly narrow confidence interval, everyone hates history.

But that's statistics.

Everyone hates statistics.

Okay, okay...I'll get to the point.

You heard Danny mention the Corn War. I feel like I should inject briefly, just to fill in a few of the blanks you might not know, if you haven't read the proper books, well, because you hate...

Anyway, corn. By 2030, essentially every inch of arable land in the United States was planted with corn. Why? Well, there were a lot of reasons, but foremost among them was a federal subsidy paid to corn farmers to produce enough corn for Ethanol research...

Yawn. I know: it's already boring. Hang in there; this bit is important.

Ethanol was an additive we used to put into gasoline to make it burn a little cleaner, so we wouldn't punch such a big hole in the ozone layer and melt the polar ice caps and drown all the polar bears and cause the ocean levels to rise and consume all the cities and homes along the coast...and, well, some of this you probably know.

Yeah, there used to be polar bears.

They drowned, because they couldn't swim far enough to get from ice pack to ice pack. It was sad. Admittedly, I wasn't born yet, but I imagine it was sad.

Anyway, the government paid farmers all kinds of supplementary income to grow corn, but lobbyists and lawmakers from states that still made oil-burning-gas-guzzling cars—yup, cars used to run on oil and gas, not that long ago— hated the idea of alternative forms of energy. So they voted against any kind of clean energy bills in Congress, but they also voted for more and more money for farmers, so they would seem like decent guys.

Yeah, most of them were guys. A few were women.

You see, ethanol refining states were also states where they made cars, lots and lots and lots of cars.

So corn farmers grew absurdly wealthy (for farmers). Sugar beet, potato, and citrus farmers—who wanted more money—converted their acreage to corn, because, well, why not? It was free money. People started growing corn in their backyards. They grew it in city parks, as far north as Aroostook

County, Maine and as far south as Danny's beloved Hinds County, Mississippi, a place perfect for sugar beets.

But...

There's another of those big 'buts.'

Heh, no laughing.

But since Congress didn't allow scientists to use more corn for ethanol or clean energy research and they kept paying for hundreds of millions of tons of corn to be harvested, American society ran into a truly inspirational problem:

What the hell were we gonna do with all that corn?

The answer is what led to the Corn War, or as it's referenced in those history books you hate to read, the American Agricultural War of 2034. It ran until 2041, with over forty million Americans dead from starvation, disease, domestic terrorism, or outright combat.

Nine years. That's a long time to wage civil war. But we did.

Why? Corn.

You see, we had to do something with the corn. So we started putting it in everything, and I do mean everything. We put corn into cheese, bread, cereal, French fries. (French fries!) It was in diapers, playground material, road paving, clothing, support beams for new construction projects. We couldn't find enough places for corn. The United States government would put an embargo on a hostile nation, and basically that meant: *stop sending them corn*. Well, hell, that just means more corn for us, corn the taxpayers had already bought. It was piling up, boat loads, train loads, truckloads of corn with nowhere to go.

Until...

You knew we were gonna get to an 'until.' Didn't you?

Back in the late twentieth century, thanks to a trade agreement we signed in the 1990s, Coca-Cola and Pepsi Cola products were manufactured in Mexico, where labor was cheap, and enormous factories could be built for the spare change Coke and Pepsi executives found beneath their couch cushions.

There was our answer: send loads of corn to Mexico and use it to sweeten soda.

Holy crap. That was a good idea.

(Actually, it was an astonishingly bad idea.)

Why?

The pancreas.

Okay, okay. I know. I get it. You came along for a fun adventure story about teens running for their lives, and I'm interrupting with a glandular organ. A glandular organ? And not one of the fun ones, like livers or kidneys. Nope. The pancreas. Are we kidding?

Nope.

I'm deadly serious.

But because I know you want to get back to Fallon, Danny, and Emma, I'm gonna get right to it.

We started processing corn into sweetener. We'd made corn syrup for generations, and it was fine. But keep in mind: we had millions of tons of useless corn just sitting around. So instead of regular old corn syrup (a delightful mix of fructose and sucrose), we started increasing the level of modified corn sugar until we had to change the name to High Fructose Corn Syrup, and until our bodies – there's that pancreas again – couldn't process the syrup like normal sugar. So the extra calories began depositing as fat in our bellies, our thighs, our droopy, triple chins, and our tremendously round asses, and especially, notoriously, frighteningly, and some other pretty bad adverbs, in our livers.

Ooops.

And we began to get fatter and sicker. By 2025, eighty percent of America was overweight or obese. The greatest threat in American history wasn't Communism, terrorism, avian flu, nuclear war, or invading armies of brainwashed Chinese soldiers. Nope. The greatest threat in American history was our food, the very food we grew, harvested, processed, preserved, hormoned, sweetened, hydrogenated, and served up in handy-dandy individual plastic wrapping to the

American consumer, most of whom were forty- to two-hundred pounds overweight by 2032.

Finally, the American people, the ones who could still get up off the couch without having a massive myocardial infarction (that's a heart attack), decided to take back America and end corporate and government-approved poison in our food. And the Corn War began.

Yeah, it didn't go well.

The American Agricultural War of 2034, some argue it was necessary. Others disagree. I don't care. What concerns me, and should concern you, my friends, is what happened afterward.

Alas, we'll have to get to that later. But I bet you know. Right? Yeah, Stormcloud. It's what every culture looks for when the wheels come off the wagon: mind-erasing drugs.

For now, however, let's get back to the farm.

12

A Wicked Brawl, Some Truth Telling, and Seaweed Energy Paste

A short hummock of unruly grass rolled between the broken-down house and the first rows of October corn, confirming Danny's assertion that American farmers continued to plant stalks on every square inch of arable land. Fallon thought of it as a dooryard, because that's what her mother always called the postage stamp of tidy property outside their trailer. But this was no yard. This was a few hundred square feet of lawn just so Farmer Bob and Farmer Jane had a place to set up a barbecue and host their neighbors with glasses of lemonade on Sundays. Afternoon sunlight, weak with full Autumn, colored the yawning field Halloween beige speckled with jungle green. Flecks of vivid yellow dotted the hegemonic expanse here and there like spilled gemstones. The same breeze that had awakened her, rustled the stalks as the fall season, oblivious to their troubles, performed *Traditional Autumn Beauty* flawlessly.

Fallon felt Danny move up behind her. "You wanna tell me whatever it was you were planning to tell me?"

"Yeah."

She took his water glass. "I'll take that inside. There's a pump just off the porch. You probably want to clean up over by the fire pit."

"All right," he understood.

"I'll be out in a second. First, I wanna—" Breeze freshened through the stalks, carrying unexpected, sweet organic decay. Fallon turned her face into the wind. "What's that?"

"Not cucumbers, I hope," Danny sniffed. "Your tendency to smell threats before they arrive might just be the sexiest thing about you, but I'm done wrestling fifty-foot snakes, Mowgli."

Fallon closed her eyes, inhaled deeply. "Nah. Must've just got a whiff of something dead out there, maybe a squirrel or a mob enforcer, something."

"Good," he wiped his hands on his pants. "I'll be here, and Fallon...thanks."

"For what?" She stacked the tumblers, one inside the other.

"I need to talk with you is all."

She didn't answer. The breeze had delivered another salvo: putrefaction, something dead, sloppy dead, and rotting. "Damn, that's nasty. It's a wonder I didn't smell it before."

"When?"

"When I woke up." She took a tentative step toward the cornfield. Easily a half mile across, more than that deep, it might have been a slumbering creature, just another in the laundry list of monsters hunting them. "I could've sworn..."

Emma called from the barn. "Hey, guys...you hear that?"

Fallon squinted into the sunlight. "Danny...Danny, c'mere. Come over..." She saw them: corn stalks, nine, maybe ten feet high, rustling in spots, puddles of agitation, left-to-right in perhaps fifteen, seventeen places. "Danny, what's that?"

"What?" He peered along her outstretched arm.

"Those...see them, like something...some *things* are moving. See? There. It's like someone's dropping pebbles in a pond."

"Yeah. There, again. Yeah, I see them." He cupped his hands toward the barn, called in a sharp whisper. "Emma! Get over here!"

She appeared, carrying the wrench Danny had been using on the peach grader. Her red hair stood out against the barn's faded, chipped paint. Even from across the dooryard, Fallon could see that the smaller girl was frightened. "What are they? Dogs? Guys, I'm afraid of mean dogs."

Over here! Danny waved.

243

Watching oddly symmetric puddles of agitation radiate throughout the first hundred or so cornrows, Fallon also motioned for Emma. She twirled her fingers, then her hand, in a *Hurry Up, God Damnit!* gesture she hoped would motivate the little Irish terrorist to get her ass moving. "They're getting closer."

"I know," Danny estimated their invisible guests might only be twenty rows deep and closing fast. Checking the field behind the barn, he had to stand tip toe to see into it. "Over there, too. We're being surrounded."

"Yeah," Fallon glanced toward the stalks beyond the driveway. "The other side of the car. See?"

"We gotta go."

She agreed. "Yeah, let's get the hell out of here. This can't be good."

"I'll get the car going." Danny rushed off; Fallon badly wanted him back.

The first of their assailants broke through rows of corn only a few paces from Emma and were on her in seconds. She shrieked when she saw them...whatever they were...and tried running the last few feet to Fallon, but the *things* were too quick and ran her down easily.

"Fallon!" Emma cried as hairy, leathery hands closed over her arms, neck, and shoulders while others, jointed pincers wrapped about her rib cage.

Fallon watched dumbstruck as one of them—it might have been four feet tall, on its hind legs—closed a burly hand over Emma's face, blinding her and choking off the younger girl's screams. More of the monsters emerged from the stalks, behind the Chevron, beside the barn, perhaps eight or ten from Fallon's flank. Twelve, then fifteen more spilled, a foul-smelling, misshapen tide, into the dooryard. It was a frontal assault designed to frighten or dishearten her into giving up, surrendering, kneeling down and waiting to die. She didn't know and didn't care. Rather her focus narrowed to one of the creatures, a five-foot, manlike monster, lousy with powerful muscle, and patched here and there with stubby, resilient hair and islands of scarred, naked skin, all black or dark brown. Barefoot and without clothing, the thing had eyes in the front of its skull—*a predator*—but that's where the creature's resemblance to a man, a gorilla, a Halloween version of a drooling Morlock ended. Its face might have been borrowed from a short-snouted horse or a long-snouted dog. Twin fangs protruded from overhanging jaws and dribbly canine lips. A few of the company breathed with their mouths open, tongues lolling like wolves, but with vampire fangs...and luminous green faces.

Fallon had a second to think, *They glow in the dark. Their faces glow. What the hell are they?* When one of them, the tallest, pointed at Emma and spoke.

"Take that one." Its lips moved; its fangs and wolf tongue cooperated long enough for her to gather that it was in charge and that it could communicate, albeit in nearly incoherent guttural grunts. "You three. Take her."

And Fallon's mind locked into place. To her left, Danny shouted something. Time slowed; she understood that unless these creatures released Emma unharmed and disappeared quickly back where they came from, she was going to kill every one of them. She tilted her head to one side, considered the leader, and thought, *Hatchet. Sledgehammer.*

Shouting unnecessarily—all of the simian monsters closing on them could hear—Fallon warned, "Release her!" She pointed to the group that held Emma. "And go."

Tall Captain ignored her, grunting again in coarse, phlegmy orders. "Take her! Kill him!"

Fallon rushed to meet them, a miniature sledgehammer in one hand, a camp hatchet in the other, she moved immediately on the leader, feinting once with the hatchet and then crushing its skull like a piñata with the sledge. The bones of its misshapen head cracked. It simultaneously barked an obscene howl, fired a stream of hot urine into the grass and dropped a watery splash of cruel smelling shit into the first row of corn.

Spinning on the balls of her feet, Fallon didn't wait for the body to fall. Instead, she sank the hatchet deep into the throat of the second creature, and slammed the sledgehammer into the rib cage of a third, trying to flank her. Spinning, striking, crushing bones, breaking knee joints, chopping off hands, fingers, ears, toes, anything she could reach, Fallon kept thinking, *Heavier. Sharper. Heavier. Sharper.* as she cut, slashed, and brutalized her way through the throng. In less than thirty seconds, nearly twenty of the creatures lay dead, dying, bleeding or irretrievably broken in an arbitrary scatter of inhuman carnage. Fallon had been scratched with fungus-crusted claws, bitten several times, punched, and nearly wrestled to the ground.

She didn't care. Nothing hurt. She bled from a scatter of minor wounds and noticed swelling stiffening one elbow where a creature had attempted to wrench her arm off. She felt none of it.

Tasting blood where she'd bitten her tongue, she backed a few steps up the untidy lawn to find Danny clubbing one of the monsters with a railing he'd torn from the porch. Two others lay dead or unconscious in the weedy flowerbeds. "Get Emma!" Fallon wheezed, sucking breaths. She spat blood at Danny's last kill. "Where is she?"

"They took her." He stopped beating the monster long enough to point into the corn with the business end of the bannister. Perhaps a dozen creatures, realizing they were outmatched by the raging woman, had carried the smaller girl away.

Stepping to her left, Fallon swung the sledge in an upward motion, shattering another creature's jaws and snapping its neck just below the skull. "What? Are you kidding? Why didn't you tell me? Why didn't you go after her?" Welcome rage rendered Fallon impervious to the monsters' sharpened fingernails, their vampire-like fangs. She wondered

246

for half a breath if she might simply burst into flames and bring ruin and hellfire down on all of Fauquier County. That'd show them; that'd show everyone.

Until Danny took her by the shoulders.

"No! I'm going after her!"

He pulled her close. "I don't know how you're doing this. I don't. But you gotta listen. Please!" He gave her a gentle shake, hoping she wouldn't bash his brains in or cut one of his legs off. "Listen. You stay here. Take care of any that try to come behind me. I'll get her; I promise. Don't go into the rows. You'll be blind in there."

"No, Danny...wait—"

"But remember, please, that I told you I needed to talk with you about something. Please." And still holding her by the shoulders, Danny Hackett disappeared into a cloud of misty smoke.

Stupefied, she understood immediately what had happened but was unable to grasp it just yet. Two creatures approached from behind the Chevron, coming in low, their heads ducked, their simian paws dragging in the uncut grass. Fallon slowly turned on them, spoke calmly. Ignoring the cuts, scrapes, and bleeding bites on her arms and legs, she spat blood into the grass, then asked, "Did you see that, boys? Did you see him just disappear like that? Travel as smoke or mist. That's a neat trick. That's a neat trick; I've gotta admit. But...and doncha just love *buts*?" Fury intensified her focus, resonant in each syllable. "I just love *buts,* boys." The twin monsters grunted and snarled as they hunted the thin, seemingly helpless girl. Confused at her chit chat, one blinked stupidly with dark, oval eyes, then yanked handfuls of tufted grass and tossed them over its head, hoping to intimidate her.

It didn't work. She said, "And I've gotta warn you; I do. I haven't been unhappy all day, not until this...exact...moment."

Sharing a glance, the creatures leapt in tandem; Fallon focused her attention inward once again. This angry, she required only a fraction of a second to think the words, and her body responded. *Lead pipe. Ice pick.*

She wanted these two to suffer. Then she'd deal with Danny.

Danny had nearly reached the Chevron when the first of the squat, monkey-wolf-cockroach-glow-in-the-dark, whatever-they-were things materialized from the murky shadows of the cornfield. They'd used the stalks, now nearly ten feet high, as cover, masking their approach until they were almost upon the fugitives.

As ranks of monsters strode from the field, he stood still, too frightened to come up with a means to fight them, too surprised to react, and too worried about Fallon—*and Emma; you should worry about Emma, also*—to move. He thought he might use the Chevron, just demolition derby his way around the dooryard, smashing the monkey-dogs to sloppy paste on the old car's grille. That'd do it. At least he'd be able to clear the majority of them out of the way, maybe give Fallon—*and Emma*—a chance to jump in the back. And they'd be gone. They'd leave all their stuff. Who cared? He could rob a sporting goods store anywhere.

Drive. Do it. Get in. Quickly.

Then Emma screamed.

With a psychotic's mad confidence, Fallon charged the monsters, just lowered her head and attacked, one on twenty – perhaps more. Danny had no idea how many might be huddled in the corn, waiting to charge in as reinforcements.

But it was too late for any of that, too late for anything but getting to Fallon. Three of the creatures had Emma prisoner, the petite redhead nearly disappearing inside their muscular arms and jointed, insectile grippers.

So Danny ran, searching for a weapon.

At the bottom of the farm's brief stretch of lawn, Fallon battled a platoon of monsters hand to hand. Danny panicked when he saw them flank her, bite her arms, legs, yank her hair, and scratch at her face with their prehistoric claws. "You bastards," he cursed, then shouted, "Hang on! I'm coming!" With a firm kick then a quick wrench, he was able to pull one of the porch railings loose. Immediately, it felt good in his hands, a baseball bat studded with a bouquet of rusty, hundred-year-old nails.

He turned on the few creatures pursuing him, would have to deal with them first.

Danny needed to be quick about it. He waited, leaning back on one leg, timing his swing, and as the first squat abomination approached, low and fast, he unloaded with the railing, hoping it wouldn't shatter as he attempted to drive the monster's head two-hundred feet into the cornfield.

His attacker was dead before it hit the ground. If the others noticed, it didn't slow them. Danny clubbed another before the first's corpse had stopped twitching. "Eat that, you ugly motherscratcher," he spun, waited for the third monkey-wolf, and risked a glance at Fallon.

She was winning handily.

Danny couldn't fathom how she managed it. She appeared to be using her hands, just bare hands, but with amazing and unprecedented strength and power—as if she held a cudgel and an executioner's axe or an old butcher's cleaver. Limbs shattered; heads lolled on torn necks. Knees buckled; skulls caved in with audible cracks as Fallon punched and slashed through the group of howling, grunting monsters.

When the last creature attacked, it came in low, diving beneath Danny's studded bat and knocking his legs from beneath him. The two tumbled backwards twice, rolling to a stop with the pale-faced attacker pressing heavily on the teen's chest. Growling in triumph, the thing dripped drool onto Danny's face, then howled with such unbridled madness and pleasure that Danny about swallowed the monster's shriek, a warm gust, redolent of damp, rotting meat. He saw bits of gnawed flesh trapped between the creature's fangs and wondered for a fraction of a second what they ate.

Gagging, he brought his hands up, protecting his neck. He held the thing by the jaws, pressing down on its lower jaw, figuring that was the weaker of the two, but leaving himself open to be brutalized by the monster's powerful fists and wrestled about by its wiry pincers.

It hit him solidly in the ribs, and Danny exhaled all the breath in his lungs. Gasping, he had to release the thing's jaw, had to cover up his midsection.

Sensing its advantage, the monster raised its dripping jowls, offered a howl to the afternoon sky, then set about tearing the boy's throat out and lapping up his blood.

But Danny proved an instant too quick. As the creature opened its mouth to strike, he evaporated, leaving the monster confused and biting down on a mouthful of uncut grass.

By the time the ape-wolf located him, several feet away, Danny had retrieved the porch railing. Spinning it like a child's baton, he tormented the monster. "How's that taste, Bubba? Didn't figure you for a plant eater."

Raging at having been denied an afternoon kill, the monster made its fatal mistake and leapt at the boy, angry that the human trickster had fought unfairly. It was the last thought the creature would ever have.

With time, distance, and a weapons advantage, Danny reveled in bashing this creature to death, and offered the dying corpse several additional whacks, just to feel bones break even as the monster expired on the lawn. Swinging with all his might, Danny hummed the commercial jingle that had been stuck in his head since the three friends fled Baltimore's Penn Station. *You're never in the weather when you're in your weather guard.*

Then Fallon was beside him, bleeding, panting, and— unsurprising to Danny—yelling at him.

"Get Emma!" She spat watery blood onto the dead creature. "Where is she?"

"They took her." He pointed with the bloody bannister, east toward the cornfield.

250

Fallon turned momentarily to murder another of the monsters, punching so hard with a rudimentary uppercut that Danny heard its neck break. The thing folded like a discarded rag. She wheeled on him, frustrated anger transforming her from a beautiful young woman into a force of nature. He couldn't figure how she'd managed, with bare hands, to murder upwards of twenty creatures in less than two minutes, but he knew he couldn't allow her to go into the corn. These things knew the corn, would use it to their advantage, blind her, surround her.

He had to go. *That's fine,* he thought. *Actually, I can probably do it from here.*

Inches from his face, Fallon shouted, "What? Are you kidding? Why didn't you tell me? Why didn't you go after her?"

And he knew he'd have to confess, to show her. He'd planned on telling her—knew she was going to be upset that he'd kept it from her—but there were no other options now. He took Fallon by the shoulders, hoping to calm her down.

It wasn't effective. "No! I'm going after her!"

He gripped her tightly; it felt like trying to hold down a departing rocket. "I don't know how you're doing this. I don't. But you gotta listen. Please! Listen. You stay here. Take care of any that try to come behind me. I'll get her; I promise. Don't go into the rows. You'll be blind in there."

"No, Danny...wait—"

He went for his most disarming, cannot-be-resisted-by-teenage-women grin, hoping she might forgive him later, but knowing that hope was probably empty. "Remember, please, that I told you I needed to talk with you about something. Please." And Danny dissipated into the autumn breeze.

Emma and her captors were easy to track from the air. Danny watched, impressed the creatures, seemingly simpletons he and Fallon had been able to kill without much finesse, retreated through the corn in what was clearly a cover formation. The monsters took turns rotating back, then forward, forging ahead of the two who dragged Emma to scout

251

a safe path or turning back in case the unexpectedly deadly teens followed on foot.

Didn't expect me up here, though. Did you?

Under normal circumstances, he would take a moment to enjoy the breeze, allowing himself to be carried effortlessly on the wind. Mississippi thunderstorms tended to blow in with such ebullient foreshadowing breezes, that flying above the swamps and bayous ranked among the gifted young man's favorite pastimes.

Not today.

Instead, Danny dropped to the fuzzy tips of the corn stalks and hurried, propelling himself against the wind to a point a few hundred feet in front of Emma's attackers. Passing overhead, he estimated their strength at about fourteen.

Doesn't matter, he thought. *Might as well be a hundred.*

He came to rest inside an east-west row, ensuring he retook his teenage form directly in the creatures' path. Then, with concentration and a practiced gesture, just a separation of his hands like an orchestra conductor bringing a section of violins to the ready, Danny flattened a sixty-foot circle of corn. The stalks simply bent over, then lay prostrate on the dry Virginia clay, as if a UFO had landed leaving history's smallest crop circle here in the middle of nowhere.

He didn't wait long. The first of the retreating creatures emerged from the sheltering corn, this time looking harried, not at all sinister. Danny imagined that whoever had sent them would be disappointed they'd failed to retrieve Fallon along with Emma...not that their leader would offer much discipline now, not since Fallon crushed his skull and left him shitting in the daisies.

He stood quietly, didn't taunt them, call out invitations or insults. Rather, Danny tried to look as meek and vulnerable as possible, wanted this chore completed quickly. Emma had to be scared beyond reckoning. Clearing out the last of these fellows needed to be his priority, not scaring them into scattering all over the field and perhaps warning or informing whoever had sent them that the teens were a formidable force, clearly able to defend themselves.

"Hi kids," he waved. "Nice to see you again."

Three, then four, then nine of the creatures stepped into the miniature crop circle Danny had created. He wasn't sure how he knew, but most appeared pleased to have an open field of view, a clear line of attack on the lone, unarmed boy.

When the two carrying Emma emerged behind the others, Danny unsheathed that same irresistible-to-teenage-women smile he'd tried (and failed with) on Fallon. Sadly, none of the approaching monsters seemed impressed. "Shit," he said. "That's my best smile, too. I'm striking out all over the place today."

One of the creatures wrapped around Emma grunted, "Kill that one." And the stunted, homely monsters charged.

Still smiling, Danny gestured again, and like violinists in a compliant orchestra, the corn stalks he'd asked to lie flat rose as one. Coiling, snakelike, the tough, fibrous stalks slid about ankles, gripped calves and thighs, tugged tightly about creatures' waists, wrists, even necks, pulling them down, dragging them away. He watched, impassive, as the creatures' eerie faces, those pale, glow-in-the-dark visages modulated from bloodthirsty rage to surprise and then terror.

"Yeah," he said, not caring whether they heard him. "You shouldn't have come here."

His view blocked by animated corn stalks, Danny contented himself with listening as the field dragged the ape-wolves off to their deaths. Howling cries gave way to unsettling gasps and downright disturbing unnatural shrieks as the corn first strangled and then tore the creatures apart.

Cries for mercy went on for most of the afternoon, long after Danny, Fallon, and Emma had retreated into the relative safety of the farmhouse.

Hysterical, Emma shouted, "Danny! Danny, please. There's one here. One left."

253

He hurried toward the sound of her voice, the rustle and swish as she fled the last of her captors. "It's okay, Em!" He ran down one row, shifted over two, then saw her. "I'm here. Wait!"

Turning, she found him and ran in a stumbling, shuffling gait to dive into his arms. "Danny! I'm sorry." She sobbed. "I'm sorry. Are you okay? Is Fallon? I'm sorry...sorry." Inconsolable, Emma seemed as if she might unzip Danny and climb inside. She wrapped legs around his, tugged his neck and shoulders down, buried her face in his chest and wept into his already greasy t-shirt.

He tried comforting her. "It's okay. We're fine. You're fine. We're gonna go back. Just gimme one second. Wait right here. Okay? I'm gonna be right back. I just need—"

"No!" she refused to release him. "No. Don't. Please. You can't leave me here. I can't see anywhere. Take me. You gotta take me with you."

"Okay, okay," he peeled her off his chest, took her hand. "C'mon, just over here."

He led her through several rows, following the grunts and curses of the single ape-wolf he'd allowed to survive the attack. They found it where it had been standing, holding Emma hostage, when Danny unleased the cornfield, his army of clone soldiers. The creature's legs were wrapped tightly by half a dozen stalks, holding it fast as if a den of powerful snakes had emerged from a subterranean nest to feed. Other stalks held its arms down, its neck and head captive, prepared to strangle it to death if Danny so much as blinked approval.

Still terrified, Emma shrank from the creature, but Danny strode up to it, lifted its vampire, canine jaws, forced it to make eye contact.

"Die!" It choked and spat. "Die!"

"Not today, Jerry Lee," he slapped it across the snout, like he might slap a stray dog trying to bite his ankle. "Pay attention!"

"Die," it said again, albeit with less enthusiasm.

254

"Listen," Danny took its snout in both hands, twisted its face up. "Go back. Tell them, whoever it is, that I will kill everyone, everything you send against us. Tell them. You understand. I'll kill all of you, every last one."

The monster tried snapping at Danny's face, hoping to take a bite out of the infuriating fugitive before dying. But Danny proved too quick. A mere nod to the corn stalks, and the field intensified its grip, choking the creature until it could barely draw breath.

He slapped it again. "Tell them. Warn them. I'll kill you all. Never come back here." He leaned in close, only inches from the thing's oddly luminescent face, and drew a fingertip over one, glow-in-the-dark cheek. "God damn, will you look at that? Where do you live, Jerry Lee? Underground? Close by?"

The beast answered with a useless, threatening growl.

"Yeah, yeah," Danny pressed its elongated snout to one side, tormenting it. "Shut up already. You lost. Get used to the idea." He led Emma back toward the farmhouse. A hundred or so feet from the yard, he spoke briefly to the stalks. Emma understood that Jerry Lee had been released to carry the fugitives' warning to whomever had sent the ape-wolves here hunting.

From farther out the disturbing sounds of animal torture, strangulation, and dismemberment reached them in a ghastly juxtaposition with late afternoon sunlight and amiable autumn breeze.

In the dooryard, Fallon rushed to them. "Jesus, Danny..."

He raised a hand. "Wait. Please, later. I promise. Just now, let's..."

"Yeah," she wrapped Emma in a bearhug, hoping to erase the touch, aroma, even the memory of the kidnappers. "You okay?"

Emma's voice shook, rustling like corn. "Danny...I dunno. I can't...Danny?"

255

"It's okay." He pulled her tighter, completing the Emma sandwich between him and Fallon. "We'll get some water, take a break here in the sunshine, and we'll talk. It's gonna be—"

"They covered my mouth," she said, still mostly hysterical and panting. "They covered my mouth; I couldn't say anything."

"Couldn't call us," Fallon said. "We understand. But you've gotta know that there was no way we were gonna let them—"

"No," she interrupted, insisting they understand. "They covered my mouth. I couldn't breathe, couldn't talk, or—"

The last creature, Jerry Lee, burst from the rows. Bounding toward them, it might have been a frothing Rottweiler. It snarled, bared its fangs and leapt wildly up the grassy hummock.

"I goddamned knew it," Danny muttered.

Emma shoved the others away, turned to face the creature, and said quickly, just above a whisper, "Preening bird and slippery frog, save me from this big, mean dog." She said it in such a child's singsong, it had to have been something she'd written long ago, perhaps with the pen she wore night and day.

Jerry Lee pulled up so suddenly its momentum caused it to tumble and roll like a cartoon character fired from a cannon. Fallon recalled the old kid's shows she and her mother used to watch on the main screen in their trailer on the lake. She almost laughed at the comical way this monster lost its footing and piled headlong into the porch steps. Focusing her imagination, she was too tired for anything truly creative and simply thought *hatchet*. Her body responded, arming her with a ¾ bit axe. She crossed to the incapacitated creature, lifted her arm to finish it off.

Emma pressed her backwards toward the barn. Over her shoulder, the redhead called, "You should stand back, Danny, or maybe just duck." Having seen enough today to convince him that anything was possible, he complied, sheltering behind a weather-beaten stump.

Allowing her axe to fall away, Fallon asked, "What'd you do?"

Before Emma could answer, the creature began bulging in unlikely places: its hip, left breast, right shoulder, both cheeks, as if being pumped full of water, stretching itself into even more horrific bends and turns than it had as a squat, burly killer.

"What's happening?" Fallon asked.

"Watch," Emma replied. "I wish they hadn't covered my mouth. I could have helped."

Smoke puffed from the creature's nostrils, then from one ear, its throat. It twisted and writhed, throwing itself about the dooryard. Finally it came to rest on its knees, facing the two of them, while Danny remained tucked safely behind the stump, covering his head.

"There you go," Emma said. And held her breath. "This part always scares me."

Fallon pulled them both to the ground.

The younger girl resisted. "No. I wanna watch."

Smoke now streamed from the creature's eyes, nose, and mouth, as if a green wood fire burned just at the back of its throat. Its thighs expanded to twice their previous size and its stomach, which had been flat and rippled with striated muscle, inflated like a beach ball, growing dangerously large.

Fallon covered her ears.

Emma watched intently.

The explosion wasn't as dramatic as Fallon expected. There was no cataclysmic boom or any great burst of flaming innards cast about the dooryard. Rather the creature broke, splitting at its seams. Sloppy splashes of pressure released in simultaneous wet hisses made Fallon think of auto tires going flat, a dozen at once. Then unidentifiable parts, sections of gut, liver, intestines, and other organs did fire and ricochet until they fell with disturbing smacks, scattering Jerry Lee over about fifty feet of the farm's small back yard.

257

The last to go was its head, which popped from one eye, then one nostril. Billows of smoke and bloody steam puffed crazily until whatever passed for brains in the monster's head poked in disgusting, smeary coils out its ears, right eye, and nose.

Danny rose from his hiding place. "The dogs. Jesus, Emma, that's how you blew up those dogs. You...with a poem? A little kid's poem? What the holy, everloving hell?"

"The dogs explode," Emma explained. "It's faster and way more effective."

Fallon whispered, "good lord."

"This thing only sort of looks like a dog, so I didn't know if it would completely work, but I knew it would at least stop them."

"Oh...I'd say it worked," Fallon nudged a hunk of wet liver with her toe.

"Hey, you're all scratched up. Are you okay?"

"She got bit," Danny hurried over, careful to avoid the puddles of steaming Jerry Lee. "They bit her a bunch of times. We gotta get some water boiling and clean her up."

"I'm fine," Fallon said, not entirely convinced. "But let's...yeah, let's get cleaned up. Someone needs to stay out here, though, in case those others come back."

"They won't," Emma said. "He made the corn kill all of them."

"He what?" Now Fallon did feel woozy and staggered a step before Danny caught hold of her.

"Sure," Emma went on. "You hear that out there?"

Fallon hadn't, but now tuned her ears to the distant reaches of the cornfield. Shouts of mercy, cries of agony and utter despair reached her on the mild afternoon breeze. "What's that? What's happening out there?"

"You don't wanna know," Emma said.

"Actually, I do," she regained her balance, stared at both of them in turn. "We all need to know everything."

They agreed that it was too risky to discuss plans or ask questions inside the farmhouse. No one could guess what disagreeable ghoulies might come creeping out of the corn after dark. And while they felt confident that they'd dispatched all of the ape-wolf creatures with the night-glow complexion, there was no way they could know for certain.

Danny wanted to pack up and leave. "It was stupid of us to come back here. I admit it. We've gotta head someplace else."

"Where?" Dehydrated, hungry, and exhausted, Fallon sat heavily in the grass, all the while watching the corn rows as they danced primly in the breeze. She was able to ignore the cries and moans of the dying creatures, but only if she deliberately tuned them out, listening instead to Emma and Danny, the wind, and a rusty set of tuneless chimes dangling from a strand of fishing wire above the porch.

Emma handed her another tumbler of discolored water with a Kleen straw and two pills. "Take these."

She did. "What are they?"

"Prevoxycillin. We have plenty."

"No," Fallon drank, grimaced. "We need to keep those in case anyone actually gets sick."

"Sorry," Emma disagreed. "You were bitten a half dozen times. You might have rabies, feline distemper, frigging plague for all we know. This stuff," she shook the baggie Danny had stolen in Baltimore, "should be enough to get you through."

"And if we run out," Danny added, "we can steal more." He sat beside her, but facing the opposite way, ensuring he could see into the sprawling acreage behind the Chevron and the barn.

"*You* can steal more; that's what you mean to say. Right?" Too tired for a full-on brawl, she wanted answers, regardless.

"I can steal more. Yes. And we've got lots of Stormcloud, too, just in case you wanna shut down completely until tomorrow." He wasn't interested in fighting. "And keep in

259

mind, I told you we needed to talk, that I had something to tell you."

"I know," she acquiesced on this point. "But why not tell me earlier, after you found out about me?"

"She didn't tell you," he pointed at Emma. "Give her a hard time, too. Did you see that monkey thing explode? Good mother of Christ, I wouldn't have wished that on anyone. Its frigging spleen flew over my head into the bushes fifty feet out."

Both young women offered up guilty looks. Emma's lower lip quivered.

"Oh, shit," Danny tore a handful of grass—not unlike the last ape-wolf that attacked Fallon—and tossed it toward the house. "You *both* knew...about each other."

Emma tried steering them in another direction. "Do you know what the odds are of two gifted people finding one another in the same school for juvenile management?"

Danny sighed, then lay back in the grass. "No, Em. What are the odds?"

"One in twelve million just that we exist," she said. "So can you imagine what the odds are of the three of us actually finding one another?"

Danny sat up at that. "Hey. You're right. That's not just one in thirty-six million. It's one of those statistics things, exponent things. I was always dogshit at math. But it goes up like by a gazillion percent. Right?"

Emma calculated, "It's like 4 to the negative 18, truly thin odds."

"Yeah, my brain doesn't do numbers like that."

"That's not possible," Fallon said. "You've gotta have that wrong."

"Nope. It's true. Those are the odds of three gifted individuals, healthy, with their skills intact, finding one another at the same time in the same shitty reform school in Backwards Ass, Virginia." She paused, then added, "That is *if* they randomly find one another."

"What are you suggesting?" Fallon asked. "That we were deliberately brought together?"

Danny tried reconciling this massive improbability in his mind. "That's exactly what she's saying. There's no way we all landed in Blair's home for the young, sexy, and criminally disturbed by accident."

"Correct," Emma said. "We were herded there."

"Why?" Fallon asked.

"Someone wants us together," Danny said. "That seems obvious."

"So they can kill us all at once?"

"Maybe that's another someone," Emma said.

Tall Captain, the ape-wolf who'd grunted orders, echoed in Fallon's memory: *Take her. Kill him.* She asked, "Did you two hear that one? The tall one...he wanted Emma and me kidnapped and Danny dead."

"Lovely," Emma said. "Maybe they're just sexist."

"Heh," Danny laughed. "More likely, they don't know that I have any skills."

"And you were gonna let that last one go," Emma said. "Whoah, that would've been...well, we have no idea what that would've been. But if they don't know about you, that gives us an advantage. Doesn't it?"

"Yeah," Fallon said. "I guess we're lucky that one came after us rather than going back with news that we all have talents."

"I think that's called ironic," Danny said.

"Nope," Emma corrected. "It's just a coincidence. To be ironic, it has to have an added dimension that—"

Fallon raised a hand. "Em, sweetie. We're good."

Abashed, the smaller girl blushed. "Right. I guess if he just saved my life, I probably shouldn't be correcting his syntax."

He ruffled her hair. "Kiddo, I don't even know what syntax is."

"Liar," Emma said. "You're like Mr. History."

261

"Focus, puppies." Still bleeding from a dozen bites, gashes, and claw marks, Fallon turned the conversation back to practical matters. "We've gotta set some priorities and then get out of here."

"I agree," Danny said. "Our first priority should be to transfer Emma's credits into my dummy account and then go somewhere sunny, warm, with decent fried food, free library downloads, and maybe a hammock."

"Keep dreaming, big guy," Emma said.

"What? I like that dream. That's a really good one, with, you know, little umbrellas in the drinks."

"I do, too. But you've gotta remember: they found us here; they found us in Baltimore, and they found us here again."

"That's true," Fallon searched the corn, watching for any rustle that might be out of sync with the afternoon breeze. "And they're quick about it. We hadn't been in Baltimore for two hours when that snake arrived."

"Don't remind me," Emma shuddered.

"Or back here," Danny agreed. "We got here before dawn, and by midafternoon an entire battalion of those ape-wolf things showed up."

"Yeah," Fallon said. "Someone has us on satellite radar. But I can't figure how. No one has anything electronic. We haven't used our bio-wires or wrist screens. How can they be tracking us so easily?"

"Our gifts," Emma said.

"Whaddya mean?" Danny asked. "You think someone can tell when we're using our talents?"

"It's the only way." She went on, "We used them when we first arrived, when the bulls were in the yard."

"And Mr. Ugly Mountain showed up that afternoon," Fallon finished.

"We used them in the street level corridors beneath Penn Station." Understanding dawned on Danny's face. He wagged a finger at the others.

"And Old Kaa showed up in no time," Emma said.

"Kaa," Fallon considered the name, held it up to the light. "Kaa...the big snake from the Kipling story. *The Jungle Book*, that's it."

"What?" Danny asked. "What are you getting at?"

"Its eyes," Fallon said. "Did you get a good look into that thing's eyes?"

"No," he frowned. "I was too busy climbing the marinara cans, trying to escape."

"They were terrible," she said. "Actually, I think that's how Bagheera, the panther, refers to them in the story: *evil eyes*. Kaa was thirty feet long and had evil eyes."

"So?" he said. "That snake in the train station was a copperhead, impossibly long with regular, old copperhead eyes."

"No," Fallon waved him off. "Those weren't normal snake eyes."

"Again," Danny asked. "So what?"

"Why did you call it Kaa, Em?"

Now Emma shrugged. "Dunno. That's the only big snake I've ever heard of."

"You read the book?"

"Nah," she held up her wrist. "I have over two-hundred Disney films in my Prevo account. I saw the animated version. It's wicked old, from back when they drew them by hand. Can you imagine that?"

"I saw that one," Danny added. "It was in one of those sim room theaters. I swear I thought I was in a cartoon jungle the whole time. Except for the little door directly behind you, the film is total immersion, even over your head. I was maybe eight or nine, I think, and that snake scared the absolute camel piss out of me."

Fallon let it go. "The snake in the original version helps Bagheera and Baloo. They have to rescue Mowgli from the baboons or orangutans or whatever they are. And Kaa is the hero. He saves Mowgli, then tries to hypnotize Baloo and Bagheera, is gonna eat them both, I guess."

Danny interrupted. "Where are we going with this? Kaa was a python or a boa constrictor or some other kind of choke-you-'til-your-eyeballs-pop snake, not a copperhead."

"A copperhead, like you have down in Mississippi."

"Yeah, so?"

Again, Fallon hesitated, turning possibilities over. "Okay, it's nothing."

Danny sat beside Emma. "How long've you been able to blow stuff up with just a few lines of poetry? Because I gotta tell you, that's one of the more impressive things I've seen in years."

"Always," Emma said. "I can't remember when I couldn't do it."

"The dogs," Fallon said, "when you two broke me out of Blair's chop shop, I watched a dog explode, figured I was drugged or hallucinating. But no."

Emma pulled her pen lanyard over her head. "I always have something to write with, just in case I come up with one that works."

"A poem?"

"More a rhyming couplet or series of couplets, yeah." She pulled a tattered notebook from her back pocket. It looked to have been dunked, dropped, run over, and dried out a hundred times. The pages, dog-eared and wrinkly, barely stayed closed.

"Did you have work done as a baby?" Fallon asked. "You must have."

"Just my kidney extraction, when I was four," Emma said. "If there was anything else, no one told me about it. But I guess I did. Otherwise, how could I do these things?"

"When was yours?" Fallon asked Danny.

He extended his weak ankle, waggled his foot. "Three years ago. I went in to have a section of torn ligament replaced, just a few inches in this ankle."

264

"Your limp!" Emma slapped herself comically on the forehead. "That finally makes sense. You've never had it fixed..."

"I can't. They did a crap job of it. I limped home, pissed off but soon discovered that I could get apples to drop down from the highest branches, just by concentrating my will."

"What else can you do?" Fallon asked. "Now's the time. We might as well put everything on the table."

Danny plucked blades of grass one at a time, flicking them at Emma. The young revolutionary blocked them with hyperbolic drama, a ninja in a bad film. "I can ask Nature for help, real help, in certain desperate situations, like the other morning when I set that cloud of hornets on those two bulls."

"That was you?" Emma shouted, rolled in the grass. "Holy crap! That was so fun."

"Yeah," he said. "Often it—"

"She?" Fallon interrupted. "We always hear about Nature as a *she*."

"I think that might be bullshit," he said. "Nature—to me, anyway—always presents itself as a source of almost unimaginable energy, just thriving life and boundless enthusiasm for...um, growth, expansion, reaching out, reaching up...it's hard to explain. But Nature doesn't care one bit about us...all of us...the fact that it responds to me, sometimes, is a frigging miracle."

"Jesus," Emma whispered, impressed. "Do you have any idea what a big deal this is?"

"Yeah," Danny tugged at one ear. "It's unprecedented. In the history of the human race, there haven't been a dozen people like me. Nature has been content for tens of thousands of years to go on without considering us."

"There've been others like you?"

"A few," he guessed. "I figure statistically, of the billions of people in history, we essentially add up to zero. But a few have been able to communicate with Nature, to ask for things, beg sometimes, and not often get what we ask for."

265

"God damn," Emma said. "I thought Fallon's skills were amazing."

"They are," he changed the subject. "I don't understand how you did that."

"What?"

"When you rushed into the fight, you were bashing their skulls in, chopping off their legs and arms. I mean, I can't figure what you'd done. How do you get so much power in your hands?"

"Wait." Having never discussed her gifts with anyone, she had no idea what others saw when they watched her. "What did you see?"

"Just you," Emma said. "Busting heads and chopping off ugly black fingers and toes and stuff."

"What did my hands look like to you?"

"Hands," Danny said. "Why? What are they to you?"

Fallon extended one wrist, thought: *straight razor*. She watched as her body went through the familiar change, collapsing, folding together, melding into a laser-sharpened razor capable of slicing the head off any ape-wolf or prehistoric copperhead. "There. See that?"

"Your hand?" Emma asked, confused.

"No," Fallon took the extra length of light-alloy shoelace from Danny's boot and sliced it off, quick as a thought.

"No way!" He cried, sliding back a few feet. "Those are flexi-steel! You did that with your finger?"

"Or this..." Showing off now, she gripped about six inches of hair above her shoulder and, like the shoelace, sliced it off with an easy flick of her wrist.

"Oh, no," Emma took the severed locks. "What'd you do that for? I really liked your—"

Allowing the razor to fade, Fallon took the truncated locks of hair, hanging well above her ear and dragged her hand across them gently, growing the butchered strands back to full length in the span of two breaths.

266

"Now, that's a neat trick," Danny seemed genuinely impressed. "You can turn your hands into tools? Even though from our vantage point they just look like hands."

"I guess," she said. "To me, my hand looks like a straight razor. But to you, it must look—"

"What did you use on those ape-wolf monkey things?"

"A sledgehammer and a hatchet." She reached into her pocket, handed a square of cloth to Danny.

"What?"

"Your forehead. You're bleeding again."

"When did you know you had skills?" He dabbed at his cuts, inspected the cloth, then pressed down hard.

"Years ago," Fallon said. "I had a lot of work done as a kid."

"Not a lot," Emma still held five inches of Fallon's hair in her fist. "If we ever get our screens working again, I can show you posts of little kids who've basically been dismantled for spare parts. They look like jigsaw puzzles some bully pushed off the library table."

"Okay," Fallon agreed, "not a lot of work, but enough."

"What?" Danny asked. "Besides that sexy foot, the thumb, and your eye?"

"A kidney," warm shame colored her cheeks. "I...we were alone, mom and me. We needed to make payments on...shit, I dunno, a hundred things. I was a healthy kid. Why not?" She rolled to her side, lifted her sweatshirt, exposing the neat scar, about six inches of pale, white line against the tan of her lower back.

Danny stared, didn't care if the entire world caught him. More than anything in his life he wanted to drop to his knees and caress all vestiges of pain, poverty, and suffering from that scar. Nothing as devastating as an involuntary kidney extraction could possibly have come from that crooked, tattooed incision. He sucked in a quick breath. "Okay, so...yeah, you did what you needed to do."

"Yeah."

"Which one was it that finally pushed you across the finish line?" Emma sliced through the tension.

"This one," Fallon indicated the mud-colored eye her mother had purchased for peanuts from the transport soup bags at Herkimer County's Brokerage House. "I was in the bathroom, wanted a drink, and was thinking I needed the scuzzy old water glass my mom used to leave in there, and...boom. There it was."

"Your hand?" Danny asked.

Fallon focused, thought: *bathroom water cup* and the old daisy-spotted mug formed at the end of her wrist. "Wanna see a cool trick?" She took the water glass from Emma and upended it into the cup where her hand had been. If Emma and Danny couldn't see her mother's old plastic cup, they'd watch an optical illusion as the ring formed by her thumb and forefinger appeared to swallow up six ounces of rusty brown water from the farmhouse tap.

"God damn," Emma said. "It's a cup. Right?"

"Yeah," Fallon waited a moment, then rotated her wrist. The water, which from all accounts had disappeared beneath her palm, now spilled into the uncut grass.

"Mother!" Danny said. "Now that's something."

"Anything else?" Emma asked.

"She doesn't need anything else," Danny said, thinking perhaps his ability to travel as smoke might go unmentioned.

"Honestly," Fallon said. "I don't know. I keep surprising myself, I guess."

"Yeah, you're young," Emma said. "A lot of young people have no idea what the full extent of their talents are until they're much older."

"Listen to you, Franny Fourteen Years Old," Danny teased.

"Fifteen, jackass," Emma glared at him. "But it's true: lots of us don't have any idea what we're capable of until later in life."

"You've made a study of gifted individuals?" he asked.

"Cursed," Fallon corrected.

"Nah, we don't have enough wealth to call ourselves *cursed*."

"That's true," Emma agreed. "The poor think of us as *gifted*, the rich as *cursed* and more importantly *disposable*."

"That's the one I dislike most," Danny said. "*Disposable*. That covers a lot of pretty disagreeable outcomes, if you get my meaning."

"Exactly," Fallon stood, brushed dirt and grass from her jeans. She wobbled slightly, didn't want the others to see her this exhausted. "That's exactly why we've gotta hit Blair. Hit him hard. Shut him down; close his tidy little factory forever."

"Um...have you forgotten the flying monkeys, Dorothy?" Danny motioned toward the corn. "We're being watched, love. How are we gonna get within two miles of that place without giant snakes, ape-dogs, walking scarecrows, ravenous zombies, or the frigging Prevo-Ice Custard Snowman showing up to rip our arms off?"

Emma folded her arms behind her head, squinted into the late afternoon sun. "Not to mention our friend, Mr. Hyde, that bloated, slobbering fellow who just wants Fallon...for lunch."

"Thanks for nothing, Em," Danny tossed another handful of torn grass toward the field. "I'd almost forgotten about your buddy, Brontosaurus Bob. What if we steal a boat, cross that lake, manage it without drowning..."

"I'm an excellent swimmer," Emma said, still sun bathing peacefully. "Old Edward Hyde...I bet he sinks like a truckload of lead toilets."

Danny went on, "...and get to the other side only to find Mr. Drool 'n Kill, there waiting for us? That'll be delightful, another lovely afternoon out in the autumn air."

Fallon watched Emma closely. With her eyes closed, the younger girl didn't notice. "Yeah...him. I imagine he'll show up again, looking for a bar fight."

269

Danny observed the odd interchange, asked hesitantly, "So there's no convincing you? Even after today?"

Fallon shook off the distraction. "Why would today make a difference to me? We won, pretty easily, all things considered."

"Um...no," Danny said. "Look at yourself. You're bleeding from fifteen places. You look like an ad for Band-Aids and a half gallon of antiseptic cream. Do you realize what might have happened if even one of those stinky rodents had bitten off your finger? Your little pinkie, I-barely-even-felt-it-Mom finger? You'd be out of luck calling up sledgehammers, chop sticks, and razor blades."

"I don't think so."

"How can you say that when you know we—well, you and I, anyway—only manifested these skills after having work done in some storefront?"

"Exactly," she explained. "I think it's the Stormcloud, something about the injections and the body parts they either add or remove. It's gotta be the perfect combination of—who knows? Two? Three?—parts, but the meds have to play a role. Right?" There was more; she knew it. But Fallon left that part unsaid, at least for now. Perhaps after she'd thought it through, she'd try out her emerging theory on Danny. Instead, she said, "It's gotta have something to do with riding the storm."

He massaged his lower lip with a fingertip.

Fallon wanted him to agree, wanted to feel like the dots lining up in her head were supposed to spell out something useful. Still watching Emma, she added, "I don't think anything would have happened to my skills if one of those stray monkeys had bitten off my finger, my toe, my left hand—"

"How about your right hand," Emma asked without opening her eyes. "The one with the imported thumb?"

"We can't know," Danny said. "There's no way we can know. And for my fifty credits worth, I don't wanna find out. I like my skill—

Singular. I caught that, Daniel: Skill, not skills. Good thinking.

—my limp, all of me just the way I am."

"So don't come," Fallon said, more out of frustrated exhaustion than anger.

"I'm coming," he brushed her off. "You don't have to get pissed every time we talk."

"Let's eat," Emma bounced nimbly to her feet and disappeared inside the farmhouse. The screen door slammed in her wake. "Be right back!"

Danny whispered, "You want me to tell her about being able to travel as mist? That's why you're angry."

Fallon pressed fingers to his lips. "You don't have to get defensive every time we talk. Don't be that guy."

"Okay, but if you want—"

"I don't, actually." She glanced at the porch door. "As a matter of fact, I don't think you should tell her, not at all."

"Why? What happened?"

Emma returned before Fallon could explain. Toting the nylon bag they'd stolen from the sporting goods store, she had to half drag the load down the steps.

"We're not gonna eat all of it." Danny moved to help her.

"I know," she grunted. "But I wasn't sure what you'd want, so I brought everything."

"Just bread and cheese for me," Fallon said. "We might as well eat the perishable bits before it all turns green."

"Good point." Emma dug in the bag.

"And some of that energy paste," Danny said. "I could live on that stuff."

"Tastes like seaweed to me," Fallon accepted a half loaf of Italian bread.

"It is seaweed," Emma passed bread to Danny. "And all kinds of other nasty stuff from the ocean…octopus guts and whale testicles, ugh, ghastly."

Danny found a tin of energy concentrate. "More for me, kids. More for me."

271

"I'll have some, too," Fallon said.

"Alright!" Pleasantly surprised, he handed her two tins. "The blue is protein; the green is carbs."

Emma said, "but both taste like mackerel snot."

"Excellent!" Fallon peeled back the aluminum lid, sniffed. "I love mackerel snot."

"I found a marriable woman!" Danny beamed. "My mother will be proud."

"Marriage," Fallon dipped a finger in the grim looking spread. "You're living in the wrong century, History Boy."

Emma asked, "How's it smell? Like orangutan ass, doesn't it?"

"Honestly, I can't tell if it's this stuff that stinks so bad or…all of them." She nodded toward the flying monkey corpses scattered over the lawn, their bioluminescent faces snuffed out, cold and blotchy.

"Maybe we should get rid of them." Danny dropped his food back inside the bag.

"I'll do it," Emma offered.

"Heh, yeah," he said. "But we wanna eat today."

"No," she took his arm. "You wanna see another one?"

"Another what?"

"Yeah, we do." Fallon remembered the paper clips she'd fired at Bulldozer Bob, *Edward Hyde, Emma? That's not one of your 200 Disney movies.* "You have something that'll clean this place up?"

Danny understood. "Oh…no kidding?"

"Stand back a bit." She moved to what she figured to be the center of the carnage, withdrew her worn notebook, and rifled through a few pages before landing on a particular poem. "Ready?"

"You think you need the poems?" Fallon asked.

"I know I do."

"Try it without them. Just focus your thoughts," she said. "See what happens."

272

"Nothing will happen," Emma raised her palms skyward, suggesting that she'd give it a go but already knowing she'd end up looking like a grimacing fool.

"Humor me," Fallon said.

"Why?" Danny asked.

"I'm thinking those little poems might have been something she needed in childhood. You know? Just to focus the core of her consciousness. Maybe now they're superfluous"

"I've never known what that word means," Danny said.

"Jackass."

"No kidding. I have no idea what super...whatever means."

"It means that I think her poems might just be a crutch she needed as a little kid, and if she can blow up an attacking dog, an attacking enemy, or maybe even an *army* of attacking enemies, I'd just as soon she do it without always going fishing for that notebook."

"It's okay," Emma said. "I'll try." She peeked at the page again, then stuffed it into her cargo pants. "Here we go!"

Breeze over the corn freshened, causing half a million leaves to rustle gently like acres of sandpaper smoothing splintery wood. Fallon and Danny watched without moving as Emma first bent her knees slightly, leaned forward, breathed deeply through her nose, and brandished a genuine angry-little-girl frown at the two-thousand pounds of dead ape-wolves, including Jerry Lee, whose component parts lay tossed about like a bread crumb trail to Hell.

Nothing happened.

Still game, Emma tried for another minute or two, huffing and blowing great breaths, wincing and staring, all with no results. Finally, she threw her hands up. "Nope. Sorry, Fallon. I've gotta use my verses."

"That's okay, sweetie," Fallon said, unconvinced. "We'll try again another time."

Emma checked the notebook again, as if she might have forgotten one rhyming couplet in less than a minute. Bending her knees and focusing her attention on the largest toss of dead ape-wolves, she said, "No handsome boys or pretty dress until I clean this horrid mess."

Danny laughed. "What? Really? That's supposed to strike fear into the hearts of an invading army. Sorry, but I'm not buying it."

Emma ignored him.

Fallon watched the dismembered corpses. "Shhh. Pay attention."

"Okay," Danny said, then leaned in close, whispered, "You want some coffee? I need some. I think I'm gonna go make—"

Through gritted teeth, she hissed, "Just goddamned stand there for two frigging minutes, or I'm going to barbecue your ass with molten fire. Alright?"

"You have to catch my ass first, skinny," he teased, still watching nothing happen in the dooryard. "I travel as smoke and mist. Remember?"

"Yawn. That's me yawning on command."

"It's a pretty cool trick," he insisted. "You just wish you had half the—holy shit, Fallon!" He pointed dumbly at the remains of Jerry Lee not five feet away. "Are you seeing this?"

"Yup. And I think we're gonna agree not to doubt her again. Yes?"

"Um, yeah. Sorry. Whatever you say."

As they watched, Jerry Lee's carcass, then the bits of stringy, unidentifiable ape-wolf remains, bones, slabs of pink-but-slowly-browning organ, skin, hair, every last trace of him began gathering itself up and meandering, as if dragged by an invisible length of twine, to an area of dry grass down near the corn, where Emma stood, gesturing and beckoning the fallen creatures to her, just calling friends in for dessert. Across the dooryard, a patch of raspberry bushes and a scraggly evergreen shrub began twitching and shaking as if all at once infested with a family of squirrels.

"What's that?" Fallon pointed.

"Parts of him," Danny pointed at Jerry Lee's corpse as it slid head first into Emma's swelling pile of ape-wolf flotsam and jetsam. "I think a liver and a bit of flying monkey intestine shot over my head when he…well, popped."

"Holy mother of God."

"Yeah, but look at the others, the few I killed and the goddamned platoon you slaughtered…all by your selfie."

"Teach you to piss me off, cutie pie."

"Heh, sure, and I'm the one with relationship issues. Right."

Fallon tapped a fingertip on her chin, feigning deep thought. "Hmm, what was it you said? Oh, I remember: *Kleen straws. You can drink out of a public toilet with them.*"

Danny swallowed. "Yeah, alright."

Fallon put her arm around his shoulders. "How do you do it? The mist thing."

"I dunno."

"What happens to your vid-screen, your clothes? Does it all just…"

"Yeah," he slipped an arm around her waist. "Bulky shoes. I can't do bulky shoes. Otherwise, it all just sort of comes along. The wrist screen is the easiest."

"Makes sense," Fallon pulled him closer. "It's attached."

"Yup." Danny would have stood there all night.

Fallon changed the subject. "Can you believe what this little girl is doing? I mean, that's gotta be a ton of dead bodies. And she's dragging them into a funeral pyre, with her goddamned poetry, a poem she probably wrote when she was eight and had to clean up her room. Are you shitting me?"

"The power of poetry," Danny tucked his shoulder farther beneath her arm. "I should've paid attention in English class."

"Heh, you never had an English class, dumbass."

"Yeah, okay. You got me. I wouldn't know Faulkner from *Fahrenheit 451* from Fagiello."

"Not bad, History Boy. You're not fooling anyone." After the day's terrifying turn of events, neither wanted to admit that pressed up against one another was as comforting as it was sexy. Just feeling connected was enough for now. Where their relationship might evolve, neither could say. But standing together for a moment's grace, neither cared much. Tomorrow could wait. Two entirely contented minutes later, Fallon said, "Look at that. She's amazing."

"She is," he agreed. "We are. We all are. It's like we're...God's rough drafts. You know? Like the next thing coming, the next step in some evolutionary...ah, I dunno."

"You don't believe in God," Fallon said. "God died in the Cloud Wars. Jesus Christ is just an expletive these days."

"I..." he shrugged. "Maybe I believe sometimes, when I'm running from the bulls."

"Yeah, then," she said. "That's a good time."

"And when the drones hit low turbulence."

Still gesturing in a non-verbal language only she (and the ape-wolf remains) understood, Emma dragged two dozen corpses and Danny's bloody, cracked, porch railing into a rag-tag, clumsy pile nearly fifteen feet high. She accomplished it all without saying anything more than those two lines of rhyming silliness that had started Danny to giggling. When the last of the creatures' remains joined their fallen comrades, Emma stood a moment, then withdrew the notebook from her pocket and turned through a few pages. Reading silently, she shook her head, pocketed the notes, and climbed back up the grassy hummock to where Danny and Fallon waited.

"You okay?" Danny asked.

"I can't do it." Tears dampened her cheeks, blurred her vision. "I know they tried to kill us, but I can't...can't set them on fire."

Fallon took her hand. "You don't have to. It's alright. We won't be here long enough for them to smell too bad. And that moldy paste Danny likes stinks so frigging awful, even if they do start to smell, we'll just blame him."

"You sure?" Emma cried into Fallon's shoulder. "Because, if you want, I'll—"

"Not at all," Danny said. "She's right: let's just leave them. We'll probably be gone from here by tomorrow night, the morning after at the latest."

"I don't wanna eat out here."

"Neither do I," Fallon said. "C'mon, let's go in. We can take turns standing watch." She and Danny led the younger girl inside. On the top porch step, Fallon held the screen door open for Danny and Emma, then took a lingering, appreciative look at what the young terrorist had done. The stack of ape-wolf corpses rose against the twilight, an improbable testament to an astonishing young woman. Fallon silently promised she would never underestimate Emma's talents.

13

More Corn, a Nightmare, and Pork Belly Surprise

Later, after they'd eaten tins of foul-smelling paste, asked and answered a laundry list of questions, and inflated their stolen camp mattresses, Danny and Emma curled up to sleep, while Fallon took the first watch. When she was certain they'd drifted off, she moved into the field, allowing the stalks to wrap her in quiet anonymity. Like a kid playing hide and seek, she hoped that safely beneath protective waves of cornflowers, she might actually be invisible to whoever had been sending creatures to kill her.

No. Not kill me. Kill Danny. Take me; take Emma, but kill Danny. That's important; don't forget that.

She walked, following the unholy stench of imminent putrefaction wafting east from a torn and flattened spot near the center of the field. It didn't take long to get there, to assess what Danny had done.

They were easy to find; their faces—the ones clinging to life, anyway—glowed like macabre holiday ornaments strewn about the cornfield for some sinister harvest festival. At least a dozen ape-wolves lay in various stages of twisted, broken agony, decapitation, and unimaginable dismemberment.

The corn did this? Because Danny asked it to? That's not possible.

A soft, guttural cough sounded from off to her left. Fallon jumped, then focused, thinking: *fire.* Both hands lit almost immediately. She held them aloft, bringing weak illumination to the carnage. "Where are you?"

A second cough, this one barely a wheeze, came again, followed by the brief rustle of autumn stalks. Fighting the urge to run, she turned toward the sound and lit a section of fallen rows where one of the creatures lay, still knotted indelibly in a half dozen unforgiving corn plants, two clearly about its neck, and two about each muscular arm. Its face glowed pale green but dim and dying.

The creature's legs had been broken like twigs, one summarily torn off below the knee. Still bleeding slowly, much of its wound had clotted. She couldn't guess how long it might live, trapped here but was too frightened to try unraveling Danny's corn, had no sense of what it might do to her if she freed the monster to die in peace.

Fallon knelt beside it, tried and failed to form the words welling up in her chest. *I'm sorry.*

"No, I'm not sorry." She intensified both hands, brightening the flame until she was able to set the whole clearing alight. Walking a lap of the periphery, she cast fire onto the corpses and dragged her burning hands over the corn plants, igniting the battleground with cleansing flame. As the bodies and corn stalks illuminated the night behind her, Fallon returned to the dooryard and watched until the fire burned out two hours later.

All the while she thought of Danny Hackett.

She drifted off a few times, woke once when she heard him comforting Emma inside. The younger girl had awakened from a nightmare. Fallon supposed Emma would be experiencing those for weeks.

Later—she had no idea what time it was—Fallon woke from her own nightmare. She'd been standing in an open field. Young timothy grew about her ankles. She could see for miles in all directions; there were no trees, no buildings, nothing to obstruct the view.

From a distance they came, marching like single-minded soldiers, rows and rows of diabolical, homicidal corn stalks, twelve feet high, moving immutably towards her from all points of the compass. Fallon ignited both hands, threw fire into their ranks, burning thousands, tens of thousands to ash, but still they came, hell bent to carry her off and tear her to pieces.

She shouted for Danny to call them off. But the boy couldn't hear. He was in the back seat of their stolen car, transfixed by the vid screens, hoping to get a news broadcast. Fallon didn't understand how he could be so stupid. Did he not see the corn coming for her, not know that she was going to die a ghastly death here in this beautiful place?

"Danny!" She cried.

He ignored her, fiddling with wires, plugging and unplugging cables and cords behind the old Chevron's interactive screens.

The corn was upon her. Fallon withdrew inside herself, ignored the tendrils of uncertainty as the first stalks wrapped insidious leaves around her ankles, wrists, and neck. Deep inside, she located her warm core, the center of her unexpected talents. She understood immediately that this was the place where she might fan that furnace of fury and discontentment, the one that had been trying to break free from her control ever since she'd been framed for Claire Felver's murder.

And ever since Blair raped her. She'd been thinking that, but hadn't said it. How she longed to tell him, in the moments before he died, it was his brutality that had unlocked her seemingly limitless power. She'd killed the snake without touching it, had slaughtered dozens of ape-wolves, had set those two convicts on fire. She'd never been able to do anything that focused or destructive.

Until Blair.

Emma was there, inside her chest, (not at all surprisingly) sitting beside the caricature, metaphor furnace as if waiting for Fallon to arrive. "I knew you'd figure it out." The red headed girl motioned toward the bellowing fire. "Here it is. You know what you have to do." The furnace glowed red. Flames flickered and seeped from loose rivets and seams in the metal housing. The couplings holding the furnace to the floor rattled loosely as the glowing monstrosity huffed and bellowed.

Fallon let it go.

A colossal eruption of fire, wind, and loathing burst from her chest, detonating outward like a bomb, incinerating militant corn stalks for miles around. Shock waves of energy followed the initial explosion, radiating out from the teenager, crushing everything in sight. The Chevron, with Danny inside, crumpled like a soda can and was cast hundreds of feet into the uniform rows of burning stalks.

Exhausted, Fallon stood among the timothy, her chest torn open, her rage extinguished like a candle flame, and her only friends gone, both destroyed by the untethered power sleeping inside her. She dabbed a bloody finger inside her eviscerated chest cavity, swooned dizzily, and collapsed.

"Danny!" Fallon woke with a spastic jerk.

Dawn blanketed the farmyard with the innocent promise of a new day. Fresh dew soaked her jeans and sweatshirt. Both felt heavy, as if the burden she'd carry today was already too much.

Breathing in ragged gasps, her heart thudding, Fallon ran both hands over her face, through her hair. The dream had seemed vividly real, like a film in a sim room. She'd only visited one once, to see a remake of an old adventure film, *King Kong*, but recalled getting seasick on the cargo ship as the theater floor moved and the screen blew chilly salt air into her face.

"It's just like a dream, honey," her mother had said and turned Fallon around so she could see the narrow exit curtain behind them. "Just a dream."

But no one really dreamed any more.

Fallon lay back, waited for welcome calm to find her. "Just a dream," she whispered. "You're all right. It was just—"

Icy fingers gripped her heart. Fallon stopped breathing, didn't even blink. There, between her legs rose one, ten-foot corn stalk, still green but fading to dry and rustly brown—*the perfect Halloween stalk from a haunted field.*

It came for her in the night, climbed somehow, impossibly, up the grassy hummock behind the farmhouse, and planted itself beside the sleeping girl. It hadn't attacked, hadn't moved, hadn't attempted to drag her off to an end worse than her imagination could ever summon, even from her most colorful nightmares. Rather, the lone stalk had simply reached out with one green leaf and taken her securely by the ankle.

The furnace warmed again, for real this time. Fallon felt the couplings holding it to the floor of her soul come loose and rattle as the fires inside tried to burst free. Yanking her foot back, she said, "Oh, no you don't." And scrabbled a few feet away, ass clawing and digging her heels in wet grass.

The corn stalk didn't follow, just swayed gently in the breeze brushing the farm.

"Danny Hackett, I am going to beat your ass a hundred ways to Sunday," Fallon bent, took the corn plant in both hands, low near the ground, and heaved it out by the roots. Moving toward the rows, she woke her fire and set the stalk to blazing. Facing the field beside the rotting, fly-specked stack of ape-wolf carcasses, she reared back and tossed the burning plant as far as she could into the dewy green sea. It disappeared, then burned out, leaving only a ribbon of smoke rising in the morning sunshine.

Behind her, the screen door whapped shut. "Good morning," Danny groaned through a heavy yawn. "You okay? Why didn't you wake me?"

She turned, "Oh, I dunno. I thought I'd let you sleep in."

Still groggy, he missed the sublime anger. "Well... thanks. You're all wet. You wanna go change? I'm gonna see about fixing the vid screens in the car, maybe get us a news report this morning." He carried several folds of yellowing paper. "I found a paper map upstairs. It's forty years old, so some of the roads might be impassable, but if we stick to woods, we ought to be alright."

Fallon climbed to the porch. "Do you know what you're doing, Danny? Do you really?"

"With the car? No. But how hard can it be? And if I can't fix it, I think we let Emma try, you know, with one of her poems. Maybe get lucky."

282

"Not with the car, you idiot." Wriggling breaths of smoke climbed from where she'd cast the murdered corn plant. "Out there. Do you know what you're doing? What you did?"

"Yeah, well...I...no. I mean, it's worked before, so I figured I'd try again," he stammered. "Why? I took care of them, got Emma back, ended it quick and easy."

She pushed past him up the porch stairs.

"Hey, what's burning out there? What'd you burn?"

"One of your soldiers." She passed through the screen door, then turned to him. "We've gotta be careful. You can't start waking up Nature every time you're in a tight spot." She pointed to the cornfield. "There's a hundred thousand killers out there now, just waiting for you to tell them what to do."

"Hey," he handed her a Prevoxycillin tablet. "Take this."

"I don't need it.'

"We haven't got the first clue what you might be infected with." He pressed the medication into her hand. "Take it."

"Fine," Fallon dry swallowed the pill then let the door close behind her.

Danny watched her go.

Fallon had a point. He understood enough of his own limitations to know that Nature and the forces driving the perpetuation of life on Earth were powerful enough to crush him like a mosquito, to shrug off the entire human race if it wanted to. Hell, it nearly had...a hundred years earlier, with cancer, AIDS, obesity, Diabetes. Danny's grandfather remembered when over eighty percent of the population had been overweight or obese, and dying. That had been before the wars, the Corn War from '34 to '41...and the Cloud Wars. Well, those...those had never really ended.

He recognized Nature's power. Most people didn't. He understood that. He just struggled to get Fallon to believe him.

Their problem wasn't Nature. Their problem was one another.

Danny had never ordered Nature to do anything for him. Rather, he'd asked, even begged a few times, and (much to his surprise and pleasure), Nature had complied. Even when he had wanted to kill old Arlen Howard, the pedophile ghoul who had been referring elementary school kids from Jackson out to chop shops and Prevotel storefront brokers, frigging criminals willing to tattoo a six-year-old with a recall date ten years later, for a couple of thousand credits to poverty-stricken parents. Nature had helped him kill Arlen, had animated an entire mass grave of animal carcasses, had allowed Danny to make them talk, to drive Arlen mad. He'd hoped the old monster might off himself, just jump into the pit and bury his useless soul beneath a few shovelfuls of flesh-disintegrating lye. But he hadn't.

Instead, batshit old Arlen had run his pickup onto Barton's Hill and been deliciously smeared to warm dogshit by one of those hulking garbage trucks that run down there at about 80 mph every afternoon.

That'd been better, entertaining. Although, the lye probably would've hurt more.

Arlen deserved it. Referring poor kids to storefront chop shops so their parents can be deceived into selling off organs or body parts...that was a shitty thing to do. Danny would never mourn the fact that Arlen had been launched through the window of his pickup and about a hundred-and-fifty feet down Barton's Hill, face first.

Manipulating poor parents with the promise of short-term credits for long-term trades, that deserved the death penalty, an ugly one, with fear and pain and cruel, unusual punishment.

Nature had helped him do it.

Danny couldn't blame the parents. They were doing what had to be done to make ends meet. Mothers, fathers, desperate to keep their children safe, healthy, and (from time to time) happy, would agree to almost any brokerage agreement when the kids were five or six. Why not? With ten years to wait, who knew what technology might arise? Ten years meant hope. Ten years meant progress and innovation. Ten years could mean that the obese, German businessman in town for only two days and shopping for his daughter's sixteenth birthday (ten years out) might fall over dead, might lose his daughter to disease, a catastrophe, a natural disaster, hurricane, tornado, great white frigging shark, anything to be able to tell that six-year-old girl that her eye or her foot or her kidney were safe. No one was coming for her; her vid screen wouldn't start blinking and then braying when it was time to report for dismemberment. Just ride the storm, kiddies. Ride the storm and wake up with a shit-brown eye, a faulty ankle ligament, a crooked back, a leaky kidney, a missing hand.

Just ride the storm.

Danny didn't want to get angry with Fallon this morning. He understood her. He understood why she was concerned, why she felt the need to protect Emma but also why she feared Emma. He understood that Fallon would never compromise. Uncompromising women were rare, beautiful, and infuriating creatures, and Danny hoped that he'd never see the day when Fallon left him—because that's how it would end: she'd leave him—alone.

He hadn't known many, but he somehow felt confident that uncompromising women would leave him dumbstruck, stupid, and begging for mercy.

Nope. He wasn't going to get angry with Fallon. They had too much to accomplish today.

But he was angry. She was being unfair, hadn't appreciated all he'd managed to do, didn't give him credit for the care and concern he'd shown her and Emma in the past week.

Sure, she did, dumbass. She kissed you yesterday morning. You forget that already?

Feeling disconnected, he strode listlessly down the lawn. When he saw Emma's pile of ape-wolf corpses, already crawling with flies, worms and all manner of frigging nasty bacteria, he decided.

Yes, this would make for an invigorating bit of early morning exercise.

Danny sat, crossed his legs, got comfortable in the cold, dewy grass.

A wet ass. How much damage can you really do with a wet ass, dopey?

Turning his thoughts inward, he reached out to the corn stalks. It required only a moment's concentration. A simple request, he cast it across the field several times, and was about to give up, to wander back inside, apologize for whatever it was that Fallon believed he'd done, and then serve up a pot of southern chicory coffee as a peace offering.

They answered.

They were coming.

They'd been troubled by Fallon burning a few of their number late the previous night. But they understood.

Nature always understood.

And they'd help him.

Opening his eyes, Danny caught the first ripples of incoming tide, disturbances here and there about the field. Having worked similar episodes of genuine magic over the past few years, he remained awestruck—equal parts impressed and terrified—every time the natural world agreed to assist him. In Hinds County, he'd been running from the bulls investigating Arlen Howard's death and just cast his thoughts out to the swamp across old route 529. The trees, shrubs, and underbrush had responded in just a few seconds, had injured the two officers, and would have torn them to shreds if Danny had asked.

Now, the corn came to life, organizing itself into a mile-long bucket brigade. Vast exhalations of energy coursed across the field like a rapidly moving tide; Danny likened the stalks' behavior to rolling waves on the ocean.

They're agreeing. Discussing. I wish Fallon could see this.

When the stalks at the field's edge reached over to collect the ape-wolves, Danny moved closer. Brushing dew from the ass of his new pants, he sidled to within a few feet of the field, didn't want to interrupt, but needed to witness the miracle.

Working together, the stalks wrapped about the arms, legs, even the necks of the monsters. Hauling them skyward, the plant army passed bodies along, like teenagers crowd surfing at a rock concert, until the ape-wolves vanished into a shallow gulley between the field and the encroaching forest half a mile away.

When the last of the ape-wolves had been carried off, and even the remnants of Jerry Lee had been tossed away as so much fertilizer, Danny once again turned his thoughts inward, breathed quietly a moment, then sent *thank you* into the chilly morning.

Upstairs, Fallon watched the unlikely exchange and decided that similar to her newfound respect for Emma Carlisle, she would not underestimate Danny Hackett again.

After two hours of failed attempts, Danny considered giving up on the vid screens in the Chevron.

"Sorry," Emma said. She'd been sitting in the grass, chatting with him and watching as the older boy grew steadily more frustrated with the aging car. "But if it's any consolation, the peach grader works great. We just need some peach trees."

"You wanna try?" He slipped a screwdriver into his pocket. Tucked in the cramped back seat, he'd sweat through his t-shirt, despite the chilly morning. "I'm betting you've got something in that notebook for fixing the projection screen at your house. Maybe that'd work. You wanna give it a go?"

Emma played with her pen. "Sorry. I can't do anything with technology. I can't fix a toilet, can't stop a leaky sink, can't program a wrist screen, none of it. I've never been able to. Dunno why."

"That's interesting," Danny said. "You can blow up a dog as if he's got a bomb jammed in his poodle rectum, but you can't adjust the colors on the projection screen in your living room?"

"Nope. I've tried a few times. Last year, the aroma control was off on my mom's screen. We'd watch a murder mystery, and the room would smell of Florida citrus trees. I thought it was great. The worst was a cooking show my mother loves."

"Wait," Danny interrupted. "Lemme guess: the aromas were from a documentary on sanitation challenges in Mexico City."

"Close!" Emma said. "Liver transfer video!"

"Yikes. That must've been special."

Fallon looked up from their map, interrupted the banter. "I don't know how useful this thing is." She traced a county road with her fingertip. "But I think if we take 17 to 50, we can turn north on 611 and have back roads all the way to the Potomac."

"Why there?" Emma climbed inside the Chevron, toyed with the exposed wires dangling from one of the disconnected vid screens. "You know someone?"

"I'd been thinking we could visit a campground. We have several in Old Forge, and I bet campgrounds in the Shenandoahs will be the same. The spaces all have bio wire hook ups and network connections. People pay for however many days they log in while camping. A local server keeps track." She held up the map as if it might help her explanation feel reasonable. "I figured we'd sneak in through the woods, plug in, transfer those credits, watch the news, and be gone before the network rebooted and found us...hopefully around 3:00 a.m. A lot of rural networks don't turn over until the middle of the night."

"But..." Danny twirled two fingers.

"But...I changed my mind."

"Why? That campground idea feels like a good one. I think it'll work."

Fallon explained. "I'm betting that the river—"

"Which river?" Emma asked. "The Potomac or the Shenandoah?"

"Harpers Ferry!" Danny added. "My favorite class. I paid attention in that one."

Fallon frowned. "I don't give a shit which river, knucklehead. Either river will do just fine. What we need is a cottage, out of season. Granted, there might be some people out that way for autumn—"

"Leaf peepers," Emma cut in. "That's what my grandmother always called them, out where they still have trees that change colors, not the genetically, you know, weird manipulated ones that stay green all the time."

"Them," Fallon agreed. "Exactly. We need a cottage...*two* cottages."

"Two?" Danny asked. "We're living in a mostly demolished farmhouse. Forgive me if I'm skeptical, but I dunno what we'd do with two cottages."

"Listen, if we believe that someone is tracking us because of our skills...our gifts, if you prefer...then we need a place from which we can watch a place where we've logged in and deliberately used our skills."

Emma brightened. "I get it!"

"I don't," Danny said. "Someone help the dumb kid."

Emma hopped out of the car, motioned for him to follow. "We find a cottage, one with no leaf peepers—"

"Exactly."

"But it has to be near, like really near, another cottage with no leaf peepers."

"Yup."

"Oh, wait," Danny caught up. "So we go into one cottage and use all our skills, talents, curses, whatever—"

"And we log in," Fallon said. "Why not? What the hell...they're sending all manner of creepy crawlies and murderers against us. We might as well leave whole loaves of bread on this trail."

"Yes," Danny tossed the broken vid screen onto the back seat, joined them on the sunny lawn. "We leave our stink all over the place, then hide next door...no skills, nothing at all...and wait."

"By candlelight," Fallon tossed him the map. "And we watch."

"For Mr. Colossus," Danny said.

"Edward Hyde," Emma smiled up at them both. "We hide out and watch for him to come and destroy the place. That might even be fun."

"Oh, yeah," Danny teased. "While we're logged on, we can just order out for Kung Pao chicken."

"Actually, we can. Why not? I haven't had decent Kung Pao in weeks. Any Kung Pao, come to think of it."

"What if more of those...*things* come?" Emma glanced into the empty dooryard. "Those monkey-dog things. I...guys, I didn't like those."

"Yeah," Danny said, "but with two seconds to recite your lessons, dear, it's as if you've stuffed them into a microwave and pressed EXPLODE. I gotta admit; I'm not worried."

"We can't fight Mr. Colossus," Fallon said. "Not head to head. We're not that strong."

"Unless you can blow him up," Danny suggested.

"He's not dog enough," Emma shook her head. "They've gotta be a little bit dog, mean dog, for it to work. I don't think I could blow up a nice dog."

"So if he shows, we hide."

"Exactly," Emma said, eager to agree.

"But if anyone or any*thing* else should show up looking for us—"

"Hunting us, you mean," Danny said. "We hide and watch."

"Yes," Fallon took back the map. "Let's go."

"We're done working on the vid screen?" Danny asked. "I can't get it to pick up a signal. Sorry."

"Yeah, we're done," Fallon said. "You did okay today." She tilted her head toward the corn, standing silent sentry behind them.

"I didn't...you know..."

"I saw," she said. "It's impressive. But I'm not sure they know about you and your talents."

"Because they were willing to kill me?"

"Yeah."

"Then we have the advantage?"

"If you can make frigging corn tear people apart, literally limb from limb...I mean how often do you get to use that phrase and actually mean it?"

"Yeah, okay," he agreed. "Let's go."

Dogleg Lane turned left from Bakersville Road in Washington County, Maryland, about eighty miles north of Warrenton. And while several of the roads Fallon selected from the forty-year-old map now ran through treeless suburban developments packed with clone, twenty-first century, eco-friendly mansions and another cut through a five-mile swath of over a hundred-thousand solar panels, Bakersville and Dogleg Lane remained quintessential examples of thickly forested, back county, antebellum America. Progress and technology had clearly missed the stretch of Dogleg Lane where it ran downhill to the Potomac River Valley.

Stopping at one juncture to search for road signs, Fallon stepped out to stretch her legs and found herself knees to nose with an actual red fox. None of them had ever seen one in the wild. Fallon shrieked loudly enough to scare off a battalion of foxes and any other critters crouched in the shrubbery. Another half mile along Dogleg—headed for the banks of the Potomac—they spotted a family of whitetail deer, a sizeable snapping turtle, about three hundred squirrels (all of which suffered from delusions of grandeur), and even one raccoon that eyed

291

Fallon with such a look of mistrust that the teen silently promised to improve her attitude—if she survived the evening.

"Looks like Nature is out in force to greet us," Danny said, pointing to another clutch of gray squirrels, chasing one another about a fallen cedar.

"Sure is," Emma leaned against the front seats from the back. With the small wooden box beside her, she kept a wary watch out the front window, hoping for a black bear, perhaps down near the riverbanks.

"There've gotta be a stretch of cottages down this way," Fallon said. "The river can't be more than another mile or two. We'll find them, hopefully a good long row of them, all deserted."

"Yeah," Danny agreed. "It won't do us any good to drive all the way out here just to discover that we've come during Leaf Week or Corn Fest, and everyone is here."

"They won't be," Fallon said. "I can feel it. This is gonna work."

"Oh, yeah," Emma chided. "I love being twenty miles out in forgotten wilderness all night when prehistoric supernatural monsters are chasing me."

"Right," Danny said. "Especially when I go to the woods on purpose."

Fallon snorted through her nose. The two of them had a point. She slugged Danny in the shoulder, shoved Emma gently down in the back, and said, "What's that sound, kiddies? Oh, that? That's just the dinner bell."

"Not funny!" Emma yelled. "Not funny at all, Fallon."

The three friends drove another four miles into the willywags before Danny decided to try what appeared to be a well-traveled dirt road south, in the general direction of the river.

A half mile farther on, the road sloped sharply downward. "This is it," Fallon said. "The river gorge, it's gotta be."

Danny slowed, piloting the Chevron carefully and checking every few hundred feet to ensure they'd have enough space to turn around if this road proved to be a bust.

"There," Emma pointed through colorful foliage. "That's a house. Oh, and there's the water. Nice work, Danny!"

Fallon rolled down her window. The temperature had fallen noticeably as they'd dropped from the piedmont into the river gorge. "Turn here," she said. "Looks like an access road; hopefully there are more cottages along the way. This one won't do."

"Not sure I like this," Danny turned into what proved to be an even narrower dirt lane. Studded with weeks of stubbly grass and sedge growth, this lane didn't look to have seen any traffic since summer, if not longer.

"Nope," Fallon said. "It's exactly what we need; we've just gotta find…"

"Find what?" Emma asked.

Five minutes later, Fallon answered. "Find that!"

The goat path Danny had been following opened onto a stretch of sunny, scenic riverbend at least a half mile about a quarter circle of sloping lawn, summer cottages, PVC and synthetic-wood boat docks (only two of which had been pulled onto the bank for winter), and apparently empty cottages – five of them in a sloppy row. To the north and west, autumn had colored the Potomac river valley in orange, red, yellow, even pauper's gold. Winter would soon roll through with devastating conviction, but for now, the hillside and river bank strutted together in their annual act of brilliantly colorful defiance.

"Oh, I wanna live here," Emma poked her head out the window. "Can we live here?"

"Sure, Em," Danny said. "Just pick one."

"That one," she pointed to a happy, yellow cottage, a single-family place with a brick chimney and a red canoe on concrete blocks out back.

"Sorry," Fallon said. "Not that one."

"Why? I like yellow."

"So do I, but we need two together, preferably one just a bit higher up the bank…" Fallon craned to see around the bend. "There. Danny, you see it? The white one with the green shutters."

"Yup. You want me to pull down there and park?"

"No," she pointed up the slope. "I want you to stash the car in the woods behind that one, with the fibro siding, there on the rise."

Danny turned up the sloping driveway. "And no skills in this place. Right?"

"Nothing," Fallon looked back at Emma. "We don't even heat a cup of tea in this place unless it's with traditional, non-skilled, non-gifted, non-cursed, whatever you wanna call it means. We all agree?"

Emma nodded. "Sure."

"We're gonna go down there, to that place, and make all kinds of magical noise. Danny can talk the grass into dancing the hula. Emma you can blow up the hot water heater—"

"I'm not good with techno—"

"Whatever," Fallon smiled. "We're gonna stink the place up, give them somewhere to search for us."

"And that's where we're plugging in," Danny said.

"Exactly," Fallon said. "So whether it's an E-copter full of armored bulls, a vampire snake with a laser penis or the frigging Loch Ness monster, we're gonna try to draw them to *that* place and not *this* one."

"Makes sense. That way we'll know, and we'll have the advantage if it ends in another fight." Danny pulled the Chevron across the weedy grass and beneath the fiery, outstretched limbs of an accommodating maple. Twenty feet farther on, the Chevron disappeared entirely. Shadows wrapped them up tight; Danny thumbed the engine switch off. For a moment, the friends sat in silent darkness. "How's this?"

"Perfect," Fallon reached for her bag. "Nice work."

Still carrying her box, Emma pushed open the rear door. "Let's go. I wanna explore a little before the vampire snake with the laser whizzer shows up."

Danny laughed. "Yeah, if he arrives, I'm gonna run."

They made certain that both the white cottage with the green shutters and the little house with the fibro siding were empty. Fallon noted electronic combination locks on a shed behind the white cottage and a traditional key card lock on the basement and patio doors of the fibro place.

"These people are gone for the season," she said. "This is perfect."

"How about caretakers?" Danny asked. "You know…local guys with wrenches and waterproof tape and stuff."

Fallon dragged a toe in the dirt. "Gotta risk it."

"Okay. How you wanna play it?" he asked. "If anyone is tracking us and we can trust the last few days as indicators, we've got maybe two hours once the clock starts ticking."

"Let's try for less than that," Emma suggested. "Just to be safe. You know?"

"I agree," Fallon tried the back door on the fibro place. "Locked." She punched random numbers on the key pad.

"Don't hit enter," Emma said. "Too many false entries and the county cops will be here." She searched about in the fallow flower beds beneath what looked to be a bedroom window.

"What're you doing?" Danny asked, ushering Fallon to one side.

"What're *you* doing?" Fallon asked him.

"I'm gonna use my elbow to break this window. We can just open the door from the inside." He wrapped his sweatshirt several times around his arm, padding it in thick folds.

"Be careful," Fallon stepped back. "Or wait, knucklehead. Let me do it."

"Don't!" Emma called, waving a rock she'd discovered half buried in last spring's mulch. "We can use this."

295

"Oh, yeah," Danny unraveled the sweatshirt. "That's a better idea. Thanks, Em."

She sidled past him. "I'll do it."

"Careful," Danny said. "You don't want to cut—" He stopped short when, instead of bashing the small window with the rock, Emma turned it over and entered the key code engraved on the bottom. The door lock flashed red twice, then blinked green. "Holy shit! Nice job."

"Seasonal rental," she explained. "Families lease these places for a week at a time. They go out on the water all day, get themselves good and drunk, and then come home in the afternoon having forgotten how to get back in. All these cabins have a code stashed somewhere."

"Good thinking," Fallon clapped her on the back. "But we're going into the next place with a little more fanfare."

The younger girl tossed the stone into the mulch. "That'll be fun, too."

Fallon followed Danny inside. "Remember, you two, not even a whisper of any skills or talents in this place. Not a ripple."

"Got it," Danny said, and led them into the small but tidy summer house that stank with the faint memory of 10,000 Ecuadorian cigars and a squadron of wet dogs. They'd hide for the night, taking turns watching the river, the bank, and the cozy white cottage with the green shutters for any sign that they'd been tracked.

The friends needed only about three minutes to decide that while the little cabin had been essentially stripped of all its essentials – there was some canned food, a few candles, and two wool blankets in a hallway closet—the riverside cabin with the inexpensive fibro siding was the nicest place any of them had stayed since their respective arrests.

"Look at this," Emma held up a scented candle in a hurricane glass. "Lavender! We won't have to smell Danny tonight...or whatever that is: damp animal."

"Heh," Fallon chuckled. "Light that sucker right now, Em."

"When we get back," Danny played along. "I might smell, but the last thing we need to do is burn this place down."

"Right!" Fallon dropped her voice to a sinister growl. "I wonder where they're hiding now, Leopold. Perhaps, sir, we should check that bright orange glow in the sky."

"All right," Emma rooted through a kitchen drawer, found a box of wooden matches. "Wow. I didn't even know they still made these."

"They don't," Danny said. "They've probably been in here for fifty years. But don't worry. We stole some E-lighters in Baltimore. They're in my bag."

"Musty in here," Fallon wrestled open two windows overlooking the river. "Let's let some breeze in. It's nice out today. We can take turns sleeping later. We all need a good night's rest."

Danny unloaded a half-dozen cans from a pantry beside the stove. "And a feast. We'll eat like kings."

"Yeah," Emma inspected the haul. "Kings who crave canned pasta, canned tuna, canned mixed vegetables, and canned...what is that? Pork belly? What in the name of Abraham Lincoln is pork belly?"

"Canned pork belly," Danny said. "This crew's from down south. You've gotta be a special brand of southern to buy canned pork belly on purpose."

"I can't wait," Fallon whined. "Fishy energy paste, canned pork bits, Danny you know how to show a woman a good time."

Excited, he clapped his hands noisily. "Well, then whaddya say we add felony breaking and entering, vandalism, destruction of private property, and illegal E-credit transfers to our list of party games?"

"Now that's a date."

On the porch of the white cottage beside the Potomac, Fallon checked the dirt access drive and up and downstream as far as she could see. "Two hours?"

"Give or take," Danny said.

"Let's be quick," Emma added, checking the river as well. "No boats, right? No hikers, canoes, water-skiers, nothing?"

"Nope," Danny confirmed, "we're alone out here. You wanna do the honors?"

Fallon set her jaw. "Noisy?"

"Noisy." He plugged his ears.

She faced the porch door, dropped her hands to her side, then with an incoherent shout, brought them up like a two-handed gunfighter, quick as a flash. Twin balls of dense, brilliant energy slammed into the doorway with the force of a runaway bus. The door buckled then shattered into flying splinters, some of which rained over the porch and the lawn where they fell, smoldering, a few in flames.

"Noisy," Danny followed her inside.

Fallon crossed to the center of the cottage's main room, a rectangular space lined on three sides with picture windows overlooking the river and West Virginia's colorful autumn showcase. Two comfy chairs and an old, leather couch were huddled about an expensive-looking Persian rug before a brick fireplace. If she weren't about to blast the place to rubble, Fallon thought she might like to spend the summer in a room just like this one, perhaps reading mystery novels or learning to be a better cook.

She turned a full circle, appreciating quiet, middle class comfort she and her mother would never be able to afford. When she found the room's interactive, projection screen, Fallon warned the others, "Not that. We need that."

"Right," Emma said. "But what're we gonna—"

"Duck," Fallon called up anger, fear, and isolation. She felt the very stitches and glue holding her together threaten to tear open.

"What for?" Emma asked. But Danny grabbed her, pulled the two of them down behind the couch.

"Head down, Em. Hold your ears," he said. "This is gonna hurt."

When Fallon released her will on the tidy, riverside cottage, the devastation that followed might have been the result of an artillery shell. Windows exploded outward. Furniture tore open and toppled. A coffee table was lifted and thrown into the fireplace where it broke apart. A gaudy, elk antler chandelier tore itself out by the electrical roots and careened wildly into the cottage's miniature kitchen, skewering antler-sized holes in varnished oak cabinets. The couch Danny and Emma huddled behind toppled onto them, simultaneously burying the two friends while also protecting them from other flying shrapnel or burning refuse.

Yet nothing struck the large interactive screen on the wall above the fireplace. As a matter of fact, the screen didn't move at all.

Danny grunted with the effort of bench pressing the sofa off his chest. "Holy shit!"

Emma agreed. "Yeah, that was something. Where did it come from?"

Fallon brushed rubble and splinters from her sweater. "I've been bottling up my emotions for a while now."

"I'll say," Danny pushed the sofa close to where it had been. "My ears will be ringing for six weeks, but I love what you've done with the place...*Early Dresden*." He hesitated. "What's the matter? You all right?"

Fallon flipped on power to the large screen. Familiar blue and white LOGIN logos appeared over a wallpaper pattern featuring two blonde children splashing in the Potomac with a caramel colored dog. "Yeah, I'm fine. I didn't want to damage the screen...wanted to wreck the place without damaging this."

He nodded. "You're getting better."

"I wonder what..."

299

"Yeah, I do, too. I only wish we had more time for you to experiment."

Recalling her nightmare, Fallon unobtrusively ran both hands over her chest, down her ribs, across her belly. The idea that she could generate enough force to blow herself apart hadn't frightened her as much that morning as it did now.

Emma gave her a quick squeeze, pressed her face into the crook of the taller girl's neck. "That was impressive. I was scared."

Fallon mussed her hair. "You don't have to be scared of me."

"Oh, I think everyone needs to be scared of you." Shreds of torn newsprint—from an ancient stash; paper news hadn't circulated in twenty-five years—fell about them like clumsy snowflakes.

Fallon watched as Emma unspooled a bio-wire from the room's projection screen. She didn't want these two to fear her, wanted that least of anything. These were the only friends she'd made in longer than she cared to remember. *Then stop blowing shit up, dumbass. Stop showing off.*

Reading her mind, Danny whispered, "It's all right. We're all right. That was gorgeous. Noisy but gorgeous." And again, for the hundredth time in four days, she didn't know whether to clobber him or to kiss him.

Emma interrupted. Holding aloft the eighth-inch bio-wire jack, she asked, "Who's logging in first? We gotta be quick."

Fallon gently pushed Danny toward her. "Him. We need access to his account before we see if your uncle has any credits left."

"Okay," Danny said. "Then, I wanna watch the news."

"Good," Fallon started for the kitchen. "I'll see if we can steal any more food."

Emma called from the fireplace, "tuna, pasta, or veggies, please. But not so much on the pork bellies this time. Okay?"

"Got it," Fallon searched the pantry. "You two get busy. I wanna be out of here in half an hour."

"I think we're okay," Danny held the wire jack; he hadn't plugged it into his wrist yet. "There's no way the servers out here bounce every hour. No way. I mean...we saw a fox for pity's sake. Do you have any idea how rural this is?"

"I get it," Fallon dumped a half-dozen cans into a cloth sack. "Let's just stick to the plan. The quicker we get the transfer done, the more time we have to see what's going on in the news. Being unplugged for the past week hasn't been good for us."

"I dunno about that," Emma rotated her wrist, considered the dark screen. "I kind of like it."

"Well, you're just left of sane, nutsy," Danny teased. "We've known that for days."

"No, really. I remember reading a human-interest story a few months back about a guy who disconnected his, just shut it down for like...years. When the avatars did the story, he could remember the credit price of every item, every frigging thing, in the Prevo-Mart in Lititz, Pennsylvania...Greg somebody."

"Proving what?" Fallon asked. "That our brains actually work when we're not plugged in or surfing some wireless cloud for government-approved bullshit? We knew that."

"That," Emma stacked cans into a miniature pyramid. "And the fact that maybe our ancestors weren't as primitive as we think, you know, walking around actually thinking about problems and discussing...solutions, ideas, anything, trying out recipes in the kitchen, you know, throwing ingredients in. My mother told me how my grandmother used to do that."

"Some people still do," Fallon said.

"I don't," Danny said.

"You eat stuff you hit with the car," Fallon said, "most times raw."

"Guilty," he threw his hands up. "But until you've tried opossum right off the vine, you haven't lived."

"Pork belly," Emma winced.

"The best part of the pig!"

"Focus, kiddies," Fallon said. "If this doesn't work, we'll be back eating state-approved potato and spinach paste between classes of state-approved content—"

"That probably won't address any of the credit prices in Lititz, Pennsylvania."

"Exactly," Fallon said, "wherever that is."

"Relax," Danny offered. "We did this right. Even if the servers turn over every twelve hours, it's gonna look like Emma's uncle transferred credits to my imaginary friend."

"Yeah, that's assuming they're not on to you. Carter's no dummy."

"All right," Danny nearly inserted the wire jack into his arm. "But if I should get fried in the next ten seconds…"

Fallon winced. "Not funny."

"Not kidding."

"Just do it." She held her breath.

"See you on the other side." He faced the screen, inserted the bio-wire jack, entered the login code, then waited.

Emma stood with both fists tightly balled and pressed hard against her mouth.

The projection screen morphed from LOGIN to WELCOME GABRIEL OAK.

Fallon turned to wipe her eyes on her sleeve. She hadn't permitted herself to imagine what she would do if Carter had found Danny's hidden account, if Danny was electrocuted, stunned to drooling stupefaction, or if two F-Chinooks full of carnivorous bulls suddenly flew up the river. She hadn't known, and Fallon didn't like not knowing. The ambiguity bothered her almost as much as the ape-wolves, the giant snakes, and whatever else might be coming for them. She coughed to muffle the crying jags trying to escape from her chest. "Just hurry."

Twenty minutes later, Emma and Danny had—to all appearances online, even after trolling a spyware net through their transaction history—successfully moved 3,000 E-credits from Emma's hidden 'Uncle William' account to Danny's dummy 'Gabriel Oak,' an account he opened in Jackson as a means to hide credits on the off chance that he and his criminal friends might have their assets seized. Peeking over his shoulder as he navigated financial screens, Fallon noticed that he had a grand total of six-hundred in the account prior to Emma's transfer. Granted, she didn't have much more than that in her own account—not that they could log in to her savings; that would be suicide—but she had imagined someone as resourceful and street smart as Danny would have woven a more resilient safety net.

Maybe we're not all that different. She slumped onto the couch and let her imagination wander. *Closer. Why not? Let's try a bit closer.*

Then Emma unplugged her bio-wire and used the cabin's interactive coffee table to call up an evening news broadcast from the Prevotel affiliate in Washington, DC.

Two media personalities (both digital), in near perfect 3-D, appeared in the small living room. Seated at a laser-optic desk projection, the immaculately quaffed journalists read and discussed the day's headlines, sports, weather, even a few human-interest stories.

"Is this today's?" Danny asked.

"Yeah," Emma said. "You wanna see yesterday or Friday?"

"Do you have to plug back in to change the broadcast date?" Fallon asked. "At home, we have to, but my mom has an old screen."

"Maybe use voice activation?" Danny added.

"Nope," Emma pressed a button, dialed up the previous night's report, "takes too long to imprint; this is faster."

The journalists froze, then went a bit smeary, blurring out of focus before appearing again, in different outfits. Emma used the polished coffee table to fast forward through two stories, one involving a homeless riot in Miami (most of the city had fallen to the homeless in recent years) and a regional plot to sneak frozen body parts, by E-train, across the border from Maine into Quebec. The fugitives missed most of the report, but Fallon decided that *boxcars filled with iced limbs, organs, eyes, even skin* had been sufficient to turn her off whatever pork belly surprise Danny might whip up for dinner.

The simulated reporters turned to one another, then to the room in a pre-programmed motion designed to approximate eye contact with family members sitting together for an evening broadcast.

"Can we skip this bit?" Fallon asked, "maybe just scroll until we see ourselves on the screen?"

"Good idea," Emma said, then cranked the newscast up to fast playback. Sim Guy and Sim Girl beeped, whistled, and blurred through a breakneck presentation of the day's headlines and approved stories.

Finally, Danny pointed at the wall behind their digital guests. "There! That was you, Em."

"Back it up," Fallon said. "Just a minute or two."

Emma did, slowing Sim Guy and Sim Girl until they were merely talking backwards as fast as a cocaine-addicted auctioneer.

"There," Danny sat beside Fallon. "That's good enough."

Emma let the broadcast play:

Sim Guy: "The news out of Baltimore tonight is that local and state officials have intensified their search for Emma Carlisle. The teenage fugitive has emerged as the prime suspect in the bombing death of Prevotel executive, Harold Higgins. The corporate vice president and his wife were killed last night when an incendiary device detonated in their high-rise apartment."

Sim Girl—looking directly at Fallon: "Carlisle is wanted in relation to a number of domestic and eco-terrorist bombings in the greater Baltimore area, and most recently for her daring escape from the Warrenton School for Juvenile Student Management in Virginia."

Sim Guy: "That's right, Beth."

Fallon glanced at Danny. *They have names down here? What the hell for?*

Sim Guy: "Emma Carlisle joined known felons, Daniel Hackett of Jackson, Mississippi, and Fallon Westerly of Old Forge, New York. All three are currently fugitives from justice and—officials believe—worked together to assassinate Higgins and his wife, before breaking into a heavily guarded robo-pharm facility at Baltimore's venerable, St. Sebastian Memorial Hospital."

Sim Girl—with feigned, programmed, sim concern: "Amazing story out of Baltimore, Dave. Who can believe that these kids, at seventeen, could be capable of so much devastation?"

Sim Guy—with sim empathy for her sim concern: "That's true, Beth. It's terrifying. And why the administrative staff at the Warrenton School have released images in hopes that some sharp-eyed citizen will spot these criminals and immediately contact local authorities or summon assistance by pressing their red, 911 key or coding BDC-911 and their current position log into their wrist or interactive screens."

Sim Girl: "Good point, Dave. Citizens are warned not to approach these children. They are considered deadly dangerous. State and county officials have assured us that they will sound the all-clear when these fugitives have been brought to justice."

"That's enough, Em," Danny said. "So we're deadly dangerous."

"That blast," Fallon said.

"What blast?" Emma pulled up the current evening's broadcast.

"You were sleeping," Fallon explained. "Danny and I just happened to be out back, getting some air, when it went off."

305

Danny added, "about a mile or so across town, a wicked blast, took the whole top of the building off. Could've seen the fireball for fifty miles, I bet."

"Why blame us?" Emma asked.

"Because it's easy," Fallon sat back, waited for the day's updates. "Someone can blow up half the planet, and as long as we're on the run, they can suggest that we did it...for whatever reason. They've already got you on eco-terrorism. You've got about seventy-two reasons to want Harold Higgins dead."

Emma turned her palms skyward. "Yeah, I do. So fire me."

"Jesus," Danny said. "This complicates things. Now we're all wanted for murder. Every service robot, digital scanner, neighborhood card reader, highway traffic sensor and fast food advertisement screen, everything everywhere is gonna be looking for us. Shit."

"And did you notice?" Fallon asked

"Yeah," Emma read her mind. "Not one mention of your buddy, Dozer McHyde pulverizing Drone Tower III to dust."

"Holy shit," Danny stopped. "That's right. Nothing. Not a word. I mean...that would be a tough one to pin on us."

"So they don't mention it at all."

He stood, brushed a hand through the digital avatars, now set on PAUSE. "I hate the news."

"And not to drape a wet blanket over our otherwise delightful afternoon," Emma crossed to the projection screen, yanked it down sharply, like a window shade, and let it roll up into a ceiling storage compartment. "But did you catch the order?"

"Yeah," Danny said. "They have the pharmacy break in after the explosion."

"Really?" Fallon said. "I didn't notice."

"Yup," Emma flopped on the sofa. "Despite time and date stamps on both security films, we—the teenage terrorists—blew up the building and then stole meds from the pharmacy."

306

"So everyone thinks we're injured," Danny fingered the scabbed cuts in his forehead.

"Correct. Wounded in our daring assault on Henry Hornblower, or whoever he is."

"God damn," he fell onto the sofa beside her. "You're right. I hate this."

"You and me both, Cousin."

"Where are we on time?" Fallon asked.

"About 48 minutes," Emma said. "You know, give or take a couple either way."

"Let's hustle."

Danny said, "just one second. I wanna see today's broadcast. Just the bits on us...or Higgins, Em, if you can find them."

"Got it." She yanked the retractable screen back into place and pressed FAST FORWARD. Sim Guy and Sim Girl sped madly through the day's headlines, sounding again like chatty parakeets.

Fallon stood suddenly. "There we are. You see us?"

Emma rewound.

Clad now in matching sky blue with navy accessories, Sim Guy and Sim Girl projected the same image of the teen criminals, this time with a running strapline noting: YOUTH FUGITIVES WANTED FOR MURDER, TERRORISM, STILL AT LARGE.

Much of the report matched the previous evening's text, except for the added footage of Danny breaking into the robo-pharm facility at the Baltimore County Clinic. The grainy footage—clearly gathered by a security camera long overdue for an upgrade—showed Danny run into the frame, punch a burly man easily a hundred pounds heavier than himself, then turn and similarly clobber a gantry-thin elderly woman attempting to block his way.

"Nice," Fallon teased. "My mother saw that. She's gonna love you."

"Hey, she was asking for it," he defended himself. "And the camera lies. She was mammoth."

In her signature gesture, Fallon elbowed him in the ribs. *Pretty brave work, dumbass.*

He leaned against her, just for a second. *Yeah. I did it for you.*

Then Fallon panicked. "But wait! Wait…is this gonna show you…"

Danny kicked her, hard in the ankle.

Fallon got the message, clammed up.

Emma asked, "Show you what?"

"Show my massively mediocre muscles," he joked. "Did you see that first guy, Em?"

"Yeah. Jesus, he was like a garbage truck," she watched without blinking. "Holy crap, Danny. He decked you. Good lord, did that hurt? Does it still hurt? That hurts me, and I'm a hundred miles away."

"Yeah," he laughed. "It stung a bit."

Fallon held her breath through the end of the report. They were all right. The camera angle was off just enough that the mid-Atlantic region didn't get to watch as Danny evaporated into a gust of smoke. *But someone saw it. They had to. Someone out there knows.*

Sim Girl wrapped up: "…seen here in a daring raid on a robo-pharmacy just across town from the Harold Higgins bombing has led police and officials to conclude that either Emma Carlisle or Fallon Westerly was injured in the blast that killed Higgins and his wife, Monica, Friday night."

Emma saw Danny attempt to run, then freeze as the pharmacist trained automatic weapons on him. She backed this up several times, watching again and again before allowing the video to continue. When the desperate thunderhead dove over the pharmacy counter, distracting the robot guard, Danny dashed along the corridor, disappearing from the frame, a box of stolen meds under one arm.

308

She took his hand in both of hers. "Thank you. You almost got killed for me."

"Yeah," he said, "but keep in mind, nutsy, that you dove on that snake when it was chasing after me. Talk about hare-brained ideas."

Fallon hadn't made that connection yet. *Take her. Kill him.* Without thinking, she said, "Shit."

"What?"

"Um…nothing," she collected the canned food from the kitchen. "Just…you know: shit, we gotta get going."

Danny shot her a questioning look, then decided not to press the issue. "Yeah, good. Well, we left our stink all over this place. We plugged in—which might have been dumb, if they can trace our skills—and we used enough talent to bring creepy, slimy, snakes and flying monkey creatures in from three states."

"Actually, we didn't." Fallon looked to Emma, "You wanna add something?"

She turned to the fireplace. "Don't mind if I do." And from memory, the smaller girl focused her gaze on the few pieces of white birch in the grate, probably there as a decoration. "It's cold in here; I'm not a liar. Whip us up a nice, hot fire."

Flames broke out along the logs, spreading quickly.

"Nice, Em," Danny said. "Remind me to keep you around this winter."

She rested her head on his shoulder. "Yeah, but let's hope the flu vent was open, or we're gonna get smoked out in two minutes."

"It's okay," Fallon started out. "We're done, anyway."

"What about me?" Danny asked.

"No. This is good enough."

He didn't argue. It made sense: if whoever was tracking them remained oblivious to his skills, leaving Danny's particular smell all over this cottage would be a mistake. They were already risking his dummy account. Just logging on in the same room they'd destroyed might be enough to attract someone as sharp as Carter Hodges. They'd have to be doubly careful and perhaps doubly rural the next time they tried to access Emma's transferred credits. If West Virginia bulls showed up in E-copters, they'd know without any doubt that those accounts were no longer useable. However, if another ghoulie showed up hunting for them—even a vampire with a penis laser—they'd know it was their skills leaving a trail all over the county. They could manage without credits, but they'd be screwed running if all three of them had to abandon their talents.

And he understood again why Fallon wanted him to keep his skills hidden, not just from Emma, but from whomever might be watching or listening from afar. Showing off in that cornfield might prove to be his undoing.

Emma shut down the projection screen. "Let's go."

14

A Raven-Cat, Lavender, and a Bear

Later, they argued over who would sleep, who would keep watch, and who would wash dishes. Danny asserted that Fallon should clean, because she could turn her hands into sponges, cloths, even a scraper if bits of pork belly stuck to the frying pan.

Emma argued that Danny should have that duty because anyone willing to cook anything that reprehensible ought to scrape every dish to pristine, pearly whiteness if only as a punitive measure.

Danny disagreed, noting that nearly two-hundred-million southerners agreed with him and that canned pork should be appreciated as the global delicacy it clearly was.

Fallon shushed them, moving to the fibro cabin's front windows and taking a seat on a sofa that overlooked the river and the white cottage thirty or so yards below. Smoke from Emma's quickie fire still curled skyward from the chimney. "You two, hush up. Will you? I wanna listen."

"Don't shush us," Emma said. "If we're going to be living together, we need to have some rules of decorum."

Fallon said, "Leave the damned dishes. Who cares? Fibro Man or Fibro Woman can decide which of the Cheap Fibro Tots scrape pork shit off the dishes when they come back out here...next spring."

Danny joined her, carrying the one light they'd allowed themselves, a scented lavender candle Emma lit in hopes that candlelight might improve the flavor of pork belly mixed with salty, canned pasta. It hadn't. Lavender scented pork belly didn't have a prayer of catching on, no matter what epicurean experts around the globe decided.

"You two should sleep," Fallon suggested. "I'm fine here for a while on my own."

"I can't sleep," Danny said. "I've gotta know."

"I can't sleep either," Emma flopped down beside them, splaying her legs dramatically across the braided area rug. "I gotta digest Danny's dinner first."

"Fine," Fallon abandoned the suddenly crowded couch, preferring instead to kneel before the open porch window. Resting folded hands on the sill, she propped her chin on her arms. "Yeah, this is better."

Again, Danny joined her. Emma sprawled on the couch and in five minutes was snoring indecorously through her nose. She sounded amusingly like their Chevron as it struggled up hill.

"I think we screwed up today."

She read his mind. "Logging in where we blew the place apart?"

"Yeah," he frowned. "We might have turned them on to my account and Emma's uncle. Or if they already know Emma's family, her uncle's account codes might be lighting up a programming board somewhere over in Fairfax or DC. Who knows how thorough these people are? With a regional manhunt under way for murder, I'm thinking the most talented programmers are gonna be on the case."

"We could be righteously boned. You're right."

"Trying not to think about it."

"I'll try, too," she agreed.

"You were impressive today," he said.

"I've gotta figure out everything I can do," she explained. "Living at home with my mother, I never cared if there was a limit to my skills. What threats did I face in Old Forge?"

"I get it." He shifted closer, preferred whispering now that darkness had fallen on the river gorge. "I spent weeks experimenting in the swamps outside Natchez, doing exactly that."

"What else can you do?"

"Not much," he said. "You've seen about the extent of it."

312

"Maybe you'll surprise yourself," she said. "That corn thing was staggering. Not kidding, Danny. You've got to be among the most powerful individuals…I dunno…anywhere. I mean, who can command Nature?"

"Request," he corrected. "I make requests. The world around me answers sometimes."

"Sometimes it doesn't?"

"Yeah," he said. "I'm not sure, but I think it depends on the conditions. This one time I was in Baton Rouge, running from the bulls. A friend and I had robbed a grocery store. We were frigging starving, just took some bread, cheese and dried meat…and maybe a couple of beers."

"A couple?"

"Two. I swear to God."

"Each?"

"Yeah, okay…two each."

Fallon laughed. "Criminal."

"Only when I'm hungry."

"So what happened?"

"Marty Ahearn got this brilliant idea that we'd sneak across the Mississippi and disappear into the industrial complex on the west side of the city."

"But the bulls had a boat?"

"Three boats! Don't you hate that?"

"I do," Fallon teased, enjoying herself. "So you spent two weeks in lockup for a half pound of brie?"

"Brie? Never. Cheddar. It's the most popular cheese in Louisiana."

"The country."

"You're more willing to make hasty generalizations than I am."

Fallon raised an eyebrow. *Get on with it.*

"Right. Anyway, the river is polluted as all hell: old tires, lots of plastic, oily spills, crap floating through there, dead cats, foreign tourists. It's disgusting."

Interested, Fallon said, "wait a minute. Are you suggesting that Nature struggles to help you when it's all full of human waste and shit and old Buicks?"

"Exactly," Danny said. "I asked for a pretty good wave, nothing special, just a wave to give me and Marty a boost across the river. How hard could that be?"

"Didn't work?"

"Not a whiff."

"You get arrested?"

"Marty did. The dumbass can't swim...and he's the one who wanted to escape by boat."

"My Uncle Arthur used to say there's no cure for stupid."

"Ha!" Danny laughed, too loudly. He squinted into the darkness over the white cottage, then whispered, "I think he's right."

"How'd you get away?"

"I dove in...swam for it."

"In a river full of shit, plastic, truck tires, and bloated corpses?"

"Yeah, I had a nasty rash in a few embarrassing places for a couple weeks after, but I didn't have to spend time in lockup. Baton Rouge Parish lockups are unpleasant."

Fallon shook her head in disbelief. "All for a half pound of cheddar cheese, sixty credits at any Prevo Mart."

"Heh, yeah," he smiled. "Whatever. It was character building."

Fallon cast him a thin smile, her lips pressed together to keep from giggling, embarrassing herself.

"What?" he asked.

"Nothing," she leaned over, kissed him softly on the cheek, his week's worth of beard stubble tickling her lips. Without pulling away, she whispered, "You are one confounding individual, Danny Hackett. You're among the most interesting and powerful people in human history, without exaggeration, and you risk jail time for a slab of cheap

314

cheese, probably pumped full of government-approved preservatives."

Hoping she'd kiss him again, Danny said, "That color, sunset cheddar orange...you know that doesn't exist in nature."

Fallon laughed, just a quick bluster that brushed the side of his face.

Without thinking, he added, "I would always meet you at airports."

She drew back far enough to look into his eyes. They matched. She liked that. "You'd what? What was that?"

"When you flew somewhere," he explained. "I would always meet you, drop you off, pick you up. You know...at airports or drone towers."

She shrugged. "I could just take a drone home, one of the big ones, the KGS-49s. They're impressive."

"It's not the same, not even close."

She smiled, agreed. "You're right. It isn't."

"Meeting someone at the airport. I dunno..." He cast about, hoping to rake up the right words. "It says something about...both people, I guess."

Fallon leaned close again. "It does. Yeah, meeting someone at the airport. That's...important. Right?"

He kissed her, softly at first, then more intensely. Hungrily. "I think so."

"What a nice thing to say."

"I know it's a disconnected tangent," he kissed her again. "But sometimes, you make me think of disconnected things that make perfect sense in my head, but when I say them out loud—"

"Oh, heh," she ran a hand between his shoulder blades, across the lean muscles of his back. "I invented that one, Cousin. You check the fine print on that; the copyright's credited to me."

Having finally kissed her, Danny felt unexpected confidence and almost hoped to face another gargantuan snake or a herd of hungry zombies. "Why don't you want Emma to know about my ability to transform?"

Fallon changed gears with him. They could get back to kissing and airports later. "I don't want anyone to know about you. Emma saw you manipulate that corn field as if those stalks were close relatives who owed you a favor. That's enough. She...*no one*...needs to know that you can travel as smoke."

"A few friends know," he said. "Friends. I suppose they're more like acquaintances. But people have seen me do it."

She said, "Oh, I think someone important, somewhere, knows about you."

"It's why they shipped me all the way up here for something as simple as a resisting arrest charge. They wanted me corralled with you and Emma?"

"Exactly."

"But the snake," he said, "that thing wasn't coming to kidnap me. It was definitely coming to kill me. No one sends a 700-pound snake to do its kidnapping...no hands to hang on, no opposable thumbs."

"Yeah," Fallon agreed. "I can't figure that one. Those morlock things were hoping to take Emma and me, but the snake was definitely on an assassination mission."

"So maybe they don't know the *extent* of my skills."

"Did you use the smoke trick when you were arrested down south?"

He caught her line of reasoning. "No. God damn, I didn't."

"So unless your friends have told or unless our pursuer can somehow *infer* our talents and skills, there's no reason that anyone would know. And I think we keep that one hidden."

"Why? If they sent me here, they must want me with you and Emma."

"Or with Blair."

"Oh, shit," he said. "I forgot about him."

316

Again, Tall Captain of the ape-wolves played in her memory: *Take her. Kill him.*

"Fallon?"

She dropped her head onto his shoulder. Beyond the white cottage, the Potomac, invisible in the darkness, babbled and splashed southeast toward DC. She gave in; it was a night for truth telling. "I heard that that monkey-monster thing, the lead morlock, it wanted Emma and me taken."

"And me killed."

"I didn't know what to...that bothered me."

"Me, too. But so what. We're in a fight; I get it."

"Yeah." She didn't lift her head.

"I suppose that does complicate things," he joked.

"I dunno," she explained. "It might be good for us."

He laughed, "if I'm dead?"

"No, shithead, if they have no idea what you can do, then we have a significant advantage."

"Yet, they sent me all the way up here..."

"Correct again," she waved a finger. "Let's say they—whoever they are—have some idea that you're talented."

"But they don't think I'm anything like you or Emma."

"Exactly," she said. "If they—whoever is sending these goddamned creatures—had any idea what you could do, they'd murder Emma and me and take you in."

"In?"

"Yeah, wherever that is." She peered southward without a clue what she might be looking for. "This isn't all that helpful. Is it?"

He rested the side of his face against hers. "I'd always come to meet you at airports."

"I know, Danny."

Then without preamble, he slipped to the cottage's eat-in kitchen and retrieved the varnished wooden box Emma had been carrying ever since Baltimore.

"What're you doing?"

"I wanna know." He slid open the carved lid, whistled gently through pursed lips. "Holy exploding high rises, Batman."

"What?" Fallon whispered, joined him.

"Nothing. It's an old comic book refer– never mind."

"What's there?"

He withdrew a gangly-looking device, with two wire connections protruding from either end of a small, spherical nub, about two inches across.

"What is it?"

"I can't say for sure," Danny held the oddment up to the candlelight. "It's pretty dark in here, but I think it's a detonator...a switch."

"A detonator?" Fallon hissed, then quieted, glancing over at Emma draped across the sofa. "What's she doing with a detonator?"

"Detonators," he corrected. "There's three in here, and if you really need me to answer that question, we've gotta work a bit on your inductive reasoning skills, love."

Fallon took one, examined it in the half light. "Damn, so it's true: she's a..."

"Looks like it," he confirmed. "Just your everyday, one-hundred-and-five-pound domestic terrorist."

"This casts our Baltimore trip in a whole new light. Do you think she was passed out that whole time?"

"Was she? I dunno." Danny replaced the switch, slid the box closed. "I can't imagine how she managed it, though. We pumped her full of Stormcloud; she was gone."

"But..."

"Doncha hate buts?"

"Leave it," she led him back to the window. "We'll ask her once we're finished with Blair in Warrenton."

"Okay." He followed, grabbing two loose sofa pillows and a knitted blanket.

Comfortable, Fallon inhaled fraudulent lavender. The heady stink of Danny's pasta and pork belly surprise dissipated on cross breezes that cast the curtains about like loose sails on a sloop. The Shenandoah Valley had faded into a black backdrop. Occasionally, they heard unimpressive splashes from the river: fish hunting up minnows or bite-sized insects or perhaps a hawk diving to pluck unsuspecting trout from the shallows. The breeze, the darkness, the steady, predictable music of the Potomac on its journey to the Chesapeake, and the faint, flickering light all conspired to lull Fallon and Danny into a numbed sense of complacent security. Surely nothing was coming. No behemoth speckled reptiles slithered upstream. No flying monkeys swooped in to collect Dorothy and Toto. No colossal, bulldozer men crouched in the wooded shadows, ready to smash through walls, dismembering gifted teenagers.

Nope. None of it.

Fallon's eyes grew heavy. She badly needed sleep but wanted to stay awake, wanted to finish her watch and badly wanted to keep talking with Danny. Outside, Nature, Danny's co-conspirator, called up another autumn breeze, a chatty, whispering river, a nearly impenetrable blanket of darkness in a hypnotic poem for weary travelers. Fallon considered standing up, getting her blood moving, maybe even raiding the pantry again for coffee.

She thought she might join Emma for a quick nap. The younger girl lay sprawled lengthwise, leaving about eight inches of unclaimed cushion on one end.

Not worth it.

Through weak candlelight, Fallon watched Emma sleep. On her stomach, the girl's Irish red curls hid her face in a thatch of unruly scribbles. Emma's sweater had ridden a few inches up her back, showing how thin the tired fugitive had grown, even in the few weeks since her arrest. Fallon shifted back to the window, propped her chin on folded arms, and let the comparative safety and beauty of the river gorge have her. She drifted effortlessly away.

Danny stirred beside her. "What's that?"

319

"Huh? What?" She murmured, hauling herself bodily from the deliriously comfortable depths of much-deserved rest. "Whaddya say?"

He sat rigidly upright, then pressed down on her shoulders. Leaning close—not affectionately this time—he whispered. "Stay still. Don't move."

Fallon searched the shallow valley, trying not to move her head. Emma's candle had nearly burned out and cast only a weak yellow glow about the cabin walls. "Remember, no skills. Nothing."

Danny, still close enough for his lips to brush against her ear, replied, "Don't move. Something's out there."

Straining her eyes, Fallon said, "Maybe a dog? A fox? A bear? I'm scared of bears, Danny. Don't tell me that's a frigging bear."

"Shhh," he hissed. "Don't move."

They felt it before they heard anything. The air above the cabin changed in pressure, weighing down on them, suddenly imbued with too much humidity. Something descended on the river valley from the hillside. Something large, perhaps as large as a private plane, certainly an E-copter, approached from behind, from above, swooping into the valley and pushing concentric waves of heavy night air before it.

Whatever it was.

When it passed directly overhead, Fallon shrank from the windows. "Pteranodon? A big one? You know, like an actual dinosaur? Pissed off and starving?"

Danny gripped her wrist. "No sound, not a rustle."

She said, "That's too big. That's...whatever that is...that's too big for us."

"Shhh. Let's just watch a minute and listen. If we're right, it will think we were in the other cottage but that we're long gone."

"What if we're wrong? What if we've got it wrong? What're we gonna do if that...thing...comes for us? We don't even know if we can see it." Breathing open mouthed in shallow swallows, she didn't bother trying to hide her panic.

"Just watch," he said, as scared as she was. "If we have to fight, we fight together. It'll be our only hope."

"Did you feel that?"

"I did," he said. "It's like the goddamned thing pulled the whole night down on us."

"It's wings. It's gotta have huge wings."

In response, something—Fallon guessed that trout-fishing hawk—screamed a short, warbly cry then went silent, cut off mid-yelp. She pressed a hand to her mouth, stared at the darkness with renewed desperation. She knew it was just a matter of a few seconds before whatever it was heard her, smelled her, saw her through the inky blackness, and came hurtling out of the night, winged death hunting them, homing in on her noisy breathing. She pressed hard against Danny and enjoyed a fleeting moment's comfort when she felt his heart thumping a mad allegro through his sweatshirt.

"We'll fight together," she whispered. "You and me. Yes?"

"Always." He shushed her. "Now, just watch."

Something large crashed into the river with a frothy, galloping GAWHOOSH. Images took shape in Fallon's mind; whatever it was had wings as broad as an airplane and a body at least as large as their stolen car. "You hear that?"

"Yeah," Danny answered. "It's frigging gigantic, but at least we know where it is."

Struck by an idea, Fallon dropped to her stomach and slithered toward the narrow coffee table Emma had dragged in front of the sofa when Danny served plates of offensive barnyard soufflé.

"Where you going?"

"One sec," she pressed herself up high enough to blow out the flickering candle. Whatever meagre light the small flame brought to the room went out, and the friends fell into darkness as thick and unforgiving as the ambient night. On the couch, Emma snored softly through her nose, not having moved for over an hour.

Danny caught a whiff of the fragrant smoke curling from the tiny red wick that glowed another few seconds before burning out entirely. He turned to the window, whispered, "Hey, that's better. Come see."

Fallon drew up beside him. It took a minute for her eyes to adjust and for a while she thought that perhaps whatever it was had flown away, or swum away. She didn't care. It was the *away* that interested her.

But then Danny prodded her gently in the ribs, pointed silently toward the sky, a broad swath of midnight infinitesimally less obsidian than the valley, grass, forests, and ribbon of inky water flowing past.

What? She mouthed the word, too frightened to speak. In her imagination, the winged demon hovered over their cabin, waiting until they relaxed, lit a lamp, cooked up another batch of pork belly, anything to bring it down on them like an avalanche of despair. It would come, unexpected, in a cataclysmic crash through the roof, or the front windows.

"There," Danny said quietly. "See it? There. Circling."

She squinted, peered, tried looking without blinking, then blinked a half-dozen times for good measure.

And saw it.

Indistinct, what hunted them didn't immediately take on a definitive shape, except for the wings. Easily forty feet across, they flapped soundlessly, like bat wings, great feathered sails carrying whatever it was higher into the night, where it circled, searched the river gorge, dropped to rooftop level, then climbed above the southern ridge.

"What's it doing?" Danny asked.

"Dunno. Either hunting something else to eat or biding its time, watching the cottage, waiting for us to attack, to screw up, to open a door and welcome it in. We can't be sure."

"What is it?"

Again, Fallon squinted to improve her vision. It didn't work. "I can't tell. It's goddamned huge, though, bigger than our car. Almost as big as a bus."

The creature swooped low over the white cottage and spilled like black ink across the river, just a few feet above the water. It slapped the waves with its unimaginable wings then climbed again into the sky, circling patiently as it waited to make another pass.

Finally, he leaned close, asked, "Do you smell that? What's that smell?"

Fallon inhaled deeply, past the immediate stink of lavender smoke, the background layer of processed pork and salty marinara sauce, to the swirling amalgam of river water, autumn decay, and...

"What is it?" Danny asked again. "I know that smell."

"Jesus Christ," Fallon flashed to her mother's trailer, parked on the shores of the Fulton Chain Lakes outside Old Forge, and old Ms. Jessamyn's place, just across the gladiola-lined dirt path marking the property boundary. In the evenings after she and her mother cleaned up the dishes, they'd often sit outside together and drink tea or listen to news downloads on her mother's vid-screen as sunset draped the mountains and lakeshore with a golden apron. Invariably, one of Ms. Jessamyn's dozen or so cats—Lord Henry—would wander into their yard and rub sensually against Fallon's calf, purring insistently until the girl dragged a few fingers over the animal's head and along its wiry, flexible spine. An older woman, north of seventy with no family, Ms. Jessamyn wasn't the most fastidious of housekeepers, and often her feline friends—Lord Henry and Dorian, horny, tomcat devils—smelled fragrantly of piss, unchecked dander, and bad nighttime behavior. Her mother hated cats—except for Banjo, who was as much a close relative as a feline—and often kicked or shooed them away, irritating Ms. Jessamyn no end. Fallon was more hospitable but always gave her hands a good scrubbing with anti-bacterial soap after playing with one or more of the especially reprehensible visitors from next door.

She shoved the unpleasant recollection away, took Danny by the shoulder. "It's a cat."

"That's it!" He said. "Holy shit, it's a frigging gigantic, flying, raven-winged cat. What in God's name is happening to us? Fallon, why's this happening to us? We can't fight that thing. We –" It was Danny's turn to panic.

Reciprocating the comforting gesture, she pulled him close, squeezed tightly, wanted him to feel her, to understand her commitment, even here, being hunted in the darkness. "It's all right," she said without believing a syllable of it. "We can fight together."

"It's thirty feet long," Danny said. "Look at it for shit's sake."

"We're gonna stay right here, watch, and wait."

Taking its cue, the great cat swooped from above, plummeting five-hundred feet with its wings cocked for a dive. This time, however, instead of skimming the rooftop of the white cottage, it landed, four-footed with a splintering crash. The cottage roof simply blew apart. As if struck by a guided missile, the remaining windows—the ones Fallon hadn't already broken—shattered with a gritty crack, and the upper floor, where Fallon guessed White Cottage Family slept when visiting in the summer, broke into hundreds of jagged bits. The place might have been a toothpick model held together with hot glue and duct tape.

The cat creature alighted on the new roof, what had been the hardwood floor of the upstairs bedrooms, reared up on its hind legs like a stallion, and bellowed a wet, guttural growl that reverberated up and down the river. No, this wasn't a Pteranodon; this thing would eat Pteranodons on toast.

Fallon's stomach clenched.

From the couch, Emma rolled over, yawned smeary vowels frighteningly loud in the silent cabin. She stretched, "What's that? What was—"

Diving from the floor, Danny landed full on the couch, as silently as possible, to clamp both hands over Emma's mouth. Resting bodily on the smaller girl, he crushed her against the forgiving cushions, pressed hard against her mouth, and warned. "Don't say anything. No sound. Please."

Emma tried to nod, couldn't with Danny holding her immobile, and contented herself with a series of blinks she hoped said, *Yeah, okay. I get it.*

Danny slid to the floor, and mimicking Fallon's earlier move, slithered to the windows on his belly. Emma followed.

Together they watched the winged cat, close enough now for all three of them to see and smell it plainly. Neither Fallon nor Danny had exaggerated; the monster clawing holes in the white cottage's plank floor, ripping up hardwood as if digging for a family of clever mice, stood easily fifteen feet tall. At nearly thirty feet long with inky feathered wings broad enough to blanket the cottage, the cat creature shouldered the stone chimney, now jutting nakedly from the ground level like a river god's crooked finger. It crumbled to brick and mortar stones, spilling across the lawn and leaving one side of the cottage dangerously unsupported from below.

When the snarling monster stepped too far to that side, the cottage collapsed, see-sawing into a crooked right triangle. Sturdy wooden beams Fallon remembered lining the rustic ceiling snapped so loudly that Emma pressed both hands over her ears and clamped her mouth over a hysterical shriek that would have brought the hungry creature onto them in a heartbeat.

Now, however, unable to break into the lower level, the great cat flapped its wings twice, lifted a few feet into the air, and settled with a fluttery rush to the grass beside the cottage's rear entrance. It nosed the door, pressing a few times with its forehead and snout, then pawing at the entryway with a foreleg as large as Fallon's entire body.

Without warning, the cottage's porch light flicked on causing the three friends to duck beneath the window sill until

Danny risked a wary peek. Somehow, the cat's clumsy paw had flipped an outside switch.

Weakly illuminated now, it still banged away at the door, first with its snout and again with its forepaws.

"Can't get the door open," Danny whispered.

"It's playing," Fallon replied between fingers clutched tightly over her mouth. "It'll tear the place down in a second if it wants to."

Beside them, Emma scribbled furiously in her notebook. Fallon hoped that the younger girl had concocted something to create a hairball the size of a port-o-john.

"You got anything?" Danny asked, clearly as hopeful as Fallon that Emma might pen a masterpiece in ten seconds or less.

The frightened girl merely whimpered and shook her head.

"What's it doing?" Fallon checked down the grassy slope.

Danny froze. "Oh, shit."

The raven-cat had given up on the cottage's rear doorway. Instead, it turned north toward the cheap fibro cabin. Growling, an out of tune cello, it took a few curious steps in their direction, lifted its freakish head, and sniffed the air, its black eyes closed in concentration.

Fallon held her breath.

The creature inhaled again, sniffing first high, then low near the grass. It rose up on its hind legs again, and—backlit by the porch light—looked like a steroid-injected Pegasus, albeit one sprung fully formed from Hades's darkest nightmare. Dropping to all fours, the creature snarled fiercely enough to make an African lion soil its diaper, then inhaled again, clearly testing the air for something it had smelled but couldn't locate again.

"The candle," Fallon whispered. "It smells the smoke... lavender. I blew out the candle."

Danny squeezed her wrist. *Just sit tight.*

The friends waited, peering over the window sill, hoping the sudden porch light didn't reach them and that the bloodthirsty monster sniffing the air would grow bored or distracted by something else, some wayward deer or maybe a large fish stupid enough to splash nearby.

What happened, however, was something none of the fugitives could have predicted, and which left Fallon Westerly equal parts confused, enraged, and terrified.

Rising a final time to its rear legs, the hulking raven-cat creature cast a shrill cry into the night air. It echoed from one end of the valley to the other, rattling the dental work in Fallon's mouth. Mid-shriek, however, the cry modulated, falling in timbre and pitch to a warbly bellow as the monster morphed, changing shape, its wings folding inward, then absorbing into its torso, its coat, almost porcupine bristly, smoothing to dark flesh, its facial features, flattening to something vaguely simian and then, finally, to human.

"Oh my great, frigging god," Emma hissed. "It's Bear."

Where's the bear? I don't see one! Fallon thought and dropped to the planks. Having lived in upstate New York for most of her life, Fallon learned to fear and respect bears. As terrifying as the raven-cat creature was, some part of her, something primitive, awakened, freezing her to the spot. The thought of a twenty-five-foot bear, with or without wings, was too much for her to imagine. Pulling Danny down beside her, she cracked, finally losing control. Through tears, she asked, "Is there a bear? Danny, I really don't like—"

"Shhh," he pressed two fingers to her lips. "Fallon, it isn't a bear. Its *Bear*. Beatrice Jackass Bear, the one you clobbered back in lockup."

Molten anger, the comforting visitor that had allowed her to dispatch nearly two dozen of the ape-wolves with abandon, swelled again in Fallon's chest. Taking Danny by the throat, she squeezed, just enough to ensure she had his attention. "Bear? *Bear*? Where is she?"

Danny pried her fingers loose. "Keep your head down. She's right outside. She's the thing. That cat thing...it's Bear!"

She ignored his warning, rose slowly to peek one eye over the sill. Beatrice *Bear* Guenard stood, stark naked, all two-hundred-sixty pounds of her, flat footed on the grassy slope between the cheap fibro cabin and the cottage with the white siding that she—as a raven-winged feline monster—had crushed to useless kindling. Still sniffing, but now looking oddly like a football linebacker who'd forgotten her clothes, Bear finally gave up the search for whatever lavender smoke had drifted from the north side of the valley, and turned back to what remained of the cottage below. Fallon noticed that the burly girl favored her ribs on one side, was still healing from their brief battle in the dormitory quad.

Turning the knob, Bear shoved a few times—the door had gotten stuck when the west side of the house fell over— then lowered her good shoulder and smashed her way in, ignoring the splinters and scrapes she collected while bashing through the doorframe with no clothes on.

Once Bear disappeared inside, Danny risked a quick conversation. "What the hell? You beat her brains out, took you two seconds. There's no way she was a...frigging giant, flying goddamned cat-lion monster two weeks ago. No way."

Fallon said, "You're right. It doesn't make sense." Her hands shook; she crossed her arms, jamming her fingers up beneath her armpits until she could calm down. Enough adrenaline flooded her bloodstream, Fallon seriously considered charging down the hill and challenging the tough stranger to a head-to-head fight. *Don't be stupid, dumbass. She'll shift back and crack your head open for the secret prize hidden inside.*

Emma flipped her notebook shut, pocketed it. "It's Blair."

"Blair." Fallon understood.

"Jesus," Danny looked back and forth between them. "He's...what? He's making...her, it? These things? He's making things like...like *that?*"

Fallon frowned.

He read her mind. "We're gonna kill him."

"Yeah."

"What if?" Danny watched for the beefy criminal. "What if those others..."

"They will be," Emma said. "Or whatever else he's got cooked up there."

Fallon pressed a hand softly to Danny's cheek. "You wanted to know why the three of us were brought to Warrenton?"

Emma said, "Beating that one in a gazillion shot."

"Exactly."

"To what? To experiment on us? To use our blood? Our DNA? Our skills? To what? To make...*that?*"

"Shhh," Fallon pulled him down. "She's coming."

Bear emerged from the cottage. She strode purposely over the lawn, then stopped, lifted her face to the heavens, and morphed back into the raven-winged monster. Snarling at the cottage ruins, she flapped a few times to gain enough altitude, then drifted silently eastward, following the river until she vanished into the ambient darkness.

Fallon sat stunned for several minutes, listening to the Potomac on its immutable voyage.

Finally, Emma chuckled nervously. "Huh. So, it looks like Headmaster Blair has a few tricks up his sleeve."

Danny said, "Yeah. He chose Bear for her homicidal, sociopathic personality."

"But he didn't count on her stupidity," Emma laughed. "Dumb as a teenager. Dumb as a cat, hawk, monster-bird-panther thing."

"Well said," Danny teased.

Fallon stood. "We've gotta go. Right now."

"Why?" Nervous, Danny searched outside. "Do you see her? Is she back?"

"She smelled us, smelled that candle, maybe even smelled that pork shit you charred for dinner. She did, guys. C'mon," she reached a hand to Emma. "Now."

In less than five minutes, they'd loaded their meagre possessions into the Chevron and turned eastward along the dirt road connecting the cottage cul-de-sac with the forest and logging roads back to civilization.

"No lights," Fallon said. "But hurry. This car smells like a mechanic's toilet. We can't stick around here too long. C'mon, Danny. Kick it in the ass."

"Okay, okay," he leaned over the steering wheel, struggling to navigate through the darkness waiting in ambush beneath the trees. But even at eight or nine miles per hour, they soon put a half mile, then a mile between themselves and the fibro cottage.

On the paved county road, Fallon had Danny pull over and kill the engine. The unchecked darkness of the middle watch had fallen over West Virginia, and a thick coverlet of eerie silence snaked between the hardwoods to wrap around them as they stood together in the middle of the narrow lane.

Fallon closed her eyes, listened, felt for the very air around and above them.

Danny and Emma held hands, waited.

"There," Fallon raised a hand above her head. "There. You feel that?"

Danny did the same, then stuffed his hand in his pocket. "No, I gotta tell you; I think you're over—"

"Wait," Emma interrupted. "I feel it. Up there." She pointed.

They watched as Bear, approaching at flank speed, dropped to treetop level and turned west toward the cul-de-sac. Whooshing overhead like a deadly, black-ops glider, she didn't make a sound, just pressed great swaths of humid air below, swirling gusts along the street like a furnace bellows.

Ten seconds later, they heard her. Over the cheap fibro cabin in the distance, a mile away and dropping like a crashing airplane, she shrieked that same enraged cry she'd yelped from the shattered rooftop of the cottage beside the river. What followed was such an unsettling crash of splintering boards and breaking glass, each of the fugitives understood that had they remained huddled in the cabin, they'd now be engaged in the fight of their lives.

"C'mon," Fallon ushered them toward the car. "Let's go. While she's occupied."

"Yeah," Danny hurried to the driver's side. "The main road is only a couple of miles. We can turn the lights on when we get there."

15

Pancakes, Death Threats, and a Stolen Canoe

The friends found an all-night diner attached to a small hotel outside the riverside town of Brunswick, Maryland. A simple, throwback, Formica and cracked vinyl place serving eggs, energy paste, burgers, fried shrimp, and macadam black coffee twenty-four hours a day, Jenny's Diner lit the Shenandoah piedmont with garish fluorescents and incorrigible neon: blue, red, orange, green, and a yellow that had to have been invented by a blind psychopath.

"Here we go!" Danny turned into the parking lot. "Who's hungry?"

"I am!" Emma cried. "I'd kill for a stack of pancakes."

Exhausted, Fallon had been content to nap in the back, trusting the boy to find them someplace safe to hole up until they decided on their next move. She rubbed sleep from her eyes, then shut them tight against the obnoxious glow from Jenny's. "What is this place?"

"A diner," Danny said. "I figure we ought to conduct one more test. If we plug in here to buy Emma a stack of pancakes, we'll know if they're somehow tracking our vid screens as well."

"I'll eat them," Emma added. "You know…in the interests of science."

"And what do we do if Bear shows up and drops a school bus on the place from five-hundred feet up?"

"Um…" Danny thought a moment. "Well, I guess we die. So, Em, you gotta eat quick."

"Don't worry," she unclasped the safety belts and pushed the door open. "I'll make short work of them."

"You don't think it's the wrist screens," Fallon said.

"I don't," he answered. "It's gotta be our talents. Carter might be good with technology, but I've been thinking: If they could, they would have homed in on our screens, zapped us from a hundred miles out, and had local bulls bring us back, trussed up for Thanksgiving."

"Yeah," Fallon yawned. "That makes sense. And given the fact that only Blair, or someone approved by Blair, could have gifted my friend Beatrice with the ability to transform herself into a monster from a horror story, I'd be willing to bet you the cost of Emma's pancakes that he's somehow tracking our abilities."

Danny pushed his own door open. "It's how they found us, me down in Jackson, and you up in...that bear-infested place you come from."

"Old Forge."

"That's the one."

In the parking lot. Fallon stretched then leaned her head onto her left shoulder until she heard and felt a satisfying crack from her neck. "Ah, that's better. Next time, Danny, how about you steal a car with a more comfortable back seat?"

"I'll work on it."

She followed him toward the entrance. "Heh, this is just like the place back home, a busted up old diner that had been a shiny new diner pretending to be a busted up old diner."

Danny said, "Yeah, I hate places like this. But what the hell. They have pancakes."

"I bet they're brilliant, too," Emma jogged to the entrance.

Jenny's front door had been covered almost entirely with taped messages and advertisements for local music lessons, art classes, rafting trips, platform drone excursions along the river valley, even a reenactment of John Brown's famous raid on Harper's Ferry. This amused Fallon, seeing as how Brown's terror attack had come at a time in American history when skin color meant something. These days, one solid skin tone only meant that you were poor. The richest snobs in any suburb had an assortment of colors from Norwegian white to Ivory Coast ebony. Reenacting a historical event with no historical significance seemed just another waste of sunshine.

She said, "Claire Felver ate her last meal in a place like this, just down the street from my mother's trailer by the lake."

"Who's Claire Felver?" Emma held the door open.

"The woman I'm accused of killing. She was murdered the night before her fifty-seventh birthday. Actually, I think they killed her on her birthday, making it a more egregious crime on my part. They waited until after midnight, so I'd be accused of murdering an official Cleanse and Harvest patient." She slid into an uncomfortable booth. Unnecessary air conditioning chilled the diner's interior to a temperature just shy of Arctic Christmas.

"It's cold," Emma crossed her arms, rubbed her shoulders. "I need a menu. You guys hungry?"

"I am," Danny said.

"Just coffee for me," Fallon toyed with the old bio wire hook up embedded in the tile wall beside their booth. "You ready for this?"

Danny drew the thin cable from its retractable housing, inserted it into the bio jack in his wrist. "Yeah, it's gonna be okay. I know it."

"I miss wireless access," Fallon punched RESET on the wall unit.

"Me too," Danny said. "Soon. Right? We'll be able to reconnect and go back to all-day, all-night access, numb our brains with lies and pointless drivel."

Fallon frowned. "When you put it like that..."

"Oh, baloney," Emma added. "You know you can't wait to get back to Wi-Fi. I'm gonna order a pizza from the most remote stand of woods I can find and charge it to my mother's E-account."

"Yeah," Fallon agreed. "Drone pizza delivery to the end of the Earth is a nice feature."

Danny said, "As soon as we get out of here, we'll find some alley hacker to kill Carter's Wi-Fi bug. Might run us a few hundred, but it'll be worth it. Maybe down in Richmond or Charlotte."

Emma said, "Log in as your...whatever he is, Gabriel Oak."

"Got it," he punched a code when the vid screen flickered to life. "So far so good."

Fallon waved to the bored-looking, short order cook working Jenny's empty grill. As the only patrons in the place, Fallon guessed the breakfast rush was still three hours away. She assumed the woman wiping down the grill burners doubled as the diner's overnight server. *A resume to be proud of...diverse skills.* "Can we get a menu, please?"

"It's on the main page, top left. The tabletop is interactive, just off for the night. Switch is underneath, right side."

"Do you have a paper copy? Sorry. We're about out of data this week."

"Just one?" The cook/server sighed and disconnected her own vid screen from a grill-side port, shut down whatever she had been watching, and slid from a wooden stool behind the counter. Obviously, noting food orders by hand irritated her.

Fallon didn't give a damn. "Yeah, one's fine."

"Coffee?"

"Three, please. And water, purified."

She dropped off Emma's menu, three waters, then returned with *Jenny's Diner* mugs. She poured coffee that might have been brewed when President Wong was in grade school. Steam rose from the pot, but Fallon imagined smoke rising from prehistoric sludge. The cook/server, abundantly pregnant at about nineteen years old, wore enough cheap jewelry in her ears, on her fingers, and about her neck that Fallon was secretly glad there hadn't been lightning in the area. Clearly this girl would act as a grounding rod. Shorter than Emma, Costume Jewelry might only have been the second or third generation of her family standing upright on hind legs.

"That's awfully black coffee," Fallon said.

"Well, honey, there's black and there's black," Costume Jewelry brandished the pot. "This here's black."

Danny winked at her. "Makes sense."

Fallon turned the paper placemat over—*Welcome to Jenny's Diner in Scenic Brunswick, Maryland...Home of Maryland's Longest Running Railroad Line!* Happy to discover the underside blank, she asked, "Can I borrow a pen?"

"Sure, honey," Costume Jewelry drew one from a breast pocket in her apron. She had five others there, each embossed with *Jenny's Diner* in bright yellow letters, not the arrogant yellow of the neon, but close enough to bring on a pretty good sinus headache.

Emma and Danny ordered. Fallon gave in and asked for wheat toast. She hoped the bread might soften the blow as Jenny's coffee hit her stomach like an enemy depth charge.

Danny read the news, then gave up and pressed DISPLAY, allowing the vid screen to project the 11:30 p.m. broadcast across their booth's interactive tabletop. Two news avatars, similar to those who'd visited them in the riverside cottage, appeared in miniature. Sitting side by side, as ever, they chatted amiably while reporting updates on earlier stories. Danny used two fingers to rotate the avatars toward Emma and Fallon.

"Nothing new," Emma said. "It's just the same stuff as before."

"That's good," Danny peeked behind her. "There's an exit, next to the bathrooms. If you see any bulls come in this place, even into the parking lot, just say so, I'll punch in the credits for our late-night snack, and we'll head out the back."

"Yup," Fallon drew a series of straight lines top-to-bottom on the placemat.

"What're you doing?" Emma sipped coffee. "Holy gods that's bad."

"I kind of like it," Danny drank as well. "No chance any of us are gonna sleep, though. Not after this."

"Where're we going?" Emma watched Fallon. "We can't just stay here. Right?"

336

"In a minute," Fallon largely ignored them. "We'll decide in a minute I promise."

None of the friends paid attention to Costume Jewelry as she fried bacon and poured out batter for pancakes on the grill behind the Formica counter. Rather, they watched Fallon scribble rough notes. When she finished, the page didn't amount to much more than a visual representation of what had come for them in the past several days. But Fallon decided to keep the sheet just the same. Reading it over helped her feel as though they were on to something. Some clue might emerge from the page if she just stared at them long enough.

In the first column, she wrote:

Colossal Man/Gigantor
Massive strength
Enraged
Stupid/not a problem solver
Destructive
Fists/perhaps cudgel or club. Otherwise no weapons
Sewn together/Assembled from body parts? At least upper arms and hands

In the next column, she added:

Snake/Copperhead
Aware? Intelligent? Deliberate?
Twenty-five feet long
600 – 700 pounds
Evil/aware eyes
Poisonous, but two vicious bites easily treated (Not deadly?)

In the third space, Fallon wrote:

Ape/Gorilla-Wolf Creature
Pack hunter
Smart/fast
Ruthless/sneaky
Comparatively weak
Communicate?
Subterranean/Nocturnal?
Understand us? Yes.
Fangs, claws, muscular, no weapons

Finally, she added:

Blackbird/Cat – Bear WSJSM
Wings, feathered, forty feet across? Fifty?
Black cat, twenty-five(?) feet long
Silent flyer
Sense of smell? Yes
Sense of hearing? Unknown
Fangs, claws, massive strength
Nearly silent flight
Night hunter/destructive
Smart/problem solver

And in bold, capital letters, Fallon finished up with:

CAN CHANGE SHAPE QUICKLY, LESS THAN
TWENTY SECONDS

Danny suggested, through a mouthful of pancakes. "Add that over here, just with a question mark." He tapped the **Colossal Man/Gigantor** column with the end of his knife.

338

"Which?"

"That bit about changing shape," he explained. "There's no way that thing always goes around like that. We'd have heard about it, read about it, seen viral videos or downloads of it: *Fifteen-foot man-monster destroys all of Cincinnati after getting served cold chili*...or something like that. You know? He's either gotta be transported around, chained in the back of a very large, very resilient titanium truck, or he's gotta have an alter-ego, like Bear."

Emma agreed. "Jesus, Danny that's a good point. I bet you're right."

"Thanks," he smirked. "But it's just 'Danny' not 'Jesus Danny.' Mom wanted to name me that, but Dad refused. Too bad."

"Jackass."

"His middle name," Fallon said, then added CAN CHANGE SHAPE? HUMAN FORM? to the column below **Colossal Man/Gigantor.**

Costume Jewelry returned, poured out more water and coffee, spilling some onto the three-dimensional, eight-inch news avatars sitting in the center of the table. Danny smiled; Costume Jewelry apologized, but only Emma noticed the pot quivering in her hand, or how her four necklaces and silver chains all rattled when she leaned over to wipe up the mess.

Danny scrolled through news stories and related links on their table screen. "It says here..." he dropped his voice to a whisper, "...that the guy we allegedly blew up in Baltimore, he was involved with Prevotel's mid-Atlantic research division."

"So what?" Fallon asked. "Prevotel has hands in corporations, public works projects, schools, medical centers, even airlines and transportation companies. That could mean anything."

"Yeah," Danny slid the last bit of bacon around his plate, collecting as much syrup as possible. Twin drops of sugary goop spilled over his chin.

339

Fallon wiped them off with a fingertip, then tasted the syrup. "Not bad. Does it say in there why we should care that this guy got himself killed? What's the angle? Who wants him dead?"

Danny looked between her and the screen, trying to stay focused. "I dunno. No, there's nothing here that makes sense. Why kill a guy whose primary job it is to help a company that runs just about everything we use, eat, encounter, watch, ride on, in, or under get better at what they do...more efficient, you know? What's he done to upset anyone?"

"So...extremists? Anti-corporation types, like before the last war?"

"Maybe," he scrolled further through recent downloads. "But why blame us?"

Fallon never had a chance to answer. Rather, Emma turned in her seat until her knees were on the vinyl bench, her notebook in one hand. In an assertive, uncompromising voice the others had not imagined coming from the fun-loving Irish kid, she directed, "Do not press that button!"

Fallon spun on her ass, was standing, facing the grill in a moment.

Emma stood on the bench, repeated her warning. "I promise...you will regret pressing that button."

No one had paid attention. They hadn't watched the lonely, pregnant short-order cook, a child herself who most likely read the same stories they had, watched the same broadcast downloads all night long.

But she believed them.

Costume Jewelry's voice quavered. Fallon felt she could almost see it rattle by in the air. "You...you're the ones. You killed that man, his wife, the other night. You..." she pointed at Fallon, "You're Fallon Westerly. Good God, you killed a Harvest patient. Who does that? And you..." this to Emma, "...blew up that ship and Penn Station. You killed eighty-five people."

"Two," Emma didn't back down. She didn't lower her voice or attempt to calm the frightened woman at all. If anything, Emma ramped up the tension, firing the confrontation even higher. Twin sets of necrotic snake bites in her face and neck intensified her sinister appearance. "You push that button, dearie, and I promise, you...and your baby...will not walk out of here, bulls or no bulls. You understand?"

Danny clicked off the news, unplugged his wrist from the port. "Lady, you've gotta understand: those stories are bullshit. Someone is making that all up, framing us for things we didn't do."

She jabbed a finger at Emma. "She just admitted it."

He shut down the table screen. "Calm down. Please. Calm down. Nothing bad is going to happen—"

Beside him Emma spoke slowly, clearly. "You were mean, and I don't care. So let's cut down your supply of air."

And Costume Jewelry began to choke.

Emma went on. "You feel that? Yeah, dearie, you press that button and the bulls are going to find your eyeballs bugged out far enough that they'll have to scoop them from the fryer with a ladle."

The diner cook didn't hear or understand. Raking fingers down her throat, trying and failing to yank loose whatever invisible collar Emma had tightened there, she choked, wheezed an unsettling raspy gasp, then looked to Fallon and Danny for help.

Fallon wheeled on Emma. "Let her go. You're gonna hurt the baby."

"No I'm not." She stared Costume Jewelry down. "I'm making a quick point."

"Em," Danny took her hand. "Let her go."

Emma gestured with her pen. "Undo."

Costume Jewelry fell across the diner's front counter, gulping great swallows of cold, greasy, bacon-stinking air. She might have stayed there until morning if Fallon hadn't approached half to help her sit up, drink some water, catch her breath, and half to snip both her bio wire and her vid screen antenna. Fallon thought *pruning shears* and had the job done in less time than it took Costume Jewelry to drink half a glass.

She propped the top-heavy girl back onto her stool. "Sorry about that, but we can't have you calling in the bulls."

The pregnant woman didn't care. "Don't hurt my baby. Please. Please, Fallon. You're Fallon, right?"

"I am."

"I read about you, your mother, your life; I want to believe you. I do, but they have video of you leaving that lady's apartment, the dead lady."

"That's fake," she rubbed Costume Jewelry's lower back. "I don't know why...well, that's not true. I'll be straight with you. I do know why they framed me and Danny and...well, Emma less so."

"She really kill eighty-five people?" She waited, still a bit bug-eyed, for Fallon to assure her she hadn't just served the morning pancake special to a mass murderer.

"Two," Fallon said.

"Maybe three," Emma interrupted. "But they were really, really bad guys."

The frightened woman wiped tears from her face. "Okay. Anything. Just don't hurt my baby. What do you need me to do?"

"Nothing," Danny said. "Just tell us what we owe you and I'll transfer the credits right now."

"No." Her breathing slowed. "It's okay. It's on me."

"C'mon, now," Fallon said. "We've gotta pay you for breakfast. It was great...except for, maybe, the coffee."

Now she laughed, just a quick splutter, that might have been born as a cry then changed its mind halfway out.

"Really," Danny smiled. "I'm all logged in and ready to transfer over."

"Wait," confusion washed over her face. "Won't they know? Won't they be able to tell that you were here?"

Shit. Fallon thought. *If she calls the bulls later, they'll have Danny's phony account. This was dumb. We should've taken the free breakfast.* She looked to the others, cast them a glance that said, *Keep your mouths shut. Trust me.*

"You know," Fallon explained. "You would be helping us. We've been on the run a long time, and we're short of credits. So, if you don't mind, a free breakfast might be just the thing to hustle us out of here and out of your life forever. Whaddya say?"

"That's fine." Costume Jewelry couldn't agree fast enough. "I'll never say a word. Never. Just don't hurt me or my baby, and I won't say anything."

"Thank you..." Fallon handed her more water. "What's your name?"

"Deandra," she drank, smeared tears and snotty mucus on a greasy towel. "Deandra Hollingsworth."

"All right, Deandra," Danny motioned Emma toward the door. "Thanks for the pancakes. No kidding: they were great. And I promise...I promise that if you keep watching the news, eventually, not long now—"

"Maybe a week," Fallon said.

"Maybe a week," he continued. "You're gonna see that we were innocent."

Deandra wanted to believe him. Fallon read it in her face as bright as the neon lights outside. "Trust us," she said. "I know you don't want to, but we're leaving quietly, and you'll never see us again."

"Okay," she whimpered. "Okay."

Fallon followed the others toward the exit. Emma only paused long enough to shoot Deandra a threatening glance. Reading her mind, Fallon grabbed the smaller girl and half dragged her into the parking lot.

"Are you crazy? You gonna murder someone over breakfast?"

"Not murder," Emma stood her ground. "Threaten. They're vastly different things. That girl needs to be scared

343

witless of us, or she's gonna have the bulls on us. I can hear the drones already."

Danny opened the Chevron doors. "And they're gonna have my dummy account. She's right. We need Deandra just a bit terrified."

Fallon looked around the parking lot as if someone might come to the rescue, someone kind and compassionate who never threatened to kill pregnant, semi-literate teenagers who only trusted news broadcasts because she'd only ever been taught to trust news broadcasts.

"I'll go," Danny offered, seeing Fallon hesitate.

"No," she said. "No. I'm the one who calmed her down. I've gotta do it." She checked the puddles of sodium arc lighting thinking an answer might be hidden in the shadows. "Shit!"

"Yup," Emma said. "We're okay. Now we're okay."

"I got it," Fallon said. "Get in the car. Get ready to go."

"You sure?" Danny looked ready to dive off a bridge, one of the tall ones.

She understood that but also understood that there was nothing he could do for her at this moment. "Yeah, just get ready."

Inside Jenny's, Deandra hadn't moved. Staring at the fugitives' dirty dishes, she might have been a woman trying to decide whether or not to destroy evidence. She cried in heaving gasps as miserable as a month of wet weather.

Fallon didn't let herself care. Striding to the counter, she thought *hatchet* and brought a laser-honed kitchen cleaver down on an aluminum napkin holder, slicing it cleanly in two. From Deandra's perspective, Fallon used her bare hand to slice the metal box and about a hundred paper napkins as easily as swatting a mosquito.

"Help me!" she cried. "No! No, don't, please!"

Fallon grasped a fistful of Deandra's uniform blouse, breaking at least two necklaces in the process. "I just want to be sure that we understand one another, *dearie*."

"I do. I do! Please, let me live. Please don't hurt my baby!"

"Shut up!" Fallon shouted, inches from her face. "Just so we're clear on this…if I see so much as one bull, one E-copter, one drone following us for the next three days, I'm gonna assume you blabbed, and I'm gonna come back here, and I'm gonna eat that baby's heart—"

"No! Please!" Deandra shrieked, bellowing great spluttery pleas for forgiveness between promises to keep quiet. "I won't! I swear to God; I won't!"

"I will eat that baby's heart, Deandra. I swear to you…right here on this counter," and for good measure, Fallon called up the cleaver again, just long enough to gouge an intimidating cleft into Jenny's butcher block cutting board. "You understand me?"

Deandra sobbed too violently to respond.

Fallon left the girl on the stool, shook her cleaver hand back to normal, and moved to the booth where they'd eaten. Thinking *ice pick,* she drove several deep holes into the bio-wire unit. The console sparked twice in its death throes, then blinked out.

Her vision tunneled; she worried she might pass out from some kind of adrenaline overdose. Hands shaking, Fallon pressed through the bulletin board doorway into Jenny's parking lot. There, outside the nearest puddle of overhead light, she fell to her knees, sobbing herself now, and vomited up wheat toast and badly burned coffee.

Danny stepped out of the running Chevron, then waited, one hand trailing fingertips over the dented trunk. "You all right?"

Fallon gagged again, this time bringing up only wiry strings of aromatic gook from the bottom of whatever well she'd emptied. Spitting, she coughed, "Yeah. Yeah. I'm coming."

Danny waited.

Inside the car, Emma watched, disinterested. They'd done what they needed to do. To any onlookers, she appeared content with that.

Fallon rose on uncertain legs. "We gotta steal a boat."

"You want some water?"

"We gotta steal a boat." She spat again, another mouthful of stringy saliva and diner coffee. "It's three o'clock in the morning; we're outside a river town...let's find one, even just a canoe, something small."

"I'll find some rope." He opened the door. "We can tie it to the roof and be gone by dawn."

Dizzy, Fallon tumbled into the back seat, collapsed onto the threadbare cushions. "Good. Emma can pick the color."

"Of what?" The perky Irish terrorist chimed.

"We're gonna steal a boat, my favorite felon. You and me."

"Excellent! I've always wanted a boat."

Fallon groaned, "Well this is your lucky night. You even get to pick—"

"Blue!"

Danny shifted into drive. "Blue it is. Let's go."

None of them brought up the fact that Bear might still be in the area, might be circling overhead at that very moment, or that she might not be so gentle or forgiving with Deandra and Deandra's baby. If Bear or Blair or Mr. Colossal Bulldozer or Kaa the giant frigging snake or the Flying Dutchman, Dracula, Vincent van Gogh, or the Boogie Man of Bartholomew Cubbins's worst nightmare could track their skills, then Emma and Fallon had led them directly to Deandra Hollingsworth, to Jenny's Diner, and to a disabled bio-wire console that all but blinked: CHECK HERE FIRST for the most recent network access and login. They all but handed Danny's dummy account to Blair and Carter, because they'd decided to stop for pancakes and late-night coffee.

None of them brought it up, but all of them worried about it. Instead, they allowed Emma's blue canoe to distract

346

them. The three friends—even Emma—silently hoped that Deandra would see the morning and that the few seconds of talent they'd displayed wouldn't be enough to bring Bear's raven-winged panther down from the heavens.

Danny drove along an access road leading from the town of Brunswick to a run-down campground right on the banks of the Potomac. A handful of nylon tents and pop-up campers lay scattered about the riverbank. One pine log cabin – Danny noted that this must belong to the camp director – had a light burning in the window and above the front door. Otherwise, the place appeared deserted, expectedly silent and unaware that a winged monster might be hunting them from five-hundred feet up.

Killing the Chevron's lights, he turned toward the campground's boat ramp. A canoe and kayak rack trailer rested inches deep in soft mud beside the ramp. A half dozen cheap plastic canoes and two kayaks waited, unlocked, untied, for any would-be criminal hoping to escape down river with a canoe they could pick up for five-hundred credits on any E-network swap site.

They were all fluorescent orange.

"How's orange, Em?" Danny joked.

"My stepfather, Edward, has an orange kayak. I prefer blue."

"Sorry, kid," he left the car running but killed the interior lights before Emma could open her door.

"That's all right," she climbed out. "This'll have to do. Oh, look: they even left us some rope."

"Perfect."

"But be careful," Emma warned. "I don't want us scratching my car."

Peeking in the back window for a look at Fallon, Danny forced a laugh. "Yeah, your twenty-year-old, Canadian, rust-o-matic...we'll be careful."

347

15.37

Do Not Feed the Bears!

Yoo-hoo! Sorry! I'm here with a couple of notes, just for a few minutes, and then I'll let you get back to the story.

Before I begin, I want to encourage you to keep in mind the placemat Fallon used to make notes about the creatures and crawly things that had been tracking them. I know it doesn't seem like much to us. We've had the benefit of following the story detail-by-detail all along, a pretty comfortable and convenient place here in the balcony. But trust me, that placemat is going to come into play again before our friends' adventures wrap up. Don't forget it.

Oh, and I don't know if you enjoy diner food. I tend not to. However, if you're ever in Brunswick, Maryland and have an opportunity to visit Jenny's, I suggest trying the Big Scramble. It's a three-egg concoction mixed with hash browns, bacon, sausage, cheese, and served with either toast or pancakes. No energy paste, no protein goo, no seaweed, and nothing, as Emma would say, that tastes like orangutan ass. The Big Scramble. Trust me.

Anyway, our friends have left the diner, and you're wondering what's happened to poor Deandra. Aren't you?

Young, pregnant, holding down two jobs as she makes her way alone in a world that offers up all manner of cruelty, even to teenage mothers whose boyfriends have scrammed to join the military in central Asia. Deandra was guilty of nothing more than believing the news broadcasts she watched on her wrist all night in the otherwise sleepy town.

Having gotten herself good and pregnant with an otherwise useless young fellow who took off without warning the first time Deandra's belly protruded farther than a flat sheet of newsprint, the mother-to-be decided to take life's challenges by the horns and do her best to be abundantly prepared to raise a child alone. This meant having money—

thus the two jobs she worked without complaint. But it also meant education—Deandra had narrowly finished eleventh grade before taking what her own mother called an 'extended vacation' from the Frederick County Public Schools.

That had been three years earlier. Now, at nineteen (and pregnant, let's not forget), Deandra spent most of her nights reading, watching documentaries, and keeping up with informative broadcasts on her wrist screen, particularly during slow times at the diner, which working the Midnight to 9:00 a.m. shift meant most of the night.

And this, friends, was Deandra's only mistake when she suffered the misfortune of meeting Danny, Emma, and Fallon. Deandra believed what she saw and read on her vid screen.

Stupid, I know.

But not everyone can be as brilliantly introspective and insightful as you, dear reader.

Of course, she panicked when she realized she'd been cooking up pancakes for three wanted felons, one a murderer and one a domestic terrorist. That was more excitement than Deandra had known, well, since the breezy afternoon seven months earlier that had gotten her into this predicament in the first place.

(And as a note to all of you young people out there: Keep your damned pants on for a while. Trust me. Or you might just find yourself standing the middle watch at a rural diner and having to fend off murderers and terrorists, not the best tippers if the research can be trusted.)

Anyway, what happened to Deandra:

Did they kill her? No. But they scared her.

And by *they*, I'm sure you've gathered by now that I mean the servants and employees of Susan Wentworth-White: The man in the black suit, who we've known for some pages, was this time accompanied by a muscular, disheveled, disagreeable teenage girl who looked as if she might either break the bones in Deandra's neck or perhaps settle in for a triple helping of Deandra's heartiest breakfast skillet.

349

You guessed it: Beatrice Bear Guenard.

Keep in mind that despite being as frightened and weary as she'd ever been in her life, Deandra hadn't told the authorities. She hadn't called the bulls, hadn't even told her boss when the morning shift arrived to prep for the breakfast rush. No, Deandra was terrified that Fallon Westerly, the girl with the sparkling eye and the meat cleaver hand, might return to eat her baby's heart. She had no idea that just articulating such a threat had left Fallon weeping and vomiting in the parking lot. Deandra decided to forget that the unpleasant incident had ever taken place, so she was particularly surprised when the staggeringly attractive man in the black suit and the homely, garbage truck of a young woman showed up asking questions.

When her boss attempted to join them in Fallon, Danny, and Emma's abandoned booth—still empty, even at 8:00 a.m. No one wants to eat breakfast at a table with a disabled network hook-up.—Bear shot the man such a look of untethered loathing that he retreated behind the counter, noting, "Okay, well, fine…thanks. Just lemme know if y'all need anything. Deandra here will help you out as best she can." He waved pleasantly as a means of hiding the embarrassing tremor in his voice.

The man in the black suit asked Deandra a few questions about the fugitives, what they ate, how long they stayed, if they logged in to the network, what they said, and how many other customers had visited Jenny's the previous night.

The pregnant teen responded thoroughly, despite being equal parts frightened that Fallon would return to kill her or perhaps Bear might do it and then order a slice of pie.

She saw something in Bear's eyes that troubled her, an insidious hunger, animal rage or something worse hidden just behind the big girl's muddy brown eyes, but clearly wanting to escape. Deandra answered quickly, leaving no details out, not even the meat cleaver hand—even though she'd disposed of the injured napkin holder and the cloven napkins hours earlier. She'd promised Fallon that she'd never say a word, and yet here she was, the next morning, spilling her guts, not because she decided Fallon was long gone, but because Deandra wanted to be home, hidden, locked away someplace safe before whatever it was lurking behind the strange girl's eyes managed to free itself.

If Deandra had to put money on Bear or Fallon, she'd have bet on Bear every time.

So she told everything she knew to the polite, pleasant man—stunningly good looking to boot—in the black suit.

When she returned to her tables and counter service, Deandra heard the musclebound girl ask the older man, "You think you can log in? Find them?"

The attractive fellow toyed with the network box Fallon had stabbed to death and shook his head. "Not from here. No. But with so few customers in here last night, Carter can track down that account."

"You hungry?"

The man adjusted an already perfect tie. "Almost never."

"I am." Bear pulled up a menu on her wrist and began paging through breakfast specials.

I don't suppose I need to tell you what she ordered. You can probably guess: ham, bacon paste, and sausage scrambled up with several eggs and served over a rare—bloody and nearly mooing—eight-ounce steak.

Bear was hungry. She rubbed numbness from her new jaw, silently promising to gnaw Fallon Westerly's arms off when she finally tracked the fugitives down.

16

A Fifty-Year-Old Car, a Load of Brisket Pastries (with extra gravy), and Pie at 4:00 a.m.

Hadley Hill wasn't a hill. More a knoll, a wrinkle in the landscape, it rose just high enough above Owen Pond to afford the fugitives a view north across the shallow valley, over the thatch of congested hardwoods along the lakeshore, and into the rear defenses and security protections of the Warrenton School for Juvenile Student Management. The campus was protected on all sides by a brick wall topped with electrified coils of barbed wire. It enclosed the dormitories, classroom complex, quad, mess hall, and main exercise yard on nearly all four sides.

From Hadley Hill, Fallon and the others could easily make out two narrow places where the wall was incomplete: the front gate, where the main drive entered the grounds past the guard house, and the lakefront beach, just a brief spit of sand well-behaved students were permitted to use, providing they went at least six weeks with no demerits or detentions.

The WSJSM's beach lay beyond a narrow gate, a ten-foot breach in the brick and barbed-wire ramparts. A security staff member patrolled the southern fortifications day and night. The runaways knew this, so entering campus from the beach would require them to disable, kidnap, or perhaps even kill at least one innocent staff member.

If such a thing exists, Fallon thought.

"That gate will have a key code," Danny said.

"Doesn't matter," she answered.

"True. I can get through." He pointed toward the short slope of trimmed grass, an open area where the three of them would be exposed to sight lines from hundreds of south facing windows in almost every building on campus. "That lawn, there, running down from the quad and the infirmary—"

"Blair's chop shop, you mean."

"Yeah, that," Danny said. "We're gonna be out in the open for eight, maybe ten seconds as we approach the quad."

"Not much we can do about it. Right?" Emma shaded her eyes. Morning sun cast Virginia's piedmont in harsh light, making it difficult to plan their assault from this far away.

"We can be over there before dawn," Fallon said.

"Good idea," Danny agreed. "That way the staff member on duty is groggy, tired, counting down the minutes until a replacement shows up with coffee and biscuits."

"It's still a little dark," Emma took up the speculative line of reasoning. "We get through the gate silently, somehow, and up behind the infirmary before anyone sees us."

"That's where we start," Fallon pointed to the campus's westernmost edge. "In the rear entrance to the chop shop. We start it burning, then hurry through that adjoining building. What is that?"

"Meade Hall," Danny said. "I lived there."

"Meade," Fallon went on. "We roust everyone—quietly— let them know they've got about fifteen minutes to get their shit together and get clear—"

"How do we get the door codes?"

"We'll take a guard's key card," Danny explained. "They all have spares in case the network goes down and their wireless signals don't work. It's standard security protocol. I can almost guarantee they're supposed to be in a flip-lock case on their belts, but most guards keep them right in the pocket of their uniform shirt."

"Know something about that do you?" Fallon teased.

"Every lockup I've ever been in!" He found an egg-shaped rock, heaved it toward Owen Pond below.

Emma asked, "So after we let the inmates free, do they go out the front? The back? What do we tell them?"

"By the time those fifteen minutes are up, it won't matter."

Emma agreed. "Okay. Good. Sure, that makes sense."

353

"And the gate to the pond will be open or torn off," Danny suggested. "That's the easiest way out, down to the waterline and then out through the woods."

"What if they don't run?" Emma asked.

"They'll run," Fallon said. "They'll have to."

Danny understood, turned to Emma. "Can you bring it down?"

"What? Me?" She took a step backward, had anticipated such a question but not this soon. "How much of it?"

Fallon pointed west to east. "At least the main building. Blair and Carter's apartments, offices, Carter's computer center, the network hub, the online file servers...all of that, Em. Can you bring that down?"

Emma moved to the edge of the wooded overlook where Danny had parked the Chevron. Amiable yellow and blue wild flowers grew in desultory clumps. "Yeah, I think so. I mean, I know it looks small from all the way up here, but yeah, I can leave that place looking like Atlanta after a bombing run."

"Good." Fallon picked two of the yellow flowers, then a blue, twisted them about her finger. "We need another car."

Danny agreed. "For out front. Right?"

"Yeah," she said. "We could risk it, drive the Chevron around back, drop the canoe and our supplies, and then hide it somewhere for when we have to get away."

"But we've got to assume they know this car by now," Emma said. "Even though we threw a pretty good scare into Deandra back at the diner, we've gotta figure the bulls either beat information out of her—"

Danny finished her thought. "Or they pulled security tapes from the diner parking lot. I didn't see any cameras—"

"Neither did I," Emma said.

"But we've got to assume they were there," Fallon tossed the flowers aside. "If we blow this place to kingdom come and then try to get away—"

"To Jackson," Danny said hopefully, "or Equatorial New Guinea, I don't care."

Fallon grinned, just for a second. "Yes, Danny, to Jackson. If we manage to get out of here and then decide to flee to Swampass, Mississippi, we're gonna need a different car. The manhunt for us is gonna be epic, especially if we succeed—if *I* succeed—in killing Blair. You two can stick around as long as you like, but the heat on me is gonna be significant for a good long while."

Emma took her wrist. "Let's be clear. We're taking my car."

"Em, we can't—"

"Well, then someone's just gonna have to steal me another one when we get down to Swampass. Sorry, Danny. Actually, maybe one of those F-bikes. Have you seen those? *Vrrooom!*" She mock piloted an F-cycle at pretend 200 mph. "I'm a badass!"

Danny ignored her. "Why not let someone else deal with this? We can contact someone, talk to someone, inform some news agency or something. I mean, we all saw Bear. We know what Blair's doing, well, not exactly what he's doing, but we have our suspicions, pretty solid suspicions. Why do we have to be the ones to bring this place down?"

Fallon said, "You said it yourself: We're God's rough drafts. We were brought here on purpose. We don't know why, but if it was to become lab rats for some chop shop experiment in creating super-human monsters with amazing talents, destructive skills, or powers of transformation. If they framed the three of us and sent us here to take our blood, our DNA, to create more of those…whatever they are…that have been following us, then yes, I think we need to be the ones to deal with this."

"I disagree," Danny said uselessly.

"Then go." Fallon didn't mean to sting him. "Blair and maybe a hundred others like him—who knows?—are using people like us to create things like Bear…if that's what's happening, if that's the future of Stormcloud and Brokerage Houses, we need to fight back."

355

Danny plucked two flowers, sniffed at them. "I don't know how to do that, Fallon. None of us do."

She agreed. "You're right, but we can start educating ourselves right here."

"What about his files?" Emma asked. "Online files? Data? Notes on his experiments?"

"How would we get them?" Danny asked. "It's not like we have all day to hang around in that infirmary."

Emma said, "We don't have to log in or download anything. When we're in the chop shop, we'll just take the hard drive from his computer. He's gotta have some stuff saved on there. Granted, he might have saved everything in an online storage facility or a Prevo cloud. But given the nature of his work, I think he'd be more prone to keep his files local."

"Good point," Fallon said. "How difficult will it be to steal the drive?"

"Five seconds," she explained. "Literally one cable. I'll just unhook it and stuff it into my bag. We can worry about breaking into it later."

"Really?" Danny asked. "You can do that?"

"Oh, sure. Once we're somewhere safe, we can download software that'll break into almost any hard drive on the market."

Fallon frowned, skeptical. "You don't think it'll be better protected?"

"Why would it?" she asked. "It's inside a locked, illegal chop shop on the grounds of a juvenile detention center that no one wants to visit, never mind break into on purpose. Blair could probably leave files out on the desk, open with READ ME stickers all over them, and no one ever would."

Danny ran fingers through his hair, leaving it a tangle. "You're probably right. I dunno if you can break into the drive, but if stealing it is all we need to do, I think we add that to our to-do list."

"Done," Fallon said.

356

"Actually," Emma changed gears on them. "I'm more concerned with stealing another car. That could present a problem. With all the new-fangled satellite logins and remote tracking devices, computer navigation systems, and anti-theft programming, we've almost gotta buy a car or get someone to give us a car."

'Yeah," Danny added, "or find a car that no one will report missing for a few days. We drive non-stop down to Hinds County and then sink it in a bog somewhere."

"I'll take care of that," Fallon said. "I think I know exactly where we can find one just down the road."

Danny and Emma shared a glance. He said, "Bulls transported you here from New York. You were in lockdown twenty-four hours a day. How did you locate a car that just happens to fit our needs?"

"Trust me." She turned their attention back to the lakeshore. "You see this beach access, here on the southern end?"

The others craned their necks to see down to a swatch of sandy beach almost directly beneath them. A weather-beaten dock stretched fifty feet into the water. While two swim floats lay moored offshore, there were no boats, cars, tourists, sunbathers, even dog walkers about.

Fallon said, "It looks abandoned. I think because we're so late in the fall, the tourists and summer residents have gone for the season."

Danny understood. "But there's gotta be a road."

"Exactly," she said. "That's a shared beach; probably everyone who owns a home down on this end of the pond has a right of way to use it, tie up a boat, go swimming, barbecue, whatever."

Emma said, "I don't get it. Who wants to own a home that shares a lake with a juvenile detention center?"

Danny said, "I would. C'mon, Em, that school is almost a mile out. It's nice and quiet on this end."

Fallon smiled. "Perfect for us."

Danny tallied their to-do list on his fingers. "So we've gotta find some food, steal a car, stash the car out front, find someplace quiet to sleep for a while, then make our way down here." He pointed in the direction of the dock at the base of the hill. "We ought to be here by midnight, give or take, so we can be well on our way across before the sun rises."

"I'm gonna be scared," Emma confessed. "On our way over in the dark, that's gonna scare the dogsnot out of me."

Danny pulled her close with one arm. "Well, you really shouldn't have dogsnot in you, not at your age."

"I'm not the best swimmer. I was kidding the other day."

"Well then I strongly encourage you to stay in the boat," Fallon teased.

"Maybe while she's stealing us a car, I'll go buy you some water wings."

"In case we capsize in impenetrable darkness and I fall into a mile-long lake of uncertain depth with unknown horrors swimming around: sharks, dragons, giant snapping turtles, big, wriggly, squeezy snakes, pouty-lipped fish that'll just inhale me like an appetizer...sure, water wings will brighten my whole day, Danny. While you're at it, why don't you just download a taser code and fry my ass to bacon?"

"I had bacon earlier, with my pancakes," he said, straight faced. "I was kinda hoping for some fried chicken and potato salad—last meal, you know."

Fallon checked the knots and ropes holding the stolen canoe on the Chevron's roof and wondered whether a description of the car had already been broadcast this morning. If so, their trip into Warrenton might be short and unamusing. *Fingers crossed.* If the next twenty-four hours were going to work out, the friends would have to weather dangerous risks. Being observed in a stolen car was just the first of many.

She climbed into the back seat, not having seen the splashy disturbance on the water, as if something had surfaced for a moment before returning silently to the depths.

As they descended from the foothills into Warrenton, Fallon drew the flat of one palm over her head, effectively erasing the shoulder-length hair she'd sprouted while battling the snake in Penn Station. Figuring everyone in North America had seen images of her, the bald head might throw off those few who only gave a cursory look.

Danny noticed in the rear-view mirror. "Jumping Jesus's underpants, girl! You've gotta give me just a pinch of warning before you do that. Okay?"

"Do what?" Emma turned in her seat, laughed. "Oh, heh, go to the groomer. Nice, Fallon. I like it, makes you look tough."

"I don't feel tough," she said, then added. "Sorry, Danny."

He made eye contact in the mirror. "Ah, that's all right. I like this look on you, was just getting used to it when you changed over the last time."

"Yeah, well, I'm fulla surprises."

Emma whispered, "He's a seventeen-year-old guy with an active pulse. You just stick around, and he'll be fine."

Fallon passed fingertips over her head again. It felt lean, ready for battle. "I like it. I know it's unorthodox, and my mother would break my legs. But I don't mind."

"It is unorthodox," Danny said. "But that's you. You define unorthodox. I can't imagine the guys you dated back home."

"Neither can I," Fallon added, in hopes that Danny understood how few guys had ever taken the risk.

Emma found this entertaining. "Yeah, imagine that guy dancing too close with your former best friend...ouch!" She cranked up a singsong, porcelain princess voice: "No, I didn't have a good time tonight, Reginald. So would you prefer to burst into flames, get blown to ragged chunks, or just have a barbed ice pick rammed up your—"

"We get it, Em," Danny cut her off, turned onto a street leading toward the center of town. "But Fallon's right. Once we

359

get closer to the main drag, we ought to split up. There's no sense in locals seeing us together."

"Good point," Emma agreed.

"Where do you need to go?" Danny asked the mirror.

"Martin's Café & Sundries. It's a funny little place on the north side. I can't remember the streets; we were only there for about a half hour. They sell H-batteries and E-carbon inserts for vid screens, regular rack stuff like that, but they have a lunch counter where you can order coffee and a tuna sandwich. It's like something out of a movie. The bulls who brought me down must have made regular trips to Bloody Blair's Dissection Emporium, because they didn't even glance at the menu, just ordered up two brisket pastries each, you know, the handheld ones, for takeout. They must be good."

"Get me a couple," Emma said.

"I don't have any credits."

"Then Danny can get me a couple."

"We're not going to the same places," he explained. "Sorry."

Emma cast him a mock pout. Danny grabbed for her lower lip, causing the younger girl to let go with a splutter of giggles.

"Danny can go in," Fallon said. "We need food, anyway. I'm going around back...I think."

"Excellent!" Emma cried. "I'll take two pastries, kind sir. With extra gravy."

"Done," he opened his window, inviting the cool morning in.

Fallon let the breeze caress her naked scalp and realized that she was hungry, too. Wishing she'd eaten more at the diner, she said, "Okay, why not. Two for me as well."

Danny looked for a parking space. "Well, if nothing else sends me to a state penitentiary for the rest of my life, this'll do it. *Good morning, may I have six brisket pastries, please? Yes, that's right: six with extra gravy. I'm wicked hungry.*"

360

Fallon opened her window, draped an arm out casually, as if she didn't have a care. "We all have our little challenges to face this morning. Don't we?"

Leaving her friends three blocks south of Warrenton's old town, Fallon located the detached, two-car garage behind Martin's Café & Sundries. Adjacent to the store but facing away from the street, the garage itself provided cover as she ducked behind a scatter of trash bins and sneaked along the alley between the café and a network supply store on the corner. Old Ms. Martin's garage might have been a shed in its younger days, but now, upgraded with an E-charging station and a hydrogen gas hook up, the outbuilding clearly housed the family's automobiles.

Moving through shadows, Fallon hoped the Grey Panther Ms. Martin had mentioned the previous month would be inside. She knew she wouldn't be able to steal anything new enough to run on hydrogen. Hell, even the old junker might need a charge—that could take two hours. Or the lock, login, and starter codes might not be stashed in the garage. Or the goddamned car might not even be in there.

She tried to ignore the list of fears lining up like enemy soldiers in her mind. She'd simply break into the garage, see what Ms. Martin and her family stored there, and then decide if she had enough time, opportunity, knowledge, and wild, shithouse luck to get away with a car.

Stupid. She thought. *This is stupid. You're basing all of this—dangerous risk that might find the three of us in lockup for the rest of our lives, or worse—on a couple of offhanded comments an old woman made weeks ago while you were in shackles. Lovely. Just frigging lovely.*

Fallon stretched to tiptoe and peeked inside the double doors. In one bay, plugged into a copper-lined H-fueling cable, one of Ms. Martin's adult children had parked a fire engine red, Antonelli Marauder, easily the nicest car Fallon had ever seen up close. She'd read somewhere that it went from 0 to 100 miles per hour in less than five seconds, akin to being fired off the deck of an aircraft carrier. Older and out-of-shape test drivers passed out as they accelerated. Fallon couldn't fathom why anyone would need a hydrogen-powered car, but the suburbs were still the suburbs, and people had outlandish needs that had to be met with outlandish toys. Apparently, the sundries, coffee, iced tea, and tuna sandwich business had been booming in Warrenton recently.

Beside it, beneath a canvas tarp that might have kept kittens dry on Noah's ark, rested a rounded hulk of a car. Fallon wasn't sure she really knew what shape a fifty-something-year-old Grey Panther took when hidden beneath a canvas blanket, but given the sheer amount of dust accumulated on the tarp itself, she knew this had to be old Ms. Martin's beloved shitbox.

And it was plugged in, blinking green. Fully charged. *Jackpot!*

She tried the doors. Nothing. Not surprisingly—with a two-million-credit automobile parked inside—the garage was equipped with a lock. Fallon didn't panic, not yet. She could break or cut through any chain or bolt given time. That wouldn't be a problem. What worried her was the possibility that to protect that Marauder (not an old Panther; no one in their right mind would steal a 2072 Panther), the Martins might have installed...

And she found it: mounted on the side of the garage, nearly hidden beneath the sunlit limbs of a maple tree, a network security keypad flashed red.

"Shit," she whispered, losing hope. "Shit and shit and shit!" She pressed her back to the shed wall and slid down until she was sitting, knees pulled in tight, on the gravel drive behind Martin's Café & Sundries.

Danny can get in.

But he can't open the doors, not without the codes.

And Ms. Martin will report the Grey Panther stolen.

You're as good as caught if that happens.

Think.

She'd been feeling confident all morning, despite the possibility that Deandra had spoken to the Frederick County police or that video of their Chevron had circulated throughout the region. She'd not worried at the unexpected breadth of Owen Pond, at the security measures protecting the WSJSM, or the frightening notion that they'd have to cross under the cover of darkness—one thing to talk about, even brag about to friends, but another thing entirely to actually launch the boat, point its nose into the gloom and start paddling. Nope. None of that had even dented her mood. They were so close to ending Blair's tenure as a killer, a rapist pedophile, and a frigging mad scientist hell bent on using talented young people—like her, Danny, and Emma—to create unholy monsters—like Bear and her raven-winged frigging jaguar.

And yet, here she was, undone by a ten-digit keypad with something like 3.7 million possible combinations to open a hundred-year-old shed where some boring, middle-aged junk shop owner had decided to park his two-million-credit car, probably because he was balding, getting fat, unable to find a girlfriend, or some other mid-life stumble Fallon couldn't give a floating, fried turd about.

She started to cry.

Folding her arms over her knees, she rested her forehead and thought of her mother. She would have traded almost anything to activate her vid-screen and send a message to her mother, even something in a carefully cryptic code, just to feel that naked, invisible thread connecting them over four-hundred miles. Even if it only lasted a few borrowed minutes, Fallon needed a fresh burst of unconditional love.

Granted, this wasn't the end of the world. She could find Danny, bring him back here, see if he might find the keycode inside the garage, perhaps hidden with the login and starter codes for the old car. But that would mean time and energy and another delay, and she was just so frigging tired. And maybe Danny was right. Maybe they should just steal a car and head for Nowhere, Mississippi, lay low all winter, and then decide what to do next.

But she couldn't, especially not after watching Bear transform twice with about as little effort as it would take the hulking dummy to change her t-shirt. And she couldn't hide all winter; her birthday was coming, a noisy, caterwauling Eighteen Subpoena with it.

We have to.

You have to.

"Honey?" A reedy, wavering voice asked. "You all right?"

Fallon rolled to her feet, wiped snot and tears on the back of her hand, and coughed twice to hide the fact that she'd been huddled out here crying. "Yes, sorry. I'll go. Sorry." She raised open palms chest high and backed away.

"You're her. Aren't you? You're Fallon Westerly." Ms. Martin raised her own hands now, one of them holding the leather leash to a mottled gray bulldog ancient enough to have terrorized those same kittens on Noah's ark. "Wait. Hold on now. It's okay."

Fallon stopped, sheltering beneath golden maple branches. The rustle overhead whispered assurance. This woman wasn't going to call for help.

Ms. Martin approached warily. "Why did you cut your hair? Your hair is beautiful, even in those awful fake videos and pictures they use on the vid screens."

"I...heh...well, I guess I thought it would be harder for people to recognize me." She spoke slowly, still poised to run if necessary. "But since you're literally the first person I've met, and it took you all of two seconds to recognize me, well, maybe I need to re-think my disguise a little."

"It's that eye, dear." She raised an arthritic finger to her own leathery, but friendly, face. "You can't hide that eye. It's...it's just beautiful, about the most beautiful eye anyone's ever seen."

"Yeah," Fallon covered half her face with one hand. "It's been drawing attention since I was a toddler."

"As well it should. That's a rare one, so colorful. Generations and generations all captured in one place. Gorgeous. Oh, my!" She yanked the dog leash a little too violently, prompting a frustrated grunt from the wheezing, wrinkled creature at her feet. "Oh, Bully, you hush."

Fallon relaxed. "What's his name?"

"Ulysses Sitting Bull Grant, the Fourth. But I just call him Bully." She nudged the dog forward with a ratty slipper. "Go on, Bully, say hello to our new friend."

The dog staggered forward a few paces, then lowered drooly jowls as Fallon scratched him behind his ears.

"Oh, dear," Ms. Martin said. "Be careful. You keep that up, and he'll follow you down the barrel of an enemy cannon. Of course, he can't be more than about ten minutes from death, so you'll need to make that a close enemy and a short cannon."

Fallon scratched harder. "You like that, old man? Huh? Glad you wandered all the way back here today?" Of Ms. Martin, she asked, "How old is he?"

"Lord, I don't remember. He's my fourth bulldog, my fourth Ulysses Sitting Bull Grant. I've had him since I was a thousand years old, so I guess that makes him about forty thousand. Like me."

Fallon chuckled. "You're not that old, ma'am."

"I am," she said. "But it's okay. After a while you stop counting, and then after a longer while you forget to count, and then after that...well, you kind of forget math as a concept. It's delightful really." Nearly smothered in a floral print house dress with a Martin's Café & Sundries apron tied somewhere out behind her considerable midsection, Ms. Martin looked like a hunk of gaudy drapery that had come loose and decided to waddle away, bulldog in tow.

"Well," Fallon stood, "I appreciate you not turning me in."

"Oh, pish posh to that," the older woman brushed her off. "I know you didn't do anything wrong, dear."

"You do?"

365

"Of course, I do," she said. "I've been watching news broadcasts since the days before vid screens." She held up her wrist as if the bio-embedded device there had been a nuisance since her children convinced her to have it installed. "I know rhetorical bullshit when I hear it. How old are you? Seventeen? Eighteen? How on Earth could you have done all those things for no apparent reason and in such a short stretch of time?"

"I'm glad you believe me."

"It's not you I believe, honey," she explained, nodding to her wrist. "It's them I don't believe, not an honest word out of any of them in fifty...in *eighty* years! Maybe longer. I dunno. My memory comes and goes like an old radio signal."

Fallon had no idea what one of those might be. "My friends and I are going to try and create enough of a diversion that we can simultaneously put a stop to a few pretty horrible things that are going on and maybe get away to someplace safe for a while."

"Can I help you?"

"You're doing enough by not calling the bulls on me."

"Nonsense," she said. "I'm happy to help."

Guilt dipped in shame raised an undeniable flush in Fallon's cheeks. She decided to confess, even if the kind older woman decided to turn her away. "I was here to steal your car. I heard you mention it to your son when the bulls brought me through a few weeks ago, and I figured if it really was as old as you said, I might get it away from here before you even realized it was missing."

"I figured as much."

"You did?" Fallon asked, surprised, "How?"

"Your boyfriend, Danny," she tilted her head toward the store. "He just left, ordered enough food to fill a platoon of prison parolees—paid for it all with a Jackson, Mississippi account. So I figured that if he wandered in, you wouldn't be too far off, and here I was right all along. See that? Not bad for an old lady."

Fallon leaned against the garage. "Not bad at all, Ms. Martin. We never thought that anyone would link his dummy account to the news broadcasts, but I guess we were stupid. How many people from Jackson come through here on a normal day?"

"Not many, dear."

"We'll need to deal with that soon," she said. "But how did you know I was planning to steal your car?"

"Oh, I didn't figure that out until I found you here crying in your Corn Flakes, figured Michael's fancy lock had you at all sixes and sevens."

Fallon shook her head. "I dunno what that means, but if it's anything like lost, confused, uncertain what to do, exhausted, and losing hope, that's about right."

Ms. Martin moved to the keypad. Bully followed, wheezing his atonal accompaniment. She punched six numbers and pressed ENTER. Interior bolts slid open and clicked noisily into place behind now unlocked doors. "Can you get it, dear? I'm nursing a muscle pull...overdid the bench press last night."

Fallon laughed, happy in the wake of feeling so overwhelmed. "Yeah," she displayed a thin upper arm. "I find the same thing with biceps curls, can never manage more than 500 reps with 50 pounds."

"Kids today," Ms. Martin frowned. She stood aside while Fallon slid one whitewashed door open, then shuffled inside, dragging Bully along. "Here it is."

"Ms. Martin," Fallon trailed off. "I don't want you to..."

Dropping Bully's leash, she began tugging the canvas tarp back from the Panther, revealing a near mint condition automobile over fifty years old. The dog contented himself to lay sprawled on the chilly concrete floor, a neat puddle of drool accumulating beneath his loose jowls.

Fallon stepped over the animal to help. "Ma'am, I dunno what to say."

"Well, dear," Ms. Martin dropped the tarp and took Fallon's hand. "I'm not really doing this for you."

"You're not?"

With her free hand, she drew a complicated pattern in the air between them, brought her fingers together as if pulling a tissue from a box, then raised her hand slowly. Fallon watched, transfixed, as a brilliant purple, yellow, and blue snapdragon blossom appeared, as if from nowhere.

Ms. Martin handed her the flower. "You have talents. Don't you?"

She understood. "For a few years now. I'm just getting the hang of them."

"You must be pretty powerful, if they're going to all this trouble just to track you down."

Fallon thought *razor blade* and sliced through the stem as if it were a length of cotton thread. She caught the flower stalk before it fell. "I have a few tricks up my sleeve."

"I'll say you do," Ms. Martin gathered up the tarp, folded it into something resembling a pile of untidy laundry, and drew a yellowing notecard from a tool shelf littered with old paint cans. "Here are the codes. Don't lose this. Or better yet, memorize them, just in case."

Fallon said, "Thank you. I dunno what else to say. When did you..."

"About five years ago," she moved as if to untie her apron then gave up. "My boys got me a new kidney. I was on my way out, had punched all my tickets, but they decided they liked having me around. So they kicked in, borrowed a bit from me, which is pretty amusing—lend money to your sons when they want to save your life!—and here I am. Five years and one pretty amusing talent later."

"Is it just the flowers? Or can you do...other things?"

She pressed her lips together, deepening the lines in her face. "I can feel them in there. You know?"

Fallon said, "oh, yes. I know exactly what you mean. They're like songs I can almost remember or movies I think I saw."

Ms. Martin raised the same gnarled finger she'd used to draw Fallon's snapdragon from thin air. "That's it! That's better than any explanation I've ever come up with. Yes, they're like songs I might have known back in high school, nine million years ago, when Jesus Christ and Abraham Lincoln asked me to dance then fought over me in the parking lot. Ah, but those were the days."

Fallon stashed the Panther's codes in her jacket. "So you haven't experimented with other skills?"

"Why would I? I'm ancient. Can you imagine the heartbreak, realizing this late in life that you had the power of a god? No thanks, dear. I'll just stick with my flowers. They brighten the place up nicely."

Fallon understood. She had never thought that elderly people would emerge from a brokerage house with talents. Somehow, she always imagined it was a special skill reserved for the young. But it made sense: In a culture that treated skilled individuals like mutant monsters, why would someone eighty-five years old ever admit to having developed a supernatural talent? They'd only bring the stress of judgement and disdain down on themselves. She stooped a last time to pet Bully. "Thank you, Ms. Martin. Truly."

"Will you do me a favor?"

"Anything."

"Whenever you…do this thing you're planning to do, to create some disturbance and clear a path to escape, would you, please, just for a moment, think of me and Henry?"

"Absolutely. Yes. But who's Henry?"

"My husband," she frowned. "Oh, I know. I know. You younger people don't believe in marriage any more, and I guess that most of my generation gave up on it as well. The only relationships that matter to people any more are with their silly, sodding wrists. Marriage is just about gone. But Henry and I were something of traditionalists."

"Is he…"

"About twenty years ago, yes."

"Oh, sorry."

"It's all right," she said. "I just wish that he could be here."

"To see your power? Your flowers?"

"No, no, that's all nonsense, dear. No, I wish Henry were here, right here, this moment, giving my car to you."

Surprised, Fallon asked. "Why's that, ma'am?"

"Because it's his idea."

"I don't…"

"Yes, dear, he's dead," she explained. "But that doesn't mean he and I aren't still connected, oh, just about as deep as my bone marrow can go. He's in there, and today, I can hear him loud and clear: *Lizzy! You help that girl. She needs you.*"

"I'm glad he agrees."

Ms. Martin grew wistful, out of character for someone as down to earth as she seemed to be, even at her age, but wistful regardless. "He was a lawyer, a defense attorney, believed everyone deserved a chance. He got pretty angry there at the end, pretty disenchanted with the whole system, the corporate payoffs, the judges' incomprehensible rulings in favor of the wealthy regardless of circumstances or guilt, the wild proliferation of Stormcloud after the last war. All of it made him sick, sicker than he really was, in medical terms, you know? And I lost him."

"I'm sorry," Fallon said.

"He would always meet me at airports," she added. "I never had to take a drone. Henry liked to drive me in this old car, pick me up, too."

Fallon's breath caught in her throat. "He…I don't… that's nice, ma'am."

"Oh, never mind. I'm just an old lady sounding like an old lady. Gimme ten minutes and I'll be dead. That'll shut me up!"

Fallon smiled. "I promise I'll think of you and Henry when I bring that place down—"

370

Ms. Martin waggled that same finger. "Now, now, now, don't say too much, dear. I don't need to know, and I'm sure I'll learn at least the network-approved details soon enough. Won't I?"

"I swear to you," Fallon needed the older woman to believe her. "As long as I'm in my right mind, I'll never tell them that you helped me. I swear. I stole this car, and that's the end of it."

At that, Elizabeth Martin threw her head back and laughed a throaty wheeze that woke the dog. "Oh, honey, if those bastards come for me, I'll go down fighting. Maybe I'll open my mind a little and see what else might be hiding inside these old bones besides a few snapdragons in the afternoon. Might be just the thing I need to find Henry again, a good, old fashioned brawl with the police."

Fallon had no response to that. Instead, she wrapped her arms around the old woman, whispered, "Thank you. I can't tell you how much you're helping me."

Ms. Martin hugged her back. "I look forward to hearing of your daring escape!"

Fallon climbed inside the Grey Panther, entered the start code. The engine thrummed to life. "It sounds great."

"It ought to; I've been keeping it in tip top shape, ever since Henry died. It was his favorite car, one of my last real connections to him."

"And you're sure that you don't mind me—"

"Not at all, dear. It'll be as if you're taking him along on your adventures."

Fallon said, "I promise."

Ms. Martin wiped her eyes with a tissue she'd stashed in her apron, then seemed to remember herself. "Good lord, I've forgotten my manners."

"Um...you just gave me your car. We're good."

"Do you have enough food? Oh, wait...yes, that cute Hackett boy just bought about a two-hundred credits' worth.

Do you need credits?" She peered down at her wrist. "I can probably transfer a few your way."

"No, ma'am. We have plenty." Fallon warmed at the idea of seeing Danny again. They'd only been apart for an hour, and already she was hearing from strangers what a great guy he was. She pulled the car into reverse. "I'm sorry I have to leave."

"Come back if you can one day. I'll be here another fifty, sixty years. Who knows?" She wheeze-laughed at her own joke. "Bye, dear."

"Thank you."

Danny checked his wrist: 3:17 a.m.

He missed Fallon, Emma, too, he supposed, but Fallon badly. Alone in the Chevron in the middle of the night seemed as good a time as any for a confession. He missed Fallon, everything about her athletic, bald, beautiful, stubborn, confounding, irritating self. He sat with the invisible, yet tangible weight of Hadley Hill behind him and the hollow, inky blackness of Owen Pond reaching out between the short beach and the WSJSM in the distance.

Only a few lonely spotlights illuminated the quad, the grounds, and the main building of the WSJSM. Otherwise, the place lay in quiet darkness.

That's good. Fallon and Emma had driven north to stash Elizabeth Martin's Grey Panther somewhere within reasonable walking—*heh, sprinting*—distance from the front gates. He'd wanted to be the one to do that, but Fallon had insisted.

They fought about it, fought about a number of things the previous day. Now here alone, Danny regretted every syllable of it. He honestly believed that the three friends were going to be all right. They were going to lay siege to the WSJSM, set fire to the servers, bring down the network, destroy the files, and hopefully burn the main building down after freeing the students being held there. They'd be fugitives for the rest of their lives, but even that didn't worry him too badly. He had friends in Jackson who could help them all establish new identities, create new accounts, and start fresh with new, untraceable logins.

Yet, he wished that he and Fallon hadn't argued because there was still a chance that one or more of them wouldn't make it out of the WSJSM tonight.

Alone in the Chevron's uncomfortable front seat, he made an effort to banish that thought and failed. Flicking on the car's interior lights, he cast around for something to distract himself, then turned them off again, doggedly determined to stew in the ambiguity.

Yeah, okay, one of us might not make it out. He let this fear off its leash, let it wander around unsupervised for a minute or two. *But we're probably going to be just fine. We've got the advantage. We have tremendous power; we've tested it recently, discovered new skills, and fared pretty well against some difficult challenges.*

Right?

He considered starting the engine and driving away. Without the canoe, Fallon wouldn't risk the attack, not tonight. Without him...

No. Without him, she'd still find some way to get inside, *the hardheaded pain in my ass.* Running away wouldn't save her. It wouldn't save him either, certainly not from the guilt, the loneliness, and the self-loathing he'd endure after abandoning her at the eleventh hour.

Shit! He flipped the interior light on again, dug in his pack for something to eat. They had a few bits of brisket pastry left. But Danny wasn't hungry, just frustrated and scared. Before Fallon Westerly, he would never have considered attacking a facility as well defended and secure as the WSJSM. Not a chance. Even with his most determined and revolutionary-minded friends he wouldn't have risked it. What was the point? Why risk getting killed, imprisoned, or worse, dismembered to fight one minor battle in a war that ended decades ago? Fallon jamming her flag into Headmaster Blair's black heart didn't make sense. There were countless Blairs out there rolling in credits thanks to Stormcloud. Was she really going to take them on one at a time?

Feeling cramped and closed in, he climbed out of the car into marshy grass beside the small parking lot where they'd eaten dinner and planned their dawn assault on the school. Having slept in a well-hidden copse of cedars about a mile off the beach, the friends felt pretty good. Nervous, anxious, but excited to get started across the lake, they'd eaten most of the pastries and drawn makeshift maps in the sand, reviewing their roles, their timelines, and their backup plans again and again until Fallon's assault felt foolproof.

Then they'd disagreed over something trivial.

Fallon wanted to be the one to hide the Panther outside the main gate.

"I should go," Danny argued.

"Why?" she countered. "I can hide a car as well as anyone."

"Yes, but I can...avoid being seen if I need to," he explained. "If you're seen, our risk increases a hundredfold." Emma still had no idea that Danny could travel as mist. He danced around the topic; Fallon understood.

"I won't be seen."

"How can you know that?"

"Look," she leaned against the Panther, as if claiming it. "I'm driving this car out there. I'm going to hide it in the woods or down a side street. I'm going to jog back here and tell you exactly where it is, in case we get separated."

"Or one of us dies," Emma added for good measure.

"Thanks, Em," Danny tossed an old stick into the shallows. "That's really helpful."

"It's all right," Fallon softened. "I'm gonna be fine. I'll be back in an hour. I'll go when it's full dark, when the whole planet is asleep, and I won't use the headlights. Nothing to it."

"I'll come," Emma said. "I can help."

"Why not me?" Danny asked. "We know I won't be seen."

"That's exactly why!" Fallon tried not to shout. "Because if we get separated, or something awful happens in there, Emma and I need to know where the car is. You can escape back to Mississippi or someplace where no one will find you. She and I need to have a tangible means of escape."

He threw his hands up, knew he'd lost. "This is stupid."

"Yeah, probably," she admitted. "But either way, we're taking the car."

"Go ahead," frustration came off him like a smell. "Just go."

Fallon wanted to shout, *Yeah, okay!* and drive off in a rage. But a more sensible side took control. Danny had saved her life too many times to count and had done a hundred daring, risky things to protect her and Emma over the past week. She knew he was hungry, scared, and exhausted. So instead of storming off, she said simply, "No. We'll go later, when it's dark and everyone's sleeping."

Danny had fussed with the ropes knotted about the Chevron's bumper. "All right."

Now he plopped down on the damp sand, felt the cold through his pants. November would be upon them soon, and he wanted to get back home...with Fallon along for the ride, safe, happy, hopefully happy. But certainly safe. A light breeze kicked up; he listened as Owen Pond lapped at the shoreline and worried it might rain before dawn. The air didn't feel heavy enough to dump buckets on them, but any amount of rain would slow their passage and leave them chilled and weak when they landed on the opposite shore.

It looked too far away.

He mentally calculated how long it would take the women to jog two miles—give or take—from the WSJSM's front gate. Twenty minutes? Maybe eighteen?

He checked his wrist again: 3:21 a.m. They'd left about half an hour ago; he hoped to hear them puffing along the lakeshore drive any second now. Danny pulled his knees up beneath his chin, dragging twin sand trenches with his boot heels. He wrapped his arms around his shins and pulled his legs in tight, hoping to preserve his body heat. The Chevron was too cramped; he'd blow his brains out if he waited in there, not that he had a gun. He wished they'd stolen a gun, maybe just an E-taser, a mini sonic cannon, or one of those new H-tasers. Powered by hydrogen, he'd read that they could stop a fully-grown rhinoceros mid-charge, but since there were only about six rhinoceroses—*rhinoceri?*—left in the world, and all of them in zoos and touristy faux habitats with their clone and projection image 'herds,' he didn't much worry that he'd ever have to stop one from charging.

Wouldn't mind one for old Mr. Bulldozer, whatever his name is. That guy's personality would improve significantly with the periodic application of a hydrogen-powered taser, right in the nuts, if he has nuts.

He checked his wrist a third time. "C'mon, Fallon. What the hell? You walking? Maybe you're walking." This encouraged him. "How long does it take to walk two miles? A half hour? Longer? Sure." He tossed two handfuls of sand toward the water, heard them splash down with a whispery hiss. "So you're...what? Fifteen minutes out? That's okay. What can I do? What would you want me to be doing while waiting impatiently for you to get back? I dunno. Writing you some poetry? Yeah, that. Or...okay, shit, maybe getting stuff ready for us to paddle across this lake to our death? That'll be fun, too."

He gathered himself up, untied Emma's canoe, and looked around for anything even remotely useful to do. Nothing.

3:23 a.m. Thirteen minutes.

He wandered down the beach, crouched, and trailed two fingers in the surprisingly warm lake water. *Okay, if we fall in, we won't freeze. That's comforting.* Taking up a handful of soft mud, he squeezed it through his fingers. "C'mon, you two. I'm ready."

Danny waited another forty minutes, growing more anxious as each digit on his wrist clicked past. By the time Fallon and Emma returned, he'd felt the temperature drop a few degrees and watched as billows of fog began gathering on the water's surface.

Shortly after 4:00, when he was about to go after them, he heard the two women jogging slowly out the lakeshore drive, panting with the exercise, but laughing at some shared joke.

Stark, unabridged relief flooded his bloodstream only to be chased by anger. *Where the great fustikating hell have you been? I've been sitting on my ass here, freezing my bones to ice, and you take two hours to cover two miles? Were you followed? Captured? Did you have to escape from an internment camp?*

Fallon read his mind. Coming down the beach, she wiped sweat from her cheeks and held a paper cup out to him. "We thought you might want some coffee before we go."

Danny could barely make out their faces in the darkness and actually hoped they couldn't read the fear and anxiety in his. "What...no, really, what happened to you?" He fought the rising anger, dug deep for a thimble of compassion. "Are you all right? Did something happen?"

Fallon took his forearm in both hands, held tightly. "No. No, we're fine. We just thought you might want a coffee."

"For two hours? You took two hours to get me coffee?" The cup warmed his chilly fingers but had clearly been poured a while ago.

"And pie," Emma offered him a triangle-shaped takeout box. "Blueberry. Although, I gotta tell you, I dunno if those blueberries are legit. I had a slice, and they looked a little questionable to me."

"How did you pay? Did you find paper money on the side of the road? In the cushions of that shitbox you borrowed?"

"I logged in," Emma said. "As my Uncle William. I figured...what the hell."

"You what? Why? Have you lost your periwinkle-and-puce marbles? Both of you?"

377

Emma held out the box. "Nope. If we're going to war in an hour, who the hell cares if the bulls know I was here? I mean, screw it; right? They're gonna pin the damned attack on me anyway, especially if buildings start...you know...blowing up."

"So...you got pie."

"I got pie...for you."

Dumbstruck, Danny accepted the box, didn't know what to say. "Thanks, Em."

Fallon whispered. "Sorry. We needed...well, you know."

"I don't," he said. "But it's okay."

"It's not," she said. "I know. Sorry."

"I was here by myself, Fallon, while you had pie...*pie*. You could have let me know."

She elevated her wrist. "Not me. You know that."

He didn't respond.

"C'mon, Danny." While he couldn't see her face, her voice begged forgiveness. "We needed a few minutes of normalcy before all this."

"And me?" he asked. "Do I get a little normalcy?" He surprised himself with such a childish whine. They were headed together into a battle that might kill them, and he was complaining that his only friends stopped for a comforting slice of pretend-blueberry pie.

"Yeah," Emma said. "You get pie and coffee. Pretty normal if you ask me."

Danny let go with a frustrated laugh. "Okay, yeah. All right. I get pie and coffee." He dropped to the sand, crossed his legs to create a makeshift table. "Anyone bring me a fork?"

Emma produced one like a gunslinger. "Here you go. Stole it myself."

Danny sipped the coffee. "Almond milk?"

"It's all they had at this hour," Fallon sat, leaned her forehead onto his shoulder as a means of apologizing again. "The delivery guy doesn't come for another hour or so."

He drank more. "It's okay. You get used to it, better than soy."

"I like cow milk," Emma said. "Even the fake stuff. It's okay."

He turned his head slightly, whispered. "You know…I ache when you're not here. I bet you didn't know that."

"Don't get emotional." Fallon didn't lift her head. If anything, she nestled closer.

"What? I'm most likely paddling to my death this morning. Maybe a little emotion is exactly what we need."

"Ache?" Emma sat as well, blowing the mood to smithereens. "That's a pretty powerful verb you're throwing around there, bug guy. You know you have a thesaurus on your vid screen. It's under SETTINGS then LANGUAGE then RESOURCES."

Danny shoveled in two mouthfuls of pie, chased them with more coffee. "Nope. Ache. I like that verb just fine."

Fallon sniffed, then wiped her eyes. "C'mon, Poetry Boy, let's get this boat in the water. We should be halfway across by now."

"Ache," he wolfed the last bits of crust. "Pretty good word." Leaving the takeout box on the sand, Danny moved to the canoe's bow; Fallon slid around back to take the stern. Fog engulfed the beach in damp billows. The temperature dropped another few degrees.

"It's getting colder," Emma brushed a hand in front of her face. "Darker, too…if that's possible."

Hidden now in a wisp of sheltering fog, Fallon ducked beneath the Chevron's trunk, pretended to fuss with the rope. Quietly, she said, "Ache. Yeah."

He didn't hear and tossed his length of rope into the driver's side window. "Ache. I'm gonna hang on to that word."

Fallon whispered, "me, too."

Emma rooted in the back seat for paddles and survival vests they swiped from the campground. "You don't really think we're paddling to our death. Do you? I mean, call me a stick in the mud, but that sounds a little ominous."

The others flipped the canoe over and carried it to the edge of the pond. "No, I was just looking for an excuse to complain."

"Oh," she dropped paddles and life jackets into the boat. "Well, that's good. I guess, because dying…in that water…isn't on my list of stuff to get done before breakfast."

"Mine either," Fallon said, and risked a smile for Danny. "Let's go."

Emma faced the WSJSM in the distance. "Holy crap, it's dark."

"And a long way over," Fallon admitted. "This idea seemed a lot smarter when the sun was out."

"It's just a lake," Danny said. "It's the same boring, mountain lake it was twelve hours ago. There's nothing out there to fear, no boats, no waves, just the perfect, quiet approach that…hopefully…no one is monitoring."

Fallon pulled on a sleek vest, adjusted Velcro straps. She noted that it would inflate automatically if submerged for more than thirty seconds. This heartened her. "So we're undetected until we cut the barbed wire."

"If we cut it," Danny said. "We'll decide…quickly…when we get there." He checked his cargo pants for the wire cutters he'd bought in Warrenton while Fallon was talking with Elizabeth Martin.

"How can we get in if we don't cut it?" Emma asked.

Without thinking, Fallon replied, "Danny will just—"

"Will just what?"

She backtracked. "Oh, you know him. He'll just…"

"I'll leap the fence in a single bound," he added to throw her off.

Emma let it go. "Well, you are kind of a blue-eyed superhero."

"I am." He pulled on his life vest, tossed a smaller one to Emma. "And they still match, two eyes my mom gave me seventeen years ago."

She said, "maybe if we get there, you can ask one of those trees to pick us up and carry us over."

"Yeah," Danny agreed. "Or you can just blow the whole place to rubble."

Emma placed her wooden box inside the canoe. "That's my plan, supplicants. It'll give me a chance to work out my anger at having to leave my very first, very own car here in the woods for some stranger…probably turn it into a planter."

Danny held up his wrist. "4:25, kids. You ready?"

Fallon dragged the bow into the shallows. "Yeah, let's get over there. Once we're on the water and closing in, no talking. We good with that?"

Emma and Danny answered in unison. "Yup."

"Okay," she sloshed into the water, pulled the boat out farther, then climbed in, ignoring her wet feet. "We're gonna steer about a hundred feet to the right of that spotlight over the beach. That should bring us ashore in darkness."

Danny motioned for Emma to get in, then pushed them off silently. "Got it. And keep in mind: we're about ten or twelve minutes from town. So the first bulls to get here will arrive about fifteen minutes after we hit Blair's chop shop."

"Right," Emma took up her paddle. "Be as destructive as possible, but be quick about it."

"Fifteen minutes," Fallon said without turning around. "Should be plenty of time."

17

A Sea Monster, a Tragedy, and a Rally

Fallon began paddling, pulling at the inky water, and happy to be doing something physical. It focused and calmed her. She'd known that she would feel hesitant at the possibility of guiding them all to their deaths. But she hadn't expected to be quite this off center. Her hands shook; she needed to pee. Her vest squeezed too tightly around her ribs, making it difficult to breathe, and she felt somehow disconnected from her thoughts, uncertain of what she said, even as she carried on whispered conversations with Danny and Emma. They'd stayed with her. For that she was grateful, too grateful to articulate in whatever choppy terms she might manage here, scared and uncertain in the middle of the night.

Yet, she knew that if she turned around, they'd be there, Danny with slashes in his forehead from diving through a farmhouse window, a black eye where he'd been clobbered nearly senseless by the construction worker outside the Robo-Pharm facility. And Emma, with her necrotic scars, snake bites...*Jesus Christ*...in her face and neck—both of them, the only true, loyal friends she'd ever had. Fallon shivered at the undeniable reality of it all.

She'd never had that before and understood that it was entirely her responsibility, no matter what, to protect them. Recalling her dream from the farmhouse lawn, Fallon wished this might just be an immersion loop, a sim room movie she could escape by sneaking beneath a convenient exit curtain. She spun on the plastic bench, hoping.

"What?" Danny whispered.

"Nothing. I'm okay."

"You know," he said, "if a face can launch a thousand ships, you're on your way with one fluorescent orange canoe. That's not bad, really."

"It'll probably sink, dumbass," she teased. "*You* stole it."

"Consider the face, love. Can anyone really hold me accountable?"

"Shut up, and paddle," Fallon hid her smile. She didn't know if he understood how much she needed that little exchange. Maybe she'd tell him one day when they were clear of all this business and holed up someplace warm.

Paddling helped. Kneeling, Fallon found that she could reach well out in front of the boat's narrow prow, dip her paddle, and then pull hard, feeling the strain in her arms and shoulders. She thought at first that she might wear herself out doing so but soon realized that with the three of them rowing steadily, the WSJSM was growing larger and more ominous through the fog.

She felt unaccountable happiness at the silence the canoe afforded them and was glad to have decided to approach from the water. Every time her paddle thunked against the side of the boat, however, she cursed herself for a klutz and softly apologized to the others. How their paddles didn't make any noise against the fiberglass hull, she had no idea. Perhaps they did, she was just too keyed up to hear it with so much blood rushing in her ears.

Knifing through blinding swaths of cold fog, she narrowed her gaze to the lone spotlight illuminating the WSJSM's spit of sandy beach. Drawing closer, she could make out a few rowboats and what looked like a kayak overturned and tied fast to posts. The barbed-wire gate came slowly into focus. She strained her eyes in hopes of finding a place for them to slip between the intestinal coils of prickly wire.

"It doesn't look good," she whispered.

"No way through?" Danny asked. "We sort of figured that."

"You wanna cut it?"

"Unless you think it's electrified."

"Nah," Emma said. "Can't be, not with the best-behaved inmates coming and going all the time after earning privileges. We'd have heard stories of kids who needed a towel or

383

sunscreen and got fried to gristle after forgetting the fence was hot. You know?"

"Good point," Danny whispered. "So...yes, I think we cut it."

"But what if it is hot?" Fallon asked. "What do we..."

"These pliers are insulated," Danny explained. "We'll give it a quick touch. If it sparks, we'll know."

"But so will Blair," Emma said.

"He might think it's a squirrel or something," Danny tried, hoping to hear the tension ease in her voice. "Maybe a bird."

"Oh, yeah," Emma turned, felt the boat shift uncomfortably to port, then turned back, steadying herself. "That probably happens all the time."

"Let's hope."

Something splashed off to their right. All three looked anxiously toward the sound, their paddles frozen above the water. The canoe began turning slightly, its nose drifting a few lazy degrees to starboard. Danny inserted his paddle slowly, quietly, just enough to adjust their course.

"What was that?" Emma stared uselessly into the night.

"Nothing," Fallon reassured. "Just a fish. Right? Maybe a hawk or something swooping down for an early breakfast."

Danny turned east, tried to make out even the faintest glimmer of light on the horizon. Nothing. He guessed they had at least another full hour of utter darkness to contend with. "Yeah," he said. "What the hell, it's a lake. It's full of fish."

"And other stuff?" Emma asked.

"No," he said. "Just fish."

In response, another splash sounded in the near darkness. More than just a fish surfacing, this one had a personality: two spluttery tumbles and a floppy re-entry splash that caused the friends to freeze again, peering eastward into foggy nothingness.

"What is it?" Emma asked, her paddle dripping. "Do you guys know? What could it be?"

384

"Dunno," Danny whispered. "If that's a fish, it's the granddaddy of everyone in this pond."

Fallon closed her eyes and listened. Waiting to hear another splash, she felt the canoe rise gently a few inches and tried to recall if she'd seen or heard any fish or birds earlier in the day. There'd been nothing. The entire pond had been as flat as a bedsheet. She asked, "Do fish feed at night? Is that a thing? Because I can't remember seeing anything flopping around out here at all."

The canoe rose again, slowly, before sliding off the swell to settle onto the quiet surface.

Danny pulled hard on the starboard side, pressing them forward. "We gotta go."

Emma paddled as well. "Yeah, I don't like this."

"That's not fish," he leaned forward, dipped his paddle deep, tugged the narrow boat back onto its knife edge. "Let's go, kids. Paddle. Hard. We gotta get outta here."

Panicked, Fallon complied. Without thinking, she alternated between right and left, reaching out before the bow and pulling the canoe through the Stygian darkness, focused only on the single light above the beach. "Guys, what is it? What's doing that?"

"It's big," Danny said. "Something big...out here. We gotta keep moving."

Fallon yanked on the straps in her vest, felt them tighten across her breastbone and beneath her arms. "Is it...is it gonna get us?"

Emma let go with a broken, jagged sound. "Guys...I don't—"

Danny felt it coming, began paddling faster. "Let's go! Right side! We gotta pull now!"

By the time Fallon saw the frothing hummock of rolling water, it was closing on the canoe. Less than fifty feet out it came like a submarine at flank speed, thirty miles per hour or faster. She had time to suck in a desperate breath and hold it. *Mama, I'm sorry.*

From its immutable trajectory through the water, Fallon braced for whatever it was to strike the canoe abeam, directly beneath Emma's bench. There was no doubt it would do more than simply capsize them; not a chance. This thing would catapult them halfway back to Jenny's Diner. They'd land in a field somewhere a mile away. She wanted to shout, warn the others, call up a firestorm, a tidal wave, anything.

She didn't. Instead, she gripped fast to her paddle, a few tentative drips still splashing into the black water, and watched as a sea monster, as big as a city bus, emerged from the lake like a subterranean volcanic eruption. At first, it was just the snout, pushing thousands of gallons of water at them. Then the misshapen forehead, knobby with clusters of barnacles, its mouth, elongated and lined with cracked, broken, but still deadly looking teeth, each as long and serrated as a steak knife.

Fallon heard someone shout, "Wait! No! Wait!"

The bulk of the monster emerged, as if fired from an underwater cannon, in a daredevil's arc up and over their canoe. Milky white but mottled here and there with moldy gray splotches and long, pink scars, the monster might have been a whale from the overall missile shape of its head and neck – not that a whale made even a pinch of sense in a mountain pond 100 miles from the nearest ocean – but what Fallon saw next confirmed that they were once again facing an impossible foe, another cataclysm called up from the mad imagination of a lunatic bent on crushing them to jelly.

It had tentacles, at least a dozen barbed and suckered tentacles, each twenty feet long and growing crazily from a humped girdle of gray flesh perhaps fifteen feet forward of the thing's fluked tail. She had a slack-jawed moment to wonder what purpose the spindly arms might serve, when one of them flopped awkwardly forward, and she understood: they could reach the creature's mouth. Unlike a normal whale, this thing captured and ate meat, feeding itself whatever swam too close to those sinewy fingers.

She gaped as the thing went airborne, turned an aerial half circle twelve feet above Emma, then dropped with an Old Testament splash that would have showered the friends in a rogue wave of lake water if they weren't already capsizing. And it dragged its tail, not far, not all that deep, just low enough for one notched fluke to utterly clobber Emma, knocking her out as she tumbled limply from the rolling canoe.

"Em!" Fallon shouted then choked on a mouthful of water. She reached one hand back, hoping to catch hold of something. Still gripping the paddle she considered extending it, maybe getting wildly lucky and having Emma grab on so Fallon could haul her into shallower water. But she was already tumbling. Rolling twice, then twisting back over herself, Fallon felt one-foot just above the surface, felt cool evening air caress her naked ankle. Then she was turning over again, sucked beneath the waves by the sheer immensity of the monster as it struck for the lake's bottom, tugging a hundred tons of water, and one seventeen-year-old girl along with it.

Ten feet, twelve, perhaps deeper, Fallon finally sensed the undertow release her, and she kicked for the surface, her life jacket lifting her quickly through the darkness. She remembered her mother explaining that if she was ever under water and confused, she should follow her bubbles. Bubbles would always lead to safety. Now, straining to see, Fallon understood that her mother's rule only applied in broad daylight, not when mounting an amphibious assault on a fortified chop shop run by a frothing sociopath and attacked by a supernatural sea monster large enough to lay waste to Tokyo.

She let the jacket do the work and broke the surface spluttering and shouting for Emma.

Splashes and a frantic cry sounded nearby. "Fallon! Emma!"

"Danny!" she shouted, no longer caring that WSJSM security staff might hear. "I'm here."

387

"Fallon!" His splashing drew closer. "Fallon keep talking. I'll come…" His voice gurgled off, dunked beneath another wave. He coughed raspy spasms.

"Danny?"

Another splutter. "I'm coming. I'm good."

Thank Christ.

He swam closer. "You okay?"

"Where's Emma?"

"Dunno." He appeared suddenly beside her. Fallon cast her arms around his neck, nearly submerged him. "Hey…okay. It's okay."

Without letting go, she said, "I saw her. It hit her, the tail, really banged into her. Danny, she was out of it before she even hit the water."

"It's okay." He took her by the wrists, gently pulled her arms from about his neck. "Her vest will keep her afloat. She might be unconscious, but she'll be able to breathe." He kicked toward the overturned canoe. It bobbed, a faintly lit hummock. "Climb on here."

Fallon slid off a few times, then was able to straddle the canoe. Danny climbed onto the other end, keeping it steady between them like a balanced see-saw. Hyperventilating, she asked, "Why are we up here? We gotta find her. We gotta swim."

"Just stay put for a second." He brushed soggy hair off his face. "If she's close by, we can see her better from up here."

Fallon called, "Emma! Where are you, sweetie?"

They both sat quietly, listening.

"We gotta swim." Fallon suggested. "You go that way, and I'll—"

"No!" He said sharply. "Just wait."

"Why?"

They felt it move beneath them, a submerged wall of water, like a sub-surface river, that dragged them and the canoe twenty feet closer to the WSJSM beach.

Fallon clutched the hull with wet fingers. "Holy shit. It's right beneath us."

"And it has those..." He motioned with his hands.

"Yeah, like an octopus or a giant squid."

"I don't want us in the water."

She thumped the overturned canoe. "You think this is gonna stop it?"

"I don't goddamned know, Fallon!" Danny snapped. "But I sure as hell don't want to be dangling out there where I can't see or hear it coming for us."

She acquiesced. "Yeah. Yeah, okay."

"You see its teeth? It's a meat eater."

"Don't." Fallon shook with equal measures of cold and terror. "Just..."

"All right," he cupped hands beside his mouth, half shouted-half whispered. "Emma! Can you hear us?"

Fallon tried the opposite direction as the great beast made another pass beneath the canoe, spinning it like a bath toy in the current. "Em! Honey, call out to us. Please." Her voice broke. Danny heard it; Fallon didn't care. Now was the perfect frigging time to be terrified.

Spinning past her, his back now to the beach, Danny called again. "Emma!"

"Em!" Fallon spun behind him; the darkest part of the lake, a wide swath of nothingness stretched between their useless canoe and the foot of Hadley Hill. With her back to the widest part of Owen Pond, Fallon felt the cold, creeping certainty that the monster would rise silently and wrap one of those god-awful tentacles around her ankle, yank her down. She shivered. "Danny, we have to go. I can't stand this. I can't stay out here any—"

"Guys?" Emma's whisper reached them on a tumbling wisp of fog. "You guys?"

Danny brightened. "Em!" He paddled them awkwardly through the dying waves. "Em, keep talking. We're coming."

389

Emboldened, Fallon paddled as well. "We're coming. Give us two seconds, and we'll be..."

Another current, that same underwater rush as tons of sea monster hurtled along the lake's bottom, drew the canoe closer to the sound of Emma's voice. Fallon felt the creature brush against her boots as it passed this time and worried that as quickly as their canoe was shoved toward the center of the lake, Emma would be dragged even farther into the menacing uncertainty between them and Hadley Hill.

The submerged river rushed beneath them again.

"It's coming," Danny warned. "Get ready. Hang on."

Fallon gripped the slippery fiberglass with both hands, hoping only to stay with the boat when the monster attacked.

"Guys?"

"Holy shit!" Danny cried. "There she is. Can you reach her? She's right there."

Fallon turned to the empty stretch of water behind her and saw Emma's head bobbing like a lost playground ball, about ten feet off the canoe's stern. "Hey!" She tried to sound encouraging, offering meagre comfort. "Emma, can you reach for me? I'm right here, honey. Just reach out." She squeezed the hull between her thighs, holding fast while leaning back, twisting at the waist, and stretching one hand over the open water.

Emma's eyes blinked open. "Fallon?"

"Hey, you all right?"

"No," Emma cried, her voice jittering over sobs and coughs. "Fallon, my head's hurt. And my shoulder. I don't think I can swim...don't think."

"Right here," Fallon strained, her thighs burning with the effort.

"I'll go." Danny dropped into the water. "I'm coming, Em."

The swollen current began again, not rushing past this time. Rather, it rose in a slow, irretrievable swell, lifting the canoe, nearly spilling Fallon into the murky water. Still, she reached. Only a few feet to go now, maybe two feet, one more wave, one more kick of her feet, and Emma would be back with them, maybe not safe, but back together, the three of them where they belonged.

Danny splashed past. "I got her. I'm okay. Just keep the canoe close. We'll be two seconds. We're just gonna—"

The canoe climbed a rising swell. "Danny," she whispered. "Danny, no. Wait."

With less than eighteen inches separating her outstretched fingertips from the wet bulge of Emma's life vest, Fallon watched in numb terror as a grayish-white tentacle rose from the water behind the smaller girl. She saw the trickle of blood spilling from Emma's right ear, knew she'd been hit too hard to think clearly, had been hit too hard to fight back, or to call up one of her devastating poems. The tentacle was striated with a roadmap of bright scars and dotted all over with gaping, hungry suckers. It rose several feet, hovered a moment as if considering which of them to take, then wrapped snugly over Emma's shoulders, covering her face. It pulled her beneath the surface without a sound.

The girl had no warning, no time even to cry out. She simply disappeared.

Danny dove, his feet kicking up noisy splashes as he fruitlessly fought his own life vest in an effort to rescue Emma. He might have gotten ten feet down before fear and an extremely buoyant jacket hauled him back, a scared kid losing hope. Spitting out lake water, he cried. "I'm sorry! Fallon, I'm sorry! I can't see her, can't find anything. I dunno what..."

He dove again.

Fallon let him go.

Numb, her attention shifted to three figures standing on the thin strip of sand beneath the WSJSM. They watched the scene unfold in weak light from the barbed wire gate. Leaving Danny and the canoe, Fallon unclasped her own vest, allowed it to slide into the water, and then unlaced her boots, dropping those as well. She slid soundlessly beneath the waves. Kicking toward shore, Fallon allowed fury to take hold of her once again.

Eight feet down, she thought, *flippers*, and felt herself propelled through the darkness, no longer afraid that the creature would grope for her with one of its spoiled milk tentacles. If it did, she would kill it. There was no question.

Thirty feet farther along, she thought, *gills...gimme frigging gills, God damn it.*

Searing pain burned along her neck, and she thought it had worked. Risking a mouthful, Fallon tried inhaling...and nearly drowned herself.

She surfaced, coughing and choking. The beach lay only another forty yards or so away. The figures still waited, watching her. "Fine," she gagged up another ounce. "No gills." Promising she'd work on that one, she dove again, determined not to rise until she was close enough to strike.

Behind her, sopping wet and entirely unable to change form, Danny gamely paddled and kicked along, not wanting Fallon to fight alone.

The lake bottom rose to meet her. From the angle of light through the shallows, she imagined she was only twenty or twenty-five feet from the sand.

That would do nicely.

Letting her flippered feet shift back to normal, she rose, already calling the lake to her, summoning the very depths. Feeling it respond, she cast her will toward the three strangers who'd come to the shoreline to watch as their pet sea monster tore Fallon and her friends to pieces.

She heard Danny in her memory—*ask nicely!*—and called up two million gallons of dank, murky water. And dropped it on them in a mammoth wave, fifteen feet high and rolling in at forty miles per hour. When it reached her, the wave briefly parted, slicing itself neatly as if opening a passage for Moses to march out of Egypt.

Backlit as they were by the sodium arc lamp, Fallon couldn't tell who it was she attacked. But from the beefy, misshapen shadow the largest of them cast across the beach, she assumed it was Mr. Hyde, Bulldozer Bob, the one they'd outsmarted twice in the past week. Tumbling beneath the weight of Fallon's wave, the sinewy stranger rolled several times then slammed into the electrified fence. She winced from the lightning blast of blue current as fuses shorted and the transformer arced a jagged bolt of electricity into the night sky.

A moment later, power from the city grid reached the transformer above the security fence, and it exploded with a shattering crack that, Fallon assumed, woke all the inmates and staff who might have been sleeping after the wave crashed over the security wall.

Good. Let them come.

While Mr. Hyde twitched and smoked eerily in the wet sand, Fallon turned on the others. Another man lay still. Prostrate on his back, he didn't move at all; she might have killed him.

Hopefully, it's Blair.

The third figure, tall and lean, could have been a man or a woman. From here, Fallon couldn't tell, didn't really care. Being on that beach made her, him, whoever it was, as guilty as Dozer and Blair, and with another wellspring of anger and hatred, she raised her hands to strike, this time calling on the power inside, not the lake or the barbed wire, the trees or the sand. No. She'd eviscerate whoever this was in a single release of frustration and loathing. She'd—

The water rose between and around her thighs.

It was coming.

Too large to approach this close to shore, the sea monster protruded shapelessly above the surface twenty yards out. Half of it, part whale, part squid, part octopus, part nightmare lolled above the waves. It groped for Fallon with slippery tentacles.

She let them. One had been torn nearly all the way off and flopped uselessly from its muscular stalk. She hoped that Emma had managed that solitary act of angry defiance before

393

drowning. She'd come back to retrieve the girl's body; she promised. Emma would be there, floating, in her vest. Fallon would weep. Danny would try to hide his anger, his painful desire to flee for Mississippi, and they'd fish Emma out of the water together, perhaps drive her home. Fallon didn't consider the question long, though. The kindness, the gentle feelings and sadness weakened her; now was not the time to be weak.

To the creature, she said, "Oh, chumbly, you shouldn't have come in here. You killed my friend." Ducking a tentacle, then another, Fallon looked into the monster's blinking opaline eyes and recalled the vast nightmare in which she'd burst open at the seams, loosing a torrid fire of unquenchable, molten death on miles of insidious corn. When she released the fire, the sea beast took a moment before it realized what was happening, that it had been dunked in oddly resilient flames. It screamed a painfully human wail, rolling in an effort to duck its burning head beneath the shallow water. Blind, suffocating, and terrified, the monster flopped like a stranded goldfish, slapping hundreds of gallons skyward with its powerful tail and flailing about with its tentacles as it tried vainly to reach the depths.

But even there, Fallon kept the flames hot, forty feet down before they were extinguished.

Danny paddled in.

Fallon ignored him.

That's enough, dear. The voice rang inside her head. Too loud, it threatened to knock the wind out of her. *I don't want to hurt you, Fallon.*

"No!" She shouted and dropped a wall of blistering flame onto the beach, incinerating the gate, the electrified fence, and the ten-foot hedgerow. The still man—*dead man*—didn't move. His clothes caught fire; he smoldered then flickered into a human campfire, casting enough light for Fallon to see that the last silhouette, the one still standing, was a woman, a statuesque, gorgeous, late-middle-aged woman in an expensive cocktail dress, something suitable for a corporate dinner party, not so much for a mass murder in the middle of the night. Yet, Fallon realized that it was this woman's claxon voice blaring in her mind.

Stop it.

"No, you killed Emma."

I did nothing of the sort. The voice boomed, louder than before, thundering bass drums trapped inside her skull. She thought her head would collapse. She weakened, her resolve faltering. *Come to me. I'll explain everything. Everything will be all right. You know I'm telling you the truth. Listen to your feelings.*

Danny saved her. Rolling to his knees, he unsnapped his survival vest, let it fall away. Clearly in shock at the loss of Emma, the kid he considered his little sister, he smiled madly up at Fallon. "Hey, so...when this is all done, you maybe wanna go to dinner? Maybe a sim-movie?" Rising beside her, he reached both hands toward the beach and murmured quietly.

The hedges, some still in flames, some smoldering, creeped and slithered down the beach and coiled around the tall woman's legs, waist, even her neck.

Stop this. The voice warned. She watched the woman shrug off the shrubs like a passing thought. *You can't hurt me. Come with me. Please.*

Fallon smiled at Danny. "You know; a girl could get downright attached to you."

"I hope so," he said. "I mean, look at where we've been, love. I'm frigging exhausted."

She rested a hand on his shoulder. "Stay here."

He didn't argue. "Yeah. Okay."

You're not listening, Fallon.

"No." Again, resolve solidified into something hot and tangible in her belly.

The woman's voice sighed a lazy exhalation as if she'd just learned that she'd have to stand in a slow-moving line or wait for repairs on a broken car.

"You bored?" Fallon took two steps toward shore, ready to fight.

Yes. The stranger lifted a delicate hand, graceful in the rising sun, and flicked it, almost an afterthought, in Danny's direction. The boy grunted, as if kicked hard in the stomach, rose from the water and whiplashed backward, fifteen feet into the air. He tumbled a hundred yards or more; Fallon heard him splash down.

There. That's better. Distractions are all gone. Now we can—

Fallon wheeled, releasing rage and fear in a focused assault that took the attractive woman directly in the chest. She staggered then dropped to one knee, clearly not expecting such a display of focused emotion and power from the inexperienced teen. A porcelain white leg shone from beneath her dress. Muscles along her thigh and calf moved independently, rippling unnaturally beneath her skin as she regained her footing.

Fallon thought: *ice pick* and *protective shield*, picturing the smooth armor she'd read about in stories of knights, princesses, jousting, and magic swords. She had no idea if the shield would protect her from the woman's obvious power advantage, but she held her forearm up either way. Hoping just to reach the beach, she'd try to move in close, to stab the woman with the ice pick, maybe in the eye or the throat, something to eliminate her from the equation quickly, with as little effort or mess as possible. Then Fallon would bring the entire WSJSM down.

And find Danny.

Why did he take off his vest? Stupid. Now he's got to swim, probably injured, with that gimpy ankle and that goddamned monster out there.

Splashing through ankle deep water, she braced for an attack. The tall woman, standing erect, her clothing dry, her hair falling in exquisite waves over her shoulders, raised both hands this time, stared into Fallon's eyes, and released her will.

Fallon took the blow in the center of her makeshift shield. Bracing forward with her own will, she imagined the older woman's strength spilling around her, preternatural strength falling harmlessly into the pond. And it worked. Fallon stumbled, nearly fell backward, then pressed forward again as if into a powerful headwind. She could win this; she had the advantage.

The woman took a step forward, leaned into her next volley, and loosed another concussive blast of sheer, naked energy at the resolute girl. *There's no need for this, dear. Please don't make me hurt you.*

"Eat shit," Fallon growled, sounding as much like a feral animal as a seventeen-year-old. "You killed my friend...my *friends.*"

I didn't.

"I'm going to kill you." She reached dry sand, moving more quickly now. Her bare feet left wet tracks that steamed in the aftermath of her fiery onslaught. With them burning beneath her, Fallon felt the sand crackle and break as she approached the curiously unfazed woman waiting just twenty feet away. Her fire had been so hot, so precisely targeted that some of the sand had melted into glass. Fallon's feet cracked and broke it now. Shards stabbed into her flesh; splinters caught in her skin, pressed into her muscles.

She boxed up the pain and focused instead on her ice pick and shield.

Speaking normally now, the tall woman offered a reassuring smile. "Welcome, my dear. I've been waiting for you for quite a long time. I'm glad you could come."

"You killed my friends." Ropy strands of incandescent rage slithered through her arms and legs, tautened her muscles, and drew Fallon's will deep inside her chest, brightening and focusing it to a single strike, one that would eviscerate this woman, whoever she was.

397

"I can feel you," the older woman said calmly. "I know what you're planning, and I love the idea. I do. But it'll do you no good to level your anger at me."

"You killed my friends," Fallon repeated. All other thoughts escaped her. "You did." Her feet bled; she didn't feel it. Her toes blistered on the searing hot sand. Fallon ignored them. Her clothes and hair dried in the oven-like temperature. Steam rose around her, while fog gathered over the water, stark white in the rising sun.

"Do you want to know why, dear? Why I arranged for Claire Felver's death? Why I had you framed for the killing, shipped all the way down here, and why I've been so determined to bring you back? Can I offer you an explanation? You've got to be curious." She took a hesitant step toward Fallon, offered a hand. "Don't you want to know? Want to get your old life back?"

Fallon kept her last sliver of rational thought focused on the idea of a *shield*. She held it before herself like a knight then elevated her free hand to strike.

Quick as a snake, the older woman grabbed it; her long delicate fingers manacled Fallon's wrist. The compelling voice thundered in her head again. *Stop being difficult. You understand nothing.*

Fallon felt herself weaken, felt the woman's strength— not combative, just undeniable—flow into her, entering her blood stream like an injection of deliberate truth. Knowledge, conviction, possibilities, Nature, power, control…all of it coursed through the teen's body in an immutable wave that left Fallon standing, but barely, on wobbly legs, weak kneed and dizzy.

"Stop that." Her vision blurred. "Let go of me."

Don't fight me. Let me show you. You know you want me to; I can feel you letting go.

From somewhere distant, she heard what could only be Danny's voice. Faint and indistinct, but clear enough to break the stranger's spell. "Fallon! No! Get away from her!"

398

She let go. Throwing her arms open, an orchestra conductor calling for *fortissimo*, Fallon released all of her fear and confusion in one focused blast. Aimed directly at the woman's chest, a point just north of the V-shape in her expensive cocktail bodice and just south of the gaudy pendant dangling between her insignificant breasts. Fallon felt the very surroundings, the air, the lake water, the glass-melted sand, the singed hedges, even the wispy thin fog still blowing about...all of it rallied behind her and this one climactic gesture.

With a hedonistic bellow, she let go her will, cast her head back, and thinking of Emma and Danny, tried not just to murder the woman before her, but to eradicate her, to remove her very bones from existence.

But the stranger was gone.

Instead of striking her, the force of Fallon's blow cannonaded through the security wall between the WSJSM, leveling a section large enough for a freight train to pass easily. It tore through the wire fence surrounding the rarely-used tennis courts like a spider's web, and left Headmaster Blair's personal chop shop in ruins, a dusty pile of smoking rubble.

Fallon watched this happen with distracted disinterest. She cast about warily a moment or two, hoping to find the bewildering woman somewhere but didn't see her, couldn't feel her. Quieting the agony in her feet, she turned long enough to see Danny swimming gamely for the beach. Warm, unchecked joy flooded through her, washing almost every remnant of the woman's assault from her bloodstream.

A bit remained. Fallon felt it hidden there, knew she'd have to deal with it eventually.

She crossed to the man lying still on the sand. He'd been knocked insensible by her initial tidal wave and then burned nearly to death when she rained hellfire down on them. Yet, he was still alive. Sucking tiny, rapid mouthfuls of singed air, he couldn't move. He smelled of charred flesh and melted rubber. Fallon knew that she'd killed him.

He gulped two breaths in quick succession, managed, "Should've taken you apart."

She offered a sinister grin. "Headmaster Blair. I've been looking forward to seeing you again." She knelt, felt the lingering heat and couldn't imagine how the old bastard was suffering, if he felt anything at all. "I have you to thank, I suppose."

Another two breaths. "Wh…why?"

"For helping me to become a murderer." She needed only a second to think *ice pick*, then drove it into the gristly flesh above Blair's left ear. His hair and much of his scalp had been charred away, so she had only to generate enough force to drive the pick through Blair's still resilient skull.

It required surprising commitment on her part.

Blair's smoldering corpse twitched a half-dozen times, his arms and legs spastic, before finally coming to rest. Fallon withdrew her ice pick, rose, and whispered, "Yes, Daniel, I know. I know…we'll talk about it later."

Feeling that now familiar and comforting anger, she climbed the beach toward the WSJSM. She knew, for some reason, she needed to take the hard drives from the computers in Blair's chop shop and thought she might just incinerate the entire place, burning them to ash rather than taking time to dig through the rubble. But then Danny's voice welled up in her mind. *No, dumbass, we need the data stored on those things!* So with those same ropy bands of fury shaping her will into another formidable firebomb, Fallon decided to make the chop shop her first stop as she visited the WSJSM for the last time.

Moving through the devastation of the rear security wall, she didn't notice that Mr. Hyde, Bulldozer Bob, had disappeared as well.

18

Another Kiss, Emma's Annotations,
and that Peach Grader

Danny sipped lukewarm well water through a Kleen straw. He would've preferred soda, tea, coffee, raccoon urine, camel spit, almost anything other than water that tasted like the bottom of a mountain lake. He'd swallowed his share the previous night, what now felt like gallons.

His ribs hurt; at least two were broken. They were his first. He'd broken bones before, never ribs. No one he'd ever known had told him how badly they hurt. When breathing felt like being stabbed with knives—*ice picks*—he assumed he'd reached a new low.

An ice pick, that's what she'd used. Not that Blair would have lived much longer. After getting the utter dog piss knocked out of him with her tsunami and then being incinerated in her fire, old Blair only had a few threads binding him to the realm of the living anyway. What's an ice pick in the ear? Right? He was on his way out. What did it matter that Fallon hurried him along a little, gave him a push down the icy slope to eternity.

"It's what she wanted," he said to no one. "He raped her; she killed him."

She'd done it there on the sand. For a week they'd talked about it, Fallon going on and on about how she wanted him dead, wanted to leave the WSJSM in ruins. Danny and Emma had entertained the idea, but honestly, neither of them had actually believed it would happen, that Blair would be dead and the grumpy campus on the hill would look like it had been the target of a bombing run.

It did. Fallon had done it all on her own.

The older woman—she was gorgeous, eerily so—had sent such a formidable blast of energy into Danny's guts that he'd taken flight, traveled over a hundred yards, and hit the water like a circus clown fired from the deck gun of a Navy destroyer. He didn't remember much of the few seconds after that but thanked the searing pain in his ribs for bringing him around. He had no idea how long an unconscious person might hold his breath beneath the water but was glad he hadn't found out.

Surfacing, he'd done a half dog paddle, half broken-rib crawl back to shore, watching the beautiful woman try to transfix Fallon with her...what? Her mind? Her gaze? Clearly, they'd been communicating, but from Danny's vantage point, neither seemed to speak.

He took another swallow, pocketed the Kleen straw for later, then tossed the rest of the yellowish water toward a clump of snapdragons Emma had loved.

Emma.

He tried not to think about her.

She couldn't be dead. No way. The creature had hurried into the shallows, chasing Fallon. It had happened too quickly, had been less than a minute. There's no way Emma drowned that fast. No way.

It was closer to three minutes, buddy. You know it. Fallon swam a good hundred yards and attacked the beach before the monster got there.

Yeah, but...

And you know you only saw three, maybe four of its tentacles before Fallon lit its ass on fire.

But that one tentacle had been injured.

Sure. It might have been injured thirty years ago, a hundred years. Who knows?

Or Emma did it. Emma blasted that tentacle apart. Thank the frigging gods Fallon forced her to try and cast one of her 'spells' without reciting the little poem. That was lucky. Perhaps Emma managed to escape, is maybe floating out there right now, injured and lonely.

And maybe not. Okay? Maybe not.

402

"We gotta go look for her," he said. "As soon as Fallon wakes up, we gotta go back."

There'd be bulls, hundreds of them searching for the fugitives this morning. Even though no one had identified him or Fallon as perpetrators, some authority figure looking for a quick scapegoat would connect the dots, and the runaways would be named as suspects, upping the intensity of the manhunt to epic, national, intergalactic proportions.

"Shit." A queasy, unsettling feeling warred with the pain in his ribs for highest honors in Danny's morning discomfort. He didn't want to wake Fallon. She'd been nearly catatonic when he finally got her into the Grey Panther. Watching her lay waste to the school, he realized the sheer power she possessed. A handful of guards, teachers, staff members, even a few of the stupider inmates had tried to stop her...and seemed to bounce off. Yeah, that was it: they rebounded from her, several before they even made contact. One guard had tried firing a taser from nearly point-blank range, but even that failed. Fallon had motioned abruptly, and the guard somersaulted into a nearby retaining wall, blue-fire zapped and droolingly unconscious before he hit the ground.

She tore two buildings apart at the stitches, merely imploding them. Danny tried to follow her into one, hoping to carry her to safety if necessary, but Fallon hadn't needed help. With tons of rubble falling about her, the girl wandered calmly out, entirely impervious to the collapsing structures. Danny had never imagined anything like it. Falling sheet rock, floor tiles, bricks, even a half ton gargoyle or two had dropped onto Fallon, encountered some burgeoning field of tangible energy and deflected away. No one had tried to shoot her, but Danny surmised that even a bullet would have been convinced, somehow, to miss her ten times out of ten.

Fallon had a flair for the dramatic, so he wasn't surprised that she left the arched entrance, the executive offices, Blair's apartments, and the iconic façade burning as they fled in the Grey Panther. The scores of bulls, firefighters, and rescue workers who arrived from Warrenton and surrounding jurisdictions would have been impressed—it made for an unambiguous parting testament to her vengeance.

Danny smiled to himself as he entered the ruined barn, still propped up by the solitary beam old Bulldozer Bob had left. He had no idea where their fledgling relationship might go over the next few months, whether Fallon would agree to stay with him, whether they would run away someplace safe. They might even let themselves fall a little bit in love. Sure, it didn't have to be super-duper, irretrievable, everlasting, soul mate, bring a life jacket because this sumbitch is deep, love of my life kind of love—not that he would mind—but something more than two friends on the run for their lives. That might be nice.

He wandered to the peach grader he'd been tinkering with on and off for the past week. They couldn't stay; Old Dozer had found them here. He'd be back. Someone would come. Fallon had graduated from suspected murderer, whoever Claire Felver was, to pre-meditated badass killer. With all the turmoil and noise coming from the lakeshore, dozens of onlookers probably witnessed her killing Blair. Plenty of dormitory windows, staff apartments, even the south guard house had a view directly over the beach. The Fauquier County Bulls would need about ten minutes to find witnesses willing to trade freedom for testimony against the crazed, bald sociopath. The news media had painted Fallon as a killer. Now, she was one.

He flipped on the grader's primers, crossed to the engine starter, figured he'd get a little work done while Fallon slept. But not much longer. They didn't have time. Fugitives running from a murder charge don't have time to sleep. "What the hell. Right? Blair's a monster, and a rapist to boot. Screw him. The world is better off without—"

The great cat, silent as a frightening memory, dropped from the farmhouse roof, landed softly on its hind legs, and had Danny by the throat before the distracted boy could do more than suck in a raspy breath. Muscular paws squeezed his larynx closed; his eyes bulged. Capillaries in his sinuses burst, causing twin trickles of blood to spill from his nose.

The winged panther, the same one they'd seen attack the river cottage on the Potomac, drew Danny bodily from the dusty planks in the barn floor, lifting him like a rag doll until the two were face-to-face.

His mind reeled, his thoughts flashing like lightning, incoherent, impossible to follow, until one nestled firmly between his eyes: *She's gonna bite my head off. Do something. Something.*

He flailed and thrashed to no avail. Unable to breathe, he quickly lost strength in his extremities and flopped uselessly in the creature's grasp.

Its exhalations, wet on Danny's face, smelled of tangy, rotting meat. Had he been able to draw breath, he'd have used it to vomit up the remnants of Ms. Martin's brisket gravy. But Danny realized sadly that vomiting didn't matter. Thrashing and fighting and kicking and flailing didn't matter. He couldn't breathe. His throat was entirely closed, and the pressure in his skull would leave him unconscious in a matter of seconds.

Not like this. No. Lemme go in a fair fight. Not like this.

Reading his mind, the raven-panther began slowly to morph through a roadmap of smeary stages beginning with inconceivable winged monster and ending with burly, homicidal, Beatrice Guenard. Still salivating sloppily, still smelling of raw meat, the girl's paws shifted from massive, furry, clawed mitts to cigar-thick fingers, calloused palms, and beefy forearms, wrapped tightly about Danny's throat.

"How ya been, Dragga?"

He gurgled nothing that made even remote sense.

"I been missing y'all, looking fer ya fer a few days. Figured y'all was too stupid to go somwheres new. Just hadda come back here. Huh?"

Light faded from Danny's vision. He felt more than heard—didn't see—the peach grader turn on, its powerful rotating screens spinning as Bear pressed him against the metal frame.

"Now, I'm gonna kill ya, and then I'm gonna kill her, nice and neat and ladylike. Ya know, Dragga? I'm gonna kill ya both, and then maybe I'm gonna eatcha. Just you, though. I gotta take her back."

A faint voice, deep within Danny's mind, began bellowing, yawping madly in an effort to be understood. His arms and legs went numb, and he lost touch with his body entirely as all the colors in the bright October morning dimmed to leaden grey.

Now, dumbass! Do it now!

Now?

Dumbass.

Teeth gritted tightly, spittle dripping from her chin, Bear pressed Danny backwards onto, then nearly all the way over the peach grader. Unconcerned that it had started up, she wanted to watch as the last light faded from the irritating boy's eyes. Drawing her face within inches of his, close enough to kiss him, her massive chest and shoulders pushing down, her weight fully on Danny, holding his throat closed, choking him, imagining the immense pleasure she'd feel...and then feel again when she killed the girl, Fallon Westerly, sleeping upstairs—where Bear had smelled her just a few minutes earlier.

Beneath them, the grader coughed and belched out clouds of oily smoke as it roared fully to life. Bear didn't think twice about it.

When Danny disappeared into a foggy wisp of damp cloud, Bear thought that she'd popped him like a balloon. She'd squeezed too hard too long, and he'd just exploded, leaving her nothing to eat when she shifted to her raven-panther form for the flight back to Alexandria.

What she hadn't expected, however, was her weight carrying her forward, and her arms, her muscular but all-too-human arms dropping elbow deep between the three-inch grader screen. In a matter of a half second, she found herself alone in the Draggers' barn, with her arms pressed eighteen inches into a prehistoric piece of farm machinery...that was running.

Bear never had to look far for anger, and her confusion at losing track of Danny quickly gave way to fury. "Skinny. Where you at, dragga? I'm jus' gonna kill ya all over agin. C'mon back here now."

She was in such a state of rage and frustration that when the grader began tearing her right arm off, Bear couldn't quite believe it. She needed an extra fraction of a second to realize what a dangerous spot she'd landed in, and tried, too late, to shift back to her panther form.

That cost her precious seconds. Too many.

She watched in stunned disbelief as her arm, trapped now against the grader's transition frame, bent awkwardly, swelled to balloon-like proportions—someone would pop, after all—and then began tearing, like meat from a bone.

She screamed when the bones fractured, then broke clumsily across.

Bear watched in paralyzed horror as the machine tore through the rest of her floppy, useless flesh.

Splashes of gaudy blood spewed from her severed arm. She observed it disconnectedly as her senses sharpened, her vision, scent, and hearing. She was changing, her left forearm thickening with bandy muscles. Bear attempted to yank it free, but it resisted, had grown too sinewy to dislodge. A cat's forearm, her paw trapped nearly two feet inside the peach grader brushed and then dragged over what remained of her human arm, now little more than graded refuse in the collection chute where a hundred-thousand three-inch peaches had spilled over the decades.

She felt it, still alive, the severed hand tried gripping her clumsy furry paw.

Bear screamed; it emerged as a cat's howl, a jungle cry of futility and imminent death.

407

And the boy. Where was the boy? How had he gotten away? What had he done?

She turned to the barn entrance and found them: Fallon, with bloody, burned feet, looking battered, exhausted, disheartened, and Danny, rubbing his neck, rivulets of blood spilling from his nose, across his lips and chin. Fallon propped him up, held him snugly beneath one arm and around his waist.

They didn't look like much, certainly not strong or crafty enough for this.

She howled again, her ponderous wings flapping up choking clouds of dust, dry timothy grass, and old corn stalks, as the peach grader tore her other arm off.

Fallon supported Danny.

She'd arrived in time to get the grader running, to plant the idea in Danny's head. She might have lashed out at Bear, loosed a bolt of destructive energy into the dreadful cat's ribcage, but she hadn't wanted to risk injuring or even killing Danny in the process. Trapping Bear's wrists inside the grader gave her a chance to get Danny clear of the barn. Having it rip the troubled bully to pieces, well, that turned out to be an unexpected bonus.

Bear's inhuman screeching sent bolts of delightful disgust up and down Fallon's spine, but she didn't look back. Helping Danny out, she turned to the single support beam Bulldozer Bob had left after his rampage. Thinking *sledgehammer*, she swung hard, dislodged the weathered post, and stepped away, shaking her hand back to normal, as the ramshackle building collapsed onto Bear Guenard with a dusty, clattering crash.

She sat in the grass, took Danny's hand. "You okay?"

His voice cracked, squeaking like a rusty bike wheel. "You saved me."

She dropped her head to his shoulder. "Oh, my blue-eyed superhero. Let's not start counting the number of times you've saved me. It's not a competition, not one either of us can win, anyway."

He wiped blood from his face and managed a crooked smile. "Okay, but come here. I wanna show you something I discovered last night." Danny led her to Elizabeth Martin's fifty-year-old car. From the back seat, he pulled the polished wooden box Emma had insisted they rescue from her parents' restaurant in Baltimore, the reason she'd wanted to hide there rather than take off for Jackson.

"Her detonators?" Fallon took the box, slid open the top. "How'd you get the box?"

"Found it near the beach, just grabbed it without thinking."

"Okay, but we've seen these."

"Yeah, I thought so, too." He turned one over in his hands. "Look at this. These switches, they don't switch. They're molded plastic, frozen in place. And this—" He indicated the tiny fluid reservoir.

"Yeah?" Fallon assumed one of the switches caused the fluid to mix or flow or something that sent a charge into whatever explosives had been rigged to the thing. She silently promised to learn how to use one the very next time she needed to blow something up.

"It's Mercury. Well, it's supposed to be."

"Supposed?"

"It's fake. It's empty, dry. It's just plastic." He tossed the detonator onto the driveway. "They're pretend."

"So," Fallon stared down at it. "How did she manage to..."

"How do you?" Danny massaged his neck.

"Jesus."

"Fallon, she blew up a cargo ship two miles off shore. At least, she claims she did, and the news feeds agree."

Fallon dumped the two remaining detonators from the box and began flipping them from hand to hand. Thinking

409

aloud, she said, "If that's the case, then she didn't need any help."

"And she didn't need explosives."

"That would make her a lot more powerful than I am."

He shrugged. "The jury is still out on that one, love. You've come a long way in two weeks."

Her eyes widened. "Danny, that night in Baltimore…"

"We assumed she was sleeping."

"How far out was that explosion?"

"About a mile."

"Do you think?"

"Yup."

"But why?"

Again, he shrugged. "A hundred reasons. Who knows?"

Fallon tossed the detonators into the car. "Remember how she didn't want us watching the broadcasts with her…as if they might say something…"

"Something you and I weren't supposed to hear. Exactly."

"I don't get it." She drew sweat stained fingers over the box's smoothly varnished surface. "Why make us drive all the way up there to get a box of pretend terrorist equipment?"

"To kill that guy, whatshisname…Harold Higgins."

She took him by the shoulder, squeezed hard. "That's gotta be it."

"Remember that morning in the restaurant? She said she'd been awful at Chemistry. We kind of laughed because only Bloodsucker kids even get to study Chemistry."

Fallon remembered. Seconds later, Emma had been beaten up pretty badly by the behemoth copperhead, so she and Danny never thought anything about the girl's confession regarding school. "Yeah, how many bomb makers do you know who were shithouse at Chemistry?" She cast her memory back over the past few days, digging for something crouched at the edge of her mind's eye. Then she had it. "And holy shit, Danny—"

410

"What?"

"The other night, in the cabin on the river," Fallon's legs weakened. She leaned heavily against the old car. "Emma fell asleep on the sofa."

"Yeah, so?"

Fallon concentrated, bringing the image into focus. "I watched her in the light of that god-awful candle. Her...her sweater had ridden partway up her back."

"So?"

"Her kidney," Fallon said simply. "Did you see it?"

Danny thought for a moment. "You know...I can't say I noticed."

"No scar."

"She was lying. Why?"

"She never had any work done. She made that up about her kidney extraction, just so we'd think she was like us..."

"God's rough drafts." He ran greasy fingers through his hair. "You know, when I think back to that morning when those ape-wolf things attacked us—"

"The morlocks," Fallon added. *And Edward Hyde and Kaa and Moby Dick...what else, Em?*

"Whatever. But that morning...I don't remember any of us using our skills that morning."

She considered this. "Holy shit. You're right. No one did anything."

"How'd they find us?"

"You think?"

He shrugged. "Maybe."

"But why?" she asked, genuinely troubled at the burgeoning possibility that they never should have trusted Emma Carlisle.

"Because we're God's rough drafts."

Fallon stared at the desultory ruins of the ancient barn, wondered if Bear might still be alive under there. "We're God's rough drafts." She played a cracked fingernail along the

411

crooked scar where her new thumb had been attached years earlier. "She's not."

"Emma's more."

"She's the finished version."

"And there's this." Danny slid the box top completely off, passed it to her, and reached inside what appeared to be empty space. She watched him press down on one corner. Fallon heard a dry click, and gasped when Danny's hand emerged holding a thin square of wood, a false bottom.

"Holy crap, what's there?"

He reached inside again, this time withdrawing an aged hardcover book, its dust jacket ratty, worn at the spine, but still legible in the sunlight. "*Poe's Unwritten Legacy* by Arthur Wentworth White."

"Who's that?"

"Edgar Allan Poe, you knucklehead, the guy was arguably the most important writer of the nineteenth century. He lived in Baltimore for a while, died there in 1849, Richmond, too, I think."

Fallon slugged him in the shoulder. He winced and favored his ribs. "Sorry! Danny, I'm sorry! I forgot."

"It's all right." He wheezed, his voice again sounding like air forced through a dog's chew toy. "This just isn't my morning."

She helped him to the lawn. "I know who Poe was, jackass. I was asking who this Arthur Wentworth Whatever person is."

"I dunno." He handed her the book. "But if you flip through, you'll see that Emma spent hours, maybe weeks studying this guy's writings."

"What's it all say?" She paged aimlessly through the chapters. Danny was right: there were nearly as many notes in the margins as there were words on the pages.

He retrieved the book, replaced it in Emma's box and slid the top closed. "It says that we've gotta go look for her. She knows something, maybe a lot more than she ever let on."

412

"About what?"

He raised open palms to the acres of October corn. "About all of this: giant snakes in Baltimore, monstrous bulldozer men bustin' through the living room wall, fields full of creepy, glow-in-the-dark monsters, Bear as a flying panther, that frigging, slimy tentacled whale thing – I mean, what the hell was that atrocity doing in a mountain lake?"

Fallon shook her head. "Danny..."

"We have to."

"There's gonna be a battalion of bulls all over that place."

"I don't care." He slid a hand over her bald head. "We're going."

"All right."

"Emma masterminded our escape from the school. Did you know that? As if she knew..."

"I thought you had."

Danny rubbed feeling into his neck. "Nah, it was all her—now that I think on it. I just followed along, acting the part, like I'd come up with this daring rescue. Nope. It was her idea."

Fallon leaned against him. "This is getting complicated."

He laughed, held her a moment. "Grow your hair out."

"What?"

"Please," he tried another smile, wasn't sure it worked.

Fallon slipped a few inches to one side and stared down at Emma's pretend detonator in concentration. She drew her hands over the naked skin of her scalp. Shoulder length auburn hair, just a touch more curly than last time, fountained beneath her fingers. She shook it out, dug in her pocket and found a rubber band to tie it up. "Better?"

"Better," Danny regained his feet with a disconcerting groan. He hugged his ribs. "Let's go."

Fallon joined him, pulled him close. He pressed his bruised, exhausted body against hers. "You okay?"

"You staying?"

413

She nodded.

"Then I'm okay."

She rotated the bio-wire vid screen implanted in her wrist years earlier. "My grandfather used to talk about a time when people had best friends. Imagine that…a best friend instead of three-thousand acquaintances."

"Let's go back. Whaddya say?"

"I say 'yes,' Danny Hackett. As long as it's you."

"As long as it's you."

She kissed him. The two lingered as long as they dared, then packed up Ms. Martin's Grey Panther and made for Hadley Hill, hoping to get a clear view of Owen Pond and maybe, if they were wildly fortunate, even find Emma Carlisle.

Nearly an hour later, corn stalks nearest the barn ruins rustled and a handsome man in an immaculate black suit emerged. Not a wrinkle or a dust speck marred his incongruously attractive appearance. His hair lay quaffed perfectly over his forehead. His tie rested neatly cinched beneath his narrow chin. His shoes, black wing tips a hundred years out of style yet still somehow compelling, shined in the late morning sunlight.

He crossed to the crude pile of rubble burying Bear Guenard beside a still running, still coughing and belching peach grader. Tilting his head slightly, he exhaled slowly through his nose, calming noticeably as he waited beside the wreckage.

And began to change.

Thirty seconds later, the creature Fallon and Danny thought of as Bulldozer Bob, his immaculate suit in ragged tatters about his massive, muscular form, began digging through the fallen beams, hay bales, and dry rotted planks, searching for Bear.

Anyone passing would have been able to see the blistered, scabbed wounds across the monster's shoulders, as if he'd been badly burned or electrocuted. The creature tossed hundreds of pounds of wreckage to one side, howled briefly into

414

the morning, then knelt to gather up Bear's torn, bloody body.

Nearly dead and dipped in her own blood, she seemed to recognize him as her head lolled loosely in his powerful arms.

18.49

Parting Shot

You know what's funny? We call them parting shots, but really the term ought to be 'Parthian' shot. The phrase is based on a legendary mounted military unit, Parthian soldiers, who got themselves written into the history books for their uncanny ability to fire arrows backwards while fleeing on horses. You see, the trick for them was to train the horses to—

Sorry. You don't care. Do you?

That's all right.

So here we are. What a mess. Emma is missing; you're assuming she drowned or made a tasty midnight snack for my whale-squid. And you're frustrated because you, like Danny and Fallon, aren't sure if they're going to find her or what they ought to do next. You want to know what's in that book and why Emma was hiding and protecting it and—

Oh, yes, sorry. It's *my* whale-squid. You caught that? Excellent.

Anyway, the good news is: Fallon succeeded. Headmaster Blair behaved badly, inexcusably if you ask me, and she killed him. She wanted to put an end to Blair's work at the Warrenton School for Juvenile Student Management, and I think you'll agree that she was boomingly successful at that.

Boomingly. Don't you just love adverbs...in moderation?

Is Fallon a murderer? Yes. Is that all right with you? Can you cheer for a murderer? I can, and I think you should, too. For now. You're probably uncertain why Susan Wentworth White was at the WSJSM or why my Mr. Hyde was with her on the beach, waiting with Headmaster Blair for Fallon and Danny to arrive. Or perhaps you already have that bit figured out.

You do; don't you? Good heavens, you're such a special snowflake.

Anyway, it certainly is a tangled web. The hand is quicker than the eye and all that.

But it's not too tangled. Some threads lead right where you expect them to. (Amos J. Oakton, the lawyer who lobbied and litigated to get everyone the legally-protected right to sell their body parts...don't forget about him, kiddos. We're gonna get back to him soon.)

I know you're worried about Danny, and I want to assure you that everything will work out for him. However, any time anyone tries to convince you that everything is going to be all right, chances are they're lying, probably so you'll leave. I admit that I worry a little about Danny and how he's gotten himself dunked in some pretty deep waters. But I'm also hopeful that he'll decide to tap his heels together and start chanting, "There's no place like Jackson. There's no place like Jackson." Maybe he'll sneak off in that cruddy Chevron (if it's still by the pond) and try to forget that he ever met Fallon Westerly.

But he won't. Will he? Nope, because when it comes to Fallon, that boy has lost a tug-o-war with wisdom.

On the other hand, Fallon's unexpected powers certainly came through for her at the WSJSM, and if Danny's any kind of friend to her, he'll get her out of harm's way for a while. Maybe she can practice a bit, refine and enrich her skills so she's ready the next time she runs into Susan Wentworth White.

Won't that be an interesting conversation?

I hope we're both there for it.

I plan to be. Because, you see, I'm going to kill Fallon Westerly and Danny Hackett.

And Emma Carlisle is going to help me.

See you again soon!

Arthur Wentworth White   October 25, 2128
Alexandria, Virginia

417

"I hated that play. And those hats! Who wears hats like that? I mean, please, it's 1865!"

--Cicero
(Not *that* Cicero, the other one, Abraham Lincoln's dry cleaner's hairdresser)

Robert Scott began writing fiction as a creative way to engage his father-in-law, Jay Gordon's, imagination while Jay's body succumbed slowly to Lou Gehrig's disease. *The Hickory Staff* (2005) is the result of two years of storytelling over the phone, via email, and in day-long discussions of characters, plot twists, and mysteries that hopefully helped to distract Jay from his physical battles. *Lessek's Key* (2006) and *The Larion Senators* (2007) represent the remainder of Jay and Robert's collaboration, released after Jay died. *The Eldarn Sequence* has since been translated into Russian, Turkish, and Czech.

In 2009, he published a collection of short stories for young readers, *The Great M&M Caper* and *Other Fourth Grade Adventures*, comedy stories about the misadventures of a gifted underachiever. Robert's novel, *15 Miles* (2010) and its sequel, *Asbury Park* (2012), are Gollancz horror/crime releases featuring the alcohol- and OxyContin-addicted homicide detective, Sailor Doyle. His novel, *Emails from Jennifer Cooper* (2015), is a slice-of-life tragic/comedy portrayal of a 43-year-old woman struggling through a difficult divorce.

Robert studied music at Colby College before turning to education. He moved from New Jersey to Colorado where he worked as a teacher and completed a doctorate at the University of Northern Colorado. He works now as an English teacher, encouraging unwilling students to trade their iPhones for a story or two from Edgar Poe. Sometimes it works.

He is a classical guitarist and distance runner, and was named Prince William County's inaugural poet laureate. While serving in that position, he released his first book of poems, *3:17 a.m. and Other Poems, Scribbles, Rants, and Drivel* (2015).

For more information visit www.robscottbooks.com (warning: some adult content).

www.reddashboard.com

49739605R00245

Made in the USA
Middletown, DE
25 June 2019